DJ WILSON

I humbly dedicate this book to Dani, Darren, Robin and Julie, without whose badgering, encouragement and assistance this sequel would not have been written.

*"Life is not about
Waiting for the Storm to Pass,
It's about Learning how to Dance in the Rain."*

— Vivian Green

Introduction

Surviving both love and loss while sailing through the tumultuous storms life haphazardly blows our way defines our essence, oft times peeling us to the core. If we're fortunate enough to experience heart palpitating love, it's only by losing it, do we appreciate its intrinsic value. The same goes for financial security. If we have it we're good. If we've had it, then lost it, we're screwed. Righting another's grievous wrong on this ride that compensated hundreds of people millions of dollars, no matter how noble and grand I thought it seemed at the time was not without terrible costs, excruciating heartache and significant loss.

Redemption was the ultimate goal when I started this quest many months ago. Individuals from all walks of life had entrusted their short and long term financial health to a charismatic man who seemed too good to be true. Sadly, that turned out to be factual in spectacular fashion. Hope was lost and people were dying, literally and figuratively, because of it. Someone had to intervene. That someone was me — along with a cast of characters and a comedy of errors that moved this journey from one of redemption to one of restoration.

Everyone deserves second chances — some even third and fourth. But, here comes the tricky part. If that four- letter word…love…worms its way into the equation, you're screwed. Meeting the girl of my dreams in the midst of my quest one glorious early morning in Tennessee, not many months removed, was a refreshing breath of seasons wrapped up into one delicious package I came to know as Candi.

A perfect love story in the making, one that would make Ryan O'Neal proud, Candi raced into my life, stole my heart over a ninety-day span and compelled me to love again. And then the bitch went rogue, catapulting me into the arms of vivacious Victoria who so happened to be my friend ... my protector ... my solicitor. "Ethically," Vic says, "I'm required to make that point of order extremely clear."

High stepping into the role that Candi previously played on my ride to redemption, Victoria joined me on my adventure home, offering her all, be it on her back, her stomach or her side. I digress ... Victoria was a player, a master barrister at the top of her game, capable of arguing and defending any position, including mine.

Caught up in my drama, friends do what friends do when they're on three thousand miles from home, they escape ... they ride. Into the Plains of Alberta, into the land of 'Rape and Honey,' into the forests of Saskatchewan we rode. We discovered in our travels many things that made us laugh, while confessing in our deepest, darkest moments those things that made us cry. We were flawed, Victoria and I, and we knew it.

Into the hearts of an innkeeper or two, into the life of a child we rode, paying it forward, having already dodged bullets and disaster, daring tomorrow to find us ... in our journey ... in our ride. Through it all, I taught Vic the gracious art of giving. She taught me the fine art of receiving. I taught Vic that confession is good for the soul. She taught me that I couldn't love another when I still loved the one that got away. Sadly, she was right...

Then, reality knocked, slapped me sideways and brought me back into the world as I knew it before I escaped to "Oz." Seems like everybody wanted a piece of me. Guessing it had something to do with the two hundred pounds of conflict diamonds I cast upon the waters that weren't rightly mine. Then again, they didn't legitimately belong to A.J. Standford, the Ponzi scheming banker I took them from, either. But, his 2.5 million dollar bounty on my head to anyone that would listen to him from behind prison walls said otherwise.

Toss into the equation, Candi's powerful Ex who, as of late, has recently developed a nasty hard-on for me and the U.S. Marshal Service, doing their best to protect me in spite of myself. Spin these all together and you've got yourself one heck of a mess. Oh, and let's not forget Candi's mom and her Gambino Family who's also on the outs with me. Oh, Happy Day!

Thankfully, there was the D.O.G. In the confines of a kennel in Middle Tennessee, Major waited patiently for me to return, whereby he could resume his rightful place, riding shotgun in my truck. I was confident, even with my current identity compromised and my life in shambles, we could make a fresh start, Mayberry, maybe. Sounds welcoming, doesn't it?

Leaving my recreated life on beautiful Dale Hollow Lake to begin again seemed overwhelming at times. But, I'd done it before and I could do it again. First things first — with no malice left in me, I had to find Candi, hoping beyond hope that I could restore ... us. And with that, a plan that would be played out on my terms, not at the mercy of those who sought to do us harm.

All this conniving is driving me nuts. A Sam Adams in hand with my head in the clouds and my feet on the ground, I devised a scheme that could make us whole. Since no other options were coming down the pike, with the help of a trusted few, I put the game in play. The question of the day on this ride to restoration ... would it work?

Momma said, "when you play with fire, you're gonna get burned. It's not a question of if, but when." Sadly, since Candi almost took me out in the Starbucks Drive Thru the day we met ... I resemble that remark ... My question is, how bad is it gonna hurt?

Chapter 1

ood morning, barrister," I whispered to Victoria, as she awakened sleepy-eyed beside me, snuggled into the goose down bedding of our king sized, four-poster, bed. Wiping the sleep from her beautiful green eyes with clenched fists, fondly reminded me of my favorite childhood cartoon character … I smiled. Then she opened her mouth.

Victoria, you're on. I almost said, "Good morning Jon David, I loved that you held me all night long," but caught myself. I sure as hell don't want him to hear that. It's best he hears this, loud and clear! "Damn you, D, you've done it again. This is the second or maybe even the third time I've thrown my naked sultry self into your arms and all you've managed to do is cuddle. I do love snuggling, but there's only so much a girl can take when she's wrapped around you like a pretzel and can't lick or kiss or bite. If I didn't care so much for you, after all we've been through, I might develop a complex and start taking this the wrong way."

"Vic, after what we witnessed yesterday, no amount of Canadian whiskey or sensuous seduction from you could erase my living nightmare over these past twenty-four hours. Pinch me will ya? Tell me we're still in Sioux City, and I've just woken up from a very bad dream."

I remember that night … vividly. I was so close to seducing this man. "If that were the case, lover boy, you'd be sore in your bone and I'd be tender to the touch, if you catch my drift," she said, flicking her tongue across her lips for visual effect. Whispering in D's ear, she continued, as she wrapped her arms around him, "Sadly my friend, yesterday was all too real. The events that cumulated over the last few days would earn some seedy novelist a Pulitzer. Hell, it might even earn a Scorsese wannabe an Oscar."

I paused, reflecting and digesting her words. "Thank you … I think. With that type of assurance, I've gone from hoping this was a bad dream to waiting for my real life drama to be featured on a big screen in one fell swoop. Lucky me!"

Let me regress, the events that transpired over the last few days here in Calgary, Canada, the ones Vic and I are referring to, involved a girl and getting screwed royally. Vic, who has an innate gift for reading people and I, having lovingly shagged this girl over the last few months, were blind-sided — no we were downright screwed — out of a ten million dollar reward by Candice. My guess is that old adage, "you can never leave the Mafia alive," rings true, especially when your family and your ex-husband are knee deep in 'the culture.' That means she's related by blood, bullets and, oh yeah, marriage. That being said, over the past two days Victoria has been kidnapped and released, and traded for Candi during one of the darkest moments of my life to date. I, on the other hand, have been shot at, betrayed, lied to and forced to bring bodily harm to another individual who was only doing his job.

Thankfully, I'd made unsolicited restitution to many before the (pardon my French) 'shit' hit the fan. Trying to do the right thing and paying it forward are the two maxims I've spent my entire adult life adhering to. Except this time, it all went to 'hell in a handbasket' in the end. Doing the right thing, albeit skewed by my loneliness, coupled with the lust and desire for a delicious, willing and receptive Woo-Hoo drove me to my knees. I've lost the girl of my dreams, there's a huge bounty on my head and I'm in Calgary, Alberta with a sex fiend who happens to be my lawyer, my friend. "Again, am I lucky or what?"

"What are you mumbling in my ear, D? Are you positive we can't take your idea of snuggling to the next level? Give me 3 minutes," Vic purred, burying herself under the covers, her boobs coming to rest on top of my thighs, "and I'll get a rise out of you yet."

"Stop it, Vic," I stammered playfully, firmly pushing her hot breath and moist lips away from my rapidly rising shorts. Bolting from the bed, I made a beeline to my day bag and retrieved the well-traveled and equally experienced BOA. "Here girlfriend, knock yourself out. New batteries, too."

Listening to the rhythmic hum of the BOA, as well as her ever-increasing rapid breaths culminating beneath the sheets, I could attest to her ability to make the most of any fluid situation. After a few long painful minutes, being a spectator, not a participant, the humming abruptly stopped. Vic, flipping back the sheets, sported a mischievous smile and a rather ominous glow.

"Damn you, D. I wanted to take you ... and me over the top this morning. It's a sad, sad day, when all that's willing is BOB, for now."

"It's not a B.O.B. Vic, it's a B.O.A."

"What's the difference ... seriously? They're both battery operated boys."

"True, but this one is uniquely designed, as you've so aptly proven to accelerate your star-studded experience with or without my warm, manly body next to yours."

My mind raced ahead of my mouth. It's too soon, Victoria, don't press it. Candi is still fresh and raw. You'll push him away. "D, best you keep your shorts on and me flush in fresh batteries and I'll do my best to keep my hands off you on this ride ... for now."

"You always preface for now, girlfriend. That terrifies me. I dare not tread the halls with you when for now no longer suffices. Come on Vic," rapidly changing my current thought process, aka lust, while lowering, among other things, my rapid heartbeat. "Put some clothes on, will ya? I'm sure Josie has breakfast ready. Besides, I need a serious distraction to take my mind off of ... excuse me, out of ... you."

Tossing back her hair, Vic whispered, "Beneath this lamb awaits a hungry lion. You're teasing me, aren't you? I know you want me. You love my green eyes, my long auburn hair, my soft and supple, voluptuous, milky white breasts. You're standing over there right now fantasizing about my pouty lips, wrapped, deliciously round your—"

"STOP! Client attorney privileges only go so far, remember?"

I'm trying to be his best friend with benefits, not his counsel right now. How do I say this? "Not exactly, big boy. We're under the 'grandfather clause.' I attempted to get in your pants long before I became your lawyer. So there! Like I said, D, just keep your shorts on and the boy toy readily accessible. Now scram, I need to get dressed!"

"Works for me, girlfriend," snagging my Polartec jacket on the way out the door. "If you please, I'll skip showering this morning. I can see you joining me, in all your glory, offering to wash my back..."

"Among other things, D. Don't forget the other things."

"OK, among other things, which in my current condition," I confessed, lowering my eyes to my rigid rise, "I doubt my little brain could refuse."

Pursing, pouting lips, followed by a devious, determined smile that only Vic could produce, she slung a pillow at me, "Out!"

Chapter 2

The aroma of fresh baked treats filled the hallways, drawing me into Josie's breakfast room in the Inn, a welcome respite that over the last few days we've fondly called home. There, I found the 'Marines,' Frank, Ron, and Terry finishing up a five-course meal, while Josie refreshed their drinks and warmed their coffees. "You're spoiling them, Josie," giving her a morning hug from behind. "Vic, will be down soon. Better give us the light version," looking over the scrumptious fare spread across the table, "we've got a long ride ahead of us today."

"You let her be the judge of that, young man," snarled our host. "When will you learn, you can't think for a woman when it comes to food, clothes and—"

"Sex, don't forget the sex," interjected Frank. "You'd think D would've learned his lesson from all that's happened. Because once again, he tried to think like a woman … and crashed and burned, big time."

"Boys, there is more to life than just sex with a woman," Josie continued, undaunted. "You keep her pleased with the peripheral things and you'll have all the sex you can stand."

"Peri-if-feral what?" asked Ron.

"You know, snazzy clothes, jewelry, fine cars, expensive stuff," offered Terry.

"Pardon my French, Ms. Josie, wouldn't it be cheaper on us men folk if we just hired a high-priced hooker occasionally?" quipped Frank.

"Boys, someday you'll want to settle down and it will be the unselfish pampered things you've done for the woman in your life that keeps her around. It sure won't be those shriveled up little sausages you've got down there between your legs that makes her want to wake up beside you for the rest of her life."

Watching the Marines squirm uncomfortably, I shared this morning's tension wholeheartedly, "I take offense to that, Josie. There are some of us here that don't have shriveled up little ones and there are even a few of us who can and do refrain from lust." I heard footsteps approaching from behind. Vivacious, Victoria had arrived.

That's my cue. "I heard refrain and lust," Vic chuckled, strolling into the room and headlong into the conversation. Walking up behind me, Vic put her left hand on my head, her right on my crotch, "I can sadly attest, D here can refrain, both with his big head and this little one," she sighed, simultaneously patting them both, "for now."

"Vic, way too much TMI," I chuckled, brushing her hands away. Spinning around, I playfully flicked my tongue in her ear, "Girlfriend, now is not the best time to tease me. I'm on the precipice of..."

"Good for you, D," she whispered back. Spinning him around so we could both face our attentive audience, "Lady and gentlemen, he's on the verge, the precipice of no return. Finally, I've got him where I want him." *Ha, if only that were true.*

"The two of you get a room. Oh, I forgot you have a room, two of em to be exact. Take it upstairs, will ya? Not now mind you, later. Sit yourself down and I'll bring your breakfast," demanded Josie, pulling a chair from the table and motioning for me to sit like a small child, over the loud snickering of the 'Calvary.'

Embarrassed by the fuss, "Congratulations, Josie, you've found us out. I'm a bodacious flirt and Vic's a titillating tease."

"Well," laughed Frank, "I see a train wreck in the making. One of these days, you're gonna go the rails and I'd like to be there when it happens."

"Me, too," beamed Josie. "Count me in."

"Enough! You may be right. I've drawn the short straw to haul her bodacious behind across Canada on my bike, fighting off her luscious lips and roaming hands while keeping us upright, rolling forward. That is unless … one of you fine gentlemen would like the honors?"

Is he trying to get rid of me already? Say it ain't so. "You're stuck with me, Jon David," Vic proclaimed, defending her territory, as three excited 'man paws' waved furiously in the air. "Besides, we've got much to discuss on our ride. Like how to keep your 'cheeky ass' out of jail and or the morgue … or both."

"Thanks for clarifying that, Victoria. I especially liked the cheeky part. Enough bout' me and my 'ass-tributes', let's talk about getting the 'Calvary' home safely." *Going from sexy to safety is not the best transition, but I took a stab.* "Thankfully, no one saw any of you up close yesterday, so we're good in that respect. Frank, the publicity you generated trying to take the heat off me will still be there when you get back. Vic, any ideas how to diffuse that situation?"

"Move … as in out of the country," said Vic. "At least, if you're out of sight, you're out of mind. And it may not be for that long now that Mr. Generosity here has flooded the country with sparkling baubles over the last couple of weeks. Frank, can you take an extended vacation, say for 90 days… somewhere far away?"

Scratching his beard stubble, "Guess so," said Frank. The boys here can handle everything while I'm gone. I've kinda wanted to travel around Europe. I could get a Euro-pass and 'Ride, Boley, Ride.' What, don't look at me like that? James Caan said that in a John Wayne movie once."

"Sounds like fun in a Clint Eastwood kind of way," I laughed. "Stay in touch with Vic by email. Who knows, if everything comes crashing down, I may be joining you. Now to get you home. I've instructed Vic to charter a private jet to take you to Oregon, no questions asked. You'll clear customs here in Calgary and be home by dark. That work for you?"

"D, you didn't have to go to all that trouble for us," countered Ron, "but I'm not complaining. I've never flown on a private jet before."

"Me either," proclaimed Terry. "I'm thankful we could be here for you, like you were there for Frank and like he was there for us. What goes around comes around, if you catch my drift."

"I do, sir. I do. It's—"

Here we go again. "It's called paying it forward," Victoria interjected. "D has been preaching that to me almost every day since we met." Playfully patting D's head, I added, "This poor generous soul tries to live it every friggin' day."

Chapter 3

Josie scurried out of the kitchen with freshly squeezed orange juice, garnished with a mint leaf, followed by blueberry waffles topped with homemade whipped cream and boysenberry syrup, eggs cooked to order, a rasp of bacon, moose sausage, and Tennessee country ham, that she'd flown in just for me. "This your idea of light?"

"Honey, I owe you more," replied Josie. Wiping her calloused hands on her well-worn apron, she said, "This being your last day here and all, I wanted this breakfast to be extra special."

Vic spoke up between bites, "You've truly outdone yourself, Ms. Josie."

I concurred with a nod, my mouth full of waffle, and my silvery bearded chin dripping purple syrup. Swallowing my last bite, I said, "All of your meals are as special as is this beautiful B&B you call home. Now leave us be, Josie. I've got some things to talk over with the 'Calvary' and the barrister, before we scatter in all directions."

Wrapping up our conversation, I asked Frank and Vic to meet me in the kitchen, then I ran upstairs to retrieve a package from my daypack. Digging to the bottom of the bag, I realized the numerous boxes I'd brought on this ride were disappearing quickly.

Walking into the kitchen, I found the group engaged in lively conversation. It was most likely about me, because the sound of the swinging door stopped their conversation cold. Walking up behind Josie, I grabbed her in a bear hug, lifting her a foot off the floor. Teasing her, I kissed the back of her neck, breathing a whiff of lavender shampoo.

"Put me down this instant, D," Josie huffed. "Or not. On second thought, I could get used to this. Spin me around and pick me up again … please? I'd love to plant one … on those kissable lips of yours."

Ha, you absolutely are a horny little fellow, D. Victoria you are so close. "Why don't you both get a room? Frank and I will wait right here 'til you're done."

"Jealous are we, Vic?" I asked.

"Damn right I am. Josie, teach me your secret how to score with this man."

"Honey, when the time is right, you'll know," Josie assured her. "Let this man come to you. Quit trying to throw yourself at Jon David! He will come to you when he's good and ready… or desperate and dejected."

Victoria snarled, "Cold Josie, even for you."

Quickly changing the subject, I removed the small, nondescript package from my pocket. The excited look on Frank and Vic's faces confirmed my intentions, both being former recipients of the shiny baubles, held securely in velvet, draw string, bags. "Miss Josie, Frank, there's roughly 350 carats of diamonds in this bag, worth two and a half million, give or take. Because of your enduring selflessness, I'd like you to have them…with a couple of conditions."

"Jon David … I mean D, you don't owe me a thing," confessed Josie.

The sincerity in her voice, as well as her eyes, conveyed her conviction.

"Mr. D, I'm good. You've seen to that," added Frank.

"Here it comes guys, D's got some new way for you to spread his cheer," Victoria said. "This man dreams way out, and I mean way outside the box. Now don't look hurt Jon David, I'm stating facts. Continue."

"Thanks for your unwavering confidence, even if it's royally skewed… not screwed. I saw that head roll, Victoria."

"Josie, you mentioned you'd like to build private balconies off your main suites to accommodate hot tubs. This should cover it and you'll have quite a bit left over. It's the left over I want you to use to make a difference. Every month I'd like you to run a contest, offering four struggling couples a chance to get away for the weekend. Let their children nominate them with their own handwritten letters and go from there. You have an innate way of making everyone feel special. Imagine the joy you could bring to families living paycheck to paycheck. Everyone, regardless of circumstance, deserves the opportunity to reconnect, even if it's only for a weekend."

"Oh my, D. In all my years, who would have thought to let children nominate their parents? I'd love to do this for you, for us, for them. Count me in!"

"Frank, here's what I'd like to propose to you. Take some of these and buy Terry and Ron a place to live. No matter what happens in their future, they'll always have a place to call home. I know what it's like to be homeless and alone. I'd wish that on no one."

"Second, this is me thinking outside your box. Since you're going to Europe, where there's just as much need there as here, use the rest to pay your way and then some. I'd like you to travel below the radar, if you will, living modestly, but giving generously along the way. By doing so, you'll meet real people with real needs. Changing one life at a time, will change them the way I changed you, for the better."

I took a deep breath, "This is your chance to pay it forward across Europe. Keep a journal, take some pictures, come home in a few months when it's safe and write a book about the differences you made in the lives of others. Most importantly, document the difference they made in you. Can you do that, sir?"

"Can do, Mr. D. I'll act like I'm you. Yep, that should do it."

Fidgeting, Victoria whispered, "D, you're amazing! How do you dream this stuff up? You should be running a hands-on charity somewhere. I mean, it's one thing to give a few hundred bucks to United Way or the Red Cross, but it's off the charts when you single-handedly address peoples' needs by overcoming their obstacles immediately."

"Which would have helped you more, Vic, me saying I'll try to find you a job in a law firm somewhere or giving you the confidence and the resources necessary to start your own practice? Had I done the former, you wouldn't be here right now, would you? That's what empowerment does when one has the resources to back it up."

"He's right, Ms. Vic," interjected Frank. Had D not picked me up, trying to get home, I wouldn't be here either. Ms. Josie, this man believed in me so much that he flew my dog home and me from Tennessee and staked me with enough of these diamonds to start over. Yes sir-ee, I'm living proof that his kind of generosity works."

"Me, too."

"Me, three," added Josie. "I can tell you this boy stayed here almost twenty years ago when I was first getting started. He came for the Stampede and stayed long after it was over, helping me get this place in shape for my guests and never asked for a dime."

"Josie, don't forget, you did house and feed me. Guys, it's not only money that empowers people, but the confidence behind it that says, I believe in you. I've been fortunate to be your lives when you were at a crossroads. Timing… my friends… is everything."

Chapter 4

Tampa Bay

In the coal black darkness, our Gulfstream V touched down at Peter O. Knight Airport in Tampa, Florida, enveloping us in sweltering humidity; a far cry, from the crisp fall air we left behind in Calgary, just a few short hours before. Multiple, nondescript black SUVs sat just off the tarmac, engines idling, ready to whisk me, my cousin Gio, his girlfriend, my Ex, and his bodyguard, away. More important than the passengers, however, were the encrypted ledgers Candi carried, which provided in incriminating detail the Families money laundering practices, including a detailed list of their numerous off shore and Swiss bank accounts.

Helping Giovanni deplane, his crutches clanging toward the waiting car, Candi saw Joseph hurriedly closing the distance between them. *Here comes the talk!*

"Did you mean what you said earlier, Candice?" asked Joseph, grasping her hand in the process, looking her squarely in the eyes. "If you meant it, I mean really meant it, I'd like you to come home with me tonight. I've missed you. Your being with D, I'm sure banging his brains out all this time, pushed me to the brink. And I know you don't want me on the brink. I can't think of a better way to prove your sincerity than to make love to me … like you used to."

What is it with men and their penile thinking? That having sex will make every-thing all better, regardless of how tumultuous the state of the relationship might be, *I asked myself before answering,* "I meant what I said in Calgary, Joseph. Much has happened while we've been apart. I've changed; you've changed. Best you take it slow this time around. Be the man I fell in love with. You may be ready to jump back in the sack with me, but I'm nowhere near ready to join you. I'm sure you've had your share of sluts... I mean girls who've satisfied your primal urges. Go hook up with one of them if you need to get off so bad right now!" *There he goes, hanging his head again.*

"Damn you, Joseph, you still don't get it. I see that hurt puppy dog look in your eyes. I want to be courted. I want to be wooed. I want you to feel special again. Go buy a motorcycle. I'll ride with you," I caught myself saying aloud, *dreaming fondly of the memories I made with D, not him, not ever.* "I want you to convince me by your actions, that, unlike before, you want me for me, not just as an avenue to get closer to my family. Besides, you've got to prove to me that you will keep your end of the deal and leave D and Victoria alone. They deserve to be happy, without continually looking over their shoulders for you or anyone else. We're splitting the ten million. Surely you don't need to worry about collecting that ridiculous bounty that Standford put out on D? Or do you?"

"I guess that all depends on you, sweetheart," a rather familiar indigna-tion of times past, rising in his voice. "If you really created this whole ruse to retrieve the ledgers for us, I guess not. Only time will tell if we're on the same page, or if you're blowing smoke up my ass. Let me tell you straight up, baby girl, your family be damned. If you screw with me, you'll not like the results. But hey," he laughed, "if you keep your end of the bargain, I'll gladly keep mine."

Threats ... He's threatening me in the same breath, through the same lips that *wants to make love to me tonight? It's not happening!* "Go away, Joseph, it's late. I'm going to ride with Gio and Mile to Mom's. We'll continue this conversa-tion tomorrow."

Climbing into the sullen, black Suburban with Gio and Mile, Candi replayed over and over the absurd promises she made to Joseph in Calgary to keep him from harming D. *What was I thinking? Leaving D with Victoria was like leaving an injured lamb in a cage with a ravenous lion. What else could I do? D called, Victoria dropped everything and came with reinforcements. That's loyalty, love or lust. Or possibly some combination of the three. D has a way with women and men too, that's for sure, me included.*

"Candice, you OK?" asked Gio, while Mile expressed the same question to me through her eyes. "D, he good guy, you see. He save me, he fix leg. You wait, he come."

"I'm no good for him. Look at all the trouble I've brought him and the two of you for that matter," I stated factually, while the tears I'd bravely held back for so long, unleashed.

Mile handed Candi a tissue from her pocket, while Go continued undaunted, "You wait. I tell your Momma, he, how you say, special. He care for you. I know it. You know it. We fix it."

"He did, before I sold him out and got on the plane with Joseph." *I couldn't tell him what I had to do to protect him. If I did, he'd have never let me leave. Bodies would have been scattered everywhere. I did what he taught me to do, put others needs before my own. What a difference a few months makes. When he met me, I was a selfish, spoiled bitch. Now I have a hole in the pit of my stomach. Doing the right thing was supposed to make me feel better. It doesn't by a long shot!*

"You reach him, you tell him why you leave. He understand."

Sniffling and snorting was so undignified, but hey, we're family here, "How will I find him, Gio? He's still on his bike trip riding who knows where and for how long, before he makes his way home. That is, even if he goes home. His identity has been compromised. There's a bounty on his head. For all I know, he may just keep riding."

"He and you talk about his dog, you call May-jore. He not leave dog. You look there."

Cousin Gio thinks like a man, not some silly broken-hearted girl. I appreciate that! "Good idea, Giovanni. There can't be that many kennels where he lives. I'll send my girlfriend Marcy to visit all of them until she finds him. We find Major, we'll find D or at least I'll be able to get a message to him. He needs to know the truth about what happened yesterday and why. He has to know I did what I did for him, for Victoria. For once in my life," Candi sighed, "I didn't do it for me."

Chapter 5

"Call if you need me. Leave a message on this phone or email Victoria and I'll get in touch. Vic, give Frank and Josie your email address, along with my current cell number. I'm going to say goodbye to Terry and Ron. Oh, and Frank, don't tell them their homes came from me. It's best they come from you. The ideal way to create loyal, lifetime employees is to treat them the way you'd like to be treated. By this magnanimous gesture, they'll always have your back, just like you've so graciously had mine."

Walking into the breakfast room, "Terry, Ron, I can't thank you enough. Putting yourself in Harm's Way for a guy you've never met is most admirable."

"No problem, Mr. D," mumbled Terry, looking at the ground uncomfortably, shuffling his feet side to side.

"We haven't had a chance to do much good for anybody lately. That is until Frank found us and put us to work. It's a great feeling when you can give back, rather than take," Ron confessed. "Frank says you're good people. That was enough for us."

"Take care of him, will ya? Vic," I shouted into the kitchen, "wrap it up, it's time to haul ass."

"Frank, ya'll need to pack up. By the time you return the rental, your ride should be fueled and waiting for ya.

"Quit hollering, D. You know better than to shout between rooms," scolded Josie, stomping through the swinging door, shaking her forefinger in my direction. "We heard you. Why are you and Victoria in such an all fired hurry to leave? Why can't you stay here an extra day or two? I want you to sketch out the balconies and hot tubs before you leave."

"I'll talk to Vic. If she..."

"I already have," said Josie, putting her foot down. "You're staying. I'll be right back with a sketchpad and pencil. You were pretty good at sketching out the glass walls in this breakfast room. I can't wait for you to put your vision on paper."

"Josie, it's your vision. You share it, I'll sketch it."

Vic, making another pronounced entrance, burst into the breakfast room, after overhearing Josie say we were staying, "I can't contribute to the architectural portion of this conversation, but I can write, so I'd like to work on the couple's promotion. Ms. Josie, I bet if you'll keep a record of their responses, especially the best ones, I could publish them into a book for you, somewhere down the road."

"Oh, that'd be wonderful, Victoria. We could also make a framed copy for the winners as a memento to take home."

It was my turn to toss in two cents. "That's an excellent idea, but we'd best have some perimeters. The innocence of a child sees only the good things that make their parents special. It's only much later through our very own difficulties, trying to be husband and wife, that they see us as we truly are, very human and exceptionally flawed. Guess you better cut the age off at twelve." I turned to Vic for some semblance of approval.

"Agreed, D. Is that OK with you, Ms. Josie?"

"That works, Victoria. I'm so happy you agreed to stay. Good minds think alike."

Vic grinned. "Yes, they do," she whispered under her breath, "except when it comes to getting D into my pants."

Josie wrinkling her nose, "Ants, honey we don't have ants here, I assure you."

"Never mind," I countered, biting my lip to keep from laughing out loud, "I heard what Vic said. It has absolutely nothing to do with ants. Girl needs to get a life."

"You are so wrong, D," said Vic. "I have a life. Of course, since I met you, it's been twisted and turned upside down. Paying a little personalized attention to me could enhance it…for now…"

"Of course, for now. How could I not see that one coming?" gazing into Vic's sparkling green eyes, all the while trying to suppress my evil grin.

Chapter 6

After seeing Frank and the boys off to the airport, each carrying a goody bag of Josie's fresh baked treats, Vic and I began the process of putting our thoughts on paper. Getting the Herald newspaper, as well as the local CBC station on board, should not be a problem because of the very nature of this promotion. What would be crucial, however, would be the anonymity necessary to maintain confidentiality and integrity throughout the contest. Using only first names, or better yet initials, would allow the chosen recipients to be honored, based solely on the nomination of their children, followed up with due diligence as to their socioeconomic condition.

"Good job, D," Vic said. "Again, let me say two heads are better than one when it comes to working out the privacy issues that must be maintained." Reaching under the table, she nonchalantly placed her hand on my inner thigh hoping to spark an immediate reaction without breaking stride in her conversation. "Speaking of privacy issues, what say we adjourn to the room for a nap?" Feigning a yawn, "I'm suddenly experiencing a sinking spell and could use a quickie ... I mean a short nap."

"You don't quit, counselor, do you?"

"As long as I'm breathing, you're breathing… nope."

"Come on, Vic, let's you and I move this conversation to the room. I'll never get Josie's additions sketched as long as you've got your hand rumbling 'round my crotch and your tongue finger deep in my ear."

***

Bursting through the bedroom door, I said, "Lay down on the bed, Vic. Close your eyes and for once, be still and listen!"

"Here comes the talk," said Vic. "Damn you, D, another lecture, another unfulfilled moment."

"Shhh ... You're beautiful, you're flaming hot. I want you so bad that I can taste you. For now, as you so aptly alluded to, would be the time to ravish you, to give in to my desires and yours. Sex complicates a relationship — lack of sex complicates it even more. Random, lust filled sex in my mind, somehow cheapens it, especially, if you're not careful. I want us to be careful. That girlfriend is my ... excuse me ... our current dilemma."

Vic motioned for me to join her on the bed, gently patting the comforter, before beginning her rebuttal, "look pal, we're healthy, attractive adults here with normal, biological urges. You've already said you want me. You damn well know I want you." Taking my hand, she deftly glided my fingers across her navel, into the depths of her jeans.

Jerking my hand away, as if touching a hot stove, "I remember a truism from my mom delivered repeatedly early in life, 'if you play with fire, you're gonna get burned.' She was right, as usual. It was never a matter of if, but when. You, my darling, are on fire. If my hand lingered any longer where you so expertly placed it, we're gonna get scorched. I'm not sure I'm ready for that."

What do I have to do, beg him to get laid? "I am, D," said Vic. "Go with it. Now it's your turn to close your eyes and ravish me, ravishing you."

Closing my eyes, I was in a fog, as Vic's hands and lips explored every exposed surface area of my body. *Lost in the moment, this was becoming everything I had dreamed of with her and more ... then reality slapped me squarely in the face. This was not a dream, this was not a fantasy, this was the heat of the moment and it was my turn to burn.* Bolting from the bed, I tripped headlong over the oval rug that complimented the hardwood floors in our suite and fell into the emerald green club chair facing Vic. "I can't do this right now, I can't."

A woman frustrated, Vic pulled the comforter over her head and sulked. "Damn you, D, damn you."

"Vic, I'm gonna tell you another story," I continued, as I walked over to my bag and retrieved her 'newfound friend.' Throwing back the linens, I turned it on high. "Here, girlfriend, use this if you need to while I'm talking. The batteries are as fresh as you."

Emboldened, she jumped from the bed and disrobed before my eyes, addressing with my toy, her most pressing needs, while I 'numb nuts' looked longingly on. *I got him where I want him. He wants me. That's why he's not looking at me in total exhibition mode.*

With my jeans rising, I turned away from the spectacle to regain my thoughts, trying to suppress the lust infused air... permeating everywhere. Over the hum of the BOA, I continued the narrative that was briefly interrupted by her stunning, mind numbing nakedness. "Remember, when I said sex complicates and lack of sex complicates even more? I'm speaking from experience and lots of it. Candi called me a slut far too many times. Sadly, there was some truth to that moniker. Can you imagine puberty rising in a child like a pressure cooker on high with no relief valve? That is, until I went to Europe on a spring vacation and lost my virginity to a blond, blue-eyed, fourteen-year-old. Getting laid became my life mission. I couldn't ever have enough girls and they couldn't ever have enough of me. Let me regress. Only when I shot up in height and slimmed down in size during my fourteenth summer, did the girls take notice. And, boy did they take notice. When boys should have been scoring touchdowns, goals and baskets, I was scoring girls. Sex consumed me. Not so much for the act itself, but to soothe the repressed, abuse issues that dogged me as a child. I had a 'come to Jesus' moment and embraced celibacy, somewhere around age twenty, when I'd romanced eight girls in six days and still had a to-do list. I didn't know if I was coming or going, or where I was supposed to be sleeping from one day to the next. I'm not bragging. Sadly enough, sex became an out of control addiction fueled by the abuses of my past. In college, I spent many a long night trying to understand the drivers within. Study after study pointed to the same conclusion, the younger you are when you first experience sex, even abuse, the more serious implications it has in your life. Standing before you are the shattered remains of loving childhood gone horribly wrong."

Just what am I supposed to say? This is getting emotionally deep. D's trying to get this off his chest. Bite your tongue, Victoria.

"With that wealth of knowledge, I moved into adulthood, where I met an awesome girl, managed to settle down, start a family and watch my children develop into functioning adults. Sadly, however, life repeats itself. After two decades, the apple of my eye, who I lived and breathed for, lost interest in me. That's where the lack of sex complicates a relationship even more. Just imagine, the person you worshiped, the woman you adored, suddenly having no time for you, because life and her budding career consumed her. Besides, her words not mine, 'I was old enough where my wants and needs didn't matter anymore.' Damn it, they did! Much more than you could imagine. No matter how hard I tried to convince her otherwise, she refused to see me self-destructing before her eyes."

The slow rhythmic humming of the BOA stopped. Looking directly at Vic, I discovered that she had modestly covered herself. And, by her solemn expression, was composing an appropriate reply.

How do I say this and not be mean? "You're flawed, D," confessed Vic. "I get it. Hell, we're all flawed in some form or fashion. We convey admirable traits that we pray will gloss over the not so admirable ones. Sometimes they do, sometimes they don't. Your generosity covers quite a bit of your past sins. Today, you've shared some of your demons. Guess what, I'm not running? Excuse me, I digress. I can tell by the look on your face, you're not finished, are you? I suspect you have the all-encompassing random sex theory to explain. Best you go ahead, cause I'm sure that's where I come into this equation."

How'd you know?... "Random, casual sex is like putting a Band-Aid on a severed artery. It may limit the blood loss, but only temporarily. The wound is still there, the hurt is still there, compounded even more because you've failed to address the underlying problem." Rising from the bed, Vic, wrapped in the comforter, settled onto the floor beside my chair.

Vic, laying her head on my knees, "I'm sorry I've pressured you so much to make love to me. You're a desirable guy and the last time I looked, I'm a desirable girl. That's what we do, or so I thought, 'til now. No man, in my sexually active lifetime has ever spurned me. Never! The harder you teased me and oh so casually pushed me away, the more I wanted you. I'll tell you a not-so-secret, secret. For me, sex is power. Sex is a weapon. Sex is a self-sharpening tool. The vagina has and continues to be a WMD. Throughout history, sex has brought powerful men and great countries to their knees repeatedly. Sex is my ally and from wince my power comes. A life-changing lesson that was thrust upon me a long time ago." she exhaled. *Whew! There, I said it!*

Not knowing whether to stay on subject, complicated by her bold confessional, or continue with her previous questions, I chose the latter. *WMD's, aka weapons of mass destruction, are not something I want to tackle today.* The chicken in me continued, "Fortunately, I've managed to move on to some degree. The train wreck of my making still smolders on the well-worn tracks of my past. At this very moment, I'm still not over Candi. I'm surely not over you and we've yet to become an "us." There's a possibility if the stars align, there could be an 'us' in the future, couldn't there?" I waited for a non-verbal response…I got nothing. "That being said, why let a sex crazed roll in the sack screw us up before we've had a chance fire off on all cylinders?"

"We're screwed up enough, huh, D? Here's a heads up, I'm not sure I'm ready for all of you either. I mean, my body is, as you've so aptly experienced, but my mind has some heavy lifting ahead of you. Sometime soon, before we get home, you'd best hear about the nefarious skeletons jingling around in my closet. After that, you very well may not be ready for me… period. A fair warning, you'll probably have to get me in a precarious state to open my Pandora's box. That closely guarded area of my life has been off limits forever. Not even my Ex was privy to it. He had no flaws, or so I thought, 'til he did. Then it was too, damn late. By my not opening up, he found someone who did. Would it have made a difference? I doubt it. Yet, you've convinced me in the last thirty minutes, what I've failed to figure out over the last thirty-two years…to completely know someone, you have to know where they're coming from, even if it means going back to the beginning. I've buried those memories, as if they never happened to me, but someone…"

Stopping Vic mid-sentence, by pressing my fingers to her lips, "surely, that's enough for now, barrister. I'm emotionally drained, sexually frustrated and come to think of it, in dire need of a brew…not screw, geez! I saw that sneer. Put your clothes on and meet me on the patio…please."

Rising from the chair, I lifted Vic to her feet, offering her a much-needed hug, as the comforter fell willy-nilly to the floor. Wrapped securely in my arms was a very scared and frightened little girl, longing to reveal her life altering past to me. I kissed her passionately on the lips, lingering long enough to breathe her air. "I'm here for you…but, you know that already," I assured her, before bolting out the door, astutely aware of the endless possibilities, soon realized, had I stayed.

Chapter 7

Josie joined me on the patio with a bucket of chilled, Canadian Molson's, giddily sharing her vision of the private balconies and the accompanying hot tubs. Building out the ground floor decks were simple enough, but the two, second story suites presented more of a problem because of the extreme weight and potential liability. We finally agreed on two balconies for the second-floor units, with private staircases leading down and connecting to the two, ground floor hot tubs. The worst-case scenario would be that her guests might have to share the tubs occasionally.

Victoria appeared, flawlessly emerging herself into our conversation.

"Have you worked out all the logistics?" Vic asked, joining Josie and I outside.

"We have," replied Josie, "we compromised."

"Josie, I'll generate a materials list to go with these renderings to assist the contractors in pricing. Now, however, I'd like to take Victoria for a stroll through your beautiful gardens and along the golf course before dark."

"Then what are you waiting for, Jon David?" asked Josie. "Did I tell the both of you how glad I am you stayed?"

"You did, sweetie, numerous times. I promise I'll have Victoria back by dusk."

Taking Vic's hand, I led her through the lush gardens, and onto the fairway of the adjoining golf course. "Vic, baring my soul earlier drained me emotionally. I shared secrets with you I've never shared with anyone, including Candi. We do have client, attorney privileges, don't we? Plus, a budding friendship to build a lifetime of trust."

"I assure you, we're friends first and always," Vic said, followed up with a quick kiss on my cheek.

"You have get back to Sioux City anytime soon, Victoria? I mean … now that you've joined my ride, we can take the long way or the long, long way back. There's really no ideal shortcut from here. I say that to confess I dread what lies ahead. There's still a bounty on my head, compliments of Standford and WITSEC is not the least bit happy I left the good ole U.S. of A. For all I know Donny, no teeth, is looking for me and possibly even Joseph."

"To reply to your last statement, first, you're welcome to hang with me in Sioux City… at least until we know what we're up against. As to your second question, I'm good either way on the ride back. That may change after a couple of days when my saddle-sore ass starts screaming, bloody murder, for relief." She paused… "We'll have to cross that precarious bridge when we come to it, won't we?"

"We will. If it helps, I can tell you that Candi managed to soak her saddle soreness away most evenings in a great big tub."

She wiggled. "So, find me a room each night with a great big tub and we're copasetic."

"It's a deal. In the meantime, I best check in with the boys in blue. I'm sure they'd like an update on my current situation. Oh, and the dog. The kennel thinks I'm due back tomorrow."

That's a thought. Spinning him into my space, "Just what is our current situation, D?"

"Well, I've swapped my number one girl for my number one girl, number two. I have expert legal counsel close at hand and I'm still on the bike. Oh, and the Family, like Elvis, has left the building with most of what they came after. Other than that, I have no clue."

"Me either, I'm hungry," said Vic. "Let's eat."

"You sound just like—"

"Candi." *When is he going to finally hear me instead of her?*

"Yep, just like her."

Chapter 8

Tampa Bay

After an endless exchange of late night pleasantries with the whole 'fam damily,' Candi managed to make a graceful exit to her room and crawl into her childhood bed, albeit alone. *Where's D? What's he doing right now? Who will hold me while I sleep? Question after question tossed about in my restless mind, robbing me of the sleep my body desperately craved. That is until I found myself carried back in time, to a bed and breakfast in northern Alabama, where I woke for the very first time, in his arms. He said something later that morning, that I appreciated, 'Waking up to you saying good morning baby, with a smile on your face that says you're happy to be here, is more precious than gold.' I'd trade all the gold in the world, to have him here now to share those words with me again.* Using my iPad, I turned on Pandora to Sinatra, our lovemaking music. Sleep came quickly.

* * *

She slept 'til noon. Still in her PJ's, Candi followed the sounds of spirited Italian into the kitchen where she found Gio and Mile gathered around the breakfast table with Mom.

"Morning all or afternoon, whatever the case may be. What's with all the noise?"

"I tell your Momma that D save me, he save my leg. He good people," replied Gio. "I tell her, how you say, he care for you. He make you smile."

"Thank you, cousin. Mom and I have much to talk about including D… just not right now."

Her mother, however, had other ideas. "I am thankful you are all safe. But, as I recall, there is someone else that cares for you, and he too, made you smile."

"Enough about Joseph. I'm not still in love with him, I'm not sure I ever was. He is a good person, heck, I'm a good person, that we both used selfishly as an end to a means." Candi paused, "It is what it is."

"What's love got to do with it? Why can't you just be friends?" countered Mom.

Ready to spew forth something she would surely regret, Gio latched onto her shoulder, using her as a crutch and walked Candi outside. "You no win with your Momma. Not now, hmm…maybe later. She like Joseph, he part of family. D, he outsider. He no good for you. We know better. We know, D, she not."

"Thank you Gio, for trying. Sometimes Mom only sees what she wants to see. There is no big picture in her world. She can be extremely narrow minded, as well as obstinate when she chooses to be."

"Be nice Candice. She your Momma."

"Yep, I keep trying to remember that. Moving out of Florida was the best thing I ever did. As I've aged, I can only take her in small doses. Mom tries to run me like she runs the Family business. It's her way or the highway. When I was in Tennessee, it was my way. Would you believe, D, liked me for me? Even when he found out otherwise, he still cared for me, Candi. Not Candice, not part of some big conspiracy, not someone who had ulterior motives, but me. He saw through all that stuff that was just a game to me and forced me to be selfless, not selfish."

"You love him, Candice?"

"I don't know how to answer that, because I'm not sure what love is, Gio. Does he make me happy to be with him, yes? Does he make me want to be a better person? I have to say yes to that, too. I betrayed him Gio. How will he ever forgive me?"

"D good Candice. You ask, you explain, he will."

"I hope so, Gio, but first I have to find him. I know, I know, start with the dog. I'll call Marcy this afternoon and get her on that hunt. In the meantime, what about you? When are you and Mile going back to Milan?"

"Your momma say tomorrow. We stay if you need us."

"Thanks for the offer. I'm a big girl, soon, a much wealthier, big girl. I can handle Mom. It's just going to take time and space. Lots and lots of space."

Before Gio could offer a verbal or non-verbal reply, the French door to the kitchen swung open, revealing my mother, the messenger. "Joseph called. He said you were getting together with him today. He will be here at seven to take you to dinner at your favorite restaurant, Byrnes. I took the liberty to tell him you would love to go. Besides, what else do you have to do tonight?"

I have lots to do, none of which includes Joseph. Biting her lip just as Gio put his hand on her shoulder, she nodded yes to acknowledge her affirmatively while Candi thought, 'No! Hell no!'

She made the call to Marcy, no answer. *I hope she listened to her voice mail and its urgency and blocks off Saturday morning for a little detective work. If anybody can find Major, it's her. I'll throw in a girls' weekend in Calgary as a reward. I want to go back. I wasn't done there. I want to finish the ride to Jasper. I want, I want, I want. In truth, without D being a part of it, my wishing is all for naught.*

Chapter 9

Dressing conservatively, Candi kept her make up to a minimum. No Sephora tonight, just lip gloss, eyeliner and a little blush. This was a business dinner, nothing more, nothing less, she kept telling herself, over and over, while she waited impatiently for the witching hour to arrive. Promptly at seven, the doorbell rang. One trait she always admired in Joseph, he was punctual. Opening the door, Candi found Joseph standing before her in a double-breasted, black Armani suit with a red silk tie. "Welcome Joseph. Have you been on family business today or did you dress in your finest just for me?"

"Hello to you. Well, Candice you look, how can I say this nicely, average?"

"I am average, Joseph. What you see is what you get. Tonight, is strictly business. I hear you're taking me to Byrnes. Any special reason you chose it, other than the fact it's where you proposed to me?"

"I'm supposed to woo you, remember? What better place for us to make a fresh start."

"Not to blow your bubble, but it didn't work out so well for us the first time."

Probably not the best way to begin an evening. Abruptly, no forcefully, Joseph locked her arm in his and escorted her to his shiny, new, red Ferrari. "Beautiful ride you have here. Does it make picking up sluts any easier?"

"Hush please, Candice. Get in the car!"

The drive to the restaurant was made in deafening silence. Staring straight ahead, she wondered how many women he'd managed to bed with this fine ride. Pulling up to the valet, Joseph exited first, and flipped him a twenty, before stomping into the restaurant, leaving her to escort herself inside. *It wasn't hard to find him. Another virtue he exhibits is predictability. He's always sitting in the darkest corner booth, nearest the bar. He must have already ordered a Black Crown neat, because an all too familiar waitress was dropping it by the table as I sat down.*

"Lori, I'd like to introduce you to my ex-wife, Candice. Candice, I'd like you to meet Lori. Bring her a bottle of white Merlot. Be sure to leave just one wine glass. Oh, and Lori keep bringing these," directed Joseph, lifting his glass as if to offer a toast, before turning it up and draining it in one long gulp.

"It's a pleasure to meet you, Ms. Candice. Mr. Joseph and I go way back."

As far as the seat will recline, she thought. "It's very good to meet you. If he drinks too much, do you see that he gets home safely?"

"Oh, I do that all the time. I'll do anything he asks to drive his car," bubbled Lori, before catching herself with foot in mouth.

"I'm sure you do, Lori. I'm sure you do."

Joseph's demeanor was rapidly changing and not for the better, his face flushing red. "Lori, you've graciously shared more than enough. Leave us alone please, we've got business to discuss, privately."

"We'd better be quick," said Candi. "You keep downing those Crowns and you'll not remember anything we've agreed on today."

"I told you, Candice, I'll keep my end of the bargain as long as you keep yours. First, I need something from you. A good faith gesture if you will."

"What might that be?"

"You."

"Me?" she stammered, "just what exactly do you want, Joseph?"

"I want you to make love to me. I want to know you're trying to make us work. The offer to split the money was a kind gesture on your part. But, you couldn't care less whether you have any or all of it. Thanks to your Family, you're set for life. What I want is what we had and that begins with having you."

"Are you out of your frigging mind? What happened to wooing me, taking it slow, winning my heart back?"

"That will come, Candice. Right now, I can't get this guy D out of my head. You were falling for him. I saw the way you looked at him. The way you dressed for him. I bet you've been riding his cock for months. If you want to keep him safe, it's your turn to ride mine. Prove to me you're over him. Screw me the way you screwed him and mean it."

"You're drunk, Joseph. This is the alcohol talking."

"I'm not drunk enough. Watch this." Removing his cell phone from his inside, breast pocket, Joseph pressed a memorized number, then hit send.

After two rings, she overheard a too familiar voice answer and immediately ask, "Boss, you ready for me to take care of the problem?"

"Hang on, Donny. Candice, what will it be? I need to know now, not tomorrow, not next week, NOW!"

Blackmail, rape, coercion, any and or all of those words crossed my lips and settled into the pit of my stomach. Suddenly I was nauseated and on the precipice of tossing the remnants of a lunch, long since digested. Strength and bravery were not the attributes I could readily claim. Self-sacrifice, however, is one I had recently learned, compliments of D. In a barely audible whisper, she mumbled, "Yes."

"What did you say, Candice? I didn't hear you. Louder please."

"Yes, damn you, yes!"

"Donny, hold off for now. Things are actually looking up. I'll be in touch."

"Are you satisfied, Joseph?" she asked, before realizing what a bad choice of words it was.

"Not at the moment, but I will be shortly, thanks to you," as his right hand moved from the table, onto her knee. "I'm not hungry anymore. What say we get outta here and go back to my place, before you change your mind?"

"I don't really have a say in the matter, do I?"

"No, tonight you don't. Tonight, you're mine."

"Then give me the valet ticket, I'm driving. You take care of the tab and Lori. I'll be in the car." Waiting impatiently for the Ferrari to be brought up, Candi shuffled her feet along the ground, thinking back to the last time she drove with a male in the passenger seat. Bringing a smile to her lips, she fondly recalled the male, aka D, was not in the passenger seat at first, but the back one, directly behind her. That was the day I gave her an anniversary present of sorts, a toy if you will, the infamous BOA. *How I long to feel that toy inside me, along with the man behind it, beside me.* Jolted from her daydreaming, reality knocked, repeatedly.

"Unlock my door, Candice," shouted Joseph, pounding on the passenger door. "Where is your head?"

Rummaging around in the dark, unfamiliar slut mobile, she finally found the unlock button on the console and pressed it.

"Thank you," Joseph huffed, before calming down, smiling like a Cheshire cat. "I'm glad you offered to drive me home. It's changed quite a bit since you've been there. Hopefully, you'll see it for the better. Candice, I was thinking, with you driving, I've got two free hands to get you prepped and ready. Speaking of that, I popped the little blue pill before I left the bar, compliments of Lori. That girl is an amazing resource if I do say so myself."

"Joseph, you're drunk. How about I take you home and we can have sex some other time."

"I told you, Candice, I'm not drunk enough. I heard just have sex, but that's not what we're doing tonight. You're going to make love to me as if your life depended on it. Hell," Joseph boasted, "I can screw anyone I want. This is not about getting off, it's about getting inside you, inside your head. You'll prove your sincerity by the way you kiss me, touch me, suck me and fuck me. I want you to convince me there can be an us again."

Screaming out of the parking lot, Candi made it less than five miles with his hand in her pants, before the nausea returned. Grabbing the steering wheel, white knuckled, she jerked the shiny new Ferrari off the road and into a gravel parking lot where she whimpered, "excuse me, I think I'm going to be sick." Just as she opened the door, the contents of her stomach launched violently onto the ground.

"I honestly hope you didn't get any of that crap on my car," barked Joseph. "You could have at least stepped outside, you know? Hold on a second. Let me find something for you to wipe up with."

Reaching into the console, Joseph handed her a wadded-up napkin, which she used to wipe off her chin before expanding it to wipe off the door-jamb of his precious car. Bad move on her part, because as she unfolded it, a used condom fell out and spilled its remnants onto her pants. Turning back toward Joseph as if to ask, "What the hell?" she saw him snickering, mouthing the word sorry, just as she threw up again…this time into his lap and all over the rest of his precious car.

"Get out, now!" screamed Joseph, exiting the car.

She readily complied, amused that he'd managed such a hasty retreat, the remnants of her stomach sliding gracefully down his black Armani pants.

"What is wrong with you, Candice? How could you do this to me … to my car?"

"I'm sorry, Joseph. I may have a stomach bug… possibly a souvenir from your plane ride home."

Sobering quickly, he slung the goo from his pants with his fingers and wiped his hands off on the back of her jacket, "You're not getting out of tonight that easy. If you're done tossing your cookies, get in the car. I'm driving."

Regardless of how the rest of the night presented itself to be, I could at least claim one small, unheralded victory — Candice, 1; Joseph, 0.

Chapter 10

Vic and I walked back into the Inn, a few minutes shy of dusk to find Josie putting out paper plates and silverware for a feast. Before us were an enormous Greek salad and a large deep-dish pizza from Nikko's Pizzeria. "Please excuse me for not cooking tonight, but we're celebrating. Vic, you and D take a seat while I round us up a bucket of beer."

"Beer and pizza, no better way to celebrate an occasion, any occasion for that matter," I offered, in a celebratory toast to Vic and Josie.

"Not just any pizza, D. Vic, this is the best pizza in all Alberta. Their salads are almost as good as mine. The best part is, I didn't have to cook a thing. This way we can spend some quality time together without me worrying if you've had enough to eat."

"Works for us," said Vic. "Thank you, Josie."

"D, promise me, you'll come back when your storms subside. I know you've got a full plate. I've really enjoyed having you around, again. Oh, and you too, Victoria. He can sure pick his women." Realizing the hole, she was digging, Josie attempted to fast forward the conversation into another direction. "The Calvary, as you call them, were extremely cordial to me. All of them asked if they could come back next year during the Stampede."

Vic answered for us, my mouth stuffed with salad, "I'm sure we'll gladly come back whenever we can get our schedules on the same page. Why don't you just plan on us coming back for the Stampede as well? We'll take your Inn that entire week, if it's okay?"

"That sounds wonderful, Victoria. I'd like that. You're welcome any time. I'm sure by early spring, I'll have quite a few letters from the children to make into a book, just as you suggested."

It was my turn, "I got it, Josie. We're family, even after this twenty year hiatus. I promise it won't be that long again. You have problems with the construction, let me know and I'll be up here within a few days. That is if I'm not off in Europe somewhere chasing down Frank."

After cleaning up the leftovers from our feast, Vic and I adjourned to the patio overlooking the beautifully landscaped gardens and fountain. Even at night they were inspiring, complimented by the soft glow of low voltage lighting, strategically placed among the trees, waterfalls and boulders.

This is relaxing, not a care in the world. "Wouldn't it be great if we could just stay here, D?"

"It's tempting, girlfriend. Candi asked me the very same thing. I'd venture to guess you and I would both be barn butt wide within six months. Josie reminds me of my mom and how she was never satisfied until everyone was bursting at the seams from her home cooking."

"D, I ever tell you I can't cook? You wind up staying with me for a while and I promise you… you'll lose weight. However, what I lack in culinary skills, I make up in so many extraordinary ways." She giggled.

"Of course, you do, I'd expect nothing less… few which require clothes, I'm guessing."

Smart boy, this guy. "How'd you know?"

"Call it my sex-th sense. Speaking of my senses, let's go upstairs, rummage through Candi's riding gear and see if I can outfit you with enough road rags to get you home."

I am not Candi! "Seriously D, you don't expect me to wear her clothes, do you?"

"You'll need leathers, boots and silks. Surely, if they fit you can wear them for a few days, can't you? Candi has excellent, and by that, I mean expensive tastes. They're worth trying on, I assure you."

She relented. "All right D, let's do it. If they're expensive, they can't be totally bad."

"In every woman lurks a clothes whore longing to get out. I saw your eyes brighten when I said excellent and expensive. You, too, have been gifted with the desire for the finer things."

"I believe that to be true," said Vic. "I heard that for the very first time when I was sixteen, serving as a page in Congress." *Catching myself, I dared not go further, immediately changing the subject before D could ask me to explain.* "Hey, what about my overnight bag? Can I take it on the bike?"

"You can if it's the size of this backpack. Otherwise, we'll need to ship it."

Once in the room, Vic brazenly stripped down, revealing nothing but her bright green thong and matching bra. "What should I try on first, D?"

Grabbing the pack, I tossed it on the bed, "Try on the silks," realizing the befuddled look on her face needed further explanation. "They're slinky black and look like long underwear for women silly."

"Found 'em," she quipped.

Watching Vic slip into them comfortably, I realized how close she and Candi were in size. "Try on her chaps and jacket. Now her boots, please." Seductively, Vic peeled off the silks before holding up the chaps, questioning in her mind just how she was supposed to attach them. "Here, let me help you. Buckle them around your waist and I'll zip them, top down." I couldn't help but laugh, remembering in vivid detail the first time these chaps were tried on by Candi. Les, from Leather Outfitter's was way too touchy-feely for her liking.

"Why are you laughing?" asked Vic. "Are my legs fat?"

"Nope, your legs are perfect, so is your ass," I replied, complimenting her by playfully slapping her on the rear. "I've decided my next side job should be in a leather store. I mean where else can you cop a feel, over and over, helping women try on tight fitting attire and get away with it?"

"What do you mean, I haven't felt you..."

Her voice trailed away as I used both hands to lift the chaps as high as they would go into her crotch while purposely running my fingers across her.

"Yep, that would do it," she purred sheepishly. "Higher D, higher. Can't wait for you to put my other leg on."

"See. I told you it's a tough job, but somebody has to do it. Success," I announced, as I managed to zip down the other leg without lingering too long near her lady parts. "A little long in the length," I guessed, "but I can take care of that. Put the jacket on for me. That works. Now the boots, I believe they're a size nine."

Not even close. "I wear an eight."

"I got it, Victoria. With two pairs of socks they'll work. It's not like we're going on mile long day hikes."

"They fit, D, but just barely. Two pair of socks helps. What else is in this bag that I might need?" Digging through the bag she pulled out two matching red thongs, one definitely for a woman, while the other confused her a bit because of the pouch. Twirling it round and round with her forefinger, "judging by its little size, I'm assuming this banana hammock belongs to you. These have a story to tell, don't they, big fella? I'd like to hear it … now."

Playfully, "You want the long version or the short one? There's not much to tell really. I mean… it was a little innocent fantasy I played out in my mind."

"So, you and Candi played make believe? I can't see that coming from you. I'm sorry D, but you're a doer. If you dreamed it, then you damn well did it."

Remembering I did it and how I did it, two times as I recall, caused my skin to flush pink. "You're embarrassing me, Vic. I'm not sure I know where to start."

"At the beginning, big boy. That's usually the best place."

Chapter 11

Tampa Bay

Pulling up to the gated entrance of her — excuse me, his — eighth floor condo overlooking beautiful Tampa Bay, Candi couldn't help but think how much she welcomed the opportunity to bath in the wall-less rain shower she left behind, a little over two years ago. "Joseph, when we get inside, the first thing I'm going to do is take a long hot shower, in private. Please open a bottle of Pinot Noir." Waiting not for a reply, she scurried past 'her furniture' in the great room and into their bedroom, which by the looks of things was now his playroom. Mirrored panels adorned the ceiling over the bed, while a 72-inch widescreen TV took up almost an entire wall where my armoire used to sit. Surround sound speakers filled every corner, suspended from the ceiling along with a plain giant silver ring that somehow conveyed something more sinister, than simple.

In the bathroom, hanging on the inside of the door, were his and her robes, while an assortment of lubes, massage oils and pot were lined up along the edge of the Jacuzzi. Oh my, if these walls could talk, she murmured to herself, as she stripped off her clothes and tossed them on the floor. Turning the shower to hot, she stepped inside, breathing deeply the steam that rapidly enveloped her. Lingering for what seemed like an eternity, she didn't want to leave the sanctity of the cleansing water that flowed across her body. *It may seem surreal, but I can empathize with date rape victims and their desire to imme-diately scrub the memory, as well as the evidence away. Sadly, I'm on the front end of his forthcoming madness and I still can't get clean enough.* A loud banging on the locked door brought her out of her dream like stupor and back into her present, sordid reality.

"Candice, you done? I need a shower to wash this God-awful smell of your insides off me."

Turning off the healing water, Candi stepped onto the heated tile floor, grabbed the 'hers' robe and wrapped herself in it before unlocking the door. "Next."

Joseph was stripped down to his boxers and holding an opened wine bot-tle in one hand and two goblets in the other. "It's all up to you now. Make yourself comfortable. I'll be out in a few."

Taking the wine and glasses from his hands, Candi poured a generous amount. She drank it, and then repeated. If this coerced lovemaking sce-nario was going to happen, and she damn well sure it was, she deserved to be under the influence of something. *Juggling the current men in my life based on what is and what was is daunting. On the one hand, Joseph and I had something, and could very well have something again. He's got a good pedigree, he's super smart and he's a great lover — a little kinky maybe, but still a great lover. That being said, I don't appreciate being forced or blackmailed to do something I don't want to do. By all accounts that's rape. I can, however, make a concerted effort tonight to recon-nect with him, emotionally, as well as physically. I'm rationalizing I know, but what other choice do I have? I mean for all I know, D's banging Victoria's brains out right now, falling for her just like he did for me. That's his right, mind you, after what I did to him. What am I talking about, "what I did to him?" I saved him. I put his and Vic's safety above what I wanted. I wanted him then, I want him now.*

She started counting off the reasons why it wouldn't work between us. *One, he's in WITSEC. He'll always be looking over his shoulder. Which leads me to number two, my mom will say no. Not just no, but hell no! Three, he won't be able to trust me ever again, even if I convince him that at the time it was best for all concerned. Four, D, could never love me for a lifetime, the spoiled brat that I am. While reaching out for reason number five, the opening of the bathroom door interrupted my well-rehearsed arguments to myself.*

"Pour me a glass please, Candice, while I turn on some music and a few other things. I would hate for you to drink alone."

"Pandora, Joseph. I would enjoy hearing Sinatra. By the way, I don't mind pouring you wine, but shouldn't you stay with liquor? I mean putting wine on top of Crown may not sit well with you."

"Let me be the judge of that. You're not talking to a girl scout here. I appreciate your concern for my well-being, really I do, but I can take care of myself."

Sitting down on the bed next to her, wrapped in his robe, Joseph poured his own glass of Pinot.

Holding the goblet in his left hand, Joseph began stroking his fingers through her hair with his right. "Candice, what happened to us? We were happy once. We were madly in love."

"Times change, Joseph. People change. The more you immersed yourself in the Family business, the less I saw of you. Then when I did see you, it was only for casual conversation and sex, nothing more. Believe it or not, I'm worthy of your admiration. Getting my Master's in Nursing wasn't enough for you. Earning an appointment to director of Risk Management at All Children's Hospital wasn't enough either. Why do you think I moved to Tennessee and tried to find the ledgers on my own? Because, I knew if D had them, I could find them. Then I could prove to my mother and everyone else, including you, that I have a lot to contribute to this family."

Taking the goblet from her hand, Joseph gently pushed her back onto the bed. Playfully unwrapping her robe, he pointed to the big screen that had come alive, starring Candi. "Now you can watch me making love to you from every angle in the room. Doesn't the thought of that make you hot?"

"Truthfully, it unnerves me. Why would you want to watch yourself having sex? I mean you're already as close as you can get, live and in color."

Removing his robe, before sliding on top of her, Joseph continued, "It adds another sensual element, just like the mirrored tile I installed on the ceiling."

He massaged her temples with his thumbs, and she closed her eyes, losing herself in the familiar music of Sinatra. Minutes passed, before she felt his lips touching hers, leaving the taste of expensive whiskey and wine. His hands moved swiftly to her chest, as his lips trailed down the nape of her neck. He grabbed and twisted her nipples simultaneously, then she felt his hot breath and lips replace his fingers as he kissed them, one at a time.

The results of the little blue pill were evident. His hardness pressed between her thighs hoping to find a wet spot that had sadly failed to materialize. Wrapping her arms around him, she rolled Joseph onto his back and using her hands, guided her nipples into his mouth. "There you go… don't stop," she directed, moving her body up and down his generous package, using the expertise of her gyrating hips to engage him all the more.

So, help me, he does feel good. Yet without protection, he was never getting inside me tonight. That, I am sure would be another argument. Taking matters into her own hands, she slid down the length of his body, before coming to rest on the generous manhood she used to lovingly adore. Enveloping him, taking little time to breathe, she hoped to quickly appease his lust-driven appetite, if only for the moment.

Grasping his hands, she placed them where hers had been so that he could hold himself firmly in the soft sleeve of her breasts while her palms slid firmly under his thighs. Using her hands to thrust him upward and forcefully into the oral vacuum of her making was more than enough to take him to the edge. Pressing his perineum with her left forefinger and thumb vaulted him over the top.

"That was incredible, Candice," Joseph said softly, his legs still shaking, the color drained from his face.

"You're welcome. I forgot all the fun we used to have, once upon a time. Thank you. No arguments, please. We need to get dressed. I have to go home."

"Wait! You're not staying? I'll be ready to go again in ten minutes, twenty, tops."

"Slow, remember? We're taking it slow. What you've had is but a taste of what's to come if you continue to play by my rules. I'm making a sincere effort here," she lied, wiping his remnants from his chest, before swiping them across his lips."

Taken aback, Joseph quickly regrouped. "I got it, Candice. We can get as kinky as you want. You can tie me up, spank me, whatever, I'm yours. Just stay. I don't want you to leave tonight. I deserve the opportunity to do you."

"Not tonight, Joseph. This evening was all you."

"Candice, damn you, I want things back the way they were before D started messing with your head."

"I keep telling you, D has nothing to do with it. Sure, he was fun, but to me it was nothing more than gamesmanship. For the record, I won. Excuse me, *we* won. Now get dressed and take me home. Otherwise, I'll call an Uber. I'm spent. It's been a long, long day."

Chapter 12

"Vic, I wanted Candi's first motorcycle ride to be memorable, so I dreamed up an event that will allay her fears and replace her apprehension of being on the back of my bike with unexpected, unbridled pleasure. Thanks to your desolate, straight Iowa roads I was able to do just that. Dressed in our matching thongs, chaps and raincoats, at least until we got out of town, I used the BOA to pleasure her while she simultaneously pleasured me. Riding along the cornfield-defined highway, under a moonlit, starry sky, we were able to mutually climax with no one else the wiser."

Oh, my God! Men! "The same 'boy toy' you've been sharing with me?"

"Come on, Vic, that's all you managed to glean from the conversation, geez? It was exciting to take her mind off the bike and have her focusing solely on herself."

She laughed. "You focused on her, D. She focused on you."

"Whatever. It worked. Only one time on our ride did she ever scream in terror. Of course, there were some extenuating circumstances."

"In that case, I want you to recreate her ride with me. I've never got off on a motorcycle — a plane maybe, a car for sure, but not a bike. That intrigues me. I deserve to know how you managed to pull it off. I say, that, right? You owe me. Call it professional courtesy."

The memories of that night came rushing back in vivid, brilliant colors. "You're serious?"

"You bet your sweet ass. I want to experience what Candi felt. I want the chance to feel you while you're feeling me, cruising down the back roads at 50 mph. But, I'm not wearing her thong. I've got my own for that."

"Vic, you're twisted."

"D, you're the one that's twisted. I'm just the pretzel that wants to be entwined with you."

Sounds like a book title. "It's a deal, I'll never win this argument. Pack all your necessities in the backpack. The rest we'll ship to your house, along with Candi's. Don't look at me like I'm crazy, we're traveling light. If you run short of anything, we'll buy it. That's all I know to tell ya. Look at this as an adventure, girlfriend."

If we live through it. "By the looks of things already, it's going to be a fun, fun ride."

We slept soundly, spooning through the night … me in my shorts and Vic in the silks she evidently appreciated.

* * *

"Wake up, sleepy head, today we ride." Rising, I immediately began packing our gear.

"What time is it, D?" she asked, knowing by the looks of things it's still dark thirty.

"6:30, girlfriend."

"You're dreaming. It's still dark outside. Come back to bed … please."

"Vic, we ride early, we stop early, long before dark. This schedule works, I promise."

"It does… 'til it don't.' I'm the 'don't' caveat. I am not a morning person." *Why on earth haven't you figured that out by now?*

"Got it. We're leaving at eight. That gives you an hour and a half to wake up and get your happy face on. I'm going downstairs for tea. What can I bring you?"

"Coffee, please. Black, and plenty of it." *Three, maybe four cups tops, to get my act together and put on a happy face for this man I've entrusted with my life … for now.*

Chapter 13

Walking into the gardens, I cut off three red, Mr. Lincoln Roses and added them to her breakfast tray. "Here you go, Victoria. A carafe of Josie's finest blend, along with a freshly made breakfast sandwich and flowers to say how grateful I am you chose to entertain me on this lonesome ride home."

He can be really sweet sometimes. "I know you care, D. These little things you do mean a lot. Thank you."

"You're welcome. Drink up; eat up. I'll be back in a few to bring our gear down. Right now, I've got a few calls to make."

It was a little after eight a.m. when I made a call to Jim, my current baby-sitter in the WITSEC program. It went straight to voice mail. I left a message.

"Morning Jim, thanks again for your assistance. I've probably screwed myself right out of the program. I got it. I'm leaving Calgary this morning and will be back in the states in a few days. I'll check my messages late tonight to see if you've got any news for me. Later."

Now, I needed to call the kennel and check on Major, my blond labradoodle. They've been great at taking care of him on short occasions, but never for this long. After two rings, it went straight to voice mail. Another dead-end call, another message.

"Hi, guys. D here. How's Major? Is he walking you every day? I'm running behind schedule at the moment. It may be another week before I get back. If you need to reach me, best to send me an email and I'll call you back within a couple of days. Thanks."

Enough with the phone — two calls and two messages, no live people. Emails and texts are totally the future. Once upstairs, I was pleasantly surprised to find Vic adorned in leather, carrying on a spirited conversation with Josie.

"Which way are we going, D?" asked Vic. "Josie said there's a really great mineral spa we need to visit in Moose Bone."

"Moose Jaw, Vic, I'm pretty sure it's Moose Jaw," I chuckled.

"It's a bone of some sorts, whatever. I'm giving you a heads up. If we're going in that direction, we're stopping."

"Honey, it's Moose Jaw, like the bone. That's what I said," assured Josie, almost apologetically.

"I got it, Josie. We are going that way and if Vic can manage to be 'Miss Iron Butt' for a day, we can make it."

You just watch me! "I'll do whatever it takes to be pampered in a spa, D," pressed Vic. "You say ride, we ride."

"We ride." Giving Josie a hug goodbye, I carried our gear to the bike while Vic worked out the details for Josie to ship the rest to Sioux City. Bringing the bike to life was her cue that I was ready to go. Rushing out the door into the early morning sunshine, Vic looked stunning in black, her long auburn hair tied into a pony tail. "Let me guess, you've ridden long distances before?"

Climbing on behind me, grasping a bulging handful of blue jeans between my chaps as she settled into me, "Yep, but not with someone as well packaged as you."

"Cute, girlfriend. Cute." With that, we were off. The mountains behind us, the route before us passed through endless miles of prairie and rolling hills along the Trans-Canada Highway, a 4,800-mile ride that starts in Victoria, BC, and ends in St. John's, NF.

One hundred and twenty miles into our ride, I felt a distinct tapping on my shoulder.

My ass is numb and I have to pee, but I won't be a pansy in his eyes. "How long before we stop, D? My butt is on fire."

Laughing, I said, "Iron butt you're not, Vic. Whiney butt, maybe. We'll be in Medicine Hat within the hour. Can your pansy ass wait that long or you want me to pull over now?"

Shifting her weight from cheek to cheek trying to squeeze off her bladder, she extended a gloved forefinger across my shoulder, pointing forward. *I ain't no pansy, asshole!*

"That's my girl," I laughed. "Ride, baby, ride."

A sign that read, "Welcome to Medicine Hat, home of the world's largest teepee" greeted us at the city limits. After crossing the South Saskatchewan River Bridge, I pulled into a Shell Canada Station to fuel, stretch our legs and clean off about every species of bug in Alberta from our windshield.

I breathed a sigh of relief. "Finally, D. Help me off, please. My butt is completely numb, and I can't feel my legs."

"Gladly, Vic. I'm proud of you. You've got a great bladder tucked away in there, I might add."

"No, I do not. I usually have an overactive bladder, but now I can't feel it either."

"Walk it off and by all means pee and re-pee while I fuel and scrape the bug juice off the windshield. You're doing great. You think you can make another 300 miles today?"

"Does that get us to Moose Bone ... uh jaw?" *Whatever the hell it is. I should be in a good mood. I asked for this ride. Suck it up girl.*

"It does. I promise we'll stop every hour or so from now on. I needed to make sure you could deliver on your end," I confessed, eagerly slapping her numb butt, "before I make reservations at the Garden's Resort."

"I'll make it, big boy. Go ahead and make the reservations. Set me up for an hour-long massage while you're at it."

Making the room reservations was the easy part. Trying to get Vic scheduled for a massage at a specific time was a little more difficult. I finally convinced the receptionist at the spa to give her a one-hour body soak at five o'clock, followed by a one-hour massage at six. That was their last slot of the day. Three hundred miles in five and a half hours can be done easily enough, but we'd have to limit our sightseeing opportunities.

Fueled, scraped and cleaned, I brought the bike to life and rumbled up to the front door.

Pain relievers, I need pain relievers. "D, do you have any Aleve close at hand or should I buy some while we're here?"

"Close is a relative term on a bike. Go ahead and buy some. You hungry? I remember seeing a Tim Horton's here my last time through — great coffee, awesome donuts and sandwiches. You game?"

"I am. Let me grab the butt relievers and we'll be off."

Vic is a refined young woman, a little gruff around the edges, but still refined. I didn't hit on her, wouldn't either, because in my mind I didn't stand a chance. That's how I remember Candi, too. Had she not almost wiped me out in the drive-thru at Starbucks, I would never have struck up a conversation with her. Look at me, a little too much belly, a little too many crow's feet and my hair and beard boasting a few too many shades of grey.

Walking back to the bike, she stood there for over a minute watching me completely zoned out. "You look like you are miles away, D. You, OK?"

"I am. Just wondering why you're here, Vic, and what you saw in me the first time we met?"

A pity party, that's what he was dwelling on? "Let's get on the road. Did you make a reservation for me? I'm not ignoring your last question. We can talk about your self-absorbed pity party when we get to Tim's."

Cranking the bike, I answered over the roar of my slightly baffled exhausts, "Tim Horton's, not Tim's. And yes, you're all set for a two-hour soak and massage that starts at five. We've got about six butt-numbing hours ahead of us with stops."

Joy! "Let's ride."

Stopping on the other side of town at Tim's, I ordered a large coffee and two, double chocolate cake, donuts, while Vic ordered a soup and sandwich combination. Sitting in an out of the way booth, Vic followed through with her offer to answer my last question.

"What's got into you today, D? First, I enjoy being around you. You have a way of making me feel special. Sure, you've got some road wear on you. Who doesn't? Yes, you're flawed, like me. That's why I think we get along so well. I read people, but don't trust them. You trust people, then read them. That in itself makes me a little more opportunistic because you're always challenging me to come up with ways to protect you from you."

"I sure could have used you a long time ago, pre Standford, pre-Candi. Maybe my ass wouldn't be in this crack."

Placing her hand on mine, "D, whatever happens, I'm here for you. That's why I chose to ride. After all the nut-busting events you've gone through, I didn't want you to be alone. Lots of windshield time is manageable when you're happy, but, trust me, it sucks royally when you've been screwed to the max."

"We still don't know if I've been royally screwed, or semi-screwed. Best we clarify that."

"You're right. I'm jumping to conclusions while you're still dreaming about that illusive snatch, excuse me, gold at the end of the rainbow. Whatever happens, we'll get through it, one way or the other."

"Thank you, Vic. I grateful you've got my back. Now eat. I've got a little over five hours to get your beautiful, whiney hinny soaking in a glorious… hot tub."

On the bike and on the road, I stopped to show Vic the world's largest teepee on the outskirts of town. Well, stopping is a relative word. I drove through the parking lot and onto the concrete pad holding the teepee in place. Circling the monument, I announced, "This is Medicine Hat's claim to fame. Now you can say you visited the largest teepee in the world."

My dad used to swing us through photo ops like that when I was young. "Thank you, tour guide. You could have stopped long enough for me to pee-pee in the teepee. Get it?"

"I get it. You make a funny. Hey, if you've really got to go again, I can find you a bush."

That's not happening. "No bushes for this girly-girl. I'll wait."

Chapter 14

Cruising at 125 kph, or a little over 75 mph to those of us who don't use the metric system, we made good time on the Trans-Canada Highway, traversing mile after mile of endless plains and prairie. With one stop for fuel and two highly anticipated potty breaks, along with a thousand multicolored splatters on my windshield, we crossed into the city limits of Moose Jaw, SK at 4:45 with 15 minutes to spare. Well, that's not exactly true. It took me another 12 minutes to "man" find the resort, leaving Vic roughly two minutes to find the spa.

"Hurry in, girlfriend. I've got this. When you're done being pampered, you'll find me imbibing in the bar."

"Hi, Lisa. I'm D," I announced to a bouncy, twenty something blond, who also happened to be the front desk manager. "I believe you have reservations for me tonight."

"I remember. You called from the motorcycle in Medicine Hat this morning. I booked you a deluxe king suite. It features a large garden tub fed from our mineral springs."

"Sounds wonderful, Lisa. Hopefully, I'll get to try it out. First things first, point me in the direction of the bar, if you please. Once I lug our gear to the room, that's where I'll be."

"Certainly, follow this long hallway on the right, and take a left at the end. The lounge will be the third set of double doors on your left. Can I set wake-up call for you?"

"No thank you. We've ridden hard today. It may take us an extra day to recover. Can I let you know in the morning if we'd like to stay another night?"

"Certainly, sir. Here are your room keys. Your room is located on the second floor facing our indoor pool. You'll also find two free drink coupons, as well as two breakfast coupons for 50% off our buffet. Thank you for choosing to stay with us."

Walking to the elevators, I couldn't help but think how special the Canadian people as a whole treat us Yanks. Unlike home, bike riders here are treated even better. I could get used to this, possibly even permanently. The room was more than just a room. It was a four-room suite, featuring a separate bedroom with a king-sized bed, a sitting room composed of a couch and two club chairs, sporting a 42-inch flat screen with a mini-bar; and a floral, ceramic tiled room specifically crafted to house the garden tub creating the advertised spa experience.

That tub was calling my name, but then again, so was the bar. The bar always wins after a long day's ride. *Tub you'll have to wait.* I washed my face and hands, giving myself the once over in the mirror. Then, I snagged the sat phone and began the quest to find those ice-cold Molson's that started calling my name a hundred plus miles before.

Lisa's directions were spot on. "Barkeep, a bucket of Canadian Molson's if you please. It's been a long day." Finding a table facing poolside, I settled down to wait until seven o'clock and Vic's highly anticipated return. The bartender, plopped a bucket of six iced down Molson's on the table, and received my customary thank you nod as I twisted off the cap and drained the first one without taking a breath.

Opening the second, I thought I'd better pace myself, considering the last time I drank at least six in a row I woke up in bed the next morning with

Candi's cousin, Giovanna, while the girls slept elsewhere. Picking up the sat phone, I dialed my voice mail and discovered one new message.

> *D, this is Jim. Call me tomorrow after twelve my time. Meanwhile, based on an email I received today your cover is no longer intact. I'm sure after all the recent events, you knew that already. In any event, you leaving the country has put your protection by WITSEC in jeopardy. Let's talk tomorrow and see what story we can come with that may keep you in the program. Be safe. Oh, against my better judgment, I've forwarded this email on to you as instructed. It's graphic porn, pure and simple, and one hot babe. My guess is you know her and this is intended to make a statement, validating a short seven-word message: Her Actions Speak Louder Than Your Words.*

Downing the second beer, I opened a third, twirling the emptied second bottle, round and round on the table with my fingers. My mind was now in overdrive. *Should I get up and find the business center and access my email or should I wait on Vic to appear to watch it together? I'm sure I've seen Vic with an iPad at some point on this ride. Best we watch it in private, rather than in a room with too many innocent eyes.*

Finally, at ten after seven, I felt a tap on my shoulder, followed by a kiss on my cheek, announcing rather subliminally that the pampered priss had arrived.

D looks wasted. "How many I need to down to catch up, D?"

"How many are in the bucket, girlfriend?"

"None. Unless there's another bucket somewhere."

"Well, that's how many you need."

"I count four empties on the table and two on the floor."

"In that case six, not counting the six on the way."

"You've had enough. Let's get something to eat. We can order room service if you'd rather skip the restaurant."

"You bring your iPad with you?"

"I did. Thankfully, it didn't take up much of the precious room you gave me for packing."

"Then room service it is," I concluded, before sliding off the bar stool and spilling onto the floor.

Helping me to my feet, Vic asked me point blank, "This drunken stupor have anything to do with Candi? The last time I saw you plastered was the day she hung you out to dry at the airport."

"I think so. We'll need your iPad to be sure. It's in an email that I've heard about, but have yet to see."

How am I going to do this gracefully? "Wait right here. Hold on to the table, please. I don't want you falling on the floor again. I'll order dinner from the bar menu and have it sent to the room. What would you like? On second thought, I'll order for you.

Chapter 15

"**D**amn Canadians!"

"Excuse me, D," said Vic. "Did I miss something?"

"Not the people, the beer. They have way too much alcohol in their beer. I keep forgetting that 'til I don't."

"You're making no sense, whatsoever. Walk with me to the bar while I order." Holding me up with her shoulder, she steadied me on the counter and ordered, before escorting me like a paid professional to the room.

"It's a group of rooms, Vic. Take me to the tub room. It's been calling … my name … all night."

"I'd love too, D. But first, we've got to sober you up a bit. Hot tubs and alcohol don't mix. They served me two flutes of champagne while I was in the tub and it went straight to my head. Your head's there already. You don't need any additional help tonight. Thinking outside the box, you'll hate me for this later, a cold shower would sure do you good."

"You said shower. I want a bath, girlfriend."

"How bout' a shower first and then a bath … with me if you're so inclined?" *Wishful thinking, but he's wasted. Therein lies my hope.*

"Whatever works, Vic. I'll follow… you lead."

Guiding me into the bedroom, she sat me on the bed and quickly removed my boots, followed by my clothes — all of them. "Nice little package there," she giggled. *It would be wonderful to bring it to life while the night is still young.*

But first, she had to get me relatively sober. Stripping down to her underwear in case her shower idea goes wrong, she left me sitting on the edge of the bed and continued with her plan.

I heard the shower door open and the water turn on, as Vic reappeared in a semi-state of undress to assist me into the large walk in shower.

"You're going to hate me for this, D. But I'm one selfish bitch, tonight. I need you at least halfway coherent," were her last words to me before pushing me headfirst into the freezing ice-cold shower.

The first thing I immediately felt were my testicles drawing up inside my body, before falling back down due to the weight of the ice hanging off my Johnson. The pulsating water continuously pelted my skin like sleet, turning it a strange, pale blue.

The next words I heard, "That's enough ice water for now, let me help warm you up," as Vic opened the shower door, adjusting the water dial to hot, and stepping inside to join me.

"I'm sorry, D. I didn't know what else to do to bring you out of your fog. You forgive me?" she asked, using one hand to caress my back, the other to massage and warm my low hanging, ice encased, fruit.

"There's nothing to forgive. You're just what the doctor ordered," I cackled, as her gentle caress awakened me from an earlier unresponsive and frigid state.

"Better, D?" *He sure feels better from where I'm standing. What I would give to...*

"You betcha. I'm sorry I let myself get wasted without you being there to prevent me from making a total ass out of myself."

"I'm sorry, too. I'm here now," purred Vic, her hands wrapping round my neck, her lips gently touching mine. Lost in the moment, reality knocked, then knocked again. Room service had arrived. "Damn it! Hang on, please. I'll be right there," she shouted over the cascade of the falling waters shower. "Timing is everything and nothing. Stay right where you are, D, while I get the door."

Timing is everything, I agreed as the alcohol induced fog slowly lifted from my brain. *You're an idiot, D. What were you thinking, putting yourself in such a defenseless position?* Stepping from the shower, disobeying her recent directive, I wrapped myself in an oversized towel and stood just inside the door. I waited until I heard Vic say goodbye, before stepping out of the bathroom and into the glaring stance of one very frustrated looking woman.

Not a good listener, this man. "You don't follow orders very well do you, sir?"

"I do most of the time, except when I'm on a tear ... then not so much."

"Well, then, I'll pass on my dessert idea first. Dinner is served. Put your shorts on and join me. Oh, don't bother hiding your excitement. It's refreshing to know I still have it in me," Vic cajoled, her hand grabbing at my tented towel, before I managed to swat it away.

We quietly shared Chicken Cordon Blue for two with mixed steamed vegetables and twice baked potatoes. Vic ordered two bottles of white Moscato and was into her second glass of the first bottle, before we finished our meal.

What a hell of a day. "I'm going for a buzz of my own if you don't mind now that the tables are turning. Join me, D?"

"Not likely. Beer and wine don't mix, silly girl. That I've learned too many times the hard way."

"Your loss big boy ... more for me."

Chapter 16

There's a big pink elephant bouncing spontaneously around the room tonight. Best we address it. "Spill," said Victoria, "what happened with Candi that shook you to the core while you were in the bar?"

"Earlier today, someone sent an email with an attached video clip to Jim at WITSEC with a seven- word message to forward to me. Jim said it's pure porn, made specifically for my viewing pleasure."

"What was the seven-word message?"

"Her actions speak louder than your words."

"Hold that thought while I get my iPad, D. Here, you might as well retrieve the email. If you're uncomfortable with what's on the video, I'll be glad to screen it for you. Not as your lawyer, but your friend."

Logging in, I retrieved Jim's email, hit download attachment and handed it back to her. "Knock yourself out, girlfriend, I'm going to fill the garden tub with hot mineral water and continue the spring thaw of my frozen testicles."

"It's downloaded, D. You sure you don't want to watch it with me?"

"If you'll allow me to borrow your famous catch phrase, for now, no. You watch it Vic, and give me the cliff notes version."

She pressed play and watched as Candi came into view in the process of mounting a man while pressing both breasts into his mouth, his face intentionally obscured. Judging by the size of his frame, along with the content of the message, one could confidently assume it was Joseph. He was really good looking with his clothes off. Throwing off her robe, she watched Candi kiss the length of his body before centering on the stiffness of his girth rising large between his legs. Pressing herself around him like a sleeve she eagerly devoured him. Expertly replacing her hands with his, Candi lifted his legs rhythmically, thrusting him continuously into the deep hollows of her throat. In a few minutes, it was over.

Catching her breath, trying to suppress the arousal the video inadvertently created in her, Vic picked up the iPad, her wine, as well as, the opened bottle and walked to the tub.

"Well, do I get the long version or the short version, Victoria?"

Change the subject or you'll change the mood. "What about some music, D?"

"Sinatra would be awesome. It's on Pandora somewhere."

"I'm sure I can find it. Any particular reason you like Frank?"

"Memories."

"Memories, as in mob memories — aka Candi?"

"I plead the fifth. Best let it go."

"Duly noted. Mind if I join you?" she asked, peeling off her clothes.

"I have a choice?"

"For now, no… you do not." Slipping into the tub, she tossed one leg over me, as remorseful tears formed in the corners of her eyes. "I'm sorry, D. I know how much you care about Candi. I'm even sure she cares quite a bit about you. Circumstances change, forcing people to change. Especially, when they must rise to meet the challenges necessary to survive. Damn it, D! The short version is she was making love to, I can only assume, Joseph and she was totally into it. Remember, I'm good at reading people as you've so aptly stated. Sadly, the video didn't look staged and she didn't look coerced in any way. From my perspective, Candi looked really comfortable taking the lead while delivering spectacular results."

"Stop it, Victoria, you've said enough. I'll take that drink now." Turning on the jets to the tub, I watched the steam rise, casting a shimmering glow on the woman beside me. Feelings that I had fought so long to suppress were waging an all-out war in me ... and winning. Wrapping my arms around her, I shared her consolation with a kiss that escalated into lip sucking, tongue probing passion, before I pulled away.

"Please, don't stop," she breathed in my ear.

"You don't understand, girlfriend."

"What's there to understand? You want me."

"I do, but there are things about me you—"

"And I want you ... now!"

"Oh, screw it!"

"Gladly," Vic retorted, repositioning herself on me, kissing me with abandon.

Her tongue danced playfully, while her hands strategically positioned me to enter her for the very first time.

I've waited too long for this. Maybe I should lighten the mood. "Damn, you feel good, you, old bastard."

"Damn, you feel better, you tight, greasy cunt."

We both laughed, realizing our banter had broken through the thick ice that had separated us for so long. "Victoria, you do realize our relationship has risen to the next level," I murmured, while her breasts jostled up and down in my face. "Slow down, girlfriend, I love the tub, but I love the bed more. Tonight, I'm going to give you what you want, even if it takes 'til morning." Rising up I made it to the seat of the tub, before Vic's hands and lips held me captive.

"Do not move," she directed on her upstroke between breaths. "I've got you... right where I want you." Gliding up and down, she was determined to bring me close repeatedly, expertly using her hands to stop any notion of me getting off ... before her.

"Enough, you've teased me enough. It's my turn to return the favor," I playfully retorted, pushing her off me before spinning full circle and stepping onto the tile floor. Holding up an oversized towel, "my lady, if you please." Like an obedient child, Vic rose from the water, stepped out of the tub and into my waiting arms. Wrapping the towel around her, I picked her up and carried her to the bed. "The next scene in our sonnet is about to unfold." Flipping back the comforter on the opposite side, I coaxed her onto the crisp linen sheets. "I want to taste you, all of you, from the nape of your neck to the tip of your toes. Hold that thought," I quipped, before retrieving her thong and wine from the tub room.

"What are you doing, D? I don't want my underwear on." *I've come too far with him tonight to back up!*

"There's a method to my madness. Humor me. Lift your feet, now your legs. Good, I've got it from here," I said, as I pulled her thong almost to its final resting place before my tongue got the best of me. "Now close your eyes, lay back and enjoy the ride." Lingering a little long in the moment, I felt her skin shiver along the insides of her thighs as they subconsciously pressed against my cheeks. Setting her thong in place in the next moment was not what she expected.

"Please, D, don't stop. I was so close—"

"No kidding, a little more agony, a whole lot more ecstasy, if you please. The best is yet to come." Climbing over her, I positioned myself between her thighs while my lips ravaged the nape of her neck, first on the left, then the right. Rocking back and forth, I continually teased her knowing that the only barrier between us was the silky fabric of her thong.

"Oh, D, I want you back inside me."

"Soon, girlfriend..."

Leaving her navel, my tongue traced the outer edges of her very wet thong before moving down her right thigh, across her knee and calf, ending at her feet. While massaging the bottom of her feet with my hands, my tongue playfully probed between each toe before starting its long-antici-pated climb to the glistening dampness of my making. "And, so it begins," I teased, pushing her legs apart with my elbows while I breathed in the scent of her excitement created by me. As my tongue flicked feather-like, Vic's fingernails clawed deeply into the linens.

"Make me come, D. Please, make me come," she whimpered, she pleaded, she begged. The fires within her raged. my experienced, deliberate tongue quickened, multiplying each exquisite sensation tenfold.

Trailing the edges of her thong, my lips and tongue teased and probed from the bottom to the top, from the top to the bottom, repeatedly while her body desperately tried to push deeper into me as she used the sheets for traction.

Screw this. I grabbed his head in my hands and pulled him into me as deep as my damn, thong would allow. "Now, D! Now!" she screamed, pulling the thong to one side, pressing against me with all her might.

With little chance to breathe, I pushed and pulled on the outer edges of her sweet spot as my tongue danced… darted and played. Tossing, turning, bucking, screaming, Victoria exploded the moment my two fingers entered her, settling near the elusive G-spot. Wave after wave of sensation coursed through her body, wobbling her knees and flushing her skin, rose pink.

"I think I'm dying," she whispered between halted breaths. "No man, until now, has ever taken me where you did tonight. Damn you. And you did it with just your hands, your lips, your tongue."

Taking a moment to reflect, "Sadly, girlfriend, it's all downhill from here. It's all about the newness, the long time coming, and anticipation of the unknown that took you where you've never been before. Of course, my expert oral skills helped carry you over the top," I confessed, rather proudly, "if I say so myself."

"Not just over the top, but over the rainbow, times two. Oh my, D. I have nothing left for you. I'm sorry. I'm spent. I can't move."

"I'm good. Let's just lay here so I can bask in your after-glow, your sweat, your juices. Girl, you have soaked the sheets. Lay still, I'm going to get a picture. You've brought new meaning to the words, wet spot."

"There will be no pictures taken, period. Now bring me a towel, preferably dry. Tonight," she stammered, pointing to where she laid, "this my friend is your side!"

Chapter 17

Waking in a reversed spoon sometime after daylight, I felt two perky breasts rubbing my back, while a very determined hand massaged me to life. "Good morning to you, girlfriend. What's happened to the 'I'm not a morning person' I went to sleep with last night?"

"She's still here as you can readily attest trying to take care of some unfinished business."

"I haven't brushed my teeth."

Men! What's with the tooth-brushing? Thankfully, I've heard that before and know what to say before he leaves the bed distracted. "I have, so we're good. Raise up a little, D, so I can slide my other arm under you. You know what they say, two hands are better than one when we're trying to make your little pistol shoot straight and true."

"I'm not sure, I've heard it quite that way before, girlfriend, but knock yourself out."

"I plan to, D," she whispered, as her breasts made circles on my back, while her fingers massaged both appendages hanging from my body.

Pressing tightly into me, Vic inadvertently discovered my Achilles' heel, my oh so sensitive neck. The moment she started biting and kissing my neck and ears I rose hard and fast to the occasion.

What a pleasant surprise! "That works. Mental note, neck and ears, hard in two."

"What'd you say, girlfriend?"

"Never mind, I've got this." Pulling me over onto my back, we kissed, her hands continuing to massage and caress. "My turn."

"It's all you, baby. Let's ride!"

Ha! My body said yes, but my mind kept saying no. I rocked and she moved to my rhythm, minute after minute, until glistening beads of sweat formed across her brow calling on me to invoke desperate measures. "Roll on your back, please." Taking this new position gave me sufficient leverage to drive deeply and forcefully, establishing a new rhythm I could use to my advantage. "Dig your fingernails into my back, Victoria, do it now!" Pulling her legs down on each side of me created a vice, which, when coupled with the pain of her nails in my back, took me where we both wanted me to go, to the land of knee wobble. Licking the salty sweat from her forehead, I collapsed on top of her, daring myself to move.

"Are you OK, D?" she asked, pushing me off her chest to breathe.

"I'm better now, thank you. I believe we have moved from the superficial to the sublime in our rapidly ever-expanding relationship. Vic, I never did get a chance to ask you how your soak and rub was yesterday with all the wrestling that's been going on here lately. Did you enjoy it?"

"It was wonderful, D. They have a stone massage that I want to try if I ever have a chance to come back here."

"Thanks to your semi-iron butt and bladder we made great time yesterday. Would you like to hang out here another day? I've heard there are some touristy places that might be fun to visit."

"Sure, like what?"

"The Tunnels of Moose Jaw — some venue that played a part in Prohibition back in the twenties. Rumor has it Al Capone stored liquor here at one time."

"The mobster?"

"Yep."

"You just can't get away from it, can you, D?" *What does Candi have that I don't?*

"Nothing, absolutely nothing. However, their influence throughout history is everywhere, Vic, from Sinatra to Capone and who knows what else we'll find on this ride."

"I wasn't talking about that. I was talking about you and Candi. Whatever you had with her, you still have it bad for her. Even after the video, you're still holding out hope, aren't you?"

"Let's just say, I'm eternally optimistic when it comes to people until they prove otherwise."

"I give up. Two times she has screwed you or is it three? Do me a favor, remember, until we get back you're stuck with me. Wine me, dine me, make me laugh and fuck me. Can you at least do that until I get home?"

"I'm sorry. You're asking me questions that I don't know how to answer. My mind's a wasteland. I'm seriously flawed, remember? Back to your question, I can do those things and more. Know this, until I've come to terms with the past what you see is what you get. That being said, make your hot rock appointment, then we'll plan the rest of the day around it. We'll have fun on the tunnel tour. I'll wine you, dine you and fuck you, in that order, or some combination of the above. Will that work, barrister?"

How am I supposed to answer that? I want in his head, as well. "It will, for now, D," Vic relented. "At least until it won't."

Chapter 18

Victoria scheduled her one-hour 'hot rock' stone massage at nine in the morning, which gave me time to book a tour to the tunnels, and plan the rest of our day in Moose Jaw as well as momentarily reflect on us. Completing the first one through the net, my daydreaming mind instinctively took care of the rest of my quiet time. I warned Vic about what sex does to casual relationships — it screws them up royally. It's one thing to be friends with someone, even pseudo sexual. It's completely another when you stick your fingers and other appendages into another person's pie. You can't manage to un-stick it. What'd she say, 'sex is power, her vagina's a WMD ... or something like that?'

I've yet to wrap my head around this all too new, budding idea, professional friends with benefits. I'll assume that's where we are at this moment in our relationship until one of us yearns to go deeper, possibly pushing the other away. Then again, so what if Candi screwed her ex? You're no saint either, D — more of a slut as I'm constantly reminded. Surely Candi would never willfully put herself in that position for my benefit. But Joseph most certainly would — for revenge maybe, to make a point definitely, or possibly to ensure that I stay away because he knows as long as I'm in the picture he hasn't got a snowball's chance in hell to win her back. That's just wishful thinking on my part. D, put it to rest. I've promised Vic my attention today, tomorrow and the next day. I owe her that and more ... for now.

"Wow! You look refreshed, girlfriend. Was it as good as you look?" I asked Victoria, who came bouncing into the room, sporting a radiant glow.

"It was wonderful and soothing. It's amazing what warm stones do to your body, D, especially when they take them on and off repeatedly. You should try it sometime."

"I'll add that to my bucket list. I'm more than cognizant of what hot rocks do coming ... off ... thanks to you. Does that count?"

"Noooooo ... then again, maybe it does for you, being male," she couldn't help but giggle.

"Made you laugh, check. I'm working on your list. See? We're booked for a tunnel tour at noon. Then a late lunch to be followed up with—"

"I'm in charge of that one." *Good to know sex is still on his bucket list.*

"You didn't even know what I was going to say."

"Doesn't matter, I know what I'm going to do, regardless. You're my new toy, D, that I can't seem to get enough of."

"I wear out easy."

"I'll be gentle and slow. I learned early on to respect my elders."

"That's cruel," I replied, before grabbing Vic by the waist and turning her over my knees, spanking her multiple times with a firm, open hand. "So how were you taught to respect your betters, little Miss Priss?"

"Ouch, you're hurting me. Just kidding. ... Harder! ... Harder! Is that the best you've got? Do it harder, damn you. Harder!"

"Nope." Pulling down her yoga pants and thong, I smacked her hard two times on her round, freshly oiled butt cheeks, leaving a rather distinct handprint on each before rolling her off my knees into the floor. "There, now maybe you'll respect your betters."

Standing up, she rubbed her smarting cheeks, "That hurt, Daddy."

"It was supposed to. I thought that's what you wanted ... Wait ... did you say ... Daddy?"

Memories, and not the best ones, consumed me. "It was, it is. I'll be good, you'll see. Fuck me now!" she begged, quickly kicking off her pants, before lying down seductively on the bed, her splayed legs, an open invitation. "A quickie, D? Please? ... I've been a bad, bad girl. I'll do whatever you want. Just do me...Do me now."

And for the next ten or so minutes I did, she did, we did; while my mind went elsewhere, wondering if the skeletons in her closet were rattling, because Pandora's box had just been breached.

Lying beside her catching my breath, "What the hell happened, Vic? 'Daddy, do me.' Where'd that come from?"

Vic was quivering, ashamed of the demons that had reared their ugly heads. "Now is not a good time. I'm sorry. Please, let's not spoil the moment. Besides, don't we have some place to be?"

"We do. I'm not pressing you, but at some point, you and I have to have a heart to heart."

"I told you I'm flawed. Just think of me as damaged goods with a hearty appetite and a bass-ass attitude."

We dressed in silence. Thirty minutes later we were in the Tunnels of Moose Jaw listening to colorful characters in period costumes describe the history of the tunnels running back and forth under the city streets. Originally, they hid Chinese immigrants who worked in sweat shops above ground by day and slept in the tunnels at night. Then during the time of Prohibition, the tunnels were used to smuggle alcohol, among other things, to the states, mainly Chicago. Rumor has it that Capone was a central player during that time, thus the Chicago connection.

I broke the silence. "Vic, it amazes me how far people will go to make money by spinning the rumor mill."

"Might I remind you, lawyers do that all the time, present company included."

Scratching my beard, I gave it a second thought, she might be onto something. "Good point. Come on Vic, I'm hungry. There's a great Chinese Restaurant nearby, so says Urbanspoon."

"Works for me, D. I just a 'Wong' for da ride."

"Cute, girlfriend. Cute."

Chapter 19

Tampa Bay

Last night was a blur. So was this morning, as Candi woke abruptly from a fitful, nights sleep. Joseph was here, though not physically. Thank God. His scent lingered on her skin, in her hair, everywhere. It's not a bad scent mind you, just an unwelcome one at the moment. *Girl, get your act together. You did what you had to do, nothing more, and nothing less. Besides, it's not like you haven't had his scent on you before. Two years later, mind you, he's back in your life and you can either embrace him or reject him. The latter, until I am sure D is safe is not an option.*

A shower, that's what I need, a long hot shower. Surely, I can think clearer without these awful sensory distractions overpowering my thoughts. Grabbing my iPad, Candi turned on the Sinatra channel, loud enough to be heard over the pulsating water. *This is our music, D's and mine, not to be shared with anyone, especially Joseph. Last night was surreal.* Washing, scrubbing, cleansing every inch of her body, she longed to be clean again, to breathe again, me.

Dressed in her work out skins, Candi traipsed into the kitchen to make a black and green tea before a much-needed walk. *This stuff is addictive. I have D to thank for that. If he were here now, I'd complain in person.* Clank, drag, clank, drag came the sounds from somewhere down the hallway, announcing Giovanna was nearby, his crutches leading the way.

"Morning, Cuz."

"Morning, Gio. When you fly out?"

"We not leave, we stay. I make sure you OK."

"I've got this, I really do. It's just going to take time. Besides, what can you do that I can't?" My phone whistled, notifying me of a text message, interrupting my conversation as well as my train of thought.

It was from Marcy. Candi glanced it over before reading it aloud to Gio. "Found Major at Borderland Pet Resort, call me."

Gio could detect the excitement in her voice, "It's good, yes? You leave message. He call me, I tell him story."

He has a point. Much better odds for D to call him than me. "Great idea, Gio. I am grateful you're staying for a while. Hold that thought. I need to call Marcy back. Excuse me for a moment."

She pressed send. "Girl, you really wanted that trip to Calgary, didn't you? How long did it take you to find Major?"

"I did. But more than anything, I want you to be happy. D seemed to make you happy. I found his dog at the third of five kennels on my list. I hope he still wants you. Candice, what's the message you want me to leave with them?"

"Tell them that D needs to call Giovanna, ASAP. Hold on a sec, Marcy."

"Gio, do we dial the country code along with your number when you're in the states?"

"Hmm ... think so, Candice."

"Marcy, I'm back. Write this number down, along with the country code. Read it back to me. Thanks. Can you leave them a hundred-dollar tip ensure they won't forget to give him the message when he calls in?"

"I can. Anything else, Candice?"

"Not at the moment, girl. You've earned that trip to Calgary and more. I just remembered. The family has to attend a masquerade benefit for All Children's Hospital two weeks from today. Can I fly you down here for that weekend?"

"Let me check my work schedule and make sure I can get someone to cover. If I can, I'll fly myself down late Thursday or Friday morning."

"You'll do no such thing. After all you've done, I owe you. I'll send the plane. Call me back with your schedule and we'll work it out from there. Bye, Marcy."

Candi ended the call, "Gio, now that you and Mile are staying for a while, would you like to attend a benefit ball two weeks from today at the Marriott Waterside? It should be fun. We can even dress in costume. Marcy's coming, I hope. Would you like to attend if you're still here?"

"We be here 'til D come. You see, he come soon. Party good I think. We be bikers. OK?"

"OK ... I left all my biker babe stuff in Canada. But, I do have a brand new red dress. I could be Pretty Woman, aka biker babe. Maybe my prince charming could swoop in and carry me away on a motorcycle."

"We go shop, Candice. Always use more."

"Whatever you say, cuz. Whatever you say," Candi agreed without thinking. *I was lost in the moment, realizing for the first time we might be able to get a message to D sooner rather than later. Will he come for me or has he moved on and out of my life? Questions compounding questions consumed me and there were no concrete answers to settle my already troubled mind.*

Chapter 20

Over a scrumptious late lunch of beef and broccoli with fried rice at Jamie's Chinese Restaurant, it seemed like a good time to plan the next leg of our journey home. "Speaking of the ride, how's your butt holding up so far, girlfriend?"

"Pretty good, not counting the welts from this morning," Vic replied, sheepishly.

I laughed. "It's decision time. Are we going the long fast route or the long, long fast route home?" Option one is to ride south through Williston, ND and the Bakken oil fields, which will be jammed up with trucks and oil rigs. Or do we ride due north and then east to Winnipeg, Manitoba before heading south to Sioux City and home? Regardless, we're three days out hard riding through North Dakota and possibly even five days out with stops through Winnipeg."

Only time will get Candi out of his head. "Choices, choices. Have you been both routes before? Which is the most scenic, D?"

"North, for sure. There are thousands of lakes in southern Saskatchewan filled with millions of ducks and geese heading south this time of year. Plus, you'll most likely see quite a few deer, a couple of moose and maybe even a bear or two."

"Ooh. I've never seen a bear in the wild before and I've sure never seen a moose, except on TV. Let's go north, if that's OK with you."

"North it is. If I can remember the number of an outfitter friend from up there that I hunted with a while back, maybe he can put us up for a night. That is, if he's still in business. I'll look him up on your iPad when we get back to the room. Speaking of moose, I'll run you by the city's claim to fame, Canada's largest moose on the way to the resort."

"First the teepee, now a moose. What is with the Canadians having to have the biggest things on display?"

"Cold winters, baby — cold, cold winters. What else do they have to do on those long winter nights, but dream, dreams and make up big things?"

"D, I could think of a wide array of things to do on a cold winters night … with you." She winked … *He so caught my drift.*

We arrived at the resort late in the day, it was too late to think of eating again, but not too late to drink. "No more Molson's for me today. I'll be a good boy and split a bottle or two of wine with you if that's OK, girlfriend?"

"D, surely you know by now, you don't have to get me drunk to take advantage of me.

"I do. Tonight, I'll try to forgo getting in your pants. I'm rather hoping to get in your head."

"Oh…" *Imagine that. Now, he wants in my head?*

After numerous searches, I found Greg's number in Tisdale, SK and made the call to his home /office. No answer. Another friggin' voice mail! *Rarely, does any human voice answer the phone anymore. Is it like that for everyone or just me?*

"Greg, It's Jon David, don't ask. I'm an asshole; I got it. A lot has happened since Texas. I'll fill you in later. My lady lawyer friend and I are in Moose Jaw on my bike. We'd like to stop by. She would really like to see a wild bear or moose in the woods if that's possible. We're not hunting mind you, this trip we're strictly tourists. If we shoot anything it will be by camera. I'll pay you whatever you need to make it happen if you can pull this off on such short notice. Leave a message on this number. It's a sat phone, which I check periodically. Thanks, Pal. We'll catch up tomorrow if you're around. Or not. Later."

Vic and I snuggled on the bed and drank our wine as we watched some chick flick on HBO. We were each waiting for the other to bring up the events from earlier in the day. Sleep crept up on us, silencing the demons we would eventually have to face head-on.

* * *

My alarm went off at dark thirty. I hit snooze, realizing I was completely clothed and cold. Vic on the other hand, sometime in the night managed to snuggle under the comforter without me. "No fair, why didn't you wake me?"

Rousing faintly, "I tried. You were out like a light. Do you know how loud you snore on your back? I finally managed to push you on your side so I could go back to sleep. What time is it, anyway?"

"Dark thirty. I've never heard myself snore. I've heard I can raise the roof, especially when I'm tired. I'm sorry. If you'll excuse me, I'm going to the gym and grab a quick workout. You're welcome to join me."

"I'm fine right here, thank you. I will consider a ... joint ... workout if you're not too stinky and sweaty when you get back," she countered, before rolling over and dragging the comforter over her head.

Twenty minutes on the treadmill at its highest incline at only 3 mph gets your heart pumping at 80%. Twenty minutes on the nautilus afterwards didn't slow it down either. I returned to the room untouchable, stinky and sweaty on both counts. After a quick shower, I emerged from the bathroom to find Vic awake and patiently waiting for me, gloriously clothes free. Not one to miss an opportunity, I accepted her subtle, non-verbal invitation. We romped and rolled just long enough for my hair to dry, but not long enough to stop the sweating. "We should have wrestled first, girlfriend. I left way too much of me in the gym."

"By the feel of things, you left quite a bit in here, too," she acknowledged, rather candidly, casting a gaze far below her navel.

"You make joke, funny girl. Share another shower and I'll clean you up for free. Then we pack, we eat, we ride."

Chapter 21

And ride we did, pulling out of the parking lot just after 7:30, heading west on the Trans-Canada Highway before going north on Canada Highway. 6. In a little under two hours we made it to Quill Lakes. Stopping to stretch at a wildlife viewing area, I grabbed my binoculars and gazed out over the thousands of ducks and geese, swimming and feeding in the lake. "Here Vic, look through these," I said, offering her the glasses.

"Wow, there are millions of them, D. And they will all fly south for the winter? I wonder if any of them will come through Iowa?"

"This is a main staging area for the Central Flyway. Seems like most group here and head south following the food as they go. I'm sure many will wind up passing through Iowa."

Handing me the binoculars… tugging, willy-nilly at my sleeve, "I have to pee … so bad."

Looking around at the vastness, I opened my arms wide, "The world is your throne, girlfriend."

Seriously, D, don't you pick up on the important things? "Uh, I don't do natural. I'm a girly-girl, remember?"

"I do remember quite a bit about you, especially your exceptional skills, both with your clothes on and off. None of which have anything to do with your aversion to peeing in the great outdoors." Grabbing some Kleenex from my saddlebag, "this is the best I can do. Turn towards the lake, drop 'em and let it fly. The bike will shield you from the road. Besides, it's not like there's bumper to bumper traffic today."

"OK," Vic relented, "but look away. I've got to take off my jacket, undo the chaps, unbuckle the jeans, wiggle down my underwear..."

"Quit talking about it, Vic. Like Nike says, 'Just do it!'"

Off in the distance, I noticed an 18-wheeler approaching fast. This could be fun. Timing is everything. With Vic bent over in all her glory, her milky white cheeks contrasting nicely with her black leather, I let the bike quietly roll backwards, grabbing my phone to capture this memorable Kodak moment.

Making eye contact with the truck driver, I pumped my right arm up and down giving him the universal signal to lay down on his booming air horn. Rapid-fire pics from the iPhone captured what transpired over the next few moments. The horn, startling Vic forward in the middle of her business, before she lurched backwards and fell butt first onto the ground, right into her recently created wet spot.

Looking over her right shoulder, her face flushing multiple shades of pissed, "Damn you, D. Damn you!" she managed to say before breaking out in laughter. "Ahhh—" was the last thing she muttered, before finishing up her business where she sat.

"Girly-girl, no more!" I shouted. "You've just received a taste of country, along with a much greater appreciation for the words, wet spot."

Asshole. "Yep, that's me. A little taste of country, among other things, on my ass, my jeans, her chaps. At least I don't have to sleep in it. Quit laughing. Don't just stand there. Get off the bike and help me up. ... Now!"

"Gladly," I replied, grabbing a micro fiber windshield cloth from my windshield bag, to wipe her off as I went. "I'm glad you can laugh at yourself. You'll laugh even more when you see the pics."

"OMG, pics, for our eyes only, period. You upload them and I'll castrate you while you sleep. Just a thought. Remind me to stop at a bathroom every hundred-miles or so from now on, will ya?" I had to laugh, it was funny. I grabbed the cloth and cleaned up my mess. "You owe me big time. What am I saying? I owe you, big boy. Paybacks are a bitch!"

Our little roadside sideshow behind us, we made it to Melfort, SK in time for lunch at a local haunt that's famous for their burgers as well as their Sushi. I remember thinking, yuck, what a combination, yet the food was outstanding my last time through. Thankfully, we were not disappointed. Vic and I both had bacon Swiss burgers and fries, leaving the Sushi for the locals.

"Next stop, Tisdale. You have a chastity belt with you?"

"What are you talking about, D?" Like I need one?

"You'll see. Plus, I believe there's another world's largest something in Tisdale awaiting you."

"I can't wait. About that chastity belt—"

"Can't explain it. You'll have to experience it firsthand."

* * *

Riding east on Canada Highway 3, we passed farm after farm that stretched for miles and miles. Slowing down enough to talk over the road noise, "Vic, did you know farmers up here can start harvesting grains in the morning until late at night for a solid week and never cross the same ground twice? That's just how big these farms are here."

"Bet it's a lonely place to live in the winter," offered Vic.

"Yep, that's why they have such big..."

"Things, I got it. Even then it would get old, huh?"

"Ice hockey is big up here, just like football is at home. Communities come together at least once a week during the season. It's a long season, too. There's a photo op coming up on the right. I expect you to help me make a memory. Close your eyes girlfriend. Don't open 'em 'til we stop."

Pulling off the road in a well-traveled wide spot, I stopped. "You can open your eyes now, Vic." By the looks of things, it was a jaw dropping moment.

WTF? "Are you serious, D? What were they thinking? A man did that, no doubt. No woman in her right mind would ever have approved this sign. Yep, this is a serious photo op. Hell-o, it's a photo worth hanging on my wall. How do we do this for maximum effect?"

"Well, you could start by standing there with nothing on but your chaps. That would surely get my attention."

"Be serious. Stop thinking with your little brain." *The one I've recently grown fond of.*

"I always think with my little brain first … before jumping on to my big one."

"Bet you wish that was reversed don't you, little pecker?" she asked, patting me on the crotch before assuming the position. "How's this?"

Both hands outstretched, palms up, just to the right of the sign said it all, as in WTF? The wide- angle lens of my digital camera captured it perfectly:

Welcome to Tisdale, the Land of Rape and Honey

"Now to explain, Victoria. Rape stands for rape seed which is where canola oil comes from. It's grown here religiously as a cash crop and usually more valuable than wheat."

"And the honey?"

"Bees are used to pollinate these crops. Hives are everywhere, thus the honey and a statute of the world's largest bee. OK, maybe the second largest," I confessed.

Shrugging her shoulders, "I'm glad you clarified that to me. I'd hate to brag about seeing the biggest bee, just for somebody to tell me I was wrong. I'll take the sign over the honeybee any day. Can you imagine being welcomed into a town like this at home? Bubba would have a field day."

"Would make for an amusing argument for the defense."

"Not hardly, that is unless Bubba went both ways. Which, come to think of it, I've heard he does. Now that would be an amusing defense."

"That even hurts to think about it."

"My point exactly. Thanks for stopping, I think."

"Girlfriend, just a few more miles, conservatively speaking, and we'll be there."

"Great. I can't wait to shower and wash off all that remains of the lingering wet spot."

Chapter 22

Making memories, that was my goal today. Forty-some minutes later, I pulled into Mistatim — population 73 — made a left across the railroad tracks and pulled up to the Mistatim Hotel and Bar.

"What's this, D?" *Surely, we're not stopping here? Maybe D wants a beer.*

"Our home for the night."

"You're joking, right? This place is a hole in the wall and I don't even know what that means."

"You're about to find out. Let's go inside and see if they have any rooms."

"After you." *Be good, Victoria. D has a method to his madness. Or so he says.*

Sauntering inside and up to the empty bar with Vic reluctantly in tow, I inquired, "Bartender?"

"Name's Will."

"Sir Will, I'm D. Do you have a suite available for tonight for me and my beautiful, scrumptious friend?"

Looking around the room in the motionless bar, Will replied, "you're in luck, we've just had a cancellation. All our rooms are suites, so pick your poison," he continued, throwing down a half- dozen keys onto the bar top.

Vic spoke up, "Will, is it? Good to meet you. I'm Victoria. Can we see the rooms first, especially the ones with a tub?"

"Miss, I'm not sure what you're expecting, but you're welcome to look around. You do know where you are, Ma'am?"

"I know we're in Canada. I know we've just come through the land of … rape and honey. And now we're here."

"D, right? You'd best show her the rooms on your own. I wouldn't go up there with her for no amount of money."

"Come, Vic. Will is right as rain. I'll be glad to show you the rooms." Walking up the creaky wooden, L-shaped staircase, eventually turned us down a long narrow blank hallway with white painted doors, half missing their numbers. "Quaint, isn't it?"

"Hell-o! Quaint is not how I'd describe it, D. More like a boarding house I'd picture sitting next to the Bate's Motel."

"Come on, give it a chance. Let's at least look at the rooms." Rummaging around in my hand, I found the key to room number 6. "Here let's check this one out."

"I hate to tell you, D, but this is room nine," quipped Victoria.

Flipping the number right side up the way it was supposed to be before it lost a screw, "see I told you it was a six. It just needs a screw."

"Oh, God. Who would have thought? … Me, too!"

Laughing at her sexual shenanigans, while opening the door, I flipped on the light. "Ladies first."

"Uh … no way … no way in Heaven or Hell are we staying here tonight. There's a bed, a lamp and a fan. D, there's no bathroom. Where the hell is the bathroom?"

"I think it's at the end of the hall. I believe it's communal," I continued, dragging this out for all it was worth. "At least sit on the bed."

Against her better judgment, she did, as the springs slowing sank within inches of the floor. "No way. It's not happening. We'll ride all night if we have to. I'm not staying here."

"Are you sure you don't want to check out the bathroom … just in case?"

Grabbing my gonads, Vic looked sternly into my eyes while tightening her grip to my great discomfort. "What part of no do you not understand, little brain or big brain, whichever one of you is listening at the moment?"

"Uh, at the moment, they both are. Vic, you can let go now? … Please?"

"I need a drink."

"Me, too, although a little Novocain would be better."

Releasing my testicles and taking my empty hand, she dragged me out of the room before I could turn off the light or close the door.

"Will? Two Molson's, please," Vic announced. "Thank you for letting us look at the rooms. We're gonna pass. How far to the next town? We're going east."

"It's at least a good hour to Hudson Bay. You might try the Porcupine. I believe they have a few rooms with a shared bath."

Choking on my beer, I mouthed, "Thank you."

The look on Vic's face was priceless.

"Ma'am, I hate it for you. We have the very best rooms in town. I'd love to have your business tonight."

"Tell her the truth, Will. Not only are they the best rooms, they are the only rooms in town."

"Yes, ma'am. He's correct. Unless you count the hunting lodge across the railroad tracks on the other side of town. Now that's a fine place but you have to be hunting with them to stay there."

Taking a swig of Molson, Vic quickly changed the subject. "When is your busiest season?"

"You're looking at it. On Friday and Saturday nights when everyone's had too much to drink after Karaoke, we fill up quick. Like tonight, maybe."

"Drink up, Vic. I guess we ride."

In three turns of the bottle she obliged me.

Chapter 23

Turning left out of the parking lot onto Railway Ave, in less than 30 seconds, I gave Vic the scenic tour of Mistatim, passing the single pump gas station/general store combination and the Postal Office. Taking a right on 2nd Ave. and then another immediate right, drove us directly to the timber framed lodge, my original destination, less the delectable detour. *Many fond memories since the early nineties have been created here. Duck hunts, goose hunts, bear hunts and deer hunts weaved their way into my life and those I called friends. I've watched Greg's children grow up and have children of their own. How I miss those days.*

I wonder if this is the hunter he was talking about? "Why are we stopping here, D? We're not hunting."

"Ah, but we have cameras. Maybe we can persuade Greg to let us shoot something with those."

"Good luck with that. Greg, you said? Sounds like you know him better than you let on."

"Come on girlfriend, let's check it out." Greeting us at the front door was Debra, Greg's wife and lifelong companion. Exchanging hugs, "By the looks of things, I see you got Greg's message. It's really good to see you. How long's it been Jon David, seven years?"

"I didn't get his message, I'm glad he got mine. Seven sounds about right…give or take."

"He's out scouting for you now. We don't have another group of hunter's due in 'til late Monday. Excuse me, Miss. I'm Debra. This man has no manners to speak of. And you are?"

"Victoria. After where we've been, it's both a pleasure and a relief to meet you."

Speaking up before the conversation went south, "I took her to the Mistatim Hotel and let her check out the rooms. She was not impressed."

"That sounds like something you would do. So, she doesn't know she's staying here tonight?"

"She does now," I relented.

"Now I understand your last statement, Victoria. Jon David, go get your luggage. Victoria, come with me and I'll show you to your room. I'm sure you'd like to relax and maybe even have a bath after riding all day with this clown."

"That sounds marvelous, Debra. If you only knew. Bring the bags to our room, Jon David," she instructed before turning and sticking her tongue out at me.

Dropping the gear in the bedroom, I pounded on the bathroom door over the sound of running water. "Your luggage, Miss. Should I wait for the tip or come back later?"

"Kind sir, if you're naked, you can claim your tip in the tub now. Otherwise, later please. I'll be clean and fresh and ready to give you a tip to remember."

"Works for me." I walked into the great room, its walls adorned with North American wildlife trophy mounts of all shapes and sizes. In the adjoining library, a new addition since my last visit, were numerous exotic mounts from Africa. Greg has been a busy boy, during my long absence. Sitting down at his desk, I flipped through his journals until I found me, proudly kneeling beside a rather large black bear, many years and far too many, unheralded memories ago.

"Where are you, D?" Vic called out, bouncing into the great room, dressed in sweats and a camo t-shirt that read Mistatim Outfitters. "You like? It's a gift from Debra. You have one just like it, only bigger."

"Cute, girlfriend. I never quite pictured you in camo. It's … well … different."

"Different good or different bad? You'd better say good. If the host gives you something to wear, you damn well wear it."

"Gotcha. You look delicious, in a woodsy sort of way. How's that?"

"It'll do. One question. Why did you take me to Will's place and put me through that torture earlier knowing damn well we were coming here?"

"Wine you, dine you, make you laugh."

"You left out—"

"Shhh … Look around. These walls have ears. Besides, with you, that's a given. Did you happen to take a gander at all the mounts?"

Gazing up and down and side to side, Vic tried to embrace the moment. "They're beautiful, D. Did he, Greg isn't it, shoot all these?"

"I think so, Debra too. But there may be a few strays mixed in. You know, shot by others, but displayed here. Come on, let's go for a walk. I'll show you around town."

"Didn't we like do that in like 30 seconds?" What'd I miss? What did I miss?

"Kinda, but we were riding. This will be the walking while exercising tour."

All the streets in town are hardpan gravel and make an excellent base. That is until they get wet and soggy from rain and snow and quickly turn to sticky, clingy muck. Vic and I wandered up and down the two main streets as well as a couple of the side streets before stopping by the little community store. Stacked floor to ceiling with everything you could imagine, food, hardware, automotive and farming gear in every size and shape imaginable, this store was the lifeblood of the town. And why not? The next closest town is almost an hour away. "Could you live here, girlfriend?"

"Absolutely not. This gives new meaning to the words quaint and rural. I thought I knew what rural was being from Iowa. This takes the cake, hands down."

"It's a hard life here, especially with the long, cold winters. But these are good, strong people in this town who use the gifts God's given them to survive and thrive. Look around you; almost all the houses are small, neat and maintained. Nothing pretentious here, excluding you."

"Smart-ass. I can see that, otherwise you'd pack up and haul ass to the big city."

"Want to go grab a beer with Will before we head back?"

"Absolutely. Now that we're not staying there, let's give him some business. I want to talk to him about some long overdue upgrades."

Three Molson's apiece, four and two if I'm being honest, two games of darts and an hours-worth of banter and local gossip later, it was time to go. "Will, thank you for filling us in all on the happenings going on over the last year."

"My pleasure. Not much happens here, but when it does I don't easily forget it. Tonight, is Karaoke. Remember? If you're not doing anything after eight, come on back."

"I can tell you right now we probably won't. I've got some unfinished business to undress about that time," Vic said winking, before latching onto my arm and escorting me out the door, mid-sentence.

"Subtle is not your middle name, Victoria?"

It's taken him long enough to figure that out. "Nope, as long as I'm breathing and you're breathing, we're good. Remember?"

"How could I forget," pinching her on the rear, leisurely swinging her hand in mine as we traipsed back to the lodge.

Chapter 24

Walking into the den, Debra emerged from the kitchen, wiping her hands on a towel, announcing dinner would be ready soon. "Greg's back and in the basement. He asked me to send you down when you got back. Victoria, I could use some extra hands in the kitchen."

Hands I've got. I hope that's all she needs. "My pleasure. I have to warn you, I burn toast."

"She has other skills, don't let her fool you, that more than make up for her lack of culinary charm. She's a high priced … lawyer and worth every penny."

Walking into Greg's shop, I found him busily laying out an assortment of clothes for our adventure tomorrow. "Jon David, it's great to see you again. How have you been? You kinda dropped off the face of the Earth a few years back. I tried multiple times to reach you, but my cards and letters were returned and the last phone number I have for you now belongs to some character named Lodi."

"It's a long story that's still being written. It's best you stay in the dark. I'm here now and I'm coming back. We had some great times, didn't we, Greg? Duck hunts, grouse hunts, bear hunts. We did 'em all. I enjoyed the fellowship. I guess that's what I've missed most, the fellowship."

"You've got another opportunity tomorrow, if only for the day. She wants to see bear and moose, yes?"

"If possible. I know nothing's guaranteed."

"Speaking of that, I've got to issue you a license so you can carry a gun in the woods with you. I've laid out all the clothes I have here on the table. Bring your friend down after supper and try them on. We'll leave early afternoon. I found an active bait area twenty miles north that has a two-person film stand over it. We'll haul the four wheelers with us and use them the last five. To make it memorable, we've gotta cross three beaver dams. You think that will be a problem for her?"

"Only if we wind up wheels up like that last bear hunt you dragged my ass on."

"Oh, I've got side by sides now. They're a whole lot more stable. Except when they turn over, then they're a bitch."

"Copy that. Then I'll do my best to keep us upright and wheels down."

The intercom buzzed. Debra announced, "Dinner is served."

Catching up on old times and sharing new stretched our meal into a two-hour ordeal. "You been staying up on the news?" asked Greg. "Somebody just made a whole lot of people millionaires. It's all over CNN. Rumor has it that the only connection anyone has come up with is that they were all victims of that banker, A.J. Standford, and that Ponzi scheme he ran out of Texas."

My tea glass slipped slowly through my fingers before I caught it just as it reached the table, while Victoria choked violently on her last sip of water. "You OK, Vic?"

Catching her breath, "the question is, are you OK, D? And, so it begins."

Oblivious to our conversation, Debra spoke up, "If only … we were so lucky."

Startled, Vic inquired further. "Debra, would you like to be a millionaire, too?"

"Heavens no, Victoria! We've got all we need here. It's just … there is this seriously ill six-year-old, neighbor girl, Missy Bryan, who has a rare disease called MDS — Myelodysplastic Syndromes — that is waiting for a clinical trial and stem cell transplant that could possibly save her life. The only hospital that has done this procedure before is in St. Petersburg, Florida. All Children's Hospital, I believe is the name of it. They say it will cost upwards of a million dollars U.S. because it's still in the experimental stage. So far, between the farmers and ranchers, here and in Tisdale, we've raised 180,000 Canadian in the last three months. I'm afraid she'll run out of time before we can raise the rest."

Without looking over, I felt Vic's piercing green eyes staring right through me all the way to my heart. "Victoria and I would like to make a contribution before we leave. Right, Vic?"

"Yes, Debra, D and I would be glad to help," said Vic. Everyone, regardless of circumstance deserves a second chance and sometimes even a third. Miracles happen every day. Don't they, D? Sometimes, you just have to run across the right miracle worker. You're lucky, I happen to know—"

Grabbing her knee in a vice grip before she could utter another word, "So Victoria, how did you like the moose balls?"

"What?" taken aback by his abrupt change in the current conversation, "Uh, well, I ... Debra said they were meatballs, not moose's balls."

"Meatballs made with moose meat, not moose balls, silly. Think about it."

"Whew, you scared me because I liked them a lot. I was hoping Debra would show you how to make them for me when we get back."

"Honey, Jon David knows. I taught him how to make them a long time ago," chuckled Debra, much to my chagrin.

"We don't have moose meat in Tennessee, ladies. It's a little tough to make them when you're... moose-less."

"It's getting late," announced Greg, "thank you for your generous offer to help Missy, every little bit helps." Looking directly at Vic, "come down stairs with me and try on some hunting clothes I've gathered up for you, Miss."

"Wait, we're not going hunting ... are we, D?"

"No, in a manner of speaking, yes. Greg has been so kind to create for us an impromptu adventure. Don't bother asking for the details, it's a surprise."

"Then a surprise it will be," Vic proudly exclaimed, "I wear a size 10, in some things a 12 in Misses, just so you know."

The table erupted in laughter, laughing not so much at her, but with her. Nope, that's not true, we were laughing at her and the naivety she brought with her to this place. The laughter continued long into the basement.

OMG! "These clothes stink! What is that smell, D?"

"A little urine, a little blood. Wouldn't you agree, Greg?"

"I would, and maybe a little musk and bile thrown in."

"And you expect me to wear them on this body," Vic asked, before tossing them on the floor.

"They've been washed, Vic. They're clean, I promise — just not scentless," I explained, gingerly trying to allay her fears.

Vic, picking up a man's size small, "Then, I'll take these. But, I'm wearing my own clothes under them and you're not stopping me." *There. I've said it, whew!*

"Not a problem, Miss. No perfume and you'll have to wash what you're wearing tomorrow in scent-free soap. Where we're going we need to smell like we belong," shared Greg convincingly. "Here, Miss, you'll need these rubber boots, plus a hat and gloves. Rummage through this box for those. D, I'm done here. She's all yours."

"Tell me again, why do I need to wear all this?"

"For our surprise adventure, Victoria. Humor me or at least try to."

I'm totally confused. "An adventure? How long will we be gone?"

"Eight hours, maybe, ten tops."

"Joy, D. I've got to smell this horrendous odor for an entire day? I bet you're going to make me pee in the wilds again?"

"Nope, you pee in a bag."

"Thank you, Mr. Wise Guy. Now I have even more to worry about. How am I supposed to do that?"

"If you can sit it, you can hit it," I assured her, cracking a smile that hushed her up. Moving beyond her incessant whining, "thank you, Greg. I'd like to borrow a truck and take Vic on a tour of the countryside right before dark."

"Pins and Greenies are feeding ten miles south. Honkers are feeding about five miles west. Is that what you're looking for?"

"That's the bulk of it with a little light show thrown in."

"You're in luck. Skies been screaming the last few days around 7:30."

"Come upstairs before you leave and I'll have you some directions to the fields. Keys are in the four-door green Dodge I call the Green Mule."

"Why are you men talking in code? Speak English." *I mean, I'm standing right here.*

"It's another surprise. Date night, just me and you and for once on this ride, bike-less."

Chapter 25

"Time to go, Vic. The green mule awaits. Don't look so lost, Vic. It's a truck silly."

"Good to hear, D. With you, I never know what your surprises consist of."

"Every moment with me is a pleasant surprise, is that what I'm hearing?"

"You nailed down the surprise part. I'd be going out on a limb to say they're all pleasant. Earlier tonight sure was. I'm sorry if I bubbled over too much at dinner. I was trying to reassure Debra that we, mostly you, had this. God, it feels good when you can jump into the impossible and make it possible. Aren't you proud of me, D? I've come a long way from the pompous, amorous bitch you met that night in the casino."

"Proud as punch, Victoria. We make a fine team, you and I. Especially, since I'm the one that's always giving."

"That's not true. I'm giving too. Why the hell do you think I'm riding back with you?"

"To get in my pants, my wallet, my head … I'm kidding. I do seem to be rubbing off on you. I pray that's a good thing."

"It's an honorable thing, a great thing… especially for me."

"Hold that thought, we need to ride." Opening the passenger door, I palmed each butt cheek and pushed Vic up and onto the bench seat before she could protest about the smell. "Roll the window down, girlfriend, then hang your head out 'til we're moving."

Choking on the aroma of blood, man sweat and gunpowder, Vic murmured, "This truck smells identical to the clothes you expect me to wear tomorrow."

The Green Mule's diesel engine rumbled to life, bellowing white smoke into the late evening sky. "Can you read a map, girlfriend? I hope so, since you're the designated copilot tonight."

"If I can get through law school, I can surely read a map." Spinning the paper, that Greg had hastily sketched, 'round and 'round in my lap, "Uh … which way is north?"

"That way," I said, pointing over my left shoulder, while wrestling the stiff steering wheel of the mule onto the road.

"On the map, dumb ass. How'd you expect me to read a map if I don't know where true north is?"

Surrendering to her logic, "It's all north up here, Vic. This is Canada. I'll make it easy for you, just tell me which road I turn on going this way," pointing my forefinger forward. "Where do we turn off the big straight line, the first or second squiggly one?"

"The second, I guess, then right at the third. You impressed?"

"I am, barrister. I am. Now, let me impress you with a geography lesson. Did you know Saskatchewan is divided into townships, comprising 36 sections? Each section is then subsequently divided into four quarters, with each quarter comprising 160 acres. Using this as a mathematical system, one can determine specific geographical locations on a map. Just not this one. However, most all roads run north and south and east and west. They're influenced by the sections, more so than not. Just thought I'd throw that out for you."

I didn't understand a word he just said. "Coming up on the second right, D. All we've seen so far are miles and miles of grain fields and ponds. Is that all there is to see in this country?"

"Not quite," I responded, slowing to a crawl. Easing over a small rise, off to our left was a pond, no bigger than the size of two football fields. Flight after flight of mallards and pintails were dropping gracefully onto it, looking for a place to rest for the night. Pulling off the road and into the wheat stubble, I turned off the Green Mule. "Sit back and watch, Vic. If we're lucky, the best is yet to come."

Fifteen minutes of quiet is too much for me. "I'm tired of waiting, D. Please, let's go back. We have ducks in Iowa. This is no big deal."

"Persistent patience is one virtue you must learn, Victoria." Taking her hand, I rubbed her fingers across my cheek. "Relax, feel me, feel the moment. Close your eyes and allow your senses to come alive within you. Listen, just listen."

Soon the quiet was broken by the deafening chatter and beats of thousands of beating wings. The skies were pulsating, they were alive with ducks. In awe, we watched the dusk turn to darkness, obscured not by the approaching sunset, but by the multitudes of Mallards and Pintails circling patiently, waiting their turn to land in the now full pond.

"Oh my," she exclaimed, "it looks like we're in the middle of a quacking tornado."

"A duck tornado to be exact. There's strength in numbers. Nature has a way of protecting its own." Vic and I sat motionless, watching flight after flight of puddle ducks, gracefully easing their way into an already crowded pond creating a nonstop, tornado like vortex that continued long after dark.

"Amazing, D. That's what it is, amazing," she confessed, snuggling tightly against me, her head resting on my shoulder. "Beauty is all around us, but we're too busy to see it. Had you not stopped and made me wait, I would never have made this memory. Thank you, Jon David," purposely trying not to contaminate the innocence of this moment.

"You're welcome, girlfriend, you're welcome. Time to head back." With the sun well below the horizon, I rumbled the Mule to life heading north. An eeriness enveloped us in the darkness before we reached Highway 3 just as I'd hoped. Driving off the road into rape stubble, I stopped again.

"What's going on, D, this is spooky, scary? The sky is eerily pulsating, almost like a green and blue flashing strobe light. Wait, now the lights are dancing. Now they're gone!"

"I ordered a light show for tonight's viewing. Victoria, may I present the Northern Lights. Mesmerizing, fearful, exhilarating were the words I used to describe the Aurora Borealis the first time I experienced it unawares at the conclusion of a very successful afternoon duck hunt."

"At first I thought we were under attack by aliens."

"I can see that, especially if you've never seen anything like this before. I was trying to find you a poem to read to you tonight while we watched the show. Although not true poetry, I found this in a Discover Magazine article on my phone. "'Streaks of light toss about with abandon. Suddenly, for a second, all the light melts away and the sky is full of darkness. Just as quickly, the lights blossom again in pulsating waves and arcs, and in undulating movements across the whole Heavens, sometimes stabbing the ends of their folds toward the earth, dripping with the green of grass and the red of blood.'"

Oh my. "That was beautiful, D. That describes it wonderfully."

"I thought it did, too. Two more firsts for you tonight, girlfriend. What was it you were saying about my surprises not being all too pleasant?"

She relented. "Never mind, D. Never mind."

Chapter 26

I dropped Vic off at the front door, and returned the Green Mule to its familiar parking spot, in the back behind the garage near the retriever kennels. *Which reminds me… Major Dog. I'm sure he's ready for me to come home. Note to self … call the kennel tomorrow and follow up.*

Coming in through the shop, I came across a recently tanned bear rug that looked ready to ship to a lucky hunter somewhere in the states. I'm sure Greg wouldn't mind me borrowing it for the night, I convinced myself, as long as I returned it in the morning, unscathed.

Throwing the bear skin over my shoulder, I carried it into our room with high hopes. With Vic in the bathroom doing whatever girls do before bed, I laid the bear skin on the floor and sprawled out on it in all my glory, waiting patiently for my squeeze to appear.

Stepping through the bathroom door, wearing nothing but her Mistatim tee, she froze. "Where'd that bear rug come from, D?"

"I borrowed it from Greg for tonight." Taking nothing for granted, "This could be another first in the making if you're so inclined. Ever made love on a bear skin rug, girlfriend?"

Taken aback, "Can't say that I have. Nor can I say with conviction I've ever had the urge to want to. You?"

"I plead the fifth."

"Oh, that's right, my bad. Standing before me is the man whore. No, what is that Candi calls you, a slut? How many times have you had sex on a bear skin rug, give? Is it a man's coming of age, a rite of passage when you kill it, you eat it or screw it? I'm sorry to blow your bubble, D, but my naked body is not going to lay down on that ... that ... animal."

"It was just a thought. To answer your question counselor — twice. My first time was planned and hot in front of a roaring fire. The second time was both accidental and memorable and not in the way your devious mind works."

Amused, Vic responded, "I got the first time nailed by your smile, sounds like you could entertain me with the second."

Rather embarrassed, now that I think back on the memorable part, I began. "Seems like yesterday. I dated a very athletic girl named Leah once upon a time who loved to wrestle. Her motto was 'if you pin, you win it.' I won, but lost more. On one particular, not-so-sober night, our wrestling escalated from the bedroom to the den floor where I was winning. That is, I was until she rolled me over onto the bear skin and wrapped me in it to pin me. Once I realized what was happening, I fought my way out while she rolled me back in using the bear's paws as her inducement. You happen to know how sharp a bear's claws are? Here, feel these," offering Vic the opportunity to run her fingers across its claws before continuing.

"They're sharp, D. I got it. So... what happened next?"

"Leah started swiping at me with the paws and growling like a bear. The next thing I know, I'm squealing like a pig and bleeding like one, too. Somehow, in my flailing, she caught me square in the nut sack, ripping a gash eleven stitches long."

"You're serious?" *I know you are, because no one could dream that up. Poor guy.*

Grimacing at the thought while inadvertently protecting my jewels with both hands, I assured her I was. "As a heart attack. I even remember the entire ER staff on duty coming by my treatment room and snickering after they learned my injury was caused by a dead bear and a live broad. Stop laughing, will ya? It hurts even now thinking about it."

With belly laughing tears cascading down her cheeks, Vic attempted to speak, "You just carry that ... that ... what did you call it? Uh, nut sack ripper back where it came from. I'll be waiting right here for you to show me ... show me your scar."

With the yet to be christened bear rug hanging lifelessly over my shoulder, I returned it rather glumly from wince it came. Nothing ventured, nothing gained, I suppose. All I'd managed to lose tonight in this humiliating ordeal was a little man pride and my eager beaver-ness to wrestle Vic long into the night. Settling for the remnants of a faded afterglow, instead of the glow of my making.

Chapter 27

The second vibration of my iPhone alarm roused me awake. Vic and I were 'pretzeled' as usual. Her right leg tossed over and between my legs, her left arm under my back holding me securely in place. "Hey girlfriend, I gotta turn off my phone."

"No, D, sleep. Sleep," she murmured, perfectly content to lay here for a few minutes more. At least she was until the chirp, chirp, chirp of my phone followed the vibrations. "Never mind, I'm awake now," she grumbled. "Please silence that nauseating alarm."

"Will do, if you'll kindly get off me. Please...." *Where was the phone? That was the question of the day. It wasn't in arms reach of the nightstand so it had to be on my belt wherever I left my pants.*

"I still hear it on my side of the bed." *Of course, it was somewhere far enough away that I would have to get up to silence it.* "You lay right there, D. I'll get it."

"It's in my pants."

It sure is. "Don't move a muscle," Vic said sternly, rolling onto the floor in search of my pants. "Found it." Swiping the screen, the alarm stopped. "I'm going to brush my teeth, D. Want to join me?"

"You told me to lay still and not move. Make up your mind."

Men don't have a clue sometimes. "I want to kiss a fresh mouth this morning, among other things. Humor me." *Geez...*

"What brought this on, you amorous, girlfriend?"

"Am now. You started it, big boy."

"How so?"

"You said it was in your pants. Now…I want in your pants. I see what you're thinking. You should know by now it doesn't take much to get me started. It's up to you to carry me across the finish line."

"Message received and understood." Joining Vic in the bathroom, we furiously brushed our teeth, hoping the other would finish first because we both surely needed to pee. "You finished? I have to go. Bad!"

"I have to go. But, I can't go with you standing in here, D."

"Hmmm … But you can go on the side of the road. What's up with that?"

"This is different. Besides, remember what got me wet? Out!"

I relented. Vic had a point. Knees locked, I waited and waited and waited. "Women!"

"Sorry, I had to freshen up, you know. Never mind. Men!"

Finally! Men are so much more efficient. Raise the lid, pee; shake it off when done. Women take forever. And when two or more go together, forget about it, time stands still. Emerging from the bathroom to the sounds of a low hum, I realized, tossing back the comforter that I had been replaced.

"What? This morning is a joint effort." Extending her free hand, Vic pulled me next to her. "You drive."

"With pleasure." Taking the BOA in my right hand, I eagerly returned it to its rightful spot. Kissing and caressing each other with wanton abandon completely caught up in the moment, I whispered, "Would you mind if my titillating tongue fought it out with your battery-operated boy?"

Haven't heard that line before. "Not at all, D. In fact, I'd love it. Don't forget, I wanna play, too."

Spinning round on the bed, I rolled onto my back and pulled her on top of me. Her moist sweetness permeated my nostrils and glistened across my tongue like honey. The vibration of the BOA against my lips created a sensation that seemed all too familiar. Candi strikes again.

Oh my! ... Oh! ... I don't know what he's doing down there, but it's absolutely wonderful. I am so ready to return the favor. Easy girl, you can do this. Relax, relax. Breathe through your nose. That's it.

What is she doing? Trying to concentrate on Vic while she was so aptly concentrating on me became an all too daunting task. Feeling her hot breaths against my stomach on her down strokes created the same glorious sensation that Candi experienced with me. Damn you, D. Stop thinking about her and enjoy the one you are with, now! Attempting to follow through on that directive, I concentrated all my energies on the task at hand, taking Victoria to the finish line. Thrusting the talented toy from above, my lips pulling and pushing from below, my thumb pressed firmly against her sphincter muscle, carried her down the home stretch. Inhaling one long deep breath, I was determined to take her across the goal before I would breathe again. Vic's sudden downward push against my face subliminally told me, along with her screams, "Yes...yes!" we had arrived. Thrashing, turning, twisting, bucking, waves of thunderous pleasure rolled through her body, signaling to me a job well done.

"Wow, girlfriend," I breathed, moving atop her, kissing her tenderly on the lips.

"Wow is right, D." Yuk! This kissing has to stop." Patting me on the shoulder was her way of signaling, move!. "Hey, not to change the mood, but you..." *How should I say this delicately? ...* "You remind me of me."

Rolling off her and onto my back, I stared at the ceiling. "That's a good thing, right? It proudly conveys where I've been. Wait a minute. You not like tasting you?" Judging by the non-response, I answered my own question. "Guess you're telling me I'm in dire need of a shower. And while you're at it spend a little extra time scrubbing me out of your beard and mustache."

Quick study, this fella. "Yep!"

"You want to wash my back, girlfriend?"

"I do...just not now. I'd like to quietly lie here alone after you bring me a warm, not cold, washcloth. Oh, and a clean towel. I'm still a little unsettled about today, especially the part about peeing in a bag. You guys whip it out anywhere, anytime, anyplace. With women, it's never quite that simple."

"Seriously, that's what you're thinking about, Victoria? We just made mad passionate love every which way, including sideways. Shouldn't you be glowing ... at least a little?"

Oh, shut up! "I was glowing, now I'm dripping. Hurry up with that washcloth, please. You're a guy, you wouldn't understand. Once I'm done, you're done. I glow, just not so much. Then, it's reality check time. What am I going to wear, will it make me look fat, will I drip you for the next hour or two? You should so be a girl."

It was in that mood-altering moment, I realized the pseudo honeymoon I had magically created between us to mask my pain during the long ride home was over. "No thank you. Manly men don't dwell on clothes and I'm relatively sure they don't leak for hours. If it's all the same to you, I'll pass. I like being a guy," I said, tossing her the towels, before stepping into the shower, alone.

My mind, now in overdrive, tossed one thought then another before colliding with an equal and opposing argument. Candi would never pass up the opportunity to shower with me. Usually she was first. Not Vic. In that instant, I realized, times change, scenes change, people change. Yet the yearning to be comforted by those who bring us comfort, not chaos, remains.

What could I have done differently that would have Candi here with me this morning instead of Victoria? Don't get me wrong; I appreciate the friendship, the company and the sex. It's been great, but as of this morning, the flame has diminished greatly. I told Vic sex ruins relationships. It takes two, asshole. You gave in, not because you had to, but because you wanted to. What did Vic say? "After the glow, then it's reality check time."

Wonder if that also pertains to my mental numbness finally wearing off after Candi's well-orchestrated ruse? You're such an idiot. She's screwing her ex. Yep, and you're screwing your lawyer. What does that tell you? It tells me we've both managed to screw our way out of each other. Who's to say we can't screw our way back in? D, you are out of your friggin' mind? Sigh ... I miss Candi, I miss Major, and I so miss us!

I'll never figure out how to pee in a bag so stop worrying about it. Just have fun, make the best of whatever situation you find yourself in. Girl, you learned that lesson a long time ago. "Hey, D, ready for me to wash your back? I'm through deep thinking and working my way back to glowing."

"Come on in. I'm done. My beard is clean...along with the rest of me, no thanks to you. I smell like ... nothing. We're supposed to use the unscented soap." *Like I have to remind her!*

Like he has to remind me. I'm glad he did, cause I forgot already. "Now why am I doing this?"

Stepping from the warm shower onto the cold floor, I ushered her in, in my stead, less one back washing. "So, you won't smell like you or more recently me, smelling like you." That confused even me. "I'll be upstairs when you're done. I'm gonna call the kennel and check on the dog. If I know Debra, she'll have breakfast waiting on us. So be quick, quick, quick...girlfriend."

"I won't be that long." *And that's the truth, no make-up, scent free sweats, just plain me. Wait a minute ... Did he just blow me off — twice? Girl, you are imagining things!*

Chapter 28

Walking outside into the crisp morning air, I rummaged through my pack before finding the phone of the week. Dialing the kennel, I was pleasantly surprised to hear a real voice answer for a change.

"Good morning, Gloria speaking. How may I assist you today?"

Morning Glory, get it? It's too early for humor. "Hi, Gloria. This is D, Major's dad. I'm running behind schedule on my trip. Kinda got held up. How's he doing?"

"Yes, sir. We got your message earlier. Major is fine. Especially since he received that box of treats yesterday."

"Treats? What treats? I didn't send him any treats."

"Your friend Marcy dropped them by. She brought two tennis balls, a box of milk bones, a bag of rawhide chews and some candy treats from PetSmart. Said you asked her to since you'd been held up. That's funny. Sounds like you didn't make it back because you were robbed. Mr. D, you did not send her by to see Major? His treats you left ran out a few days back so I figured you did."

I haven't talked to Marcy. How did she find him? I never told anyone where he was boarding. Then again, it's a kind gesture that Major I'm sure appreciates. But why? "My mind is fried sometimes, Gloria. I might have told her to run by and check on him. I guess I forgot."

"That's OK. You're on your bike. Right? I'd forget too, if I were going cross-country on a bike. My boyfriend has a crotch rocket. He makes me ride with him, but we never go far. Well, not on the bike anyway. His hurts my butt."

That's nice. Join the crowd. I don't care. I want to talk about Marcy. "She happen to say anything or leave a message for me?"

"Let me see. Found it! Yes, sir, she did leave a message. What kind of bike do you ride? Is your girlfriend riding with you? If not, maybe when you get back you can ride me."

Really, you don't even know me. Silly, precocious girls. Boys, look out for this one! "Gloria, the message, please. ... What was the message?"

"Oh, I'm sorry. Call Gio ... somebody ASAP. She left a number, but it has way too many—"

"Numbers, I got it. Giovanna is from Milan, Italy."

"Italy, I've always wanted to go there. Have you been? Duh! I'm sure you have... otherwise how would you know him?"

"Gloria, I hate to interrupt you, but give me the number and I'll see if it's different from the one I have for him." Reading off the numbers, including the country code, I recalled it was the same number I had stored in my old phone – the one I turned off and tossed in the bag the day Candi left me standing on the tarmac. "Thank you, Gloria. And thanks for taking such good care of Major. I'll be back by the end of the week. I've got to run. Bye now." Click, push end, whatever. Enough!

Question after question, rolled round and round in my head. *Call Giovanni. What's up with that? Is he trying to warn me about goings on in the Family? Does it have something to do with his health? Did Candi put Marcy up to locating the dog to get that message to me? Why is it that all these recent memories I managed to bury under a boulder over the last few days are surfacing in real time? Three times already this morning I've caught myself daydreaming about Candi, while in Vic's embrace. Now this. As Vic likes to say, big boy, you are so screwed!*

I heard the front door open and turned to find Vic standing before me in sweats, her hair in a pony- tail, her fair skinned makeup-free face, two shades up from pale.

"There you are. I've been looking for you. Debra has breakfast ready."

"I've been on the phone with the kennel. Major had an unexpected visitor who left me a message to call Giovanna."

Vic, arching her eyebrows, "Gio visited Major in Tennessee?"

"No, Candi's friend, Marcy did and left a message for me to call Gio, ASAP."

"What's up with that? You think there's more trouble brewing with the family… or with Candi for that matter?"

"I don't know. That's where my mind was going before you bounced out the door."

"If you want, I'll call Giovanni from my phone and find out what his news is."

"Thanks, but this one's on me. If someone went to the trouble to find the dog to get a message to me, must be important."

Damn right it must be important. D has stirred up one hell of a hornet's nest with his theft and subsequent generosity on behalf of others. "Might I remind you, Miss Debra has breakfast on the table. Can we talk about this later? I'm hungry."

"Me, too. Let's eat," I concurred, hoping that a pleasant meal among friends would put all these goings-on in my head in the proper perspective. Before us, spread across the table, were blueberry scones, corned beef hash, eggs over easy, sausage links and thick country bacon.

I'm going to ask this time, before I eat any meat. Vic, whispering to me, "Is any of this wild that you know of?"

Laughing, I shouted to Debra who had disappeared into the kitchen. "Debra, Vic wants to know how many wild animals are on the table this morning."

"Shush! I could have asked her myself." *Boys!*

Debra appeared, wiping her hands on a dishtowel. "Victoria, everything on the table is from the market in Tisdale. There's nothing wild on the table, well, except maybe your boyfriend sitting over there."

I smiled. Vic blushed. "He's not my boyfriend. We're just friends."

"Of course, you are," countered Debra with a wink, "and the bear in our woods aren't wild either."

Vic blushed again.

It seemed like an appropriate time to change the subject. "Speaking of wild, where's Greg this morning?"

"Last I saw him, he was loading up the four wheelers for your trip. You should have a few hours before you leave. Is there anything you'd like to do until then?"

"If possible, I'd like to visit the little girl, Missy, said Vic. Wouldn't you, D?"

"I would. Debra would you try and arrange that?"

"Gladly. Eat up and I'll make the call." Appearing in the doorway, Debra happily announced, "We can go when you're done with breakfast. You're in luck, Missy is having a good day. You'll make it even better since she loves company."

Chapter 29

Thinking long term during the two-block walk to Missy's house, I wasn't sure how we were going to play this and still remain anonymous. Before discussing it with Vic, I decided to involve both Greg and Candi, without their knowledge. Hey, what are friends for?

Debra led us to a little two-bedroom cottage, nestled in the trees on a lane with a white picket fence out front. Perfect place to raise a family — healthy ones. Warmly welcomed by Mrs. Bryan, we were introduced to Missy, a beautiful, but frail, blond haired, green eyed little girl, lying in a hospital bed in a room, wonderfully adorned in pink frills and ruffles. Pictures of happier times adorned the walls, while stuffed animals and dolls filled the corners. "Hi, Missy, I'm D. This is Vic. We're on a motorcycle ride across Canada. We stopped by to visit Greg and Debra and they told us about you. We're here to help."

"I'm sick. The doctor said I can get better, but I have to go to Florida first."

"Missy, have you ever been to Florida?" I asked, cradling her hand in mine.

"Nope. Soon ... I hope."

Jumping into the conversation with both feet, "Don't say, I hope so, say I know so. And when you get better you're going to Disney World, along with all your family. How would you like that?"

Missy laid back on the bed, closed her eyes and breathed deeply the oxygen that was making her comfortable. "More than anything. Can I be a Princess? Can I see Mickey and Minnie and Pluto?"

"Close your eyes, Missy. Make this wish with me… when I get better, I wish I could go to Disney World. Wishes do come true, especially for precious little girls like you. You must believe. Do you believe, Missy?"

"Oh, I do, I do. I believe with all my heart. Mommy did you hear, we're going to Disney World?"

Ah, through the innocent eyes of a child lies mankind's eternal hope. Looking around the room, there was her mother, Debra, Victoria and me. "You see all these people here? And all your dolls and animals, we're wishing with you. Big wishes aren't so hard when you're loved by so many." Knowing by her actions the recent excitement had taken its toll, Vic and I took turns giving her a hug and kissing her forehead, before saying good-bye.

Pulling Missy's mother aside, "there's light at the end of the tunnel. I have a friend, Candice Parker, who will see to it that Missy makes it to All Children's Hospital in St. Pete, shortly. And Victoria, whom you've just met, will see to it that your family has a wonderful holiday at Disney World before you return home. Sadly, I don't have a crystal ball. Neither you, nor I know for certain if the procedure will be successful. Only God above grants that wish. That being said, Disney World is a magic place for kids and a healing place for parents. Honor Missy's wish for me please, no matter what happens."

Holding her hands in mine, she cried, I choked. "Wishes come true for big people, too. We just have to believe with all our heart like Missy." With that, I was gone, walking quickly out the door, wiping the tears from my eyes before Vic and Debra saw my tear stained cheeks.

What's this? D's been crying. Victoria, too was moved, "What did you tell her Mom?"

"I told her that Candice Parker will help make the trip to All Children's possible—"

"Really D, Candice?" asked Vic. "Won't she be surprised?"

"And that you would send them to Disney World with or without Missy."

"Of course, I'd be honored to do that. But, why did you tell her with or without her daughter?"

"All we can do is provide the opportunity. Only God decides the outcome. Let Disney World be the dream they all aspire to. Let it be a trip to rejoice in the healing or to heal through the suffering. It just needs to happen, regardless of the outcome. I made her mom promise me that she would go. If I'm not around will you see to it, Vic?"

"I'll see to it. Why would you say if you're not around?" *What am I thinking? D is being pragmatic and for once, I'm the dreamer.* "Never mind, I just answered my own question without you opening your mouth."

"Good girl."

Debra, overhearing the important aspects of our conversation, spoke up. "Jon David, you made Missy's eyes glow when you promised her Disney World. I've never seen her that happy in a long time. Excuse me for eavesdropping, but did I overhear you correctly, you or someone you know will make her trip to All Children's possible? Can you really do that?"

I'd better interject for D before he gets put on the spot and says something he can't take back. "Debra, D or Jon David, as you call him, has many valuable connections. If he says he can make it happen, it will happen. Don't ask me how, just know that it will, sooner, rather than later."

"I don't know what to say to either of you. It's a miracle that you happened to ride through here and stay with us. What's even more miraculous is that diamond story that's flooding all the news channels right now making instant millionaires to so many people. Had that not been on my mind, I don't think I would have ever troubled you with Missy's story. It's a miracle, that's what it is..."

Gazing at D, his reddened, brown eyes reluctantly meeting mine, "It really is a miracle, Debra. Much more than you could possibly ever fathom or imagine at this very moment. A miracle in the making that is both up close and personal to all of us."

Enough Victoria, "Come on guys, I'm sure Greg is waiting for us. Debra, thank you for sharing Missy's crisis. We're fortunate to have friends in high places who have the wherewithal to make any mountain, surmountable."

Clasping my hand, Vic lifted it high into the sky as we walked, "We certainly are, D. We certainly are."

Chapter 30

Now to drag Greg, kicking and screaming, into my drama. "Ladies, wouldn't you like some tea? If you'd be so kind to heat up the kettle, I'll be back after I talk to Greg for a few."

"You'll find him in the shop," said Debra. "That's where he always is this time of morning."

"Thanks, Debra, I'm heading that direction. I'll be along soon. While you're bonding, do me a favor, teach Vic how to pee in a bag."

"Get out! You're a mess."

Damn straight! "D," said Vic, "I think she means you're a hot mess!"

"Hot mess it is then. Vic, you explain to Debbie the hot part, while she explains the Ziploc protocol," I added, watching a foreign object sail over my head, signaling it was way past my time to disappear.

I found Greg busily packing a bag for us, complete with binoculars, head nets, water bottles and snacks. "Is there anything you're not sending into the woods with us?"

"Good morning to you. Hey, you're the one taking this girl on her first hunt, not me. If it was only you, I'd let you pack your own bag. I'm doing my best to cover your ass... as usual."

What a great lead in to my next question. I couldn't have timed it better myself. "Speaking of covering my ass, I need a ginormous favor. We've just returned from visiting Missy. I promised her mom that funds would be immediately forthcoming to make the trip to St. Pete."

Bewildered, Greg asked, "You do that?"

"Nope, but you can on behalf of someone else. It's a long story, the less you know the better. Hold that thought, I'll be back." Returning with it to the shop, I dug deep into the bottom of my bag. Ripping one package open, I asked Greg to hold out his hands and close his eyes. Pouring a smattering of diamonds into his hands, I clenched his fingers and pushed them into a doubled fist. "Greg, before you open your hands, know this, there's a certain amount of risk that follows. I'm sure there's another way, but the urgency of Missy's situation demands action."

"Got it. If it helps her live a long and happy life that's good enough for me."

"Agreed. Open your hands."

Greg's mouth dropped. "Are these real? Where'd you get them? Wait. The news, diamonds are all over the news. Did you get a package? Can't see it, you, giving all them away if you did. What I can see, clear as mud, you're the benefactor behind the headlines. I'll be damned, you're the reason these instant millionaires have been springing up everywhere over the last few weeks. Go ahead, deny it…tell me I'm wrong."

"You're not wrong. Honestly, you're 'bout dead on. Our secret, OK? Remember, you can't deny what you don't know or something to that degree. Anyway, you're holding somewhere between three hundred and four hundred carats in your hand, plus what's in this bag. Half should more than cover Missy's expenses and then some. Take Debra on a 'round the world cruise' while you're at it, on me. My way of saying thanks."

"I don't …we don't … you don't have to pay me. Being able to help her is enough, D."

"I got it. But, don't forget, after all the publicity I've generated, there's a risk you'll make headlines. I'd rather you not. First, I need you to go to Toronto to the diamond exchange and quietly sell enough of these on the open market to satisfy the hospital. Second, everyone and I mean everyone up here and in Florida needs to know that Ms. Candice Parker, from Chattanooga, Tennessee is the generous benefactor behind Missy Bryan's ability to secure the treatments."

"Who is Candice Parker? I've never heard you mention her name before."

"She was or is, I don't know exactly which at the moment, someone very special to me. Let's just say that her connection to a well-known Family, as well as to children's healthcare makes her a viable benefactor and leave it at that."

"OK, Jon David, whatever you say. What do you want me to do with all the left-over diamonds and money? It belongs to you, not me."

"Medicine Hat has a Teepee. Tisdale has the bee. Why shouldn't Mistatim have the world's largest duck?"

Greg rolled off his work stool laughing. "You're joking, right? Mistatim having the world's largest duck. That's amusing, then again it would bring in lots of tourists … and traffic, and people who don't know how to mind their own business. Nope, I don't like that idea one bit."

"I was joking, Greg. Just put it away for me. Invest it where you can get your hands on it if I find myself in a bind. Don't you dare be afraid to use it! I'm sure there will be more Missy's that cross your path down the road. You'd better surprise Debra with a trip of a lifetime. I've known you long enough to say this out of friendship… I'd better not hear that you've taken her on some African safari that you think she might like. Deal?"

Extending his right hand, we shook on it. "You do know Debra likes to hunt as much as I do," confessed Greg, a broad smile beaming across his face.

"Remember what I said. Just this once make her the Princess and you be the frog."

"You've made that crystal clear. I got it. Ribbit … Ribbit, that's me."

"I also know you've still got many questions and I'd like to tell you more. I will soon enough." The intercom buzzed. "Boys," announced Debra, "Lunch is ready, and D ... your tea is cold."

"We'll be right up," I replied. "Tell Vic to put the tea cup between her boobs 'til I get there. That's bound to warm it up PDQ."

"I heard that," shouted Vic, in the background.

"The walls have ears, huh Greg?"

"Not likely. Women have ears and they hear everything."

Only when they want to, not so much when they don't, my attention turned once again to Candi.

Chapter 31

With lunch behind us, Vic and I changed into the 'smelly' camo Greg generously provided for our impromptu adventure.

"Here, D, carry this," said Greg, handing me a Remington 7MM short mag bolt-action rifle, along with an extra clip. "It's my gun. You're sighted in and good to go."

A gun? Really? Come on, we are going hunting. "D, I thought you said we were shooting with a camera. What's with the gun?"

Greg looked at me shaking his head. I took the lead in answering her. "Protection, Vic. Up where we're going there's a bunch of horny old trappers who haven't seen a woman with teeth as beautiful as you in twenty something years. I've got to have something to fight them off with ... or not. Greg, on second thought, I'm sure Vic can take care of herself."

Asshole ... "Whatever, bring the gun." *I'm not that stupid, even if I do look like it... dressed in this God awful, smelly set of hunting clothes.*

Greg brought the Green Mule to life, its white smoke reminiscent of our last adventure. Traveling north on Second Avenue, the paved road quickly turned to hardpan gravel, interspersed with rug boards, created by the endless farm equipment that traversed the sections. After five miles, we entered the Crown Provincial Forest, the equivalent of our National Forests, where the road turned into a trail, then later into a path with 18" deep ruts. Bouncing,

120

bobbing, weaving, leaning, we held onto the handholds as the Mule rocked and rolled us along at 5 mph another 30 minutes to our drop off.

"You remember this place, Jon David?" asked Greg, after we stopped. "This area is where you took down that old 600 pound boar with the clawed up face."

"I remember. Because of you, we turned the trike over three times trying to haul Brutus out. Didn't get back 'til four in the morning." The expression on Vic's face — another Kodak moment. "Don't look at me like that, girlfriend. There are no absolutes when you go deep into the wilderness. You get in when you get in, you get out when you get out. That is if you're lucky."

What has he roped me into today? "All this jostling around getting here, I have to..."

"Pee? Go ahead, you're among friends," I chuckled, handing her a Ziploc from my pack. "Come on, I'll go with you. This I've got to see. You wanna watch, Greg?"

Boys! "Absolutely not, it's bad enough to pee in a bag, let alone in front of you. Not Greg, nope, not happening."

"That's OK, I'll pass this time around," snickered Greg. "I'll get the machines off and warmed up while you take care of her business."

"Thank you, sir. Come on Vic, let's go find you a tree." Walking off the trail and out of sight, I found a downed Trembling Aspen about two feet off the ground ideally suited for a woman. "Will this work for you, barrister? Looks like the proper height and circumference for you to hang your sweet cheeks over."

I can't believe I'm doing this. ... What was I thinking when I agreed to go on this so-called adventure? Wait just a minute; I never agreed to anything. I went with it. "It will work. Give me a minute. I've got to unhook, unzip, and untie." *Boys just unzip and let it fly, lucky them.* Balancing myself over a downed tree, while trying to hold a Ziploc bag is NOT my idea of making pleasant memories!

"Hold that thought. Better still hold it. I'll help you. First, I have to go."

"Too late, D." Relief! *Ahh… that's better. Oh wait, the bag's almost full! Stop girl! Remember your Kegels.* "D, I … uh … need another Ziploc."

Turning back to her in full stream, I started drawing golden figure eights on the ground as only a man can. "Just dump it out and fill it up again. I'll be there in a sec."

Like I can go anywhere. He's such an ass sometimes. Wait a minute. Why is he peeing on the ground and I'm peeing in a bag? What did he just say, pour it out and fill it up again? "D, how come you're not using a Ziploc? What did you mean pour it on the ground and fill it up again? Something stinks!"

"I never said you had to pee in a bag… now. You just assumed—" were all the words I could get out of my mouth before a golden, liquid filled Ziploc glanced off my shoulder. "Hey, you almost hit me in the chest with that."

"I was aiming for your head. Damn it! I missed." She finished. "You think you're so cute. Why did you give me the bag if I wasn't supposed to use it?"

"You're the inquisitive lawyer in our midst. You're supposed to ask the hard questions," I replied, laughing loud enough for Greg to hear me at a distance.

"Jon David, Victoria, all OK?"

"I'm fine, Greg. D, on the other hand, will not be once I get my hands on him." *I can tell by the looks of things already … this is going to be a long, ass afternoon.*

Relieved being the understatement of the day, Vic and I joined Greg as he was securing our gear on one of the 4x4 Polaris Rangers. "D, you explain to Vic about the beaver crossings?"

"Not yet! Figured we'd dress 'em as we hit 'em."

Has he been drinking? Have I missed something? "D, what are you talking about ?"

"We're on an adventure to remember. Right? Are we having fun yet? Don't worry, we will." And we were off with Greg leading the way. Moving into the forest and beneath the tree canopy, the fresh smell of peat permeated the air. "What do you smell, Vic?"

Like I know ... "Stale dampness, like mildewed shoes."

"It's peat, like peat moss you use in the garden. We're driving across peat bogs at the moment." The ground would give way beneath our tires, leaving deep ruts, but only for the moment. In less than a minute, the ruts would disappear as the peat sprang back like a sponge. I saw Greg stop ahead, motioning me to ride up beside him.

"First beaver, Jon David. You wanna go first?"

"Nope, it's all you. Vic, you can walk or ride, your call. Both are tough. If you ride, be prepared to hang your body over the side farthest away from the ground."

Feeling sheer terror, "What did you just say?"

"If I start to turn over, throw all your body weight to the opposite side. Whatever you do, don't get out unless it flips you out. I'll use your weight as a counter balance to offset mine and the machine's. I can see the whites of your eyes. Look, beaver build great dams, but they have holes in the top. Sometimes we hit them, most times we don't. Here we go. Hang on." Following Greg, I inched our way across the first one, tilting to the left, then the right, before bottoming out fifty feet from the other side. I got this. "Vic, can you hop up in the bed and put all your weight on the back?"

"What good will that do?" *Seriously, at 138 pounds dripping wet what difference will it make?*

"It will put more weight on the back wheels. I need traction. When I start rocking it back and forth, your weight will help the rear wheels grab and I can jump out of this hole. Trust me!"

Climbing into the utility bed, Vic stood silently holding onto the roll bars knowing just enough about physics to be dangerous. *This will either work or it won't. It's the won't that concerns me. That and 'trust me.'* "I'm ready. Just do it."

"Good girl!" Rocking back and forth between forward and reverse, I finally felt the rear wheels catch propelling us backwards. "Now forward," I shouted, throwing the Ranger into 1st gear, holding the accelerator to the floor. We cleared the first hole easily enough, but the rear wheels landed where our front wheels had been. With the throttle wide open, the Ranger automatically threw all its torque to the rear wheels, standing it straight up in the air while I was doing everything I could to keep from falling out. Easing back on the gas the front end began to fall. Suddenly two hands appeared over the front, then two arms and finally an entire body, Greg's, his weight dropping the front end quickly to the ground.

"Now go!" shouted Greg. "Floor it!"

The front wheels grabbed traction and I lurched forward, not stopping until I made it across the dam with Greg sprawled out across the front and Vic... Where's Vic? Satisfied I was on solid ground, I turned back to see Vic rising to her feet on top the dam, rubbing her smarting cheeks with both hands. "What happened to you?"

Asshole. What do you mean what happened to me? "What's it look like dumbass, I fell off?"

"You OK? Watch out for the holes!"

"Watch out for the holes. No shit, Sherlock. If you'd been watching out for the holes we wouldn't have gotten stuck, and my ass wouldn't be stinging like it is right now!"

"I'm sorry, girlfriend. I told you to hold on."

"I did, I was, 'til superman Greg here climbs on the front like the Hulk causing me to forget what I was supposed to be doing."

"Like holding on?"

"Yep, like holding on. When you punched it, I watched my life flash before my eyes. One minute I was standing in the bed, the next minute I was standing in the air before I landed on my ass. We have two more of these to cross? No thanks, I'll walk." And I did until I stepped off into a bottomless hole that didn't stop until my aching butt was on the ground again. "A little help here!" Vic yelled, watching two grown men laughing their asses off. "I know, I know, watch out for the holes."

"She worth it?" asked Greg.

"She is. Let's go get her. Vic, we're coming. You hurt anything?"

"Only my pride," *What else could I say? First, D warned me to hang on. Then he told me to watch out for the holes. I'm batting a thousand today for all the wrong reasons.*

After a little maneuvering, Greg and I each took an arm and lifted Vic straight up out of the hole that unwillingly held her leg. "Are you sure you're OK?"

No, I'm not all right! "Hold on a minute, D. Steady me please. I think this time I bruised my you know ... hoo-ha."

That's a first. Trying not to laugh, "Want me to take a look at it? Greg has a first aid kit on his machine."

"Shhh ... I'll fine," Vic answered the little boy inside the man, grabbing my arm and squeezing it to the bone to get me to hush.

Greg, hearing his name, coupled with first aid kit, stopped and spun around. "Is she OK? Did she hurt something?"

If her grip on my arm could kill, I'd be dead. "Only her pride, Greg. Only her pride."

Chapter 32

Finally, we were off again, screaming through the woods, zipping across peat bogs, climbing over logs and crossing the last two dams with ease. The last leg of our journey flew by.

Greg slowed his machine to a crawl, motioning for me to do the same. Then he made a 360° turn and stopped. "You're on your own from here. Now you walk. About one hundred and fifty yards up on the left there will be a timber cut. Follow it until you see three orange flags on a Jack Pine. Go into the woods there and follow the flags to the tree stand. I'm going to check more baited areas and will meet you back here at seven. Any questions?"

D shook his head no. Of course, he did. "Excuse me, Greg. I have one. How far is it to the stand, as you call it?"

"It's another thirty minutes of brisk walking, Victoria. Why?"

"Just in case I have to, you know, go again," she replied uncomfortably.

"The two of you better take care of any business here. I don't want you screwing up my bait areas."

"Copy that, Greg. That's why I brought along extra Ziplocs. Vic's bout got the hang of it."

Greg laughed, seriously? Damn him, and damn D, too, while we're at it. "I do have the hang of it, thank you. It's takes a whole lot of work to be a woman around boys playing with their toys." *Come to think of it, even more so, when they're playing with me...*

Greg's Ranger roared to life. "I'm outta here. If you're gonna do that, do it here. Not in my tree stand!"

Well, Vic knew just how to push his button and mine too, for that matter. "I'm not saying a word, girlfriend. After we start walking in, you'll have to be quiet as in no talking. Whatever you need to get off your chest or out of—"

"I'm fine. I just don't like you making fun of me. I'm doing this for you, you know."

"That's hilarious. I thought I was doing this for you, Victoria."

"I still don't know what 'this' is, D? You're carrying a rifle, a backpack and me into the woods. I can only deduce we're going hunting."

Embracing her in both arms, I whispered, "we're going sightseeing… trust me."

Why is it when men say, 'trust me,' I always find myself catching my breath before thinking WTF is next? "Let's do this. What are you waiting on?"

Women, can't live with them, can't live without them. "Nothing, absolutely nothing. Follow me."

Walking quietly to the cut, we made the left into big timber where the undergrowth was at least six feet high on both sides of the old logging road. Twenty minutes into our trek with my mind thousands of miles away somewhere in Florida, I felt a tug on my sleeve.

Mister outdoorsman is clueless. "D, did you hear that? I think something is following us."

"I'm sorry. What'd you say, Vic?"

"I said, I think something or someone is following us. When we stop, it stops. When we walk, it walks."

Trying to allay her fears, I pulled the rifle off my shoulder and chambered a round into the barrel. "There, whatever it is, we'll be ready." I motioned for Vic to follow me, then stop. Walk a few yards more, then stop again. Nothing. Guess her imagination is in overdrive right now. Then, off to my right I heard branches breaking in stride. Vic closed up behind me, close enough that I could feel her breath on my neck.

I may not be a hunter, but as a full-blown, cautious female, I am constantly aware of my surroundings. "I told you, didn't I? There is something out there."

"You have a great sense of hearing, Vic, I'll give you that. There is definitely something following us. Let's keep walking until I can figure out what it… is."

Great. … And he's the one with the gun. "A bear? I mean, what else will stalk you up here?"

"It could be anything. The quicker we get to the tree stand the more we'll be able to see," which sounded much better than the safer we will be. Over the next rise, I saw a glimpse of the three orange flags dangling from the long-needled pine. "Vic, it's not far, now. See the flags. We go left there."

And that's supposed to give me some sort of relief? "I see them. Does that mean the tree stand is close by?"

"It's closer than it was when we started." We were being tracked that's for sure, but by the lack of aggression it seemed more about curiosity than a meal. Reaching the Jack Pine, I pushed Vic off the cut and onto the trail. "Wouldn't you like to know what's been following us?"

I'd like to know if it's going to eat us. "You're gonna protect me, aren't you?"

"Of course, I am, unless it's a grizz. Then all you have to do is out run me."

Fat chance in these rubber boots. "Wait, there aren't any grizzly's in this part of Saskatchewan. You said so yourself."

"You're a quick study. See you have nothing to worry about." Taking her arm, I led her underneath the low hanging branches of the pine just deep enough for us to watch the trail. Maybe five minutes at the most passed before we heard loud snorting, followed by small trees crashing to the ground, announcing the arrival of our tracker, aka Bullwinkle. Stepping through the undergrowth exactly where Vic and I made the left, an old bull moose appeared, snorting, thrashing, shaking the brush from his antlers.

Oh my. That moose is at least fourteen hands high. It's big enough to ride. "Will it bite?" I mouthed to D, hoping in that instant he could read my lips.

I slowly put my forefinger to my lips, telling Vic, "Shhh!" We watched in amazement as the old guy sniffed and snorted the ground around him, doing his best to pick up our scent. After a couple of minutes, he caught wind of something else that raised his awareness, whereby he tilted his head high and trotted off into the brush out of sight, but not out of our memory.

Chapter 33

"**M**ind blowing, D. That was incredible. Did you see how big he was? Did you see how wide his antlers were? Did you know it was a moose all along?" Question after question rolled out of her mouth. "That was awesome."

It was impressive I had to agree. "Too many questions," I whispered, "let's go find the tree stand and I'll answer them up there." Hiking down the trail, the forest enveloped us, its immense density obscuring the late afternoon sun. "There, over there," I directed Vic, following the flags along a line of sight straight to a dark green ladder disappearing high into a tree. "You first."

Of course, me first asshole, I wouldn't stay down here by myself. "Wait, what if there's something up there, D? Then what?"

I laughed. "Then you'll tell me and I'll come up and shoo it off." The ladder rose a good twenty feet through the branches to a metal tree stand built for two. Following closely behind her, I made sure Vic knew I was there by the constant cheek pinching I administered each time she stopped. "You're almost there. Just a few more feet. Crawl on your belly through the rail, then stand up and I'll hand you my gun and gear."

Climb the ladder, pinch my butt, crawl on my belly, suck my— "I got it. Stop pinching my butt. I'm nervous to be this high in a tree. You're good at barking orders, aren't you? The next thing you'll tell me to do is blow..."

"Stop with the drama. That's not a bad idea though," I chuckled. "I could use a little stress relief."

Vic smacked me on my head, my big one as I climbed up beside the stand. "Ouch! What was that for?"

"For wanting a blow job at a time like this. Remember, I'm only along for the ride."

"You brought it up, girlfriend. I was trying to oblige. You have to chill out. Whacking something is bound to calm your nerves. It sure works for me." I grinned ear to ear, the boy in me, anyway. Then, the man in me relented, "Want me to do you? Bet that would calm you down."

You're dreaming. Hey, if I could unzip it and whip it out, I might take you up on that. Men! "Good luck with that. Taking my clothes off and putting them back on would kill any mood enhancement generated by your lips and tongue." *Ooh ... I shivered. On second thought, nothing ventured, nothing gained...*

"Who said anything about lips, I was gonna—"

Asshole, I was so close to taking you up on your offer. "I thought this was about me, remember?"

"It is about you, this is all about you. Here, take my gear," I added, passing it to her waiting hands, "and don't drop it." Settled in on the six-foot wide stand with an aluminum safety railing, I mounted the mini-tripod for the camera and assumed the hurry up and wait position. "You might as well take a nap. We've got at least an hour or two to kill 'til show time."

"Just where am I supposed to be looking and for what exactly?"

Handing Vic my binoculars, "Look through the manmade cut-out in the trees. What do you see 40-plus yards out?"

"I see a barrel chained to a tree, and a little bear and a big bear. Oh, that's so cool ... bears."

"Here, let me see," taking the glasses from her hands, looking in the direction of the bait barrel. Sure enough, there was a 300-lb. sow wrestling around the 55-gallon drum, jam-packed with molasses covered oats, but no cub. "Are you sure there were two bears?"

Hell-o. "I am. The little bear was a third the size of the big one."

Turning the camera to video, I handed Vic back the glasses and began filming the momma bear flipping the drum over and over trying to shake the food onto the ground before she finally settled down and started licking out the grain through the two-inch diameter hole in the end. "Where'd the cub go? You were so good at finding it the first time, let's see if you can find it again."

"See, I am good at other things besides the obvious you already know: gambling with other peoples' money, criminal law and sex."

Giving Vic a fist bump, I concurred wholeheartedly, still wondering what happened to the bear cub as I searched right and left through the camera's viewfinder. Her hand clamped down on my leg. "What? I complimented you, girlfriend. I'm sure you have many more talents that I've yet to see…or experience, first hand."

Chapter 34

I found the bear, D. It's ... it's—"

"Good job, Vic. I'm proud of you. Where is it?"

Shut up and follow my finger, pointing directly below us, "There."

"Oops ... That's not good with momma nearby." Somehow, we were scented or seen and the not so little cub was coming up our tree to investigate. Trying not to make a commotion to attract the attention of momma, I started whispering "Shoo! ... shoo! ... We need to get it to go down!"

Like, I could do that great white hunter. "D, give me your water bottle."

"You can't throw it at him. If you knock him off, momma bear will come running and we'll never get out of this tree."

Geez! "Who said anything about throwing it, I'm gonna squirt him. Hopefully the cold water will shock him enough to make him turn around."

Handing her the bottle, I watched Vic perform her magic. With the bear, not more than six feet below us, she squirted it directly in the face. To my chagrin, baby bruiser began to lap it up like a dog, swallowing as much of the 32-oz. water bottle as Vic was willing to give him. Knowing we were quickly running out of options, I grabbed the rifle and released the safety, just as a big tree branch snapped off deep in the forest. The baby's ears perked up signaling danger, and he immediately scampered down the tree and joined his mom. Soon after, they ran off into the timber.

Ha! "Told you it might work! Good idea, huh? Come on, you can tell me I'm golden."

Who am I to burst her bubble? I knew what the branch breaking meant, only because I'd seen this scenario play out two times before. Whispering, "That was a great idea. You did good. Sit very still. Act two is about to begin. Train your glasses on the barrel and wait." I flipped the camera on and watched.

Out of the deep woods, a shadowy cinnamon colored behemoth emerged and lumbered across open ground to the barrel. Judging Yogi's size by comparing him to the 55-gallon drum, I estimated him to be two feet taller than it was and at least 600 pounds. Yogi picked the barrel up like it was a feather and tossed it against the tree. Then he jumped on top of it and rolled it around like a trained bear from Ringling Brothers. Finally, he, too, gave up and began to lick out the grain through the two-inch opening, just like the sow before him.

"He looks mean, D. I wouldn't want to have a run-in with him."

"Look at his right ear. It's missing. This is the dominant bear 'round here. This is his bait, his food, his territory. Everyone else is trespassing."

"Including us?"

"Including us. He should be gone by dark." But he wasn't. Yogi was thoroughly content to stay with the barrel for the next hour, eating the grain one lick at a time.

The darkness gradually enveloped us…it was almost six o'clock. I knew we had to go if we were going to meet Greg. "Vic, do you think you can climb down the ladder quietly?"

Are you an idiot? "With Yogi down there somewhere? Nope! Shoot Him. You have a license and you have a gun. Shoot him!"

"Too much work. I'd have to gut him, skin him and haul him out. That would add another six hours to our adventure. Of course, if you'd like to make love on the rug we could make out of him, I could be persuaded to change my mind. Besides, the gun is only for protection."

"Then protect me, D. Shoot the damn bear."

Handing her the rifle, "You shoot him. Then you can make love to me on your bear skin."

"But ... but, I'm not having sex on a bear skin rug. Understood?"

"Understood. Loud and clear. Shoot him for the meat then."

That's a thought... "What if I miss?"

"Then we'll have one very pissed off bear to contend with."

Handing me back the gun, Vic spouted off, "Never mind." Asshole!

"Vic, hunter's pay big money for the once in a lifetime chance to shoot a bear this size. I wouldn't want to deprive anyone of that opportunity. That fella's gonna make some husband a happy man when he gets to wrestle momma around on that big old hide."

Ooh, yuck! "That's gross, D."

"You talkin' about the bear or the wife?" *I surprise myself sometimes.* "Don't knock it 'til you've tried it, girlfriend. Not to change the subject, but Greg will know something is going on if we're not back by seven. He'll come looking for us."

"What are we supposed to do until then?"

"Well, we could tell stories, couldn't we?"

"I'm drawing a blank, D. What stories would you like to share?"

Retrieving her hand from the rail, I placed it on my lap. "Be patient, I'm sure something's bound to pop up." I laughed at my crude attempt at humor in a tree stand ... in Canada ... with a menacing looking bear, feeding not 120 feet away. She wasn't amused.

OMG — men! "Seriously, D. You wanna fool around now? It's hard to get in the mood in this tree, even if it is with you."

"Vic, don't you know by now, men only need an opportunity and possibly a place? It's you women who pretty much always need a reason."

"How well I know. Remember, I told you, you'd have to get me wasted before I'd shared the skeletons in my closet?"

"I do. Sadly, I don't have anything to drink or smoke to bring that about. However, I possibly have a little something you could swallow." She punched me!

Chapter 35

"Fear is an amazing thing. It blurs the lines between fight and flight. It courses through your veins and brings on a rush similar to amphetamines. It makes you wholly appreciate living in the past, the present and the future… if and when it comes. Close your eyes, D," Vic said, rounding up the courage to bare her soul. "Don't interrupt me until I've had my say."

Whew! Where do I begin? "My mom and dad divorced when I was ten and because my dad traveled with work, my older brother and I lived with mom. Michael, all of thirteen, took it upon himself to be the man of the house, which included disciplining me. If I got in trouble at school and he found out about it before Mom got home, he would spank me with his hand or a belt and send me to my room.

"At first, I hated it and couldn't stand being around him. But, … I can't believe I'm telling you this, by age twelve I began to enjoy it. I would purposely make up things just so he would spank me. It excited me and he knew it. He stopped, but I didn't. I wanted spanked. I wanted punished. If not by him, I'd find others that would do it. By age fifteen, I realized how much power I had over men, teachers, principals, and counselors, just by letting them cop an occasional feel when I was bent over their knees.

"I kind of told you I was a congressional page in Washington for my junior semester in high school. How do you think that happened? My hoo-ha and my desire to be spanked opened doors I never dreamed possible. What was amazing was that I never had sex with any of them until that Washington year when this chief of staff forced himself on me. He raped me repeatedly and threatened to send me packing in disgrace if I ever told anyone.

"I was too scared to say no until the end of the semester when I filmed us having sex. I had him spank me, tie me up and have sex with me in every way possible. I wanted something on film he could not refute. And I got it. My last day in Washington, I met with the congressman in private and showed him just enough to get that asshole fired and me a full ride to the college of my choice. I had it coming, and I knew it, but I made it work to my advantage.

"Like your Momma said, you can't continually play with fire and not get burned. There, now you know. I'm a terrible person, D. I told you I was flawed ... Please say something. D?"

I was speechless and ashamed. I was hurting with her, for her. "We're all flawed, Vic. Remember? Everyone has a past. Don't let anyone tell you different. It's how we scrape the, — pardon my French — shit off going forward that defines us. Are we stained, you betcha? Does it linger… every day? Does it make it harder to succeed and easier to fail? Absolutely!

"Our minds are constantly at war with our past convincing us of our unworthiness when the road gets tough. If everyone gave up and quit living because of the baggage of our yesterdays, I'd venture to say there would be very few of us left to make this world a happy place."

I paused, took a breath, then swallowed, "Did you deserve it, who am I to say? Could I have been one of those men? It's unlikely, but possible. Anything is possible. You put yourself in a vulnerable position, Victoria. Good men, bad men, all men are subject to fail without notice. Especially when the power of a receptive and willing Woo-Hoo as beautiful as yours is drawing them like a moth to a flame. Remember what I said earlier, men just need a place and an opportunity. Sadly girlfriend, you provided both.

"Are you the only one? Hell no! I've dated many a girl who were assaulted, abused and raped by brothers, fathers, cousins, uncles and close family friends. People of authority, people of trust, who you know damn well knew better but were somehow provided an opportunity. Sadly, sexual abuse of a minor sees no gender. It occurs both with males and females. Guys seem to fare better outwardly because there's no stigma associated with it for them. Inwardly, though, the damage skews their sense of morality. Girls, as you well know, suffer much more in so many ways…by acting out or suppressing their emotional turmoil 'til some event triggers it's eruption."

"I hurt for you, Victoria. I hurt for all of those like you and me who are scarred for life because corruptible men can't keep it in their pants." Wrapping her up in my arms, I felt her tears on my cheek. Likewise, she felt my tears for her. Sitting quietly in the darkness, we held each other tight … two scarred individuals who crossed paths, maybe just so we could help each other heal. And in the silence, we did. With each moment that passed the heavy loads of our sordid pasts were spirited aloft into the night's star-filled sky.

Reality beckoned. The pervasive sounds of a rumbling engine off in the distance signaled Greg was on his way to retrieve us. Rousing the woman nestled in my arms, I said, "Vic, it's time to go."

"D, I don't want to leave. It's healing here."

"An hour a go you couldn't wait to leave!"

He'd better not laugh at what I'm about to say. "Well, that was before I bared my soul to you."

"Confession is good, girlfriend. I'm humbled you trusted me enough to share your demons."

"I trust you, pal, I always have. From the very first time we met when you wouldn't make love to me, I knew."

"Speaking of sleeping with you. I'd like to go back to the way we were before, you know, when all we did was sleep together without the sex."

I saw that coming ... I knew it. Pursing her lower lip, "You don't want to make love, have sex, or whatever you want to call it, anymore?"

"It's not that. We've had amazing comfort sex. It's been pleasurable, but it's not real. That is, as long as I'm always thinking about Candi when I'm making love to you."

She hit me, hard. Pounding my shoulders with both fists, "Why can't you let her go, D? After what you've seen, after what she's done to you, you still think there's hope?"

"What do you want me to say? I'm a horrible romantic. I can't get closure 'til I see her again. I have to know."

He's right. How do I compete with someone who's constantly on his mind? "I can't promise you I won't jump you, but I will do all I can to help you get the answers you seek. I got it. You can't open another door before you close this one. All I have to say is the quicker you get me home the better."

As Vic wrapped up her heart wrenching conversation, Greg came roaring down the trail, his Zenon headlights piercing the darkness. Stopping within fifty feet of the stand, "There a problem up there? You been shaking that tree in the dark and forget what time it was?"

"Yep, we been rocking this tree and testing your stand, especially the rails. Did you know it can support Vic's hands and my legs in a 69 embrace for an hour?"

"Stop...you ruined it right there, D. I was beginning to believe you 'til you said an hour. No one could last an hour like that ... 10-15 minutes tops. But you can keep on dreaming since that's what old men do when they can't perform like they once did."

"Yep... The real reason we're still here is that big 600-pound Yogi bear over there at the bait. He's been hanging around for the last two hours. He's somebody's trophy, that's for sure. Vic wasn't too keen on heading back with him wandering around. Besides, I didn't feel up to walking back in the dark. Glad your ass finally showed up."

Greg laughed. "You're welcome. Miss, you can come down. With all the noise we've made, Yogi's run off by now."

The headlights lit up the tree, making it much easier to climb down the ladder in the dark. With Vic in the passenger seat and me standing in the bed, we made great time to our machine and eventually the Green Mule and trailer.

I'm bumfuzzled. Where are the infamous beaver dams we crossed on the way in? Once the boys loaded up their toys and we were all in the truck, Vic asked, "Excuse me, Greg. We didn't cross the beaver dams on the way back. Why?"

"Oh, we don't go that way in the dark. Can't see," answered Greg, snickering. "Besides, it's not safe."

Did he just laugh? "D, did I miss something? Why is he laughing?"

How should I say this and not get clobbered? "Vic, per my instructions, Greg took us over the challenging route on the way in. You have to admit, it was more memorable than the ride out—"

Little boys and big toys! "Memorable? It's only memorable because of my bruised ass and my sore hoo—"

"Ha! You're just mad because you fell off and we didn't."

There's some truth to that. I actually had a wonderful time, so I guess I'll let him off the hook. "Thank you both for making this day possible. It goes to the top in my lifetime book of memories."

"You're welcome," said Greg. "I'm glad it worked out for all of us."

"We've got some great film to add to that book of yours," I added. "I especially like the scene that shows your sweet cheeks hanging over the log, peeing in the bag."

Son of a bitch! "D, you didn't film that, did you? Show me. I want to see what's on that camera. Now!"

"You can catch it on the news at eleven. I'll have it edited and on the air by then," I joked, right before Vic punched me hard in the groin, then squeezed.

"That hurt? This hurt?"

"Yep."

"There's more where that came from if I ever hear of it making it to You-Tube. Our eyes only, big boy. You got that?"

"I got it ... ah hem ... you can let go now, Vic. I got it."

Boys. ... hell-o! I'm in a truck full of juvenile delinquents. Lucky me!

Chapter 36

Dinner was served late. Debra didn't seem to mind. Such is the life of an outfitter's wife. Grilled salmon, fried potatoes and green beans were our fare for the evening. The wine we shared was a sparkling Moscato, followed by her famous Saskatoon berry pie topped with a dollop of vanilla ice cream. "I can't thank you both enough for riding through here on your way home. Greg and I want you to know you're welcome anytime, not just during hunting season."

"Thanks, Debra. It's good to know I still have a few friends left. Your hospitality has been over the top this trip. Vic, I'm sure it's because of you. Usually, I'm left to fend for myself after a long day's hunt, sitting around with a bunch of old farts, sipping whisky, drinking beer and telling lies."

"They weren't all lies," Greg interjected, rising from the table. "What time are you heading out in the morning? Debra will need to know to have breakfast ready."

Looking at my not so early riser sitting beside me, my mind said seven, but her mind meld purred eight. "Eight should be early enough." Judging by Vic's approving nod, Mr. Spock's talents had struck again.

* * *

We crashed. Sleep came quickly. My morning came quicker as I bolted from the bed somewhere around 3 AM in a cold sweat, realizing I was supposed to call Giovanni on Italy time. Six hours ahead or is it six hours behind? It's too early to think, that's for sure. I eased quietly from the bed and crept out the door to keep my rumblings from disturbing Vic. Rummaging through my bag, I found last week's phone as well as his stored number. I pressed send. On the fifth ring, Gio answered groggily, "Ciao."

"Gio, D. Did I wake you? I'm sorry. What time is it in Italy?"

"Cuze?…D? … That you?"

"Yes, sir. I'll call you back later if you'll tell me a good time."

"Good now. Me sleep. Now not."

"My bad. Six-hour time difference or seven. I can't remember. What time is it there?"

"Phone say five one five."

"Where are you, pal? That's eastern time."

"Me and Mile in Tampa, Candice, too."

"What's going on? Why are you not in Italy? How did you find Major? Has something happened to Candi?" I hit him with rapid-fire questions, wondering if I was prepared for the answers that would follow.

"You speak, slow … D. Mile, me OK, Candice not. We stay. You come, we go home. She find dog, find you. How you say … my idea? When you come? Candice sad. You come now."

"Gio, it's not that easy. Candi chose Joseph over me when she got on the plane. Candi chose Joseph when she screwed his brains out sometime in the last few days. Why would she now choose me?"

"She protect you and lady friend lawyer, Victoria. She good girl. You see, she explain. She no screw Joseph. You wrong … she not like him now … She like you."

"I could protect us, I was protecting us. She blew it."

"She make right. You see, D. Joseph bad, you good. When you come, you see."

"I want to talk to her. I can't promise anything. I'll call back at eight. Answer your phone, OK?"

"OK, D. You see. I wake her."

"Not now, pal. At eight, Gio. Thanks." I hung up without saying good-bye. Shame on me. Too much to process this early in the morning. I can see Candi taking the ledgers to claim the reward, especially if it appeased Joseph. Maybe even to protect me? Still, why would she screw him on film? Who does that today? Open ended questions that deserved a damn good explanation. I wanted to believe Gio. I so wanted to believe Candi. Is there a method to her madness? Damn you, woo-hoo ... Damn you!

Walking the streets for the next two and a half hours was not my best idea to date. It was friggin' cold and dark. My only saving grace was the cloudless, starry sky that shined down on me. Even though it looked somewhat criminal in nature, me strolling through town in the wee morning hours, it did provide me the solitude to lay out a plan of action in my head if I chose to invade Florida and mount a rescue operation of sorts.

Rescue operation? You're dreaming, D. How long has it been since you played soldier? How many years have passed since you had at your beck and call, the power of the Tactical Air Command and the Special Ops team you fondly referred to as family? Where are those guys now? How many made lifers through their service to our country? Who can I still count on to mount an operation to assist me in my quest? You are so getting ahead of yourself. First things first. Talk to Candi, hear her side and then decide. How can you rescue someone who may not want to be rescued? You are such a ... a ... PUTZ!

Tampa Bay

Strolling through my neighborhood in the early morning hours to clear my head, waifs of sulphur emitting from the neighbor's lawn sprinklers permeated the heavy and humid air. Even growing up here, my stomach still churns, each time I breathe in that horrendous odor. *Come to think of it, I never experienced this problem in Chattanooga. I liked living in Tennessee. Regardless of what happens, maybe I should go back. Life was simpler there and drama free. I've taken a month's leave of absence from work. So I've got some time to think about it. First things first, beginning tomorrow, turn in the ledgers to the Family, unlock the encryption codes to prove their authenticity and collect the reward, before splitting it with Joseph. Will that satisfy him? Will he continue to drag me back into his life? Too many questions, compounded by very few answers. Oh well …* I sighed before being rattled back into reality as my phone vibrated, then chirped twice, signaling incoming text messages from Marcy, no less.

Text 1:

> We're good to go after next Thursday, Candice. I've got work covered. Booked a flight on Southwest, Thursday late. See you Friday.

Text 2:

> Any word from D?

I replied to both:

> That's great. Wish you would allow me to send the plane. Will be great to spend time with you girl. We're going to have fun. LOL. Sadly, there's been nothing from D. Thanks for asking.

The rest of the morning Candi filled with catching up on the news. The instant diamond gifted millionaires continued to make headlines across CNN, MSN and FOX. So much for being discreet. Most of D's recipients were quiet for the most part. It was only a select few that couldn't keep their mouths shut, relishing in their 30 seconds of fame. The afternoon was a different story.

Gio hobbled into the kitchen with Mile in tow, plopping down on the bar stool next to Candi. "We go shopping, Candice, for party."

"Not now, Gio. It can wait," she countered, knowing she had nothing left in her arsenal of excuses to delay this spree.

"We go now!"

Candi relented. Snagging her Mom's keys to her X-5, she helped Gio into the front seat as Mile climbed in the back. "I remember there's a leather place up in New Port Richey, but I don't remember the name."

"We go, we find. Let's ride," directed Gio, pointing his forefinger forward across the dash.

Candi laughed, "That's it, Gio. The store, it's called Let's Ride." His puzzled look was priceless. She didn't attempt to explain, pulling through the security gates and driving northwest towards Port Richey. Conversing with Mile in Italian while en route to the leather shop, she learned she was ready to go home with or without Giovanni.

Gio, sensing her unhappiness, more in her tone than her words, wormed his way into their conversation before she could find out why. "She not want to see you hurt. Mile miss D and you, how you say ... together?"

Speaking only Italian now, "I can't fix us by myself, he has to want to as well. I'm sorry you were dragged in the middle of this. It's not your place to make it better. This is all on me. I lied to him, not once, not twice, but three times. And he knows it. Why should he care what happens to me?"

"He good man," countered Gio. "His eyes speak so."

Oh ... his eyes, his brown bedroom eyes. "I remember the first time D kissed me by the waterfalls. He was gentle, yet powerful, selfless, but confident. He knew how far he was willing to go with me ... I am sorry, you don't need to hear all this." After her confessional, Candi felt Mile's hand patting her right shoulder.

"D, good for you," Mile added, before lifting her hand off Candi's shoulder, hesitating just a second, before slapping Gio squarely on the cheek. "You be good."

A litany of Italian curse words filled the SUV as Gio rubbed his face, smarting from the sting of her open palm. "Mile ... she say I should be good for her like D for you," he laughed as Candi pulled into the parking lot of Let's Ride.

Timing is everything, whew! "Come on guys, let's go make me into a Pretty Woman, slash biker babe or bitch, for that matter," she mumbled the last words softly under her breath. *A well-deserved moniker Joseph assigned to me at the end of our tumultuous and troubled marriage, forever and a day, ago.*

An hour later and twelve hundred dollars lighter, Candi had chaps, boots, a jacket, a belt and a red thong. Her plan was to wear her red silk Donna Karan Caftan Gown to the Gala before changing into leathers for the party that followed. She wasn't sure about the red thong. *That was for D's eyes only, on his bike and with my toy, if and when, the stars aligned and we were together again. Mile, not to be denied, found a pair of Italian red leather pants, size eight and a matching vest while Gio came away with a patch for his jacket. Oh, and a sizable decrease in the thickness of his wallet. Treat her good, Gio, I thought, or she will take you for all you're dumb enough to give her before she kicks your rear out the door.*

Just for kicks and giggles, the three of them had dinner out at Byrne's on the way home. Candi was hoping to meet up with Lisa again to see if she remembered her. Sadly, she wasn't on the schedule. *Probably off somewhere laying her head in the lap of the guy with the red Ferrari. What do I care? I don't, but then again, I do. What idiot in their right mind, sincerely trying to get back together would bring me to his local haunt and introduce me to his fave bimbo? I hate to admit it, but we're both playing the same type of game as Gio and Mile. Only our stakes were much, much higher.*

Finally, home, her cup overflowing with being social, she said her good-nights to everyone, turned on Sinatra, snuggled up to a pillow and fell asleep. It was not the sound of the alarm that roused her from sleep, but Gio's strong calloused hand jostling her shoulder.

"You get up. Candice, now! D, he call in dark. He call back, say talk to you." Pointing to the time on the phone, 7:30, "D call 8:00."

Chapter 38

Mistatim, SK
Tampa Bay, FL

It was 7:55 Eastern time and I found myself sitting alone in the not so fragrant Green Mule hoping to dredge up the right words to begin the conversation with Candi at eight o'clock sharp.

Do I act mad? I'm not. Do I act hurt? I was. Now, however, I'm just … totally numb to it all. We had great times together, many of them firsts, and told many lies that are going to be hard to overcome unless we both somehow manage to forgive, forget and move the hell on. What choice did I have? What choice did we have? I pressed send.

On the fourth ring, Gio answered. "Ciao, D. I wake Candice. You talk, I leave. Ciao."

"Ciao, Giovanni. Thank you." I hesitated, hoping that Candi would speak first. That didn't happen. The silence was deafening. It surely was not golden. Clearing the emerging lump from my throat, I began, "Candi, you wanted me to call, so here I am."

I've waited days for this moment and now that it's here I'm speechless. Say something, anything. "D, are you still on your bike? How are you? Are you in Canada or back in the U.S.? How is the weather where you are?" *Question after stupid question rolled off my tongue like olive oil off a hot Teflon skillet, to the point that I'd somehow managed to forget the first few questions I'd asked to begin this long, anticipated conversation. Girl, you are hopeless!*

"Candi, surely you didn't go to all this trouble to find me just to ask me about the weather? What's going on in that twisted mind of yours?"

He's right ... speak from your head, your heart ... "I miss you. I've missed you since the moment I stepped onto the plane. Just listen. Let me finish, I know you think I screwed you and by all accounts I did. D, I didn't have a choice. Joseph and the boys were not coming back without you, one way or the other. That is, until I convinced them otherwise. I was in it for the money, nothing more. Our pseudo relationship was a means to an end. I thought he believed me then. Now, I'm not so sure. God knows, I've tried to protect you and Victoria. Believe me ... or not. I also know I've hurt you. I'm ... I am so sorry. Say something, D. ... Please."

"Candi, I gave you the ledgers to Fed Ex to your Mom. You didn't send them. This could have all been averted had you done that one simple task. You played me. After all the confessions and tears, you played me. The question of the day, the week, the year, is why?"

"I didn't play you, damn it! Joseph was determined to take you out. He was jealous of the way I looked at you, dressed for you, cared for you. He knew something unexpected had happened between us on our ride. There could never be an us. I mean, unless you were out of the picture. I couldn't tell you. You wouldn't have let me go. Had I not done what he wanted, both you and Vic would be history."

"I've managed to take care of myself so far and you too, for that matter. So, this was all for me, for Vic? I'm humbled." *Bite your tongue. Don't go there, D. Not yet. Hear her out.*

"Please don't be catty. If I could see you, hold you, kiss you, you'd know ... I'm speaking from my heart."

"Is that what it takes Candi, holding me, kissing me, blowing me, screwing me, for me to know beyond a shadow of a doubt you're telling the truth?" *You had to go there. Didn't you, dumb ass?*

Where'd that come from? "D, I never said anything about sex. Where did that come from? Why are you being hateful and mean when I'm trying my best to apologize?"

"Never mind, Candi. You're right; you didn't mention anything about sex. I took unnecessary liberties, especially after seeing you banging Joseph's brains out on the internet. I can only surmise you were telling him the truth also, in little increments, one bump and grind at a time."

What did he see? There is absolutely no tape of me having sex with Joseph ... or is there? OMG! "D, I need to know. What did you see and when?"

"A few days ago, Jim at WITSEC received an anonymous email with a video attachment that was forwarded to me, showing you banging someone, I'm only assuming now mind you, Joseph's brains out."

"Listen to me please. This is important. What was on the video? What did the room look like? What was I wearing? What exactly was I doing?"

You've done it now. Foot in mouth has moved to head up ass. "I can't answer any of those questions, Candi. Vic watched it and shared the highlights, if you will. The man's face was obscured, but his generous package wasn't. She said you looked like you were really getting into it, on it ... whatever the hell you were doing."

That bastard, Joseph had the camera rolling the whole time. "I can explain ... On second thought, there's nothing to explain, it is what it is. Yes, I had sex with him. Yes, it was good. Let's just say I did it for old time's sake. Are you happy now? Wait! Wait! Is Vic still with you?"

"Yep… Candi, I wasn't happy then, I'm not happy now. And it has little to do with you and Joseph. That's your business. After all, you have a much longer history with him than with me. More than anything, I want to believe you. I'm trying, but as of late, you've made it extremely difficult. I want things back the way they were. Is that even possible? You screw me and tell me what I want to hear. You screw Joseph and tell him what he wants to hear. I have one question for you, do you even know what the truth is anymore?"

I deserved that. What am I supposed to say? "D, I did what I had to do. I didn't knowingly have sex in front of a camera to purposely hurt you. I'm better than that. You know I'm better than that. No matter what happens between us, promise me you won't watch the tape without me. Please have Vic, along with your friend Jim at WITSEC erase it, destroy it, get rid of it. It could ruin me, my career ... us. I'm sorry ... so sorry." Candi pressed end, threw the phone on the bed and buried herself in a pillow and cried.

She hung up on me, crying. You are an even bigger putz! You had to bring it up? She started it; I finished it. No, you started it and you finished it. She was caught unaware. D, you are one hypocritical SOB. Now what? Call her back ... and say what, 'I've been sleeping with Vic, so we're even?' Doubt if that would go over well ... Say something comforting, meaningful, worthwhile. But what? She was crying because of my cruel, venom spewing mouth. I needed to make her stop crying. I pressed send.

Candi, between sniffles, answered, "Yes."

"Don't hang up again. I'm no saint either. I'm far from perfect and way out of your league. Your family wants nothing to do with me. I'm too old for you. I'm out of shape. I can go on and on. You could tell me to stop, you know?"

She snorted, "Stop!"

"Thank you," I stammered, breathing a sigh of relief. "I was beginning to get a complex, talking myself right out of us. There are a thousand and one reasons why we shouldn't be together, but there's one very important reason why we should… we complement one another to the ten-thousandth degree. Oh, there's actually two — I make you laugh."

Candi stopped crying long enough to laugh at my silliness. *That's what I like so much in him, he does make me laugh even when I absolutely want to cry.*

"It's never been about the money, I know that. I've always known that. You wanted to prove your moxie to the Family. Congratulations girl, mission accomplished. Me, I wanted to bring out the best in you. You are smart, attractive, self-assured and selfless. Don't you go swelling with pride on me just yet. That last trait has only manifested itself since we've been together. I consider you a masterpiece in the making, a work of art in progress. Now, I'm only supposing here, what you saw in me was someone who's been kicked to hell and back and still manages to come up swinging with a smile on his face. Someone who makes lemonade out of lemons and convinces you beyond your good judgment it's good even when you know the lemons I used were rotten. Yep, I've been trying to tell you there's a fair amount of good in everything and everyone. More times than not, however, you find yourself digging a little deeper in the cow poop to find it."

Surprisingly, hearing his voice, though far away, I feel shades better. "D, where are you?"

"I'm in Canada. Leaving this morning, heading south. Why?"

"I don't know for sure, but there may be someone looking for you. I'll do what I can to find out more. If it's all on my end, I'll deal with it from here. If it's beyond my reach, watch your back. Call me every day until you get home. Promise? Again, I'm sorry. No, it was not for the money. No, it was not to hurt you. I could go on and on. But I won't. It's enough for now. I'll leave it at that. Give Major a hug for me when you get home. Bye, baby."

I feel like I've aged ten years this morning. I'm emotionally raw. I'm mad. Joseph, that son of a bitch, 'Prove to me you're sincere in getting back together. Make love to me, show me.' I'm gonna be sick … and I was … repeatedly, that is until I got over throwing up and came up with a plan while my head rested on the porcelain throne. To be more precise, it was a slick, ass wipe, lie every time your mouth is open, lawyer speak rebuttal. Paybacks are a bitch, especially when they're launched from a powerful one and then you die!

Chapter 39

ell, big boy, what kind of mess have you gotten yourself into? That's the question of the day. What happened? She cried … you caved. Sums it up. Call everyday. Really? Someone is looking for me — whoopee, take a number and get in line. I emerged from the truck to find Greg, smoking his pipe on the basement patio, looking somewhat out of sorts.

"Jon David, I'm going to meet a diamond broker tomorrow. You stayin' another day?" asked Greg. "You want to take my hunters out for me?"

"I'd like to, but I can't. I need to get Vic back to Sioux City and me back to fight the monsters waiting for me at home. I promise, I'll come back soon enough and hang out. Just me and you. OK?

"Works. Victoria calls you, D. What … should I call you … now that you're not … you?"

"Call me anything you want," I chuckled at his reasoning, then sobered quickly to the absurdity of it all. "At this point in my life it doesn't matter. I have no permanent identity to speak of. Recent circumstances have seen to that. I'm doing what I can one day at a time to survive amid the chaos."

"You're a survivor. You'll come out on the top of all this, yet. Especially, if you keep changing lives, like Missy's, for the better. I almost forgot why I came out here looking for you. Debra said breakfast is ready whenever you and your lady friend are."

"Her names Victoria, Greg, Victoria. Why can't you remember it?"

Sheepishly Greg stared at the ground, "Every time I think of her, all that comes to mind is smoking hot. Do you think it has something to do with her red hair or her—?"

I laughed, "all the above, I'm sure. Damn you need a vacation with Debra in a bad way. Your bride is just as beautiful and smoking hot as she is. Go away, spoil her, pamper her, wine her, dine her and make love to her. Stop lusting over Vic."

"I'm not ... uh ... lusting. I'm appreciating."

"Whatever," I relented, since trying to argue with his little brain was going nowhere. "I'll go rouse smoking hot and we'll be up shortly."

* * *

Somewhere buried beneath the covers was my friend, my confidant, my attorney. "Vic, it's time to get up. Debra has breakfast ready and we have a long ride in front of us. Today is Iron Butt II, 459 miles to Winnipeg."

Rousing sleepily from her current dream, "what time is it, D?"

"It's a little before seven, girlfriend," I replied, rubbing her shoulders with my left hand and running my fingers through her hair with my right.

"Don't stop, D. I could lay here all morning with you caressing me."

"I'm sure you could. But like you said, the quicker I get you home the better."

"Don't remind me. I only said that so you wouldn't have to keep fending me off."

"I know. Thank you," I added, "it goes both ways, especially since you're so smoking hot!" I was in the moment again before I caught myself, continuing to stroke her hair. It wasn't fair to continue to build on something we'd both agreed to suppress for now. I can't believe it. I'm the one saying, "for now." Who would have thought it a week ago? Surely not me.

Vic giggled. "Smoking hot. You think so? Where did that come from?"

"Greg, he thinks you're smoking hot. Me, I know it," I answered, rising from the bed before Vic had a chance to reply. "I'll have your coffee poured. See you upstairs."

Vic and I dined alone. With a new group of hunters on the way, Greg and Debra were busy preparing for their arrival. "Vic, I talked to Gio this morning." No response. "And Candi."

No shock there. It's about time he reached out. "Really? How did that go?"

"It was emotional. I made her cry. From what I gathered the video was as much a surprise to her as it was to us."

"You told her?" *Of course he did. What happened to subtle?*

"Not at first, but later on in our conversation. She asked me specifics which only you could answer, unfortunately. Like what did the room look like, what was she wearing, etc?"

"So… Candi knows I'm with you? I bet that rolled her."

"Truthfully, if it did, it didn't register. She was very apologetic from the get go and was dumbstruck that she had been filmed, live and in color. Pleaded with me to have you erase it, as well as Jim. It could wreak havoc on her professional career if it got out."

"D, it's on your email. Remember? You'll have to do that. You think blackmail?"

"Possibly or some type of coercion. Whatever brought it about devastated her."

"It would me, too," said Vic. "I could see her slimy Ex using it as leverage to make sure he got what he wanted. Poor Candi. So what's next, D?"

"We go home. Two to three days hard riding. I hope you can handle it. I hope I can handle it. When we reach Winnipeg nine or ten hours from now, we may need to sleep in tomorrow."

"Whatever you decide, I'm good." But she wasn't. *I don't want our trip to end, not like this, anyway. Why can't we be friends and still be intimate … at least occasionally? I told him I wouldn't press it and I won't. However, if the opportunity presents itself again, like this morning, I'm going to encourage it. I will not take no for an answer, Candi be damned!*

"Vic, you mind clearing the dishes from the table while I pack the bike? We'd best get on the road."

"I've got this, D. I'll be down in a few."

After strapping on our gear, I found Greg scurrying around in the shop. "Let me know if you have any problems selling the diamonds tomorrow. I'll try to find you another buyer abroad, if I can."

"I got this, D. You've done your part. Now it's up to me to do mine. Candice Parker, right?"

"Yes, sir. Compliments of Candice Parker and her family. That takes you and me out of the loop ... I hope."

Vic found the boys playing with their toys. Walking up to Greg, she kissed him squarely on the lips. "Smoking hot? I like," she purred in his ear. "Thank you for the wonderful compliment."

Greg blushed crimson, "Uh ... you're welcome. Take care of him."

"I'm trying, but it's not easy."

"You've made his day, Vic. Let's get out of here before Greg gets any ideas."

"Oh, I've got lots of ideas already," Greg countered, as Debra joined us in the shop.

"Debra, thanks for everything. You and Greg have made Vic feel welcome."

Of course they did. "It was a pleasure meeting some of D's friends. I hope we'll see each other again," Vic said, giving Greg a wink that seemed to take him over the top.

Taking Vic's hand, I led her away. "What was that about, girlfriend? You raised his blood pressure twenty points."

"I like compliments, D. Haven't heard any from you in a day or two. Besides, looking at that bulge in his pants, that's not all I raised." She grinned. *D got my hint loud and clear. Of that, I'm certain.*

Chapter 40

Flustered and speechless, I entered Winnipeg into the GPS, routing us east along Canada Hwy. 3, before turning south across the vast plains on the Saskota Flyway to Yorkton. I only got as far as 2nd Avenue, about three hundred feet to be exact, before I felt a tap on my shoulder. "Yes?"

All this excitement amongst the men, I damn near forgot. "Turn left, D. Take me to the Mistatim Hotel."

"It's far too early for alcohol, girlfriend. Care to tell me why?"

"I have a proposition for Will. … One that I hope he won't refuse."

"Seriously, Vic, I didn't realize how much he turned you on." The spontaneous sideways slap on my helmet said otherwise.

"Smart ass, a business proposition." *Men and sex…sex and men. Go figure.* "Stay here. This won't take long." Vic climbed off the bike and ran into the bar/hotel, finding Will snoozing behind the counter. "Wake up, Will, it's Victoria."

"Victoria … good to see you again. I was resting my eyes," said Will, focusing his sleepy gaze on her as she stood before him clad in black leather.

"I'd like to invest in your establishment. You need to attract more women, which in turn attracts more men. If you reduce your room rates by five and turn them into two full baths each, one for each of the remaining rooms that will help you with your occupancy. Plus, add flat screen TVs with pay-per-view options, new pillow-top mattresses, sturdy, non-squeaking beds and a couple of pieces of decent furniture."

"That's well and good ma'am, but it takes money to do that. Money that I don't have."

"Will, that's where I come in. I'm prepared to invest up to $400,000 US to make this dream a reality. In return, I get, say forty percent ownership." I let him digest that for a moment before I continued. "Can you live with that?"

"Let me get this straight, you're gonna put up $400,000 to help me attract more women?" asked Will, sporting a 'who the hell do you think you are' demeanor.

Cleavage stare, figures! "Stop looking at my boobs," Vic pleaded. "Read my lips. More women, means more men, more alcohol sales, more rocking and rolling in your rooms, more everything. Got it?"

Scratching his chin as he pondered the thought of a female partner, Will stood up and extended his hand. "I got it. Can we shake on it?"

"We can," she replied, extending her right hand, handing him her card, Victoria R. Lawson, Attorney at Law. "Even better, I'll draw up the documents when I get home. Meanwhile, you need to have a contractor you trust write us a proposal for ten tiled baths with tub and shower combinations. Then send me a list of the rest of the items you'll need. I'll shop for those in the states, first. I've got to run. Call me when you have it."

"Well, that was a quickie, Vic. Was it as good for Will as it was for you?"

"That's yet to be determined. You're now looking at the new minority owner of this fine establishment."

I scowled.

"Seriously, after all your preaching about paying it forward, don't give me that look. I had an epiphany the last time we were here. Private baths, new beds and new furniture, equate to more women, more men, more partying, more sales. I volunteered to help him do it with my, I mean your ... I mean our money."

"Congratulations. You can be unselfish when you wanna be."

"I'm not that unselfish, D. I asked for forty percent."

"In that case, you'd make a great Madame if you decide to eventually turn this into a whorehouse," I chided. "Can we ride now?"

"We can," she beamed, thoroughly proud of herself, even if she did ask for part ownership. *Giving comes hard for me. I'm a lawyer first, but I could be a Madame second, a damn good one, I betcha!*

With our last detour behind us, we were on the road rolling down Highway 3 to intersect the Saskota Flyway that would take us to Winnipeg. Reaching Yorkton, I announced, while pulling into a Canadian Shell for fuel, "Last pit stop for quite a while. How are you holding up, girlfriend?"

"My butt is tingling, along with my hoo-ha," she laughed. "Otherwise, I'm good."

"You're a tingling troubadour. A rare find up here, your lady parts notwithstanding. Let's hope that's all you have to complain about two more stops from now." Turning left onto Yellowhead Highway, driving southeast, we crossed into Manitoba just after eleven. There was not much to see for the next five hours, but an endless supply of rolling hills, sporadic farmhouses and miles and miles of black asphalt. On the outskirts of Winnipeg, I squeezed Vic's knee. "Your hoo-ha still tingling, girlfriend?"

"I forgot what eight hours on a bike feels like. My face is wind-burned, and my hoo-ha and ass are numbing. Plus, my legs are frozen stiff in their current position. Other than that, I'm good."

"That answers my next question. We need to get you a room with a big soaking tub."

She squeezed me as tight as her thighs would allow, "That would be a Godsend."

The iPhone found us a boutique hotel called Maria's where I booked the red bricked road suite, featuring a two-person tub with adjoining wet bar. Twenty minutes later we were driving into the parking lot as the rain began to fall. "I couldn't have timed it better if I'd tried. Go check us in please, Vic. Leave a key at the desk. I'll be along in a while."

"Gladly, D. My back thanks you. My ass thanks you and my hoo-ha adores you."

"Hey, girlfriend, I didn't tell you. They have a spa. Bet you're ready for pampering, round two. It's probably too late to book a massage tonight. See if you can schedule one for first thing in the morning."

"You don't mind?"

"I do not. One day, give or take, won't make much difference. Will it?"

For a brief moment, Vic processed my request ... *I had clean clothes, what few there were, compliments of Debra, plus another night with D ... and a tub.* "Ab-so-lutely... no difference!"

Chapter 41

After I'd gathered our bags and carried them into the breezeway, I sat down on a weathered wooden bench and made my first call to Gio who answered on the second ring.

"Ciao, Giovanni. It's D, can you talk now?"

"D, ciao. ... Yes, can talk. We good. Candi not so good. What you say? You hurt her?"

"No, sir, I don't think so. It wasn't me. Joseph, most likely."

"Joseph, no like. She sad, D. You come, she better."

"No promises, Gio. I will try."

"You come, big party next Saturday. Mile, me bad bikers, Candice, Pretty Woman in red, then biker babe."

"Bikers, a party, Candi in red and leathers? A costume party in Tampa?"

"Yes, Child's Hospital ... mm mm ... I sure."

"A benefit for a Children's Hospital. How bizarre? Let me think about it. I'll see if I can make it work. I'll call you back in a couple of days and let you know. Ciao."

My second call was to Candi. She answered on the umpteenth ring as I was pressing end.

"D, I'm here. I didn't want you to hear me this way."

"Candi, I'm letting you know I've made it to Winnipeg. You're crying? Has something happened? Are you still upset from this morning?"

"What do you think? Of course, I'm upset. It comes and goes. Joseph used me to get his point across. Me ... me of all people."

"Yeah, well you're probably right. There was a message that went with the video that I forgot to mention ... something like 'her actions speak louder than your words.' Sounds like a man scorned, because a woman screwed, huh? Candi, you're going to have to deal with it. It's a cluster with a capitol F, I got it. Best you put on your big girl panties and face it head on. You recovered the ledgers. Surely, you can recover some clandestine video and destroy it. Speaking of the ledgers, you collect?"

"I turned them in today and unlocked them to prove their authenticity. The money is being wired to an offshore account in my name. I promised Joseph half to make him leave Canada without you."

"There's your leverage, use it. Coupled with that Woo-Hoo of yours, you can move mountains. I'm sorry ... Did you find out who's looking for me?"

"Not yet. Again, that's a Joseph issue. D, that was a terrible thing to say. You said Vic was with you?"

"I did. She is. Didn't want me to ride back alone. Surprisingly, you're both about the same size. She's wearing your leathers, your boots, your helmet."

"That's convenient ... Uh ... You sleeping with her?"

"What kind of question is that? She's a friend. She's my ... my lawyer."

"You are sleeping with her! I knew it! How long did that take?"

"Candi, don't go there. You left me standing on the tarmac with my heart in my throat, remember? You screwed me, long before I did anything with her. If you'd been honest from the get go, we could have worked our way through this, together. I'm hurting, too. Nothing happened between Vic and I ... until the email arrived showing you bouncing off the bed on his balls."

"I told you, I did what I had to do. You wouldn't understand. You had to be there. It happened. OK?"

"Same here."

"I need to go."

"Me, too," I pressed end.

Chapter 42

Tampa Bay

Damn him, damn him, damn him! There's going to be hell to pay today. Joseph and his clandestine video is the reason D is screwing Vic and not me, not yet anyway. It's one of the reasons, anyway ... No, it's the most important reason, damn him! Conveniently, the money — the all-important money — rewarding me ... bite your tongue girl ... us ... for the year-long effort transfers today. I got it. I AM SO PISSED! ... Let the games begin!

Over the next two hours Candi planned a memorable evening that was going to be even better than she originally imagined. Her first call was to the Grand Hyatt where she booked two adjoining suites for the evening. Her second call was to two actors who, depending on what was up their nose at the time, could go either way. Her third call was to a friend from high school, Kyle, who owned a one-of-a-kind specialty store. Her fourth call was to Joseph, to make a date for this evening to celebrate their windfall, which had arrived in her Cayman Islands account moments earlier, according to her email.

"Joseph, it's Candice. The money's in the bank!" she shouted into his ear. "Let's celebrate tonight. Bring your account numbers along and I'll make the transfers giving you what you so rightly deserve. Say seven-ish? I look forward to it. Oh, don't bother picking me up. I'll meet you at the Hyatt ... in the bar."

That concluded steps one through four. Now, onto five, I must go shopping. I dressed in sweats and a tee, pulled on a hooded Tampa Bucs over the t-shirt, donned a matching baseball cap and took off to a store I'd only seen, but never visited before. Ah, today was a day bursting with firsts. I am empowered, I am frustrated, I am scorned ... hear me roar and roar and roar. Joseph, on the other hand, will feel my wrath and the gnashing of my teeth.

Two hours later and two productive stops behind me, Candi slipped into my skimpiest black dress, revealing her finest attributes, displayed prominently, for Joseph to drool over. Taking a page out of D's book of Maxim's, the thought of having sex, any sex, clouds a man's judgment in any language. Arriving at the hotel a little shy of five o'clock, she checked in both rooms and found her two man hungry friends, stage named Max and Mike, sitting in the bar where they exchanged hugs, keys, various sundries and cash, lots of cash. Three shots of Patron Tequila each to take the edge off and strengthen her resolve, like she needed any help, the three of them adjourned to the second suite to prepare for an evening, she hoped Joseph would soon never forget. By 6:30, everything was in place. Candi left her two beefy studs sipping on champagne and snorting blow while she strolled casually to the bar to await Joseph's arrival.

Promptly at seven, Joseph sauntered up to her table, dressed in a navy-blue Armani suit, his eyes flushed with desire, his tongue panting profusely, feasting on this fine specimen of a woman who once loved him — a woman radiating an unrequited fire in her eyes ... but for a much more sinister reason.

Joseph struggling to translate his Viagra induced thoughts into words. "My, you look stunning tonight, Candice. Spectacular might be a better word. Before me is the girl I remember, the girl I fell in love with many years ago."

"Good to see you, Joseph. Thank you for the glows. You sir, are quite dapper tonight as usual. I've brought my iPad, business before pleasure you know," she quipped, flicking her tongue across her glistening lips, compliments of Buxom's Trixie. "I've ordered you a Black Crown, neat. That is what you drink, isn't it?"

Settling into the booth beside her, Joseph breathed in her perfume before whispering in her ear, "It is, thanks for remembering."

The waiter delivered two shots of Patron with a water chaser, along with a dish of quartered limes and his Black Crown, four fingers deep in a tea glass.

Gazing at the surprisingly large amount of alcohol in the tumbler, Joseph raised the Crown to his lips, before pausing to speak, "our last night together, when I was drinking these didn't turn out as well as I had hoped. I promise tonight, I'll pace myself."

Her stomach rolled. "That's so unlike you, Joseph." Sliding her hand into his lap, running her fingers across his slowly rising package, "Tonight, I'm prepared to get wasted with you, before delving into the kinky side, you're so aptly fond of ... now."

"Really, Candice?" Joseph replied.

"Really, Joseph. Drink up… the night is young. Before we get too under the influence ... and under the covers, do you have the account numbers for me to transfer the funds?"

Reaching into his inside jacket pocket, Joseph retrieved a folded piece of expensive linen paper and tossed it to me. "Here you go, Candice. There's two separate accounts there. Please divide the monies between them."

"I can do that," she replied, creating two distinct wire transfers to two anonymous offshore accounts. "There you go sir, 2.5 million in each. I expect you'll receive email conformations to that effect, shortly." In less than two minutes, Joseph's phone vibrated confirming that to be the case. "Do you feel richer now, Mr. Moneybags?"

He nodded, then smiled ear to ear. Raising his half empty glass into the air, Joseph offered a toast, "To us!"

"To tonight," she replied. "May this evening make you a lifetime of memories. Shall we order dinner?"

"I'd settle on an ap-pee-tizer and another one of these," slurred Joseph, holding up his now empty glass.

"My pleasure, anything to make you happy." She ordered bacon potato skins and stuffed jalapeños, plus another four-fingered drink for Joseph. After thirty minutes, eight shots of Crown and her fingers wrapped around his pleasure pistol, Candi had him exactly as she envisioned, silly putty in her hands. "Joseph," she cooed, "I reserved a suite for us tonight." Holding up her iPhone in record mode, she asked, "would you like to go upstairs to the room with me and allow me to do wild and crazy things with you, to get kinky with you in every way possible?"

"Yes, yes, oh yes," he oozed.

"Say it, I, Joseph, am of sound mind and freely offering myself willingly to Candice Parker to use as she desires." Joseph, repeated it clearly and precisely two more times, surprising even me, being eight shots into the wind by my calculation. "We're done here. ... Aren't we, Joseph?" she asked, getting a silent nod of approval before signing the check and escorting the man with the raging hard-on to her room. Sliding in the key card, she opened the door to the aroma of multi-scented candles permeating the air. Ushering Joseph to the bed, she undressed him, paying careful attention not to wrinkle his suit. *Why the hell that concerned me, I do not know. Guess it's the woman in me, appreciating the finer things in life… Armani being one of them.*

I digress. My first stop today was an adult toy store — Todd's Toys. It was filled floor to ceiling with every imaginable sex fantasy related toy under the sun. I described my fantasy for Joseph to the store manager, Paul, and he supplied me with number of devices to make the evening a success. First came the four aluminum posts with ring eyelets to affix to the bed frame. Second were two pairs of hardened steel muff cuffs, followed by an assortment of masks and hoods, a pair of nipple clips and a braided leather whip for good measure.

"Joseph," she breathed, "lie back on the bed and extend your arms," whereby she cuffed his wrists to the rails. "Good boy, now spread your legs," allowing her to cuff his ankles next. "There, you're secure and helpless ... little boy." His eyes were wide like saucers, lustfully devouring me in his mind as she slipped off her dress. Easing herself on top of him, she kissed and nibbled her way to his lips before placing a blindfold over his eyes. She could tell he was thoroughly enjoying her display of dominance; that is until she replaced her warm and wet tongue with a large black leather deep-throat gag, that she snapped securely behind his head. *Show time!*

Donning a mask that would completely obscure her face and hair, Candi opened the door to the adjoining room allowing two well-endowed, masked intruders to enter and take her place on the bed. Mystery man number one climbed onto his chest, pressing his knees into Joseph's armpits, resting his banana stuffed hammock, a breath away from Joseph's shrouded face. Now for part two. Raising the foot board, aluminum posts to their highest position, she lifted Joseph's legs into the air, offering mystery man number two unbridled access to what she assumed was virgin territory.

Candi fantasized watching these two man-beasts in rhythm, pummel and pound Joseph into submission making him their bitch for the evening. Just that thought alone made her want to join in and make it happen, almost. But, that was not her purpose here. Her purpose was to repay an eye for an eye.

Holding a small digital camcorder in her hand, Candi removed Joseph's mask and began filming close ups of him with these two now naked men poised at the ready to feed him orally and pound him anally. Thrashing, twisting, turning, first to the left, then to the right, Joseph fought the shackles to no avail. Tears of fear welled in his eyes, the lifeblood drained from his face, anticipating his pending fate. His distant gaze begged the question, how could she violate and humiliate him in this way? It was easy.

Candi whispered softly in his ear, "Paybacks are a bitch, aren't they, sweetheart? Who knows, someday you, too, may be a movie star of my making."

Patting each of her well-endowed actors on the shoulder, Candi announced, "We're done here ... or not." These guys with their raging hard-ons seemed oblivious to her current request. She screamed, but not too loud, "We're done here! Take it to the next room, gentlemen. Joseph has had enough."

Leaving Joseph motionless on the bed, Mike and Max eventually obliged walking through the adjoining door, and slammed it shut, never saying good-bye. Candi had a few words left in her, as well as a leather whip in her hand. "Joseph, baby, was it as good for you as it was for me?" she asked, striking him on his precious package that she used to lovingly adore. He winced. "I know you can't talk with the gag in your mouth. I kind of like it that way. You can't lie to me ... if you can't open your mouth. Huh, baby?

"You got me ... good. How dare you hurt me, again? You used me ... to make a point you had no right to make. We're done, it's over. We're through." The whip slapped skin again, and again, and again. Realizing she was enjoying his pain a little too much, Candi tossed the whip on the floor. "I'm prepared to call us even. The question is, are you? Let it go, Joseph. Let us go. Let D go. What's happened here will never leave this room, or will it? It's your call. Let me know what you decide." She tossed the muff cuff keys on the bed between his ever reddening, welted legs.

Walking around the room, Candi collected the four miniature wireless cameras she installed earlier to film every angle of this truly memorable occasion. Coupled with her handheld Canon, a video editor should be able to compile, at the least, a five-minute incriminating flick. Lastly, she lowered the foot posts to bed level and tossed a towel across his shrunken junk. "Lay here for a while and experience firsthand the wrath of a woman scorned. A woman with Family ties. Oh, but you know that already. How silly of me. When I get around to it, I'll call the front desk to send a maintenance man to your room. Hopefully, he'll release you. Worst case he'll take advantage of you and leave you for the maid to clean up in the morning. Later, sweet cheeks," she chuckled, before exiting with my bag of toys.

Aww, I didn't get to use the nipple clips. Like I said, paybacks are a bitch ... even worse when the bitch is pissed!

Chapter 43

ell, that went well, D. Finesse is not your middle name. Your mouth, Victoria's other orifice notwithstanding, is a WMD, as well. Why not let it go, asshole? I could use a shot, a beer or both. Loading my two bags on a luggage cart, I swung by the front desk, snagged the room key from a Linda and wheeled the cart into the bar. "Bartender, if you please, two six packs of Molson's, six limes and a bottle of Milagro Silver Tequila if you have it. Oh, and a couple of shot glasses."

"Certainly, sir. Are you having a party in your room?"

"I'll let you know, Michael, is it?" I replied, doing my best to read his name tag from across the bar. "Can I call you after I've downed at least six of each if I happen to need more?"

"Yes, sir. I'm here until one."

"Thank you, Michael. Kindly quarter me a lime and open a Molson so I'll have something to keep me company on the way to my room." Following the cart that I aptly pushed with one hand, I used the other to drink Tequila from the bottle, suck on a lime and chase it down with a beer. I am one talented S.O.B. One beer, two bottle shots and half a lime later, I arrived.

Victoria was, from all indications, naked from the waist up, lounging in the Jacuzzi with the pulsating jets at full blast. "Mind if I join you, girlfriend?"

"Mind if I join you might be the better question, D. I wondered what happened to you. I can see you stopped by the bar. How many do I need to catch up?" *This scene looks all too familiar.* "Per chance, have you been talking to Candi?" *Of course, he has. Why else would he have started his party without me?*

"Two shots, the other half of my lime and one beer. And yes, I talked to Candi."

"Did my name come up?"

"Right again, Vic. You're two for two."

"I bet she pressed you on our ... uh ... sleeping arrangements."

"Yep, you are on a ... roll. Drink up. I think I'd best take my clothes off this time before jumping in." Taking a moment to look at our surroundings, the room featured a red brick floor to the tub and a short pile, beige carpet surrounding the bed. The walls were half brick, highlighted by two arches separating the bedroom from the tub and the living, dining area. Soft white, low voltage lights were strung on each side of the archways, illuminating a barrel ceiling in the middle. "I can only assume this room has a theme of sorts? Red brick road, instead of the yellow one. I get it."

"They all do, D. It's unusual, that's for sure. How did you happen upon this hotel?"

"I looked up romantic hotels with garden tubs. Voila!"

Romantic hotel, for me? You've still got it, girl! Newly inspired, Vic downed two shots, sucked two limes and was half way through a beer when I, deliciously naked, albeit somewhat out of sorts, joined her in the tub. "Are you going to tell me about your conversation with Candi? It didn't go well, by the look of things."

"What is there to tell? She finally got around to asking me if I'd slept with you and I told her yes. That set her off a whole lot more than I would've imagined ... considering."

"Considering that she was on the big screen going down on Joseph?"

"Something like that. Wait ... What do you mean going down on Joey? I thought you said she was screwing his brains out?"

"I never said that. You just assumed. I said ... Candi looked like she was into it. All I saw was his rod in her mouth using her boobs to heighten his excitement."

Hmmm ... "Hey, I taught her that man-selfish skill set the second or third time we were together. Come to think of it, you've mastered that technique with me."

Good that you remembered, especially after all you had to drink that night. "You caught me. I confess. I watched her do it on the video and thought I'd give it a whirl. You liked ... didn't you?"

"Of course, I liked. Who wouldn't? Then again, I was trashed. No wonder I kept thinking about Candi that night when I was making love to you. Go figure."

That's my cue. "Want me to do it again?" Vic asked, without waiting for a reply, moved her hands from the sides of the tub into the churning, bubbling water. She felt my stiffness rising to greet her. Vic smiled. "Guessing by the feel of things, this means yes?"

Embarrassed, "It doesn't infer anything, Vic. What you're holding in your hand is a heightened response to the previous out of body experience we shared ... I think."

"I think not," she countered. "It's a typical male response to a sensuous, naked woman about to go down on you." Keeping her nose out of the bubbling froth was no small feat, yet, somehow, she managed to breathe deeply on every fourth or fifth upstroke without passing out.

Raising my voice to match other parts of my body, I countered, "You don't have to do this, girlfriend. I'm a big boy. Remember?"

This may very well be our last night for a while, possibly forever. I turned my eyes, before I released him from my lips to reply. "I know I don't. But I want to. I need to, for me and for you. Lay back, relax and close your eyes. Remember our first time? ... Our first kiss? Allow me to create the sequel." And over the next ten glorious minutes, she did.

Chapter 44

Vic is blessed with incredible skills, orally speaking, of course. I could think of another profession or two where her talents could put food on the table and a new Mercedes in her garage every other year. My mind, clouded in a semi-alcohol induced fog exacerbated by the body numbing effects of the Jacuzzi, traipsed back and forth between her and Candi.

Victoria, comforting me, soothing me, embracing me was more than my friend. She was my kindred spirit. And she was ... good. Feeling myself reaching the point of no return, compliments of her exquisite technique, I purposely lifted her off me and raised her up to my waiting lips.

"I'm not finished," she pouted, but I wasn't listening. "You're not finished. You're almost there."

"This is not a marathon, girlfriend. Kiss me," her lime tainted breath combined with the awkward taste of me, teased my senses. My hands roamed her voluptuous body, gliding effortlessly across her silky skin, compliments of the bath beads she must have added earlier. "You feel incredible, Victoria," I whispered, moving my hands down her back, coming to rest on her rounded, supple cheeks. Massaging them in tandem, I pressed her against my loins, her breasts, inadvertently tickling my chest. "I am perfectly content to lay here just like this, touching you, feeling you, exploring you..."

His hands, oh, his hands ... the strength they exude, the tenderness they project. "Me, too," she breathed. "This is purr...fect." *Like two well-oiled, finely tuned machines, we were gliding effortlessly back and forth across each other, my hands clasped around his neck, pushing and pulling the length of my body across him, matching him thrust for passionate thrust.*

"We're very much alike, you and I. Star crossed spirits who have discovered the innate ability to sense the hurt ... the pain of the other, before administering the appropriate healing response ... accordingly. Priceless." I turned off the jets. The clearing, bubble free water revealed the long, sinewy features of the vixen between my legs. "How beautiful you are tonight, Victoria."

Lifting her to her feet, rising from the tub, I stepped onto the brick tile, extending my hands for her to join me. Using the plush, oversized towels draped across the rack, we padded each other dry in silence. Guiding Vic to the massive plush, pillow-topped bed, I sat her down on its edge, kneeling deftly before her. Placing my head on her knees, I lingered, relishing the heat radiating from her silky, soft skin.

"Lay back for me, please," I said, placing her feet against my shoulders. Burying myself inside her, I drew across my lips the nectar of our making. Purposely, methodically, I teased her, making exaggerated circles with the pointed tip of my tongue, my hands continuing to massage her magnificent cheeks. Long, deliberate wide gliding licks propelled Victoria to involuntarily press her nails into my scalp each time I swept a sensitive area. This is my calling... there's no better place to be, buried tongue deep in a woman up to my eyeballs... who so happens to be my friend.

Something has inherently changed in this man. The passion and the lust have gone from his eyes. I see tranquility. D is relishing in me, pleasuring me, enjoying me for me. He's giving me what I wanted — needed — in this twisted relationship. What did he say, kindred spirits? Drifting into a far- off dimension, my overstuffed closet of well-worn thoughts lifted, allowing me to appreciate every sensation he was creating in me, a woman with needs. Gone was the busyness and gamesmanship

I equated with mutual satisfaction in sex. This was about me, about D ... enraptured in me. I could get used to this. My body, a slave to his techniques, no longer responded to my desires. It responded obediently to his overwhelming desire to make me climax...which I did, to his delight ... and mine.

Chapter 45

Rising from the carpeted floor and moving to the bed, I longed to finish what Victoria had started minutes earlier when my current iPhone on the nightstand began vibrating repeatedly.

My legs quivering, the after effects of his pleasantly pleasing tongue opened to receive him. His damn phone is ringing! "There's no way in hell you're going to answer that. Is there?"

I looked bitten. "I'm sorry. I always turn it off." Except this time, I didn't. Why? Glancing nonchalantly at my phone, I saw it was Candi calling me back. "I probably should answer this," I muttered apologetically to Vic, in an awkward moment of incredible insanity.

Who would have thought? "Go ahead, D. I'm sure you're talented enough to talk and screw at the same time. Aren't you, big boy?" glared Vic, determined to hold my hardness in her hand, guiding it deftly into her, before I could say no.

I answered cack-handed, possibly even a little nonchalantly, hoping to mask my present entanglement.

"Candi," I paused, taking a deep breath. "Everything…OK?"

"D, Jon David…whatever your name happens to be today…we need to talk. Really talk … without our emotions getting in the way of reason."

"Now is not a good time," I replied, my body responding to the effects of Victoria's legs wrapped round my hips, pushing and pulling her moist, hot self onto me.

"Are you riding?" asked Candi.

"You could say that." *What? Does this girl have, ESP?* "Give me a few minutes to get to a place where I can stop and I'll call you back."

"Tell Victoria hi for me ... Bye," quipped Candi, in a voice armed with an uncanny sixth sense. *Female karma maybe?*

D, is so busted. Wrapping her arms around my neck and daring me to stop, Vic whispered, "Hurry D, come for me. Then you can run off and call her back."

I faked it, my first with this auburn-haired, vivacious vixen. Rocking and rolling on the bed for the next few minutes, I exaggerated my release, my mind, a thousand miles away. Turning directly into her gaze, "I shouldn't have answered the phone, that wasn't fair to you."

"Fair to me? It wasn't fair to you. You thoroughly satisfied me, this was all about satisfying you." Rolling off the bed, Vic gathered her clothes, ran to the bathroom and slammed the door. *I wanted D to know I was upset. But I wasn't, really, I wasn't. What hold this girl has over him, I'll never know. My Woo-Hoo, as he calls it, is just as hot and tight as hers. Geez!*

Way to go, putz! You've agitated the two women you care about most in less than five minutes. You're on a roll! You're shooting snake eyes with your one-eyed monster to be exact. Quickly dressing and against my better judgment, I left Vic stewing in the bathroom to go outside and be verbally accosted by the other woman scorned.

I am a glutton for punishment. What can I say? I pressed send.

"Hi, Candi. Where were we?"

"Hi, D. I hope I didn't make you stop riding just to call me back."

If you only knew... "It's fine, Candi. I needed a ... break."

"Your sleeping with Vic is none of my business. Really, it's not. I mean you're a desirable man... she's a beautiful woman. I got it. I am jealous, but not like you think. I wish it was me instead of her you were sleeping with ... screwing — whatever you're doing."

"Stop rationalizing, Candi. It should bother you. ... that is, if you still care. Your Joey porn sure as hell bothered me. Vic comforted me the best way she knew how. I'm sure Joey did the same for you."

"You stop it, dammit! Joseph is crazy jealous of you. He manipulates people and he's good at it. He wants us back the way we used to be using any means necessary. It's not happening. Don't you get it, having sex with him was the only way I could prove to him it's over between you and me. I don't want it to be. I pray you don't want it to be. It's not ... .is it? If I could see you, talk to you ... maybe we could find our way through this. Anyplace, anywhere ... you name it, I'll be there."

"I don't know if it's over or not. I'm complicated, you're even more complicated. I would like to see you again, Candi. Right now, it's a good three days before I get home. I can't make any promises. All I can tell you is I'll try. Even then, I'm not so sure we can heal this circle of trust. It makes my head hurt thinking what you're going to say next. You've made being us damn near impossible." I paused, allowing my last statement to sink in as another thought emerged. "Not to change the subject, but since we're speaking of home, did you find out any more about who specifically might be looking for me?"

"I've dug around as much as I dare without tipping my hand. Donny has gone MIA. No one has seen him since he checked himself out of the hospital in Calgary. The last person to talk to him that I know of was ... eh ... Joseph."

"That's convenient. Guess he can't take a joke, especially since it cost him a mouthful of teeth. By now, I'm sure he knows just enough about Victoria and Sioux City to be dangerous. Thanks for the heads up. Vic may need to take another trip when we get back. Won't she be thrilled? Speaking of Vic, I need to go. I'm sure she's wondering where I ran off to. I'll try to touch base with you in the next couple of days. K?"

"K. If I learn anymore, I'll call you or text immediately. I'm sorry that I've messed up your life. What I wouldn't give to have a do-over with you. Bye, baby."

Chapter 46

I took my time walking back to the room. I savored the baby endearment Candi closed with. Haven't heard that too much lately. It was just an innocuous word that meant the world to me at the beginning of our now tumultuous and maligned relationship.

Enough of this ongoing fantasy. Right now, I'd best suck up to Vic. It was a jaw-dropping moment as I entered our room. Victoria was sprawled gloriously naked on the bed, smiling brightly. Her right hand expertly driving the BOA as it hummed merrily along on high.

"Don't just stand there with your tongue hanging out ... finish it." Knowing she had my utmost attention, Vic turned off the BOA and tossed it on the bed. Spreading her legs as far as her hands would allow, "I've kept it warm and wet for you."

Speechless, robbed of any reasonable comeback, "I thought we did finish, girlfriend ... I finished."

"Liar. You might have faked me with your moans, your groans, but your residuals never lie. There were none. Finish," she directed, wiggling her inviting hoo-ha, before my lust filled eyes, "or I will finish on you. Your choice. Don't look so pristine and proper. We're friends, remember? I've told you, I'm all for you going back and trying to make it work with Candi. I don't think it will, long term, but you can try. In the meantime, drop 'em and ride me hard like you do that bike of yours. I'm your kindred spirit, your like mind, D. Think of this moment as the culmination of your out of body experience."

Victoria was never going to take 'No, not now… maybe later' as an excuse while my jeans were sorely rising. *What about Candi? You can't do this, control yourself. But, I couldn't. I'm a slut or so I'm told. Twisted is a better word.* "I surrender," I confessed, letting my pants fall where they lay, while I laid where I fell, on her, then in her. Riding Vic slowly and deeply, I pumped hard while she pushed harder, until our rhythmic motions carried me over the top, spilling into her the long sought out evidence of my making. I collapsed.

"There, that wasn't so difficult was it, D? You needed release. Since I'm the releaser, it's best you take advantage of it … of me … whatever."

"You do have a way with words, girlfriend. Among other things…"

"Of course, among other things, D. I'm a talented, well-versed attorney, sporting a hungry mouth, as well as a cheeky ass to die for. Fortunately, you and only you have been on the receiving end of those last two attributes in quite a while."

Slapping her firmly on one of her attributes, "thank you for the privilege and honor to partake of your delicacies," I smirked, while dodging a barrage of pillows tossed at my head.

"I'm hungry. What's for dinner?"

"Of course, you are." We ordered in, two center-cut prime rib dinners with all the trimmings, watched a pay per view action movie and fell asleep, romantically entwined.

* * *

Morning broke early at 5:30, allowing me a solitary escape to the hotel's in-house gym, before rousing the sleeping beauty. Fifteen minutes on the circuit, followed by thirty minutes on the elliptical was enough to get my heart pounding. Stopping by the coffee bar, I picked up a large black and green for me, and a Brava Latte for Victoria. Kissing her gently on the cheek while waving the Latte across her nose brought her out of a deep sleep. "Wake up, girlfriend. You've got a spa date at eight."

She smiled. "What time is it?"

"Almost seven. You've got an hour before you go."

"Come with me. I bet they have a couple's massage for two."

"I'll pass. This is all you. We need to leave immediately afterwards, so don't go getting too relaxed. I'm not going all the way to Sioux City tonight since it's almost six hundred miles, but we do need to get as much windshield time in as possible."

"I can skip it if you want."

"Nope, Victoria needs pampered and schmoozed. All that I can do for you is..."

"Oh, I know what you can do. And we have one more night for you to do it!" she winked, flicked her tongue across her lips and smiled.

"You weren't kidding when you said the only way to keep you out of my pants was to get you home. I'm trying, girlfriend. ... So, help me, I'm trying."

Chapter 47

I was dressed, packed and loaded by nine, waiting for Vic by the bike when she bounded joyfully through the front door, her radiance inferring success.

"Thank you, D. That was wonderful. Now ... I'm more than ready to ride!"

"We ride," I exclaimed, bringing the bike to life and driving south on Lord Selkirk Highway for 60 miles before the road turned into U.S. I-29 at the border. Passing easily through U.S. Customs into North Dakota gave me an instantaneous sigh of relief. The trepidation that immediately followed was my not knowing what lay ahead — for me, for Vic, for Candi.

I set the throttle lock on 80 mph and we cruised straight through the rolling, barren hills of 'scenic' North Dakota to Grand Forks before stopping at the Pilot / Flying J. Truck Stop. Rigs of all lengths, loaded with drilling equipment and supplies, filled the parking lot as far as the eye could see. We were in the middle of history, the Bakken Oil Fields, brimming with black gold providing thousands of jobs for those brave enough to endure the frigid desolate winters here.

"How are you holding up, girlfriend? You've been quiet all morning. Care to tell me what's wrong?"

Of course, I've been quiet. Who wouldn't be, knowing our pseudo whirlwind romance is coming to an end? "I'm sorry. I've been thinking. You realize, we'll be home tomorrow? All the turmoil that we've evaded in Canada the last few days is about to slap us silly. Our fairy tale ride will be over and we'll have to start slaying those nasty old dragons that surfaced while we've been gone. It depresses me. Welcome back to the real world, ready or not."

"I envy you, Victoria. Just think, your new world is ahead of you. A blank canvas, compliments of me, thank you, that is all yours and yours alone to dream and do as you desire."

"D, I'm grateful. You're welcomed to be a part of it. Excuse me, you are a part of it."

"Copy that girlfriend, heavy baggage and all." I wouldn't wish my life upon anyone right now with all its uncertainties and twists and turns, especially Victoria. "Thank you, it's refreshing to know somebody wants me for what's inside, not just for my incredible looks."

She laughed, looking at my flat, helmet hair, my wind-blown beard and my bug splattered leathers. "I'm hungry. Want to wine and dine me somewhere or will you settle for a delicious Subway since we're already here?"

"Subway works for me. Order me something light, please. We need to ride another few hours to make sure I have you home by noon tomorrow."

"Why noon, I don't have a deadline?" Vic asked, backing away.

"Ah, but I do. I need to make St. Charles tomorrow night." With Vic, out of sight ordering lunch, I made reservations for us at a Holiday Inn Express in Watertown, SD, a short three-hour ride to Sioux City. I followed that up with reservations at the Ameristar Casino in St. Charles, Missouri, just west of St. Louis.

Lastly, I texted Jim at WITSEC informing him of my location and my ETA to Tennessee:

Jim, in country. Estimated time home — two days.

If we need to talk, call me after noon tomorrow. I'll be in the truck and alone.

That should do it. Moving my bike from the fuel island, I pulled up by the front door. Vic was waiting on me in a booth with half a turkey, avocado club on whole wheat and an unsweetened tea. "Good choice, Vic. It's scary how much we're alike."

You got that right. "Didn't think you'd want dessert, at least for now. That's what you have me for isn't it big fella?" she winked, knowing she couldn't be any more obvious of her intentions.

"Surely you jest, Victoria. After riding all day, on your numb ass and all, you'd still be willing to get frisky with me? Does that Woo-Hoo of yours ever get sore?"

Yep, tender to the touch when you've rode me hard and rough. "Hmm ... let me think ... If it did, I'd never tell you." *By the look in his eyes, my sheepish grin gave me away.*

"Liar, liar, panties on fire..."

"It's worth it. You're worth it. Hell, even I'm worth it," Vic retorted, convincing us both that tonight there should be one final episode of togetherness.

Chapter 48

Three hours later as the sun slipped below the horizon we made Watertown, SD. All I knew about Watertown was its exit on the interstate, featuring The Terry Redline Art Center and Museum. The hotel, a block down 172nd Ave had a surprising number of restaurants nearby.

"This will more than suffice, won't it, Vic?" I asked trying to be polite. I'd made up my mind to stay here, regardless of her reply. "Besides I get points."

"Holiday Inn? Seriously, D? They don't have big soaking tubs."

"Ah, but they do have luxurious pillows and firm, comfortable beds. I can attest to that."

"Good point," she exclaimed. "I know how you so prefer king beds over tubs when you're making love to Royalty." *Give it a rest, Victoria. He damn well knows your intentions and his capabilities. If the truth be known you're in-satiated with him because you're jealous ... of Candi ... and she's not even here.*

"You're a quick study. I believe I've told your highness that before. Check us in if you please." Bowing before her, my right hand, sweeping downward, then upward, "your man servant will caress and carry your soft and supple ... um ... bags to your room." Made her smile, good boy!

Unstrapping our gear, I stowed the tie downs in the right saddlebag where I'd thrown my phone from earlier this morning. It was vibrating and beeping multiple sounds, signaling voice mails, missed calls and un-retrieved texts.

To my chagrin, it showed six missed calls, six new texts and three voice mails. Three missed calls from Candi, two from Jim and one from Greg. Onto the texts: three from Jim, three from Candi and one voice mail, respectively, from each of the three. Isn't it good to be back in the good ole U.S. of A. where we're always connected whether we choose to be or not?

Candi's texts in order:
> Call me.

> I have news. Call me.

> Donny is somewhere in St. Louis.

Jim's texts in order:
> Call me.

> Can't wait. Talk today.

> Our deep cover sources informed me that someone is seriously looking for you. Time to relocate.

Pure joy. I knew for sure we weren't followed since we left Calgary. No one, and I mean no one knew where we were going ... not even me. Relocate? Yeah, right!

It was after 8 o'clock Eastern when I dialed Candi. It rang once before going to voice mail ... figures. By now, Jim is home with his family. It can wait until tomorrow. He's given me a heads-up. That's more than enough.

I listened to Greg's excited voice mail, disregarding the other two. He'd sold over a third of the diamonds yesterday, and raised more than enough money for Missy with a few thousand left over for Debra's trip. Listening further, Missy was scheduled to make the trip to Children's Hospital by week's end. Excellent. Good news always outweighs the bad in my book — anytime, anywhere.

Chapter 49

I turned the phone off and tossed it back into the bag, before picking up the room key Vic graciously left for me at the front desk. Opening the door to the room ever so slowly, I heard Vic's sweet and tender voice echoing over the sound of rushing water coming from the tub.

"What took you so long, D? I was lonely. I'm taking a bath. Would ask you to join me, but—"

"I got it, I got it ... the tub is too small for the both of us. Rub it in, girlfriend," I huffed. "You know what I've decided? You're a little too feisty for your own good ... when you don't get your way. Over the last few days you've been wined and dined, pampered and probed, ridden and rode. Think of it like this, tonight you can go back to being you." Vic didn't seem to appreciate that last statement by the abrupt slamming of the bathroom door. Oh well, that's all I've got for now. My butt is bone ass tired.

Unzipping my leathers, I kicked off my boots, stretched out sideways on the bed and flipped on the news. After twenty minutes of murders and political mayhem, CNN finally got around to the lucky folks and their diamond dilemmas. Speculations and postulations were rampant, featuring guest after wayward guest supporting their individual hypothesis of who was behind the sudden windfalls and why. Little do they know ... they're all wrong.

I switched to Andy Griffith and zoned out. Ah, those were the days ... Mayberry, Aunt Bee, Barney and Opie. Life was simpler then. Wonder where in the world today I could find myself another Mayberry? Surely, there is a town, a village, a community that has insulated itself from the envy and greed that's befallen humanity of late. That's worth a Google, I surmised. Now where in the world is Vic's iPad? I could get up and rummage through her stuff, but being the southern gentleman that I am, I thought better of it. I did what most men are prone to do when they're relaxed and comfortable, I yelled, "Yo, Vic! Where's your iPad?"

Yo? Did he just say, 'Yo, Vic'? "I have it, D. I'm catching up on emails and current events in the tub. Let me rephrase that," she shouted through the closed door, "I'm catching up on you." *How one man's unselfish quest for redemption could stir up so much shit is beyond me. Why couldn't these blessed few keep their investment healing treasures to themselves like D asked them to? Humanity at its finest. Geez!* Moving on, where was I? "D, I'll be out in a few minutes. Can you wait? What's for dinner?"

My body relaxed, my brain in slow-mo, I struggled to correlate her string of questions into an appropriate reply. "I can wait. You can assist me in my quest for Mayberry. I'm surprised, why didn't you just say I'm hungry?"

"Duh! I inferred it, didn't I?" This yelling back and forth through the door has to stop. Rising from the tub, Vic towel dried quickly and made an orchestrated entrance, tossing her iPad to me with her glorious naked self -attached. "Here you go, D, for your viewing pleasure..."

"Girlfriend, it's gonna be hard..." I hesitated, "looking up something on your iPad while my Googling eyes are drooling over you in your current state of attire."

She grasped the slowly rising bulge in my shorts and quipped, "I'm counting on it."

"Victoria, would you believe me if I told you I'm mentally and physically spent?"

"I would, especially after all the miles we've covered today. He," she continued, proudly massaging my tented masculinity, "conveys quite the opposite."

So much for looking up Mayberry. I purposely redirected her gaze with a push of my hand. "Turn a deaf ear to the one-eyed monster, Victoria. Remember he's a notorious slut. Besides, mind you, I'm taking liberties here. ... I thought you were hungry."

My valid argument caused her to release her death grip, but not before speaking pointedly to my little brain, "I am hungry ... What's ... for ... dinner?"

"That's my girl! You know who's in charge. Get dressed in your finest jeans. I'll call us a cab. We're going to Dempsies' downtown. We'll eat, get drunk, and—"

Vic's eyes lit up, she jiggled her booty in my face, "Screw?"

"I didn't say screw, I said sleep. You weren't listening!" Vic pounded me with one of the signature pillows while her breasts, bouncing off my chest, hardened the little fella, positioning for a full-frontal attack. "Stop it! ... Please?" I whined. "Let's get through the first two. If there's anything left in my tank, you're welcome to it."

Vic relented. *D, makes almost saying yes but not really seem sufficient, even when I don't want him to.* Following my lead, she quickly dressed.

Chapter 50

Ten minutes later and twenty bucks lighter, compliments of the Lake Cab Company, we found ourselves nestled into a corner booth in Dempsies', courtesy of Milly our most accommodating hostess. The walls were adorned with pictures of the Old West and saddles and cowboy hats reflecting the hard times long passed.

"In celebration of our last night together, Victoria, will you share a bottle or two of wine with me?" Nodding her head to the affirmative, I ordered the first bottle of Pinot Noir to kick off our evenings' festivities.

"To us," she toasted, raising her glass to mine.

"To many more tomorrows," I replied, clinking my glass with hers. "This vintage Pinot is only fitting, this, being our last night together for a while. I remember serving you this very same wine, sans the crystal, the first night we met."

"Red solo cup. How could I forget the night I undressed before your lust filled eyes ... and all you wanted to do was cuddle? I remember, you rejected me asshole ... my first!"

"I didn't reject you, Vic, I rejected the thought of me betraying Candi. We had something ... something… wonderful in the works."

"And you still might," she countered. Raising her glass again, "to Candi, wherever she may be." *Biting my tongue, I still could think it ... or on whomever she may be.*

"Thank you, Victoria. To Candi, may she be safe as well."

Vic, me thinks you're lucky your mouth didn't overload your ass with that one-liner.

"Speaking of safe, it may not be the best time to bring this up, but I'm gonna need you to disappear for a while as soon as we get back tomorrow." Knowing I'd immediately struck a nerve, I continued briefing her as best I could on the possible threat Jim and Candi conveyed to me.

"What do you mean leave? I'm going to be home tomorrow for the first time in almost two weeks. I have a slew of things to do. So much to catch up on." *His eyes, his beautiful brown eyes, projected grave concern for my safety. Damn, I'm not going to win this argument. As ludicrous as it seemed I wasn't sure I wanted to.* Exhaling, I relented, "where would you like me to go?" *There were numerous places I could safely retreat to, none of which would make me feel as safe as I am right now.* "Can I go back to Tennessee with you?"

"I'm trying to protect you, Vic. Getting you out of my immediate circle is my goal. Do you have any relatives or friends far away that you could go visit for a few days?"

Too much to process ... Wait! Wait! I need to think. "You're wanting me to go somewhere far, far, away aren't you? Hard to reach, harder still to find?"

"You got it. It's been confirmed from two reliable sources that someone is hell bent on finding me — us. I don't need to be worrying about protecting you. ... Remember, I didn't do so well the last time. I need to be proactive, protecting me."

"Damn straight, you're my best client. Can't have anything happen to you."

"Vic, I'm your only client." I grinned ... "Thanks, anyway."

"Hush ... I'm thinking ... Um, I forgot to tell you, I — we — got an email from Semper Fi, Frank. Read it in the tub. Wanted me to tell you he's in Copenhagen, Denmark staying at some hotel ... whose name escapes me at the moment, but I do remember something about it is across the street from

Tivoli Gardens." D nodded like he knew exactly what I was talking about. "You been there?"

I nodded yes, "A long time ago."

"Worst case, I could go hang out with him." Vic threw that out to gauge my knee jerk reaction, before she swapped her seduction panties for her business suit, and began her rebuttal as my twice tried and thrice tested attorney. "Too far, never mind. I'm your counsel. By the looks of things, you're going to need me, sooner, rather than later. Best I stay in the country. Got it?"

"Yes, counselor, loud and clear. Still doesn't answer my question, where can you go?"

"Non-siblings I gather? In that case, I have a cousin in Blue Ridge, Georgia, about two hours north of Atlanta. Her husband is a ranger and he carries a big gun," she said, holding her hands about twelve inches apart. Vic smiled, "big, D, big — at least twice the size of yours. Will that work?"

Humor, that's what we need right now. "I'm not going to touch that last statement. Bound to be TMI forthcoming. Thank you, Victoria for bringing levity into the room, even if it was … at my expense," I chuckled, taking her hands in mine, pushing them seven inches apart … possibly … eight. We laughed.

Still I had to get her on a plane to Atlanta before I could relax. "After all that, yes, it will work! But, I'm not leaving you until you're wheels up, no arguments," I blasted, pounding my fist on the table hard enough to rattle the silverware.

He does care. Hell, I care. "Don't take this the wrong way, D, but suddenly I'm not very hungry. Can we split an appetizer and possibly another bottle of wine?"

"Your wish is my command." I ordered the Grand Sampler, featuring a generous selection of their best sellers, along with another bottle of Pinot Noir. "Drink up girlfriend, the night is closing fast." And we did, sipping slowing through the second bottle, feasting on the platter and talking about our broken dreams, as well as the demons buried in our past.

"D, why were you looking for Mayberry? Is there really such a place in this great big world?" she asked, hoping I would answer her last question with a resounding yes.

"Surely there is, I'll just have to find it, idyllic, though it may be. I'm sorry, I'm running on empty here, Victoria. My friends are few, my family nonexistent. After all we've tried to do to repair a horrible wrong, I feel like I've been relegated to victim status. Working my way up from the bottom, I adhered to the principle if you treated people as you wanted to be treated, good things would come your way. That, I'm sad to say, has turned out to be more, false than true.

"Most people, I've come to realize are your friends because of what you can do for them. It's only when your endless supply of giving is exhausted do you wake up one day in a cold sweat to discover you have none. What once was in the hundreds, I now count on two hands. Jim, from WITSEC, said 'it was time'" … I could barely bring myself to utter the next words … "'to relocate.'"

"At first the idea repulsed me, but the more I've thought about it, the more I've warmed to it. Do you realize I've struck out building a life from the ground up three times so far? Somewhere on this planet there has to be a simpler life, lived by genuine people without self-serving agendas — people who are the real deal, respecting you for you, not just for what you bring to the table. If I can find it, you'll find me on the next plane."

He's losing me. "What if this utopia you dream of doesn't exist as you imagine it, then what?"

"There has to be, doesn't there? But, God forbid, if there isn't, to answer your question when that dream stops so will my breathing."

No, you don't. I am not throwing you a pity party right now, damn you! "You have value, you have worth. One billion dollars in diamonds you've given back to the people who could ill afford to lose their life savings. You've helped me, Frank, and now Missy and who knows how many others. You're a rare breed, Jon David," I assured him, clasping my hands around his as he subconsciously twirled the stem on the wine goblet with his fingers.

I'd had my say. I was done talking. "Drink up, Vic, it's been a long day." Calling the cab driver, who dropped us off earlier, I asked for a pick-up in fifteen. "My, what a depressing last night together this has turned out to be. I'm sorry."

"There's nothing to be sorry for, D. I wish there was more I could do. You manage brokenness well, except when you don't — by drinking too much, that is."

I laughed. "I've surely exposed you to a few of those episodes here lately, haven't I girlfriend? Honestly, what did it get me?"

"Laid. It got you laid," Vic replied somberly. "I shared in your pain, your hurt, your grieving. I commiserated with you the only way I knew how. I gave you my best, I gave you my all — I gave you me."

Chapter 51

Vic was dead on when she said she gave her all. She gave me her heart, her mind, her soul. That's what kindred spirits do. "That's what I love about you, Victoria. You're either all in or all out. There's no such thing as in between." Speaking of that, someone else, as I recall, was much the same way — Candi.

I left a Franklin on the table for a seventy-dollar tab and escorted Victoria outside to our waiting ride. Wrapping my left arm around her, Vic laid her head on my shoulder while we rode in shuttered silence back to the hotel. In the room, I sensed Vic had something profound to say by the longing in her eyes so I plopped onto the bed and waited.

"D, I'm so going to miss you. These last two weeks have given me a renewed sense of purpose and direction. You've challenged me, encouraged me, and pushed me to be the best I can be. I thought I was good, but you've made me much better. You've made me hurry up and wait patiently for life to come to me. It did with the ducks, it did with the bears, it surely did with the stars scattered amongst the northern lights. I will never be able to repay you. This I promise, whenever there is an opportunity to pay it forward, rather than allowing it to slip through my fingers, which is what I'd normally do, I'll embrace it and think of you."

"That's more than enough, girlfriend." Running my fingers through her beautiful auburn hair, I continued, "it's only fitting that we end this ride the way it began. I'd like to hold you and sleep with you tonight. In my tank, there's nothing left." The darkness enveloped us, both literally and figuratively. Sleep came quickly for me.

I turned away from him, as he spooned me. *Lying beside me was the man of many a woman's dreams… my dreams too, damn it. A man who dreamed, not of me, but of another. Filling my lungs for possibly the last time with his scent complimented by his Allure cologne I'd recently grown fond of, I cried until I had no more tears left in me. Sleep this night was my enemy. The events over the last few weeks with D played out over and over in my head. What could I have done differently? What could he? Would Candi save their relationship or would he somehow find his way back to me in his quest to find peace in some mystical town called Mayberry?* Somewhere after two, Victoria drifted off.

* * *

My phone vibrated, annoyingly announcing 5:30 a.m. I turned it off. In the stillness and quiet of the morning, I planned our day. Breakfast, followed by a three-hour ride, should put us in Sioux City before eleven o'clock. If I drop her off to pack and repack while I go load the bike on the trailer, she should be able to catch a flight out, any time after one. I don't care where it goes on her way to Atlanta as long as it takes her far and fast away from me.

I gathered my shorts and shoes and dressed in the bathroom, doing my best not to disturb my friend. I found the adequately furnished workout room on the ground floor empty and dark. Turning the flat screen on to local news, I sweated profusely for twenty minutes on the elliptical, followed by ten minutes of free weights. That's all the time I could spare and be on the road by eight.

Making us a coffee and tea had become a morning ritual that sadly after today, would end. I like her, maybe even love her, if I dared to go there. But I can't, not now with so much left unsaid between Candi and me. With a little luck, Major and I could make Tampa by Saturday with a week to spare before the all-important ball. I needed a plan. Over the next fifteen minutes, wandering the vacant halls of the hotel I got a semblance of one. Gio, and possibly others would have to be enlisted to make it come together. Returning to the room, I kissed Vic on the cheek waving the fresh brewed coffee under her nose that I'd picked up along the way.

"Hmmm, that smells wonderful, D. Guess that's my cue to rise?"

"Yep, I'm sorry. I wish I could let you sleep longer, but we've got much to accomplish today and little time to waste. I'm gonna grab a quick shower. Drink your coffee and for your reading pleasure, I brought you a USA today to peruse." My solitary shower completed, I found Vic dressed and ready to ride.

"Don't ask. It's no fun showering alone. I'm ready when you are." *But I wasn't. I don't want to leave, not this way, not like this. Last night we crashed hard, landing in the reality of his making. We were no longer playing make believe, we were no longer living a dream. D is fighting for his life, he's also fighting for mine.*

Chapter 52

A quick breakfast behind us, we were on the road ten minutes shy of eight. The crisp morning, Dakotan air was refreshing, if not exhilarating, cruising south on I-29 at 80 mph. Prairie turned into plains and plains turned into cornfields, silently signaling our closing proximity to Sioux City.

I changed my mind. Vic was not leaving my sight. Exiting onto 4th Street a few minutes after ten, I weaved my way to the Crown Plaza, where I found my truck and trailer exactly where I'd left it many weeks before.

"Wish I could say we're home, but that would be an understatement. Again, I'm sorry, Victoria. It is what it is."

"No apologies, D. I told you I have no regrets. I have a new career path, more than enough assets and you. I'm set. Just promise me you will take care of you."

Loading the bike on the trailer, I quickly tied it down while Victoria tossed our bags in the back of the truck. Her last statement deserved an answer, but not before I climbed under the truck looking for any strange device or object that might have randomly appeared while I was gone.

Seriously, all I see are his feet sticking out from under the truck. "Uh… umm … lose something?"

Confident no one had attached a tracking device or possibly an IED (Improvised Explosive Device) to my truck, I emerged, shaking my head no, before replying. "I promise. Second, I was making sure I would honor that promise, beginning here, beginning now." The fifteen-minute drive to her house in my truck took some getting used to. No handlebar to hold onto, no wind in my face, no bugs in my teeth ... rough life ahead I guess. "Vic, how long do you need to transform from biker babe to lady of leisure?"

Lady of leisure, sounds like he's calling me a—. She smiled. "Thirty minutes, give or take. I do need to go next door and pick up my mail."

Watching her walk away without her ever present leathers reminded me so much of Candi. Hopefully soon, Candi ... soon. We'll see if Humpty Dumpty can put us back together again. If not, there's always Victoria, who was screaming my name, over and over again, in real time.

"D, wake up! You could help you know." Geez, men!

I looked up to see Vic, dragging two large boxes, her mail scattered across the ground. I jumped from the truck and offered my assistance, gathering her wayward mail, before tackling the heavy cardboard boxes.

"They're clothes, D, Candi's and mine. You might as well open them and put Candi's in your truck, along with her leathers I left in the back. Bring my bag into the house. I'll repack it. Then we can leave. Want something to drink?"

"Water, please." Her well-appointed house, I assumed awarded her in the divorce, was a '60s red brick Craftsman in a quaint neighborhood with manicured lawns. Not the kind of place for singles like Vic, but families with kids or possibly retirees. Hardwood floors, solid core doors, and ornate crown moldings highlighted an interior that was sparsely furnished. Compliments of the divorce I am certain.

"I'm sure I have that," Vic winked, rummaging around in her near empty refrigerator. "When does my plane leave?"

"Hold that thought. I'll let you know before you're through packing." I summoned SIRI, flights and times departing Sioux City, Iowa this afternoon. Ah... technology... a powerful tool, and an even more powerful enemy that has contributed greatly to our mostly sedentary society.

Vic tossed me a bottle before she peeled off her days old clothes and jumped into her very own shower, breathing a welcome sigh of relief. With little time to wash and dry her hair, she was perfectly content to scrub her body clean with her own body wash for a change. Beaming from her instantaneous makeover, she was out the door in twenty, repacked and ready to ride ... I mean fly. "So, when does my plane leave, D?"

"One Ten, going to Chicago O'Hare, I'll book your next leg at the airport." At least I hoped I could. "It's 12:15. We'd better go, girlfriend. You need to make any stops along the way?"

"I do, lots of them. But they can wait. The quicker you see me off, the quicker you'll be on your way."

"If you need to make stops, I'll find you a later flight. It's OK."

I thought long and hard about his generous offer. "Will you leave me at the airport to catch a later flight?" *I knew his answer before I asked.*

"Nope. I'm staying until you're on the plane, wheels up."

"I thought so. Never mind."

I had us at the American Airlines desk at 12:40 where I bought Vic a ticket to Chicago and a voucher that would put her on the first available flight with open, first class, seats to Atlanta. "Here you go girlfriend with twenty minutes to spare. By the way, did you call your cousin and tell her you were coming? Just wondering."

"I did not. Didn't exactly know if and when I'd get there. Will call her from Chicago. Give me a hug and a kiss, Jon David. Then get your ass on the road."

I obliged wholeheartedly. "Thank you, Victoria, for being there for me ... in so many ways. I'll miss you, girlfriend."

"I'll miss you. ... Now go, before I start getting teary-eyed." *Too late, the tears cascaded across my cheeks while I tried to walk away.*

Catching her arm, I spun her around and wiped her tears off with my fingers before resorting to my sleeve. I whispered, "We created something special, you and I, that can never be taken away. Remember that, Victoria.

... In the words of Arnold Schwarzenegger, 'I'll be back.' You can count on it, girlfriend." Vic pulled away, kissing me one last time on the cheek before passing through security and out of my sight, leaving me with a hollow feeling in my stomach and a lump in my throat. I hope you know what you're doing, D. I didn't. I really wished I did.

I exited the short-term parking lot with my bike in tow and drove to the cellphone waiting area. I made a call to Jim. ... and got his voice mail.

"Jim, it's D. Heading home ... alone. Call when you can. I've got a days-worth of windshield time ahead of me before I stop."

Chapter 53

At twenty past one, American Eagle, FLT 2289 lifted off into the northeastern sky, carrying Victoria Lawson, Attorney at Law away from me, further still away from harm. Five hundred miles and seven plus hours away, the Ameristar Casino, my last overnight stay before the lush green mountains of Tennessee would appear in my windshield.

Driving south on I-29, I skirted the Missouri River, driving through an abundance of cornfields all the way to St. Joseph, Missouri. There the terrain changed, turning into rolling hills to Kansas City and east on I-70 to St. Louis. Driving my Tundra after a month on the bike was a welcome respite no matter how much I loved two wheels.

Sirius radio and I got reacquainted after a long absence. I also enjoyed the artificially created luxuries I'd done without, i.e. A/C and heat. One never appreciates what they have until it's gone ... Lately, that's the story of my life. Traipsing through my mind were the memories I'd made with Candi from Tennessee to Alabama and all points West, followed by those I'd made with Vic on the ride back East. What do I bring to the table that would make either one of these beautiful young women want to spend their bright futures with me? That was the million-dollar question I can't seem to answer.

My phone vibrated then rang, number blocked. Had to be Jim. Or was it? I answered reluctantly with a question.

"Yes?"

"D, is that you? It's Jim."

Relieved, I exhaled loudly, before continuing, "Hi, Jim, it's me. Thanks for the head's up. What can you tell me that I don't already know?"

"My sources tell me someone from the Family you've been recently ... uh-hum humping ... is trying to collect the bounty Standford put on that ugly head of yours. I'm led to believe they know where you are. It's possible they have compromised your recent flavor, excuse me, flavor's phones and have tracked them to you and your location."

"That's encouraging. I've changed phones every week, even used the Sat phone, off and on, you gave me."

"Doesn't matter, D. We're talking NSA stuff here. Somebody with extremely large gonads, throwing around large sums of cash that wants to find you bad enough, can, as long as you leave any type of electronic trail."

"Sucks to be me, huh? ... Mayberry ... It's sounding better by the moment."

"What? ... Mayberry, who said anything about Mayberry?"

"Inside joke. I can toss this phone and use pay phones from now on. Then again, sounds like it wouldn't matter one way or the other. I'll continue to use both. Give 'em something extra to decipher."

"You're dead on. They can still find your general location if they're monitoring the people you're talking to. That aside, we probably need to relocate you. You got that message. Right?"

I shrugged. "Loud and clear, Jim. Loud and clear."

"How long you think it'd take to wrap up your business concerns and be ready to move? I can assign an agent to stay with you 'til then."

"I hate to tell you this, after all you've done for me, but I'm inclined to take a rain check on your offer. I'm tired of starting over. I'm thinking about retiring to an island somewhere and writing a book. If I do, I'll send you a postcard along with a signed copy."

"You're serious? We did a good job of protecting you, that is, until you started thinking with your dick instead of your brain."

"I do resemble that remark. I got it. Me and dick were out of sorts at the lake. Lonely ... is my one word description. Actually, I thought I'd found something that made us both happy ... and who knows it still might. Funny thing is, it's gonna play out over the next few days one way or the other."

"I don't agree with you leaving the program, that's my official statement. On the other hand, I understand. If you're off grid — off radar — you're no longer in our system waiting to be hacked or compromised. What can I do, if anything, to help?"

"Send the Calvary if and when I call. I'm snatching the dog tomorrow on my way through and heading south. I'll be in touch. Thanks." I pressed end.

Chapter 54

Thank God for windshield time. *Make a plan ... weigh it ... revise it ... trash it ... make another one. Over the next few hours that's what I did. The only thing I knew for sure was a costumed Benefit Ball for Children's Hospital happening in Tampa next Saturday night, ten days from tomorrow. That gives me two days to pick up Major and grab my stuff, two days to get to Tampa and then a week to put my convoluted plan into action. Do I meet up with Candi immediately or wait? Wait until you have a plan in place, said my big brain. Got to get in touch with Giovanni to make that call.*

On the outskirts of St. Charles my phone vibrated, then chirped with a text from Vic:

Arrived in Atlanta, renting a car. Call if you can.

Of course, I can when I get to the room. And say what? I had approximately ten minutes before I descended upon the Ameristar to come up with an answer. If it doesn't work out with Candi — and there's a fifty-fifty chance it won't — will I welcome Victoria back into my life? Would she welcome me?

Women and Woo-Hoos — Woo-Hoos and women ... they're bound to be the death of me yet. Ah...But what a way to go!

I pulled into valet parking and passed the kid two twenties as he handed me the claim-check. "Park this somewhere where you can keep an eye on it. Don't want anyone messing with my bike." He laughed, I didn't.

"Yes sir," this uniformed teen replied somberly, standing straight and tall, "I'll park it in a 'No Parking' area directly across the street where I can keep an eye on it personally. Name's Jake. Welcome to the Ameristar Hotel and Casino. Are you staying with us tonight?"

I like this kid. He so reminds me of me. I peeled off two more twenties and tossed them in the console. "You're astute, son, I'll give you that. Thanks." Snagging my daypack from the back, I tossed it in the front passenger seat, before unlocking my glove box and retrieving a holstered Glock ACP .45 with an extra 10-round clip. Jake turned ashen white. "In case I win," I quipped, "won't need it if I lose. Either way, you didn't see it," handing him the other two twenties.

Because it was a weeknight, check-in was a breeze. I requested a room on the 15th floor overlooking the Missouri River. The staff, as usual, graciously accommodated. My king room was luxurious, featuring floor to ceiling windows and a sunken living room.

Yep, this will do. Not that I planned on staying here for long. Tonight, it was just me, a bottle of Smart Water and a two-hour appointment at the crap table where I hoped lady luck would shine on me, or not. First, I needed to connect with Victoria. Retrieving her number from my phone, I called her using the landline.

On the fourth ring, "Victoria Lawson, may I help you?"

"You may. The valet at the casino gave me your name and number. Since I wasn't feeling lucky tonight, he said you could fix me up. For a frolicking good time, call…

"Asshole," has to be D. "Me? … Damn good times, as I recall…at least for you…for me, not so much in the beginning… But hey, who's counting? What number is this? … You swap phones again?"

"Nope, landline. Rumor has it, spooks may be listening to my fav's phones. You made it to Jasper?"

"Not yet … Took a detour, went shopping at Lenox Square. FYI… you're too old to say fav's in my opinion. Now, I'm having dinner with my cousin at Sam Houston's, Buckhead. You've been, I'm sure."

"I have … and know it well. Doesn't crank up 'til way late, that is, at least on weekends."

"Yep, you've been here. That's what I remember about Hot Lanta. Party late, party hard … sleep in 'til two. Enough about me, you have anything new to share?"

"Not yet. I'll be back in the land of milk and honey tomorrow. After that, it's a toss-up, most likely the Sunshine State. We … I mean I need to resolve this drama quickly so you can get on with your life."

I laughed somberly. "Who knew, meeting you would keep me on an extended vacation? Take care of you, please."

"Ditto, take care of you. I could use you right now … Don't ask."

I glowed. "I won't … I'm glad … you miss me."

"Yep … Drink two for me girlfriend. Later."

"Gladly, D, maybe three. See ya!"

Five minutes later, the distinctive sound of clanging slot machines echoing across the casino filled the air. The average age tonight was seventy-plus… the white hairs outnumbering the grey hairs five to one. I landed at the third craps table I found. Though the current shooters perky breasts were entirely distracting, I found my lucky spot at the end of the table opposite her and planted. Tits of distraction aside, it didn't take me long to get in a groove.

Over the next hour, I turned five Franklins into five large. Bouncing, titillating 'Betty-what's-her-name' rode with me, matching me bet for bet until she was happier and I was significantly healthier. I cashed out. It was fun, it was fast, it was exhilarating. I needed that momentary escape from all that was behind me, not to mention all that lay ahead.

Relieved to exit the Casino floor without another Victoria-like encounter happening on my watch, I made it to the room, gazed out over the mighty Missouri River, took a deep breath and crashed.

Chapter 55

Although luxuriously swaddled in the feathered bedding of the Ameristar, the finest by any standards, I woke abruptly from a deep sleep at 4:10, fifty minutes shy of my alarm. Yes, I could lay here and dwell on the what-ifs or I could shower and shave and get an early start home. I chose the latter.

Thirty minutes later and another forty bucks lighter, thanks to the attentive morning parking valet, I was on the road traveling east on I-70 straight into St. Louis rush hour traffic. Stop and go with my bike and trailer in tow, I spent the next hour negotiating merges at 25 mph before crossing the mighty Mississippi, eastbound. Barring any unforeseen acts of God, I hoped to pick up Major by noon and after unpacking and repacking, be on the road to the land of oranges and grapefruits by four.

At least that was my plan before noticing a black Suburban with dark tinted windows, hanging six cars back as I passed through O'Fallon, Illinois. It didn't matter whether I cruised at 60 or 80, the distance between us never changed. Turning south onto I-57, I took the first exit in Mt. Vernon to fuel at the Pilot, while the Suburban stopped across the road at a competing station, never once leaving my line of sight. I made the call.

On the first ring, "Jim, it's D. I have a tail. I'm in Mt. Vernon, Illinois at the Pilot truck stop. Just one vehicle that I can tell. Number of occupants, I have no clue."

"D, don't go anywhere." ... Two minutes passed. ... "I'm back. I've patched you into the St. Louis field office."

"Yes, sir, this is U.S. Marshal Donnelley. I can put a rapid response team together, call in a chopper and be at your location in forty minutes, an hour, tops. Excuse me, D, is it, is this threat imminent?"

"How the hell do I know if it's imminent? Jim, is this threat imminent or am I blowing smoke up Marshal Donnelley's ass? Stay on the phone with me for a minute and I'll run across the street and ask."

"Donnelley, D doesn't cry wolf," countered Jim. "Threat is credible and verified out of our Tampa field office three days ago."

"Marshal Donnelley, is it? I'm gonna grab some breakfast to go. Forty miles south, give or take, there's an out of the way boat launch at the Ina, Rend Lake College exit off I-57. I think there's a Love's truck stop on the other side of the exit for reference. You know the place?"

"It seems vaguely familiar. I remember the Love's. Oh, hell, I'll find it. What do you want me to do?" asked Donnelley, thoroughly engaged in my predicament.

"I'm gonna hang out here for another ten, fifteen minutes. Then I'm driving south. I want your team to be dropped in by air, and out of sight by the time I get there. I need some answers that only I can get before you interfere — excuse me, interdict.

"If I remember correctly, the launch area is about three hundred yards long. I'll park at the furthest point, closest to the lake with only one way out. They'll confidently come to me, and hopefully you. Oh, I'm driving a dark blue Tundra, dragging a motorcycle trailer. My friends are in a jet black, late model Suburban that has no good written all over it."

"Donnelley, we owe him. Let's not screw this up," replied Jim. "D will do his part, make sure you do yours."

"Copy that," Donnelley said. "D, how will we know when to move in?"

"Good question. If and when I get the answers I need, I'll move to the back of trailer. You can take it from there. Hey, Donnelley, look for any strange motions on my part. I may need your assistance to get their undivided attention at some point. You've got fifty minutes, give or take, beginning now. Good luck." the call disconnected.

"D, it's Jim. Marshal Donnelley will be there. Between us, what questions do you want answered?"

"I want to know who's behind this, Standford or the Family. Better still if it's Joey, the ex-husband scorned."

"Then what?" Jim asked hesitantly.

"Then I'll know how fast and far I need to go or if I should stay and fight."

"D, if you stay and fight, we'd like you to remain in the program. I can help you more than you know. Remember the train wreck in Canada? You called for help, I sent the cavalry."

"I remember, thank you. I'll consider it. Thanks again for your help, Jim. Gotta go."

Chapter 56

Moving my truck from the fuel island, I parked in plain sight of the Suburban, before leisurely strolling into the adjoining Denny's and ordering the Grand Slam to go. Casually taking my time, I shopped in the store another ten minutes, buying John Grisham's Sycamore Row on tape before picking up my breakfast and traveling south.

Predictable, that's how I'd describe my escort… staying far enough back to keep me in view without causing me to rabbit. Stupid is as stupid does, I convinced myself. How could I rabbit in a truck pulling a trailer with an 800-lb. bike on it?

Fifty-five minutes since my conversation with Donnelley ended, I took the Ina exit to the right and drove straight to the boat launch ramp, a long mile off the interstate. Thankfully there were only three trucks with empty, boat trailers in the parking lot and no one loitering in plain sight. I honestly hoped they'd made it.

Pulling as close to the lake as possible, I parked the truck at a 45-degree angle, facing out and waited. It didn't take long. Three minutes later, the black Suburban slowly rolled into the parking lot, reconnoitering the surroundings, before moving in my direction and blocking my only exit. If they only knew … escaping is the furthest thing from my mind today. Live to fight another day is not an option. It ends here…questions are answered here… in some form or fashion.

I stepped from the truck and set my breakfast on the Tonneau cover. Looking over my left shoulder, I noticed subtle movement along a deeply overgrown fencerow, fifty yards away. Someone was taking up a defensive position, a good sign. Two hundred yards to the north and to the right of a shuttered public bathroom, I glimpsed a black-clad figure crouched to the right of the building. Another good sign. Off to my right, not 75 feet away, standing behind a bridge piling of the wooden pier jutting out into the water was a man with what looked like a .50 cal. Barrett M107 sniper rifle, pointed directly at me. A little unnerving, but I took comfort knowing someone with that much firepower in his hands had my back.

For the moment, however, if I was to get the answers I needed, this was my fight. Slipping into the truck from the passenger side as the Suburban continued its snail's pace approach, I unlocked the glove box, retrieved the Glock and clipped it onto my belt. Spreading out my Styrofoam encapsulated breakfast fare, I indulged, intensely watching the Suburban inch its way forward two hundred yards, then a hundred, then fifty, before stopping less than a hundred feet away. I acted completely indifferent, waving my hand in their direction, before turning my back to them and gazing at the sparkling waters of Rend Lake. How you gonna play this, D?

I heard multiple doors open and shut before turning to face four approaching individuals, only one of whom I recognized. Donnie had arrived with his entourage. He was sporting two black eyes, a distinct nose bandage and an aluminum neck brace. By the looks of things, he was not particularly happy to be here. Displaying the cause and effect of my helmet's impact with his face a week earlier, I was not too happy to be here either. I grimaced. "Damn that had to hurt! ... Bet he's one pissed-off son of a bitch!"

Guess I should stop them short. "Donnie, that you? Best you stop where you are until you tell me what you want. I almost didn't recognize you. Sorry about that number I did on your face."

The three other men stopped and looked straightaway at Donnie as he began to mumble a string of words in my direction, which for the life of me I couldn't understand at any distance.

"I'm sorry, I got nothing," I managed to say, holding out my hands palm side up.

The stocky, bald man next to Donnie spoke up, pointing his finger at Donnie's face. "His mouth is wired shut. Gotta be up close to understand him. Then it's still tough when he gets excited… kinda like he is now."

"If that's the case, Donnie, why don't you walk on over here? I'd like to talk to you and only you. Alone." Everyone looked perplexed, so I continued, "Don't worry, all my helmets are locked up in the back of the truck." That got a subdued chuckle out of three of them and momentarily diffused the tense atmosphere that enveloped us.

Donnie, hand signaling it was OK, motioned his enforcers to stand down while he walked the remaining seventy-five feet to me.

Mumbling through clenched teeth as he got within earshot, Donnie began halting, "D, you hard man to find. I owe you big time. Mr. Joseph sent me collect you."

Looking Donnie squarely in the face, "I know why you'd like to, but I'm struggling to see Joseph's angle."

"He say he promise Standford to bring you back." Donnie strained to get that thought out before shaking his head side to side, "I say Ms. Candice always been your biggest problem."

"Yep, I can see that. What did Joseph promise you to deliver me?"

Hanging his head, Donnie mumbled … "Half a mil."

"That's not enough, Donnie. Two, point five is what Standford offered for me, plus Candi split her take with him. Joseph is flush with cash already and that's without collecting on me."

"Follow orders," countered Donnie.

"What if I give you five times that to walk away… as in forever? That enticing?"

Donnie's tone deepened, attempting to sound tough, "You no position to bargain. You outnumbered… four to one."

I raised both hands in the air hoping the individual who had my back would get my not so subtle hint. Thankfully, he did. A blazing red circle appeared on Donnie's chest. "That's where you're wrong, sir. See that dot on your chest? It's coming from a .50 cal. Barrett currently aimed at your heart. I'd almost guarantee there's three more just like it aimed at each of your pals."

The color in Donnie's face faded to ashen white. "If I lower my hands and move quickly, they'll drop you where you stand. What will it be, Donnie? It's your call."

Defeated, Donnie strained to reply, "What you want?"

"I want you to buy me some time. Ten days, tops. Make the call. Tell Joseph you took me out, dumped my body in Rend Lake and were taken into custody by the Marshal Service as you left the scene. Tell him I was under their surveillance. They arrived too late. That will go a long way in making him believe you."

Shifting his weight from one foot to the other, Donnie weighed the consequences. Looking over his shoulder, he turned back to me and asked, "What about them? They gonna tell same story?"

"I believe I can get the Marshal's to hold all of you on something. None of you are lily white. Bet they can barter where everybody wins. I just need some time to sort out my current circumstances."

"I do this, can't go back," seethed Donnie.

"Welcome to my world. You're long overdue for a new career — a new life. I'll help you. I'll honor the amount I told you and then some."

"Why me?"

"Because, Candi says, deep down, you're good people. A little bad-ass maybe, but good. Been with the Family a long time, haven't you? The way I see it, Joseph has an innate way of bringing out the worst in all of us."

I continued, "I'm going to slowly lower my hands now. Don't make any sudden moves. Good boy. Now, I'm sure you've got a stash of cash somewhere?"

Donnie nodded yes.

"Use it to disappear somewhere far away. Remember Victoria? I'm going to give you her email address. When you've settled, email her and let her know how to contact you. I'll have a blind trust in place, transferring ten percent of the balance I promised you every year until it's gone. Who knows? It could last you at least twenty with the right investments. We have a deal?"

"Yep," relented Donnie. "Deal."

Chapter 57

Now, it was up to me to conclude this tense situation without blood-shed, mainly so I could get back on the road in one piece. "Come on, Donnie. Walk back with me to your guys. I'm going to ask them to lay face down on the ground. Think they'll do it if I ask nicely?"

"Nope. St. Louis boys dumb as rocks. No chance in hell." Donnie spouted, "Need convincing."

"I can do that." Pulling the Glock from the holster, I placed the barrel directly on Donnie's right temple. "Gentlemen, please un-holster your weapons and lay face down on the ground." Convinced of my sincerity they were not, each one looking to the other for the courage to take our rising altercation to the next level. That is until a barrage of .50 cal. rounds, echoing like thunder, blasted into the asphalt directly in front of their feet, sending projectiles of rock and tar flying into their faces.

That sure as hell worked well, I thought … Or did it? With guns drawn, they charged us. Big mistake. Before I could scream stop, muffled shots rang out in the distance — each one a kill shot, dropping these three unfortunate, misguided souls, mid stride. Turning to me, Donnie gave me the strangest look.

Stupid, how could they have been so dumb? "Thank you, gentlemen, for not listening to me," I shouted, watching a convergence of U.S. Marshal's appear from three directions. The first Marshal to reach me was the one who had my back. The man, who with a few well-placed rounds tried to prevent the carnage that was all too real from playing out before my eyes.

Extending his gloved hand, "D, I presume. I'm Marshal Donnelley. I warned them. I made the call. Didn't have a clear shot because of you and—"

"Donnie. I'm sorry I didn't introduce you. Donnie here is changing professions, beginning today."

Donnie grinned … kind of.

"What's wrong with his face? Why is he all bandaged up? Does he need medical attention? Can't he speak?" Donnelley fired off one question after another.

I laughed. "He can talk, just not too loud or clear. Had a motorcycle accident in Canada a little over a week ago. He'll be fine," I continued, slapping Donnie on the shoulder. "Donnie needs to disappear for the next ten days or so, Marshal Donnelley. After that, it's up to him where he goes. Right, Donnie? Can you help with making the short term and long term happen?"

"I can. You happen to get the answers you were looking for in time?"

"I think so, thanks to you. You're very persuasive with a .50 cal. and a laser sight, I'll give you that. Sure, would've stopped me in my tracks. Too bad it didn't stop them."

Donnelley chuckled somberly. "We aim to please. We serve at your pleasure or destruction. Just one call brings it all. I know. It's not the time to make jokes with three dead wise guys bleeding out fifty feet away. You tried to get them to stop. I tried to get them to stop. What was wrong with them?"

Donnie did his best to chime in, "Big balls, little brains."

Yep, that pretty much said it all. "Walk with me, Donnelley. Donnie, don't just stand there, you too." While the Marshals secured the scene, I explained in brief detail who Donnie was and what I needed him to do. He had a call to make to Joseph while we listened. Not that I didn't trust him, but I didn't.

Donnelley and I monitored his conversation on speaker, listening to him convey the message as best he could. "Package picked up. Damaged, no repair. Underwater … Call insurance. Five-O here. Later." Donnie pressed end and tossed me his phone.

"Wow, that's it? I'm impressed Donnie. No one implicated. You said a lot in a little. Yep, you've been doing this far too long."

Marshal Donnelley concurred, nodding his head.

Donnie smiled, "Not no more."

Assured the mess of our making would be cleaned up and Donnie was in good hands, I said my good-byes. As I was leaving, I called Jim on Donnie's phone. He answered on the first ring.

"Hey Jim, it's D. Party over. You sent a good man to assist. Left a mess to clean up though. Three wise guys in the dark… the fourth has seen the light.

"Would it have gone south for you if we hadn't intervened?"

"Yes, sir."

"Are you sure you don't want to stay in the program?"

"Yep … What I do know is, I'm no longer a threat…at least for the moment. Message was conveyed to Florida that I was history. If anything, it's bought me a few days."

"Might be able to buy you some more. I'll get with Donnelley and have him issue a press release to that effect. Unknown person in WITSEC was killed, along with three unknown assailants in an operation involving the U.S. Marshal Service. Will that work?"

"Yes, sir. Just reinforces what the Florida connections have been told. Later, thanks again."

Chapter 58

Cruising down I-57, I picked up I-24 east and prayed that it would take me to Nashville and home, unscathed. I called the kennel and asked them to verify Major's myriad of shots were current and to bathe him before I arrived.

Next, I called AMEX travel and asked them to email me daily flight information to, two specific cities out of Tampa or Orlando. And finally, I called Brinks Security out of Nashville and scheduled them to be at my house at 6 p.m. to pick up ten 110 lb. crates to be stored in a secure vault in Nashville until I, or my designated representative sent for them.

I wanted to call Giovanni and bounce my plan off him. I wanted to call Vic and tell her about this morning. I wanted to call Candi and let her know I was safe. So much for my wants, I didn't do either, knowing someone could still be monitoring the airwaves, even if I was using Donnie's phone.

The big blue sign "Welcome to Tennessee" greeted me at the 2 p.m. mark. I passed through Clarksville, home of the 101st Airborne, on my way to Nashville, home of the Grand Ole Opry, Bruton Snuff and Yazoo Beer. Ah, to be home again.

It was a sobering thought since I was only passing through. Where will I go next? Will I find Mayberry? Will I have Candi or even Victoria to share it with? Question after question consumed me all the way to the Music City, before I merged onto I-40 east and headed down the home stretch. The good news is, it won't be long before Major is riding shotgun again.

I had an epiphany an hour out. Marcy, Candi's childhood friend, was my clandestine ticket to Candi. If I can find her, she can get a message to Candi for me easy enough. Next stop, Kroger's in Cookeville. Sixty minutes later, I found myself in line at the pharmacy drive thru.

When it was my turn, I pulled up and asked for the pharmacist on duty. Turns out it was not Marcy, but Bruce. "Where's Marcy?"

"You just missed her. Can I help you?" asked Bruce.

"No, sir," I replied. "It's personal. She's a friend. Wanted to thank her for taking care of the dog while I was gone."

"Oh, in that case, you'd better hurry. I saw her leave a few minutes ago. She's probably walking to her car."

"Thanks, Bruce." Waving good-bye, I rounded the corner of the store in time to see Marcy entering her black, Dodge Charger, parked on the far outskirts of the lot. Reaching her location as her back up lights came on, I blocked her in with my truck and locked down on the horn.

That got her attention! Marcy slammed on her brakes, put her car in park and jumped out, shaking her finger at me. "Excuse me! Excuse me! I almost hit you. Can't you see I'm trying to leave? Move your truck — now!"

I rolled the passenger window down shouting back, "No way! I like parking here just fine." Ah, the whites of a brunette's eyes when they're steaming mad…a contrast made in Heaven. "How dare you treat my dog that way without my permission? Candi put you up to it?"

"I … uh … don't know what you're talking about. Wait … wait … D, that you lurking behind those god-awful molester glasses?"

"In the flesh. Wait … molester glasses? Candi is the only other person who's ever called them that. Damn, you girls are tight."

She laughed. "Aren't we though? If you only knew how much I know about you! What are you doing here? Did you reach Giovanni? Did you speak to Candi? Do they know you're back in Tennessee?"

"Hold on, girl, one question at a time. Yes, I've spoken to them numerous times thanks to you. Good detective work on your part to find the dog."

"Thanks," Marcy, standing a little straighter, beamed. "Don't mention it. Took me all of two hours. You do know I'm flying to Tampa next Thursday?"

"I do now. Bet that will make Candi happy. Now, about why I'm here. Need a big favor. Email Candi. Do not call her. I repeat, do not call. Tell her I need to talk to her and Giovanni. Tell her I'm OK and not to believe anything she hears, unless it's from me. As far as Florida knows, I'm history, kaput, wasted. And I need to stay that way... understand? She is not to tell anyone I'm alive. Trust me ... it's better you don't know any more than this.

"Next, please ask her to go buy two burner phones and give one to Giovanni, then email you their numbers. I'm sorry to lay this all on you, but I have no one else I can trust who cares for Candi as much as me. What's your email address, by the way?"

She looked perplexed, hesitating for the longest time, before writing it down on the pad I just so happened to have in my hand. "D, how much trouble you in?"

"Quite a bit," I chuckled. "The good news is I've been in some kind of trouble ever since I met your BFF, starting with the day she tried to take me out in the Starbuck's drive thru. Come to think of it she was on the way to hook up with you."

"I heard about that... Lucky you."

"Among other things. I'm sure you've heard extensively about the other things."

"It's those snarky bedroom, brown eyes of yours. I told her you were a troublemaker the moment I laid eyes on you." She snickered.

"Thank you ... Trouble, ah yes, that's me. Not that the menacing Woo-Hoo of hers, isn't?"

Blushing, Marcy continued, "Nope, from all that she's shared, you've successfully managed to corral that thing of hers." Her eyes drifted back towards my trailer, "Guess that's the infamous motorcycle you made history on through the cornfields of Iowa and the mountains of Wyoming?"

"It is," I beamed proudly. "Want to see the scars and the toy that started it all? I've got it here somewhere. Might give you some inspiration with your significant other."

"Ha! Not hardly. You got balls, D, I give you that — big balls. Anyone that would even attempt the indescribable things you've already done with her has to have gonads this big," Marcy said, holding up both hands, resembling the size of grape fruits. "I'd nominate you as salesman of the year … excuse me, seducer of the year."

"Hey, I resemble that remark!" *Come to think of it, I resemble many of these off the cuff remarks here lately.*

"I've heard that, too. Candice…Candi as you call her… is an open book when it comes to you. With you she's fallen in love with the lake and the mountains you call home. She's enamored by your random acts of kindness with people you don't even know. You've shared your heart, your mind, your soul with her. You've brought joy back into her life that I haven't seen since we were kids. By now, surely you know you've changed her for the better. Whatever happens next in your journey with her, remember that."

"Enough, Marcy! I'm flattered with the flowers, but it's been a two-way street. Candi has given me equally as much, if not more. She's smart, witty and intuitive. It's either black or white with her, there are no shades of grey. I shouldn't say this to you, but I will. When she makes love to me, she gives me 110% of everything. She embraces the moment…"

"I got it. I got it. You're right … Candi has said the same about you. I don't know all that happened in Canada, she's been rather vague about the goings on since she returned. But, whatever it was from all that I've gleaned from our long conversations of late, it was to protect you from the carnage she brought into your life."

"I hope you're right, Marcy. Only time will tell. I've got to go, Major is waiting. Don't forget, I'm history… two burner phones, two numbers by email only. I'll email you with the subject line Dale Hollow Lake Lover."

"I'll send it when I get home. Good to see you, D. Good luck. Sounds like you're going to need it."

Chapter 59

And with that, I was off. Driving to the kennel, not twenty minutes out, I realized the big pink elephant in the room was back. If Marcy was right, at least from her perspective, and this was all about protecting me, I had to hear it from Candi's lips ... straight from her heart. The when and the where... well, that was yet to be determined.

Anxiously waiting in the lobby with a kennel assistant in tow was my fluffy pal, washed, brushed and wagging his tail to no end when I came through the sliding glass doors. Patting my chest with both hands, Major leapt the ten feet separating us in one stride, snapping the leash in two before placing his paws on my shoulders and waiting for a long overdue hug. "I've missed you, pal. More than you know." Go figure, I got teary-eyed. Dogs, especially this one, are truly man's best friend. Major's hug today, was no different than the last one he gave me when I left him stranded here, a little over a month ago. Dogs show no anger, no malice, no indifference to us, only love, no matter how royally we screw up.

"Major, let's go. You and me, we're going to find this elusive Mayberry." Opening the passenger door, Major jumped in, immediately claiming his favorite seat behind the steering wheel. After settling up with the kennel, I was handed a basket of his remaining goodies, compliments of Marcy. Note to self. ...Thank Marcy again on behalf of Major... and me. I owe her big time.

My drive to the lake for possibly the last time was serene, as well as surreal. The beauty that I'd come to appreciate surrounding Dale Hollow Lake could never be duplicated. The lush green rolling meadows and fields were salt and peppered with Holsteins and Black Angus cattle as far as the eye could see.

Beyond them, stood the mountains casting hues of orange, yellow and red in the towering maples, ash and poplar that filled them. Then there's Dale Hollow Lake. Unspoiled shorelines, crystal clear water, pristine springs and its undisturbed mountains made this place I'd been fortunate to call home for the last five years, above all things, priceless.

My last time on the lake with Candi, no less, I took her to one of my special places along the Accordion Bluffs. That day, we wined and dined at sunset, watching the ice blue skies above us turn into a moon drenched night, complimented by thousands and thousands of stars.

Talking about getting in the mood for love — it spontaneously happens here, for free. And we did get in the mood, as I recall, beautifully... even sharing a little too much of ourselves with two others who happened to get in our way. I laughed out loud over the memory of the skinny-dipping incident. We'd made precious memories that would last a lifetime. I sighed, Candi, baby, I wish you were here.

I loved this area. Even the locals that I'd come to know and love were genuine and neighborly in every sense of the word. Every holiday was a time of celebration, filled with food, laughter, and hours upon hours of fellowship. Shared gourmet dinners over a bottle or two of wine with my neighbors at least twice a month kept us informed of the goings on in the community, in this place we were blessed to claim as our own.

My heart ached, my stomach churned, and my hands trembled, as I envisioned ripping out the established roots of my heart and soul I had anchored here to replant in another town I'd only dreamt of, thus far.

Chapter 60

Change happens… life happens… whether we want it to or not. Sometimes, it's not pretty. Sometimes it's downright, gut-wrenchingly sad. Oft times, if you're lucky, it's subtle… raising neither ripple nor flag. Regardless of the hand being dealt, to survive change we must embrace it and make the most of it or die. Sadly, in this world of instant gratification we live in… there is no other option.

I was directed through the gates with a familiar wave from Ron, the daytime security guard. "Welcome back!" announced Ron. "We've missed you. You been on a long trip?"

"Yes sir. Leaving again, soon. I've got Brinks coming at six. Kindly wave them through and give them directions to the house, along with the code to my gate."

"Will do, sir. And again, welcome back."

Coasting down my long and winding drive to the house was bittersweet… the only description I could muster right now, knowing this mountain retreat would no longer be mine. On a brighter note, if I could find one, Vic could transfer the title to my sons easy enough. My desire would be for them to accept it, appreciate it and find in it a lingering piece of me. In that I found some degree of solace, but only in that, nothing more.

My do over life began here, the geography, compliments of the U.S. Government and WITSEC. Thankfully, I was able to resurrect myself, designing and building custom homes and escapes for the well to do people who could afford the quality I spent my entire adult life creating. When I found this property, between projects, I would lie on the rocks at night and listen to the waterfalls directing me on how and where to build. In my sleep, I dreamed this house, this setting into existence. Building this home, suspended on the bluffs over the waterfalls was a major undertaking and not without risks. But, we did it. I designed it, my crews and I built it, hoping one day my sons would come here and let their children, when they have children, grow up with me. Second chances are not guaranteed. *You're dreaming again, D... in another life, maybe.*

Releasing Major from the confines of the truck, he went straight to the waterfalls for a refreshing cool drink of water while I went inside and unlocked the walk-in safe. By way of a two-wheeled cart, I handily moved the ten nondescript crates to the driveway, before returning two of them to the safe; for the boys, if and when they come. Vic, after the transfer has been completed, will provide my sons the six-digit pin to access their inheritance. Until then, it remained securely locked away.

Loading enough fresh clothes in my truck to get by, I took one last look around the house and got teary-eyed again before sitting down at the farm table and writing a gut-wrenching letter to my kids:

> *This road of life you are now on has been filled with many twists and turns. You have experienced the highest of highs and the lowest of lows throughout your marvelous journey thus far. You have ventured far beyond the shore, more times than not, successfully. You've been blessed to experience firsthand, the world, its people, its values, its successes and its failures.*
>
> *You have been blessed with the fondest of memories that warm your heart and soul, memories that reflect the happiest of times through the carefree eyes of a child. Unfortunately, too are memo-*

ries that you see not as grand, for as you've grown, carefree gives way to the world you now see as a man.

You have succeeded beyond measure in many things. You may have come up short in just a few. You continually made those proud who love you. Take a deep breath, pat yourself on the back, take just a moment to glow and be thankful for the little things that make you who you are.

You have discovered through personal relationships what it means to love and be loved. You have unfortunately experienced with this love, both heartbreak and the sorrow of loss. You have relished in the opportunities to give with abandon and learned, ever so humbly, what is expected of you through the gracious art of receiving.

You have come to see that change, no matter how large or small, is inevitable, whether you like it or not. How you choose to accept it will forever define you and your happiness throughout your life. Living in the past may be the ideal, but living in the moment is reality and that my son is life.

No matter what you may wish would not have happened, when people and emotions are involved, unless you have walked long days in their shoes, their lives are not yours to judge. We all seek to be happy and we flee from rejection and pain. As you age, wisdom will follow and you'll come to understand that true lasting happiness begins and ends within.

You have been taught from where your strength comes, where forgiveness begins and where joy abounds. You have been given through God's grace, the wisdom to know you are precious in the eyes of the One who made you and can take comfort in the knowledge that He always has your back. If you will always call on Him for the little things, you will find in life through Him, there are no big things.

You live in a world that is constantly in motion. Stopping the world to get off, when things don't go your way is not a luxury you will ever be privy too. The ebbs and flows of life remain in constant flux. Move with them, embrace them and you will always find your steps firm and your path made exceedingly clear.

With you, each new day creates an opportunity to reflect not on the "what ifs" of yesterday, but to embrace and cherish the moments of today; to believe in the hope that tomorrow will bring a brighter day. Second chances, too, will come your way, but it's best to seize this time, this place, this second and do what's right today.

You are the future. In you there is hope. You are my children. Whether we live together or apart, my heart and my prayers go with you each and every day. I long to grow old with you in my life. You fill me with joy as I watch your dreams come true.

My wish for you today is to remember where you came from and the values you were taught. In you I have given my all, in spite of what you may think, so that you may have all the tools necessary to succeed in this life and the knowledge and wisdom to discard the rest.

Finally, I pray you will look beyond my shortcomings and forgive where forgiveness is due. I'm not perfect, as you well know; nor will I ever be. I ask for you to cherish the good in me that makes me who I am and look beyond that which disappoints you, that you may find in me, not just a parent but also a friend.

I signed and dated it. Stuffing it into an envelope, I addressed it to all of them and left it on the table. I closed the door, knowing in my gut I may never be back. I was sitting on the teakwood bench near the waterfalls with Major beside me at twenty minutes shy of six o'clock when the Brinks truck arrived. I signed the necessary paperwork while the men were loading the crates and watched them drive away.

Now it was my turn. Loading Major in the truck, I said goodbye one last time to the dreams I'd realized here and to the fond memories I'd made… the best of them being those I'd made with Candi. With her, I could make new ones, better ones, shared ones. … Maybe, just maybe.

Chapter 61

Driving south on Highway 111 across the mountains, bathed in the beginning colors of fall, towards Chattanooga, and all points south, I reflected on happier times. One, in particular, brought back fond memories of a time not that long ago.

I was balls-to-the-wall, flying south in the M3 for my second romantic interlude with Candi. I'd swept her off her feet after work one sunny, weekday afternoon. We traversed the winding roads, commando, to Cloudland Canyon, before arriving at a Civil War-era B&B, where we made love for the very first time. It was incredible how much pleasure she brought me. We were entwined for hours on end in that oh-so-brief overnight rendezvous. During what was to be the first of our many nights together, I rediscovered the child in me who could never get enough of a good thing and was always longing for more.

Candi was refreshing, relishing each moment we spent together, even if it was just by phone. Sure, it was the newness of us, the mystique of me, the innocence of her that made each waking moment we spent together pleasurable… but, it was worth it … so worth it. You are one sick puppy, D. What did Jim say? Something like, 'the flavor of the day.'

Yes, I could have stopped and called Victoria when I passed through Atlanta some thirty minutes earlier. And say what? 'Hi Vic, I'm passing through Atlanta on my way to find Candi and thought of you.' That would go

over like a lead balloon. Vic's safe with her cousin and the big gun dude —
safer still with no phone contact with me ... for now.

Approaching 11 p.m. with lightning strikes dancing across the moon-
less sky, I made it as far as Jonesboro, GA, before calling it a day. Stopping
at another pet friendly, Holiday Inn Express, Major and I made three trips
around the parking lot, checked in at the front desk and crashed.

* * *

Waking sometime after five, I found Major snuggled on the couch. Candi
would blow a gasket if she were here. I wish she were ... Major, I'm sure would
agree.

Dressing in shorts and a tee, I walked, watered and fed the dog, before
tackling the Elliptical. Thirty minutes later, sweating profusely, I stopped
by the breakfast area and tossed together two eggs, bacon and syrup between
two pancakes. Yuck! I used to like this combination of sweet and salty. Not
anymore. I choked down a second bite, then spit it out, before tossing the
rest of my creation in the trash. Green and black tea it will be, I mused, riding the elevator to the room, my stomach churning on empty.

Major greeted me from the couch, his tail furiously slapping the cush-
ions, expecting the worst, but hoping for the best. I didn't care, not anymore.
Candi wasn't here to scold him and I no longer had the heart.

Showered, dressed and packed, that was a stretch since I was still living
out of my daypack, I wrestled with Major all the way to the truck, before
returning to the business center and setting up an alias email address on my
Yahoo account.

Retrieving Marcy's email address, I fired off an email with "Dale Hollow Lake Lover" in the subject line and waited ... and waited ... and waited.
Surely, she hasn't gone to work this early? It's only 6:30 ... here. Dumb
ass, she's on central time. It's 5:30 there; she's still asleep. I'll give her an
hour and log in again. My stomach growled, then roared with hunger pangs.

"Cracker Barrel, where are you?" I asked to an empty room. "Your country boy breakfast is calling my name."

Fifteen minutes later, compliments of my well-traveled GPS, I was feasting on country ham… a piece the size of a dinner plate… three fried eggs, homemade buttermilk biscuits smothered in sawmill gravy and fresh fruit… no grits. I have to have at least one healthy side, geez! My hunger abated, I felt a nap coming on. God forbid, I ordered black coffee to go. Yuk! I enhanced it to make it palatable… two Stevia packets and four little tubs of half and half. There was a time, many moons ago, when I drank four, twenty-ounce mugs of black coffee a day. I even ground my own beans… Blue Mountain Coffee from Jamaica. But, once I quit smoking and changed to black and green tea, I never went back. Now, I remember why.

That was a twenty well spent, including a small bag of beef flavored treats for the dog. I arrived at the Holiday Inn at 6:45 a.m., Marcy time, hoping her email would be there. I logged in … it was. "Yippie-ki-yay!" I screamed, "We're smokin' now!" Her email was a forward from Candi, listing two numbers…one for her, the other for Giovanni. A short message to me followed:

D, I knew you were safe. I knew it. Stay that way for me, for Major. Call when you can, the sooner the better. I need to hear your voice. Baby … I miss you … XOXO

I hopped, skipped and jumped through the hotel… acting like a twelve-year-old boy who'd just experienced his first kiss from the prettiest girl in his class. Progress D, you're making progress. Thankfully, I was in the Tundra pulling a bike and not in the M3. The police protection all the way through South Georgia was inebriating. I lost count, somewhere after thirty, of the Troopers intent on slowing down the northerners who couldn't wait to put their toes in the soothing Florida sand. I had to admit, I couldn't wait to get to Florida either and dip my … in something much more satiating than sand. I panted, Major too, but then, I was vigorously rubbing his belly.

Somewhere south of Valdosta, I dialed Gio's number, compliments of Marcy … and Candi. Three rings, then four…

"Ciao, D. Is you?"

"Ciao, Giovanni. How are you, sir? Mile? Candi?"

"Heard bad things ... not true. Happy! Mile happy, Candi happy!"

"That makes four of us. I'm going to take you up on your offer. The Benefit next Saturday, I'll be there."

"Not so good idea, you dead ... then you be alive. Everybody know."

"I have a plan. Will need you to work with me to pull it off. You in?"

"I in ... Mile in, too."

"That's what I wanted to hear. Do you think you and Mile can steal away for a few days, say Monday to Thursday and persuade Candi to come along with you?"

"You have plan, I try. ... No, D, I do."

"Excellent. You ready to ride, broken leg and all?"

"Hmm ... Cast — no can do. Not, how you say, possible."

"Is possible ... You can ride a trike."

"Yes, but no trike here."

"There is in Daytona, home of Bike Week and Biketoberfest, two hours east. I've reserved two bikes for the week, one Road King Trike for you and a Sportster for Mile. Tell Candi she can ride with you. That is until you get here. Then she can ride with me. I want to surprise her."

"You surprise me ... You surprise her," Gio exclaimed.

"Walking on the beach ... that's how I want to surprise her ... excuse me ... that's how Major and I want to surprise her ... On the beach at sunset."

"Good ... you bring dog? How ... he ride?"

"I'm working on that. May need to kennel him again. Damn, I hate the thought—"

"He too, D. May–jore ... yes?"

"Yes, it's Major. Gio, I have two whole days of solitude to pull this plan together. Make it happen for me, for us. I'll find us two rooms near the Boardwalk that has covered parking and allows pets. You want anything special?"

"Beer for me, spa for Mile ... stairs no."

"Copy that. Tell Candi you talked to me and all is well. Will call soon. You run into a problem, call me and leave a message. Thanks, Gio. Means a lot to know you're with me on this. I owe you."

"No ... owe you. Never ride trike. ... Will now. Ciao."

Chapter 62

Just north of the Florida line, I stopped for fuel, to walk the dog and reprogram the GPS to Daytona Beach, rather than Tampa. Routing east on I-10, around Lake City, Florida, moved me out of heavy traffic and onto open roads to Jacksonville. I had calls to make, people to talk to, and schemes to create in my head. Distracted driving… Damn Yankee's… I did not need distracting me when I could do it well enough on my own.

With SIRI's assistance, I found a hotel not far from the Boardwalk, the Plaza Resort and Spa, which adequately met my requirements, as well as Giovanni's and the dog's. Three males making the rules for a change, at least until the women got there. Then it's back to damn you, Woo-hoo, damn you!

My next call was to Keith, a retired Air Force Captain who I had not talked to in at least eight years. He had the connections to find a direct line to another cohort of ours, a man who by all accounts should be a Full Bird Colonel by now. Giving Keith as little Intel as possible, I convinced him rather quickly of the urgency and left him in the process of making it happen.

My third set of calls was to locate Nancy, a family friend of my mom's, who happened to live in Port Orange, Florida, next door to my mom and dad at least fifteen years ago. I wanted to share good times with her again. At least I did until I found her brother who sadly broke the news that Nancy had passed two years before. Damn it … this dropping off the face of the

Earth sucks. My life, as I knew it ... stopped. If my plans worked out, this living in the shadows would finally come to an end.

Turning south onto I-95, the Damn Yankee traffic resumed and interrupted my endless string of calls all the way to Daytona. Taking the speedway exit to the world's most famous beach, I passed NASCAR's oldest track, the Daytona 500 on my right bringing back fond memories of another time, another life. There was a time when I worked hard and played harder... a time when the fruits of my labor meant something to me and everyone else. What I wouldn't pay to roll back the clock ten years, even fifteen. You're dreaming again, D. Live life forward, it's the only choice you've got.

Major and I were warmly welcomed into the Plaza Hotel where the pleasure of his company cost me an extra hundred bucks. I patted him on the head. "You're worth ten times that," I announced, "no sleeping on the couch." Zora, the foreign exchange student desk clerk gave me a frown. "What? It's better than me telling him not to pee on the furniture. Geez! Besides, that's what the hundred dollars is for, so he can have a choice. Smile girl, he is."

In spite of my banter with Zora, I was fortunate to secure two oceanfront rooms on the fifth floor, no stairs. Giovanni would be pleased. Our room, overlooking the white sandy beaches and beautiful Atlantic Ocean was furnished with a rather inviting king-size bed, an overflowing mini-bar and an oversized three cushion wide couch that had Major's name written all over it. "We can suffer through this, huh pal?" I asked my tail wagging companion with the yellowed Wilson Tennis Ball stuck in his mouth. Playtime, Daytona Beach, here we come. On a leash, dodging cars and trucks and children, lots and lots of children, this part of the beach was not dog friendly. My bad. "Come on Major, let's go find a place on this beach that is."

I traveled down Highway A1A, through South Daytona to Daytona Beach Shores. Fewer people, fewer kids, fewer cars to interfere with a dog on a mission, retrieving tennis balls tossed into the pounding surf. Twenty minutes of fetch behind us, I settled into a lounging beach chair, courtesy of the Pirate's Cove Hotel. "Major, I met a beautiful girl on this beach the summer I returned from active duty. Wonder what happened to her? Later on, I watched my son's grow up playing on this beach. See that parking lot behind us. I remember rocking and rolling with their mom in a customized Ford Leisure Van until 2 a.m. one morning. The only privacy we could find on a moments' notice with two rooms packed with kids. Memories, precious memories of a simpler time. You worked, you played, you thrived ... for your kids, family, friends and employees. Where are they now, pal?"

Life happens ... children grow up, careers expand...businesses flourish ... until they don't. Much like the waves crashing before me, our lives continuously ebb and flow comfortably until external forces appear as subtle as high tide or as devastating as a Category 5 hurricane. My life has become the latter, leaving in its wake, devastation where once there was continuity and harmony. Second chances, though few and far between, do not guarantee us the opportunity to erase and re-record. I wish they did. Our lives reflect the decisions we make, followed by their outcomes, be they good or bad. We hope and pray for redemption and restoration, and try as we might, it's not always possible. I got it. Doesn't mean it hurts any less, knowing what was may never be again. Or can it?

I am determined to remake me, better than before, scars and all. Within me lies a strong foundation, built with sinew and blood, refined with countless beads of sweat and cleansed with a lifetime supply of tears.

My phone vibrated ... then rang.

"Jon David, Richard Little here. Keith called and said you were looking for me in a bad way. How can I help you, Captain?"

"Thanks for calling me on such short notice. Captain, I'm not. That was another lifetime ago. And you, what about you, Rich?"

"The powers that be, moved me upstairs. Would you believe I'm a one star?"

"Congrats, General Little. Has a nice ring to it, doesn't it? Rumor has it... you're running Special Ops out of Hurlburt Field, near Destin. Is that still the case? If so, I'm looking for a ballsy helo pilot to perform an off-book extraction next Saturday night in Tampa. You think you could round one up?"

"Hell, son, you're talking to the best. Remember that time in Iraq, back in '90? Of course, you do ... I'll do it. Just tell me where and when, I'll be there. They don't let me out much. It would be an honor and a privilege. You gonna need support? I can bring along a team, off-book of course. Guys out of your old unit, come to think of it."

"I don't think that will be necessary. Let me digest it a little more. I'll let you know."

Over the next fifteen minutes, I pitched him my proposed plan, less the personal details and gave him my AMEX to reserve the helo of his choice. All that he asked me to do was confirm next Friday and advise if it would be a 'hot LZ.' How the hell would I know if it was going to be a hot landing zone? Come to think of it, if it involves Candice Parker, I'd best say yes without a second thought. I chuckled, if Rich only knew ... the infamous power of her Woo-hoo and its effect on the questionable men in her life ... me included.

Feeling some sense of relief in my quest, the clouds of regret, along with the few rays of sunshine I'd subjected Major to over the last hour, turned to hunger pangs again. Imagine that, I'd failed to eat lunch or dinner. I could still make the last one. Across the causeway, Aunt Catfish on the River beckoned. Memories, too, were made there, good ones, fond ones, and drunken ones over the last twenty plus years. Of course, it helped for fifteen of those years my parents lived less than three blocks away. To my chagrin, Major took the lead, jumping into the front seat, scattering white sand across the console, the dash and me. Yep, only in Florida am I privileged to spit sand granules out of my mouth with frequency.

Dining on the Admiral's Platter... my favorite from times past... was more fare than I recalled. One thing for sure that had decreased with the grey, my appetite for fine food. Thankfully, my unquenchable thirst for fine women had only been enhanced with age. Major, not to be denied, has benefited rather handsomely from both, Candi included.

Chapter 63

My, how Daytona has grown, I reflected quietly, as Major, his head buried in my leftovers, and I stayed on Highway 1 to the hotel. What once was a snowbird winter haven has become a year-round, white and blued haired paradise, sprinkled with NASCAR fans, teenagers and leather clad bikers, depending on the month and the season. I wonder what year the majority of white hairs had an epiphany to acknowledge, 'we're too old to go back and forth, from now on we're staying?' Mayberry, it's not.

Sitting on the balcony of our room, inhaling the salty, eighty-degree air blowing west off the ocean, Major and I watched the sun's rays give way to the twinkling lights of fishing boats and ships peppered across the horizon. Two distinct plans in the making deserved an equal amount of attention, beginning with Candi and our surprise Monday night reunion, followed by the Saturday night benefit ball extravaganza.

Because I needed Gio's assistance in making the latter a reality, I focused on Monday. That was all Major, all me. Flowers, I wanted to shower her in flowers and envelope her in live music, Sinatra to be exact. Over the next hour, I researched, planned and plotted my way into, out of and through our romantic rendezvous on the beach, weather permitting, of course. "Enough," I announced to the dog, "I can't do any more tonight. Come inside pal, it's time we slept."

*****

The sun's rays broke through the sliding glass doors a few minutes after five, gloriously welcoming the day, before I closed the curtains and crawled back into bed. Some days, it doesn't pay to get up, too early. This so happened to be one of them. I fell back asleep and dreamed the strangest dream.

Candi was an Egyptian Princess and I was a commoner. I roused her from sleep this particular night and was making mad passionate love to her on an outdoor marble terrace when my phone's alarm went off waking the entire kingdom. Two palace guards captured me, the king confronted me, demanding not my head, but my uh-um, since I could do unspeakable things to her that he no longer could. Startled, I awoke with a woody that for the life of me would not go away. Rather than take matters into my own hands, I turned on the news. Yep, that works every time.

I made a black and green in the lobby and took Major on a three-mile trek up the beach towards Ormond. It, too, had changed. Mom and pop establishments that dotted the shoreline years ago had given way to massive hurricane resistant condominiums, rising perilously into the sky. Progress, what I was experiencing was progress here in Daytona made at the expense of few for the pleasure of many. Cha-ching, cha-ching, cha-ching. Tax dollars, rental dollars, disposable income dollars were flooding into this area in search of the American dream, aka, a twenty percent ROI (return on investment). Status quo was no longer an option here. Bigger, taller, better, more. Mayberry, where are you? You're looking sweeter and sweeter by the moment.

Sitting at the Plaza's outdoor bar with a Bloody Mary in hand, watching Major watch the tan lined fillies in their skimpy two-piece bikinis, I did the next best thing, I called Candi. Four rings later ... she blasted me, "D, don't you ever do this to me again, ever," before I even had a change to say hello. "Do you know how many times I've looked at this phone, hoping you would call, begging for you to call, waiting for you to call? Too many ... way too many times. — Don't do this to me again."

"Hello… to you too ... baby."

"Where are you?"

"In hiding, Candi. There's some mean people with an attitude who've been looking for me. At least they were until they found me ... kinda."

"I heard ... Fortunately, Marcy enlightened me before the news of your possible demise crossed the wires. Jim put that out?"

"It was his idea ... to buy me some time."

"D, I brought all this on you. You realize that? I wouldn't blame you if you never wanted to see me again."

"Candi, it was going to happen sooner or later. I won't lie to you. You may've helped speed the process along. You're healthier because of it, aren't you? Financially, I mean"

"Yes, I guess so. I'd trade it all to have things back the way they were on the lake."

"That's a good thought. But, it's not going to happen. Sadly, WITSEC advised I relocate. Still trying to decide where."

"D, I'm terribly sorry. I've robbed you of your present dreams, your new life and Dale Hollow Lake most of all."

"I'll make better ones. Remember someone wise once said, 'Life is not the destination, but the ride.' There's still plenty of ride left in me."

"I'm sure you will, D ... Speaking of ride, would you believe Giovanni, cast and all, wants to go to Daytona Beach tomorrow, rent a trike and a bike and ride for a few days. He wants me to go and ride behind him. Mile will ride her own. I don't want to. It's not going to be the same without you."

"Candi, I'd go for it. What's keeping you there?"

"For one thing, Marcy is coming the end of the week and then there's Joseph. That's another story in itself."

"I would go. It will do you good to get away, feel the wind in your hair, your face…"

"Stop! ... D. I miss you. I'll do it. At least when I'm riding, it will remind me of you…of us."

"That's the spirit, Candi. Tell Gio to take care of you. Oh, and watch out for moose. Bye, baby."

"Wait, D… don't go. When will I hear from you?"

"I'll be in touch."

I hung up and immediately dialed Giovanni. He answered on two rings… impressive.

"Gio, D. Candi nearby?"

"Ciao … D. No. Not here. She say she … not"

"Go … I changed her mind. She's going. I have rooms reserved at the Plaza in Daytona. I'll text you where to meet up with me tomorrow at six. Want to surprise Candi on the ocean. We'll pick the bikes up Tuesday. Too much hassle dealing with it tomorrow. Bring your gear."

"Tomorrow, D. Happy. … Ride again."

"Tomorrow, Gio. Ciao."

Chapter 64

Long into my second Bloody Mary, I remembered how much I enjoyed it when a plan finally comes together. I was cautiously optimistic that Major and I, with enough creativity and cash, could make tomorrow night one for the ages. My to do list was growing, shrinking, evolving moment by moment, as I flipped from one location to another before settling on the spot where I found myself yesterday.

The beach at Pirate's Cove was significantly less crowded than here. Besides, I heard Aunt Catfish calling me back for seconds. This time she told me to bring friends.

Major cajoled me to the boardwalk where he sniffed and smelled every signpost, fire hydrant and bench leg within a two-mile radius. After that early afternoon fiasco, I ordered in. He munched on lamb and rice with a side of green beans, while I snacked on fish and chips, sipped on Smart Water and for good measure, chased it with my last Sam. Sleep came quickly.

Thanks to a cold, wet nose nuzzling my face, C-Day was here, beginning at 5:05, long before the rooster crowed, even longer before the sun peaked its head above the far horizon. Major and I trudged south along the surf until the darkness gave way to blue sky. "It's Candi Day, Major!" I shouted. "I can't wait."

But ... wait I did until 8 a.m. for the local shops to open. Five gallons of fresh pink and red rose petals was not that absurd to the second florist on my list, thanks to the three hundred dollars I offered to make my request come true. Securing the fab '50s band, now that was a little tougher, but nothing that five large wouldn't cure. The crooner soloist and their illustrious leader cost equally as much. Sinatra impersonators must be in high demand round here. All I've got to say is for what he's charging me he'd better sound like Frank, look like Dean and move like Sammy Davis Jr.

Thankfully, the bakery had the brownies at the ready for less than ten bucks a dozen. Finally, something cheap ... excuse me affordable. After much searching, PetSmart had the twin 'milk' bottle carrying backpack for Major to wear since alcohol and glass were prohibited on the beach. I was missing something. Surely it would come to me during my last two stops in an otherwise, uneventful day.

I texted Giovanni:

Pirate's Cove, 3000-block, Hwy. A1A, 6 PM. Don't be late! Send Candi straight through lobby to beach. Thx

I paid in advance for the cycle rentals at the largest Harley Davidson store on earth and secured a place to store our vehicles. I took immediate advantage, unloading my bike and dropping the trailer in the secure lot. Which reminded me, I needed a long-distance shipper. Thanks to the guys at HD, I found one out of Ft. Myers. My last stop was the airport, where I brought two open-ended first-class tickets out of Southwest Florida International — plus one pampered dog seat — to an island in country, as well as to one north of the border.

By 3 p.m. I was finished and it was back to the Plaza and their business center where I booked two rooms in two different locations for the next three days, beginning tomorrow. The route I'd chosen took us up Highway A1A to Jacksonville, before heading northeast to Savannah, Georgia. The D.O.G. would have to stay behind. Historic B&Bs are not pet friendly. The beach condos weren't either, no matter what I was willing to pay. It didn't matter ... the Plaza has a critically acclaimed kennel on-site and that's where Major would reside while I was gone.

Probably for the best, I thought. He was going to have to ride behind Gio anyway. By my logic, Gio was a wreck waiting to happen in his thigh to ankle cast. One accident behind us was one too many already. I wish no ill will on anyone. Oops, that's not entirely true. Joseph is another story in his twisted, distorted self.

Slinging my daypack over my shoulder it was time. "Come on Major, let's do this. It's Candi day." An hour before show time, I arrived to find a fairly deserted beach. Beginning just to the right of the stairs leading across the beach at Pirate's Cove, I scattered rose petals two feet wide across ankle deep sand for the next fifty yards. At the end I made my heart, a big one, almost six feet in diameter with a dozen brownies in its center. To the left I made a smiley face using red solo cups turned upside down for the eyes and mouth and a 32-oz. bottle of Smart Water planted upright, three feet away in the sand ... representing ... well ... ME. Off to my right was a boardwalk to a private residence that by all indications was unoccupied tonight. It was there I planned to position the band and 'Frank' just out of Candi's line of sight.

My phone vibrated ... A text from Giovanni.

"Ciao, D ... Lost ... Daytona."

Of course, you are. I replied. "Not in Daytona now. Go south on Highway A1A to Daytona Beach Shores. Pirates Cove Hotel."

"Ahh ... see soon," Gio fired back.

Men, what was I thinking? They, we, don't ever stop and ask for directions. Gio was a hell of a man in some areas ... as in, hung like a horse ... slighted in others ... Maybe he tries to think with it. ... Guess I should have sent him a map with a naked woman on top with an X to mark the spot.

Chapter 65

At 5:30 p.m., I was staring at a five-piece band, plus one guy wandering aimlessly in circles beach side…he was either looking for direction, for me, or both.

"Gentlemen," I called out, closing the distance between us, "I'm D. Glad you could make it. I'll show you where to set up. Follow me." Walking the ensemble across the hard-packed sand to keep from disturbing my rose-petal laced path, I set them in place on the private boardwalk and settled up immediately in cash. "Are you familiar with the song I requested?"

"We are," responded 'Mr. Sinatra,' "just give us the word."

"Gladly. Candi may arrive a few minutes late. Seems the Crazy Italian Stallion with her has absolutely no sense of direction, except when it comes to his dick. Horse-hung, good as gold… the envy of all mankind." They laughed.

I strapped the backpack on Major and inserted two milk bottles into their holders. Just for good measure, I tied the bandana from my bike around his neck. At 5:55 p.m., give or take a few minutes, I walked him to the steps and hooked his lead to the handrail. "Sit," I commanded, (in reality I just advised) "Candi will be along soon." Scattering the last of my rose petals around him before tying them into the trail, I walked back to the band, feeling my phone vibrate as I reached the steps.

I got Gio's text that said "here."

Turning to the band, I nodded, "Let the music begin." Uncasing their instruments — salt spray plays havoc on reeds and brass — they warmed up briefly, before breaking into my long-anticipated song, Frank Sinatra's, Stranger's in the Night.

A solitary figure appeared poolside, gazing over the railing and into the ocean's waves. Dressed in dark skinny jeans and a royal blue, billowy, silk blouse, I watched her reaction when the dog she spotted at the foot of the steps suddenly seemed familiar.

Ah, Atlantic Ocean I've missed you, I breathed, looking out upon the waves crashing effortlessly on the shore. Music, do I hear music? Yes, someone, somewhere is playing Sinatra. Moving to the top of the steps leading to the beach, I spotted a beautiful service dog waiting patiently for his owner. He looks like Major. No, it couldn't be. I never saw Major wear a pack like that. If only ... silly me, you've been in the car with Gio too long, listening to his wrong turn by wrong turn directions. Stepping out of her shoes and onto the sand, Candi froze. Hanging around the neck of the Major look-alike was a sign that read, "Follow Me." Red and pink rose petals surrounded him, except where his tail wagging furiously had brushed them away. They didn't stop there. A trail of red and pink rose petals led directly toward the music's source.

Speechless, with tears welling in her eyes, Candi unhooked the labradoodle's leash and using both hands patted her chest. Only Major would know what to do next. White sand launched out of nowhere into her face and hair, followed by two massive paws firmly planted on her chest. "Major," she cried, "it is you. I am so happy ... so happy!" She hugged him repeatedly. The bandana tied around his neck looked and smelled vaguely familiar ... like me. "Go find daddy!"

Major dropped to the ground, turned and bounded off across the rose-petaled path before stopping and waiting for her to catch up. Her eyes clouded with tears with her shoes in her left hand, she ran straight to the sound of the music and the words bellowing from someone who sounded much like old blue eyes...

Strangers in the night exchanging glances
Wondering in the night
What were the chances we'd be sharing love
Before the night was through...

I stopped and inhaled the lyrics, recited the lyrics, sung the lyrics before continuing on...

Ever since that night we've been together
Lovers at first sight, in love forever
It turned out so right for strangers in the night

The music was vibrant and live. It's the little things you pick up on when over-whelmed with emotion. That, and the fact that she could see musicians gathered on the walkway when she reached the end of the rose-colored path. Before her was a giant heart with a basket of ... brownies. *That's why Major was carrying milk. I get it. Off to my left was Mr. Smiley face, defined with pronounced facial features made from red solo cups and one very distinct appendage I'd recognize anywhere.*

As the music faded it was her cue, "D, where's Major? Better still, where are you?"

Stepping from behind a fragrant, blooming clump of Oleander with Major leading the way, "Hi, Candi... surprised?"

"Of course, you surprised me, Major most of all. I thought my mind was playing tricks on me ... that is until he hugged me and copped a feel. Then I knew ... he's ... he's so like you." My tears would not stop flowing. My make-up a disaster zone. This is not how I wanted D to see me after all this time. I wiped the Sephora, mixed with salt, sand and tears from my face. "D, I must look a mess. I'm sorry."

"Hush ... You look wonderful Candi... for a raccoon." I chuckled. "I've missed you."

Turning to the band, "Gentlemen, thank you for coming and sharing this homecoming with us. I must say you performed admirably. Candi loves Sinatra and I'm becoming quite a fan myself."

Packing up, I watched them exit up the walkway opposite the way they came. Very considerate. I appreciated them for not ruining the ambiance we'd worked so hard to create.

Focusing on Candi, "I'm glad you decided to come along, baby. I couldn't bear the thought of you riding bitch behind Gio when you could be riding with me." I glowed.

"D, did you set this whole thing up? I mean, one minute Gio and Mile were going to South Beach and the next thing I knew he wanted to come here. You did, didn't you?"

"Major mostly, he missed you."

"I missed him ... I really, positively, absolutely ... missed you."

"Thank you. Means a lot. Help me gather our stuff. I see Gio and Mile ogling us over the rail."

<h1 style="text-align:center">Chapter 66</h1>

Five minutes later we were packed up, welcomed by Gio, passionately hugged by Mile and flying across the causeway to Aunt Catfishes for dinner. Dining on platters of fresh seafood, drinking Sam on draft and wine from a bottle, we conversed and laughed like we did a month ago; almost as if we'd never been apart.

Gio graciously paid the tab and we were off to the hotel with me leading the way. Candi was once again beside me, Major relegated comfortably to the back seat.

Having checked in Gio and Mile before I left, I handed them their keys on our arrival. "Let me help you with your things, Gio. You're useless with two crutches and a cast."

Gio nodded, then spoke. "Not useless where it counts ... Mile, she ride sidesaddle."

We laughed all the way to the elevator. "Gio, Mile would you prefer breakfast at seven or eight?"

"Seven good," replied Mile.

Feeling an excruciating pinch on my arm from the woman on my immediate right, Candi announced, "Eight is better."

Sensing the wrath of someone slighted, I quickly replied, "Eight it will be." Handing Candi, the room key and the leash, I helped settle Gio and

Mile into their room, while Major, the tail wagging dog that he is, did the same for Candi.

With Mile retired to the bathroom, I embraced Gio, "Thanks for coming and thanks for bringing Candi. Thanks for being you."

"Welcome, D … We happy now … You happy now … we good."

"We are good … for now. Good night all," I shouted to Mile, slapping the closed bathroom door on my way out.

I found Candi waiting for me on the balcony, Major piled comfortably on the couch.

Looking at Major disapprovingly, "old habits die hard don't they, D?"

"They do," I confessed, "except when they don't. You weren't here to scold him and I haven't the heart after leaving him in the kennel for a month. It's the least I can do, let him sleep where he wants to…" I assured her, running my fingers through her natural curls. "The same goes for you, you know."

How do I say this and not sugar coat it? "D, I had sex with Joseph because I wanted to, not because he forced me to … although he did to some degree. I wanted what he wanted, someone to love, to laugh with, to be happy with. Sadly, in his own distorted sense of reality, he believed the only avenue he had to keep me was through the pain he brought to you. What you saw on the tape was real, not contrived, but real. Look at me!" *He looks puzzled. Have I said too much?* "You have watched the video by now, haven't you?"

What exactly does she want me to say? "I have … not. Do you have your iPad? If it means so much to you, we can watch it together."

"No, No, I can't believe you weren't the least bit curious— That's not important now. What is important… there was something between Joseph and I, twice. I was working to get it back, before I took off on the Family odyssey in search of Fool's Gold, by way of you."

Candi had more to say. "D, just to let you know, I got him back for film-ing me unawares. Tit for tat … no, it was more like twat for cock." *That doesn't sound right either.* "Not for what he did to me, mind you, but for what he hoped to do to you. I poured out my soul extracting revenge. Do you know what? After I got it, I cried. I used his weaknesses that are inherent to his character to humiliate him before my eyes. I even have it on tape. Blackmail is a powerful tool that goes both ways. I don't think he'll bother us again."

"It's twice scorned Joseph, remember? Can I see what you have on him?"

"You didn't watch my video ... now you want to watch his? I'll have to think about it."

"Remember the Godfather?" I laughed at myself for asking the question. "Of course, you do. How could you not...being Family and all? Anyway, someone in the movie said, 'revenge is a dish better served cold.' Which means, as I interpret it, it's best to take a deep breath, calm down and let your emotionally charged anger subside before seeking retribution. You didn't do that, did you?

"I did, until I didn't ... as you're so apt to say. I imagined you and Vic banging each other's brains out, soothing each other, being the slut that you are, pardon me, but it is the truth ... because of the turmoil Joseph and I brought into your lives."

There are no saints in this room. It was my turn to come clean. "Candi, look at me. The sexual banter between Vic and I started long before anything physically happened between us. She was hot and she knew it. She was sexual and I knew it. She's also a damaged little girl who tried to comfort me the only way she knew how by giving herself to me, sexually. Like I told her then, like I'm telling you now, my Momma preached, 'when you play with fire, you're gonna get burned. It's not a matter of if, but when.' Sure, I was unhappy the way everything went down between us. I pulled an all-night bender the day you left. Strangely enough, I was even more unhappy that you put yourself out there to be recorded in the raw. This stuff does not easily go away once it's splashed across the web. Too many fingers touching it and voile, you're a porn star, whether you meant to be or not."

I continued, "You are correct, in your earlier assumption, I am, or was, a slut. But you knew that going in. I'm also a hopeless romantic. I wanted to recapture what you and I had, if not with you, then someone. It was wonderful. No, it was spectacular. You left me with a void that I could only describe as indescribable. I hoped I could instantly fill the black hole with Vic. And I attempted to multiple times. Truthfully, I still might be able to — but then there's you — precious, beautiful, desirable you. No matter how hard I tried to suppress your memory, I couldn't shake you out of my mind." I laughed somberly. "Even when I made love to her, I couldn't help but think of you. That's not callous or cruel or arrogant. It's factual. Sadly, Vic damn well knew it. She couldn't compete with you as long as there was a chance for us. That's why I'm here. I need to know if there can be an us again."

None of this makes sense right now. We're two screwed up people searching for the same dream we realized on that fateful day at Starbucks. "Come closer, D. Hold me."

And I did, embracing her on the balcony, listening to and watching the waves breaking rhythmically on the shore. Running my fingers through her curls, I kissed each eye, each cheek before softly pressing her lips to mine. Tongues darting, hands roaming, fingers exploring, lust replaced the tenderness I'd spent so much time trying to convey. I led Candi inside, guiding her midway onto the bed, before rising to turn off the lights.

My clothes are smothering me. I want them off and I want him ... now! Tossing my blouse to the side, I shimmied out of my jeans and waited for this man to return. I wanted his chest next to mine, his lips kissing and exploring every neglected inch of my body. I wanted D on top of me, inside me, tasting me, breathing me. I've waited long for this day to come again ... please ... let the wholeness return.

So much for taking it slow. Finding Candi undressed except for her matching Victoria Secret attire, I shed my clothes before lowering myself on her, while my lips passionately pulled her darting, dancing tongue into my mouth. Rocking my hips back and forth across her moistening thong, I moved my attention to the nape of her neck, her fingernails, grasping, scratching, clawing into my neck, my back. I breathed into her ear, "I have missed you, baby. We left so much unsaid, unrealized, unexplored." Releasing her legs from mine, I pressed hers together and pushed my rigid self between them, gliding up and down her warm crevasse ... My body was waging war, fighting my lips and my tongue that longed to be there as well.

How he drives me insane, biting my neck, kissing my ears. It's time I reciprocate. Grasping my head in her hands, Candi pulled my neck to her lips while my manhood rubbed her and that ridiculous thong, she had absentmindedly left on.

Wow ... that makes me hot! Hotter than I remember! Her lips attacked my neck with a vengeance, her teeth bit gently into my flesh. I flipped her over. With her magnificent breasts in my palms, I guided her twins across my lips, playfully tugging on each, while my hands lifted and lowered her moistness across a glistening... me. Reaching the point of no return, I slid my arms under her thighs and carried her across my chest. With her hands propped against the headboard, I immersed myself in her sweetness, while Candi pressed herself into me, attempting to relocate the razor thin cotton separating me from her ecstasy.

Mindful that I had taken her as far as the fabric would allow, I forcefully ripped off her soaking wet thong and flung it across the room. Relieved there was no longer a barrier between us, I breathed as deep as my lungs would allow, before burying myself inside her. Random oval circling with my tongue, first deep, then wide, shallow, then pointed, followed by the vacuum of my lips stiffened her body, paving the way for the pleasure of her orgasm, soon to be realized.

Tossing Candi onto her back, I resumed the position, using two fingers to massage her magic spot just below my planted tongue. That did it. She exploded...no she rocketed into the abyss... riding wave after wave of pleasure, her legs locked involuntarily around my neck. Tossing, turning, twisting, bucking, Candi moaned, then screamed, then melted into the bedding.

Catching my breath, first one minute, then two, I eased on top of her, where she warmly welcomed me. I glided effortlessly to the tempo of our making. First slow, then fast, then somewhere in between. I thrust in and out of her wet, warm vice that had no intention of letting me go. With beads of sweat dripping from my forehead, I released, pushing deeply inside her as far as her body would allow. Totally spent, I moved to her side and snuggled her head to my chest. In moments, we were fast asleep, our bodies, our hearts, somewhat reconnected.

Chapter 67

Major, being the earliest riser in the group, woke us up at twenty after five on this fine Candi Day +1. After nuzzling my arm and getting no response, he promptly walked around the bed and nuzzled Candi. She jumped… cold, wet nose to warm cheek works every time.

Feeling something or someone next to her, Candi opened her eyes to a dog's nose, planted eye level on the bed next to her cheek. "Major — yuck!"

"I think he wants to go out."

Pulling the pillow over her head, she groaned, "It's all you, D. He's your dog."

"Yep and thanks to you … a homeless dog at that."

That hurts, even if it's true. "That's not fair!"

"Who said life's fair? Sometimes, it down right sucks. The way I see it, if it wasn't for you baby doll, he'd be at home right now letting his own self out, not waiting for an escort from a fifth floor, ocean front, hotel room."

She pounded me with my pillow. Then, Candi relented, "You're right, hold on Major. I'll take you for a walk. Where are my clothes?"

I slipped onto the floor and tossed Candi a handful of twisted strings. "Your thong, or what's left of it. Guess you'll go commando today," I chuckled.

"You wish big boy, it's not good to go commando in jeans. Rubs my hoo-ha the wrong way. I know you don't want that." I chuckled. "Don't laugh — it's about proper hygiene."

"Really? ... I never knew there was a trick to it. TMI if you ask me."

"I didn't ask you," Candi growled sexily. "I told you. Slut that you are, you should always know where it's been before you kiss it, lick it, tease it…down here," she cooed.

"I bet you taste like me, baby... ... day-old salty ... hmmm ... and sweet. FYI, I've never licked a pussy I didn't pet… first. Have to test the water before you jump in, you know. Major, my boy, you will have to wait."

The dog looked painfully on the verge. Then again, so did I. "Major, I'm sorry." Candi squirmed sideways on the bed. "This won't take long I promise," widely exposing her nether regions to my wanting eyes. "Will it, baby?"

"Nope," was the second word that came to mind, before I planted my mouth where her fingers had lingered. I dove in ... tongue extended ... inhaling ... then tasting ... the flavor of our making.

Something is missing ... I remembered ... "My toy ... baby, where's my toy?"

I eventually came up for air. "In my bag," I replied, catching my breath and a short break while I got up and rummaged through my pack. "Found it," holding up the well-traveled BOA for Candi to see. "Be right back," I mumbled, disappearing into the bathroom to wash it twice with hot soapy water. If she knew where it's been, I bet she'd change her mind ... or maybe not. It's a toy and toys are meant to be shared. Or are they?

Where'd he go in such a hurry? "D, something wrong?"

"Fresh batteries, baby. I must have left it on." Grinning sheepishly, "Now, where was I?"

The insertion of the BOA, below, beside and on top of my talented twisting tongue tickler, accelerated her climactic conclusion considerably. Four body shivers, two bucking broncs, one muffled moan and three Oh Baby's, signaled we had arrived. Looking into Candi's sparkling brown eyes, I asked, "satisfied, precious?"

"I am, completely. Thank you, baby. ... Now you."

"I'm good. This morning was all you." Rising from the bed, I brought Candi her bag from the closet and leaned over the bed for a kiss. "Major prefers we both join him on his walk. We can shower later and you can wash my back.

"I'll take you up on your offer on one condition—" she winked.

"Yes?"

"Bring me a warm, wet, soapy washcloth. Then please wash me off your face and out of your beard. You smell gross."

I've heard that before. "If that's not the pot calling the kettle black. It just proves my point."

"I got it. You never petted a pussy you didn't lick ... or something like that. Was I close?"

I smiled. "Close enough."

Chapter 68

It was a few minutes after six when the three of us left the room. Why shouldn't there be four? "I'll meet you in the lobby. Maybe I can get Mile to join us for an early morning romp on the beach."

"It's feast or famine with you, D. You just can't get enough…"

"It's who I am. Seriously, who wants to hang around with a gimp all day? Might do Mile some good to get away from the three-legged stallion."

"He can't walk, but at least she can ride."

"My thought's exactly, sidesaddle."

Sex … He just had it … kinda … and he still thinks about it. I give up! "Major and I will meet you in the lobby."

Watching them walk to the elevator, I did an about face and traipsed down the hall to Giovanni's room. Pounding on the door, I listened and waited.

Meekly, I heard "Yes" through the door.

"Mile, that you? Major is taking Candi and I for a walk. You like to join us?" I heard the latch drop. Standing before me was beautiful, unabashed Mile in a short tee shirt, a very short T-shirt…and nothing more. I grimaced.

"Ciao, D. Walk good. Yes, I go. Gio no go," strained Mile in decent English.

I whispered, "Mile, you should never answer the door like this," pointing at her attire. "You never know who it might be."

She grinned sheepishly, "I know, D ... You."

Foot in mouth again. "Clothes on please. We'll meet you downstairs." With a nod and a kiss on the cheek, Mile closed the door while I stood there speechless. *Don't even go there, slut that you are.* Walking to the elevator, I had another epiphany…men have to look. Only real men don't touch. *What does that make me… a real man or real, man slut?*

Candi had a black and green waiting for me as I stepped off the elevator. "Thank you, precious. I believe this is a first. Usually, I'm the morning gofer."

"You're welcome. Don't get used to it. Let's just say it's for services unselfishly rendered."

"Understood. You can use my services anytime."

"Mile?"

"No, not Mile. My services are off limits to her all the time."

"Where's your head, D? Is Mile coming?" He grinned. ... *Geez there he goes again.* "Is Mile walking with us?"

"Yes, baby, she will be down shortly." *What does she know that I don't know she knows?* "Candi, don't take this wrong, but do you have eyes in the back of your head? ESP maybe?"

"If I did, I wouldn't tell you. What I can tell you is I know by your voice when your mind is preoccupied. Since you're a man, more times than not, it's probably sexually related. At least that's what I read in you. Then again, I could be wrong. You tell me."

I opened my mouth and removed my foot to reply. Whew! Saved by an elevator.

Mile, dressed in form-fitting yoga pants and her famous tee, stepped through its doors, immediately launching into a spirited tirade with Candi in Italian. *Safe!*

With Major leading the way and me the odd man out, I found myself walking six feet behind the dog and twelve feet in front of the women, alone. Lucky me. In the two miles up and back I managed to converse all of five minutes about food, as in what's for breakfast? Narrowing it down to Cracker

Barrel and IHOP, those being nearest the Harley shop, IHOP won. Blintzes over biscuits, go figure.

We didn't make eight o'clock, but we made 8:30, dropping Major by the kennel before IHOP called their name. Over a breakfast of crepes, pancakes and blintzes, I stubbornly ate a patty melt, we discussed our trip north to Savannah and Tybee Island. Driving the back roads wherever we could, I hoped we could stay out of heavy traffic and enjoy a leisurely ride.

"You good guide, D. You say, we go," offered Gio, anxiously waiting to get this 'show on the road.'

"I didn't do so well last time, Gio," slapping his cast with my hand. He laughed.

Candi and Mile liked the idea of staying in a historic B&B in downtown Savannah. Gio slowly warmed to the idea as long as there were no stairs to climb. "Maybe a few," I confessed. "If there's more, I'll carry you." Looking at his sincere expression, somehow, I thought he actually believed me.

Chapter 69

While I strapped our meager necessities on my bike, by way of Candi packing light, Gio and Mile filled out a plethora of paperwork, including their passport information, international driver's licenses numbers, and after asking Gio how he came by the cast, an unlimited waiver of liability with a personal guarantee for excessive damages. Confirming with the rental clerk there were no recently reported moose sightings in the area, we collectively breathed a unanimous sigh of relief.

Reasonably assured that Gio left his video camera in the trunk with his crutches strapped on top, we rolled out of the parking lot at ten o'clock sharp. Shouting to Candi over the engines roar, "it's been a long day already, baby, and we're just getting started."

Leading us north along Highway. A1A, I followed the coast line north, passing through Ormond By the Sea, then Flagler Beach, before stopping at the St. Augustine Lighthouse and Museum. Rising into the sky like a giant black and white striped barber pole, the lighthouse seemed like a great place for the ladies to explore. But, then again, I was traveling with women who thought with their big brains and stomachs.

First, Mile ... "Food?"

Then Candi, "I'm hungry. There's nothing to eat here."

Followed by Giovanni's final interjection, "Beer?"

Defeated, I was outgunned and outnumbered. "SIRI, find us Italian." And she did, directing me to Trip Advisor and Benitto's Italian House, boasting eleven hundred favorable reviews.

"Follow me," I said, watching the lighthouse disappear in my rear views, driving forward through St. Augustine, the oldest continuously occupied city in America. Just proves I do pay attention to the city limit signs here and not just in Canada.

Winding through the town, we rumbled across 400-year-old cobble-stone streets, rattling my teeth, while I thought of another mode of transportation. Fifteen minutes of lefts and rights behind us, we arrived at an odd looking A-framed building. I had Siri confirm it twice, putting me in the doghouse with her all familiar voice. "D, you have arrived at your destination. I am not telling you again!" Geez … What is it with me and women today? I can't catch a break, even with an inanimate one.

"Italian. We're having Italian," I announced. "You can't judge a book by its cover. This may look like a Swiss Chalet, but it's Italian through and through. Judging by the stares I was getting, I tossed out my last line of defense. "Don't trust me, trust Siri. Besides, maybe it's Italian Swiss." Fortunately, they did.

Looking to my spicy Italians for guidance, they ordered four of Benitto's specialties to share, Chicken Piccata, Eggplant Parm, Chicken Parm, and Flounder Francese. By the end of the meal, Gio and Mile praised the talented chefs of Benitto's for their authenticity. Candi and I, not to be outdone, added our two cents to Trip Advisor, 5 star reviews, 1101 and 1102.

"You good guide, D," replied Gio. "Where we go next?"

Before I could answer Gio, I felt Candi move in close.

"What have you dreamed up for the rest of today, D?" she asked, as her lips briefly touched my neck.

I chilled. Regaining my composure, "it's tough being a tour guide with hop along here," I replied, pointing at Giovanni and the cast he rode in on.

"Doing my best to visit places we can ride. Next stop, Bonaventure Cemetery, Savannah. But we need to get there by four. The dead pack it in around five."

"I've heard of it, D. Johnny Mercer is buried there. Sounds like fun. Let's ride," confidently assuring Mile and Gio it was an integral part of D's master plan.

So much for staying on the back roads, interstates were designed to make time. I-95 did not disappoint, dropping us into Savannah proper by 3:30. Allowing the GPS to route us, it guided us up to the main gates with ease. I stopped, made a generous donation to the Historical Society and snagged a map.

Riding through the ornate iron gates of Bonaventure, time literally stopped. Before us, huge, centuries old live oaks lined the main roads creating a majestic live canopy, dripping of Spanish moss, dancing at times to the recurring oceans breeze. Monstrous concrete pillars, vaults and tombstones of all shapes and sizes, paid homage to another time, another era. Even in death, its residents could still make an eternal statement of their values, their beliefs, their worth. Many of the tombstones in the Jewish section were lined with small stones, signifying someone had visited the grave and reminding those entombed that they were not forgotten.

Looking at Candi, I could tell this place moved her as well. "Speak, baby."

"D, this is beautiful, serene, peaceful — a place for healing troubled souls in the land of the living, not the dead."

After spending a generous ninety minutes, exploring, discovering, photographing a simpler time in our past, we rode out through the gates and back into reality. I wanted to return and linger with the memories we made, but today called…

'Live like there's no tomorrow.' I planned to.

Chapter 70

Cruising through downtown Savannah on the way to the B&B, I was overwhelmed by the sheer number of squares — twenty-four in all — that the founding fathers located throughout the town's initial design. Gathering places of green space under massive live oaks where neighbors packed tightly in zero lot line homes could be … neighborly.

After quite a few calls and internet inquiries, I settled on the Kehoe Inn on Habersham. With only three steps to negotiate to access a first-floor room, this B&B was centrally located in the heart of the Historic Area. Rolling up to the entrance, I watched Gio and Mile give it the once over. before Gio turned to me.

Gio nodded, "Works, D. Mile like. Candice, you? Stairs?"

Patting Candi on the knee, "check us in, please. I'll bring the Italians and our bags along shortly."

"With pleasure. Our room does have a garden tub, doesn't it, D?"

"I can't remember," was not what Candi wanted to hear by the pouting of her lips. "I recall one of them does. For my sake, I hope it's yours."

"I'll let you know soon enough."

"I am sure you will sweet cheeks," I quipped, slapping Candi firmly on the rear as she walked past the bike.

"Gio, there are only three steps." Unstrapping all our gear, I tossed my bag over my shoulder and carried their bags in each hand.

"I help you, D," offered Mile.

"Names pack mule D, to you," replying to Mile, before addressing Gio in my next breath. "Remind me, the next time we ride together to treat you like Candi. Each of you is entitled to one backpack, no more."

Gio hung his head, "D, all Mile, not me. I bring toothbrush and your Dee-odor… Right Guard."

I cracked up. "Mile, did you pack Gio any clothes?"

Reaching into a side pocket of the second bag in my left hand, Mile grinned, producing two, stallion sized, banana hammock, man thongs.

"I know where her heart lies, pal."

Gio sported a sheepish smile, "not her heart … how you say … it is her…"

"Multiple orifices, I got it. You look confused. Sorry, orifice. If Mile has a hole you fill it."

Gio nodded, Mile too, "Si."

Wrapped up in sexual shenanigans bouncing back and forth between the three of us in the parking lot, gave Candi ample time to check in and return.

"I have rooms and keys and no people to fill them. What's taking you so long?"

"It's my fault, baby. We were lost in translation. Don't even go there. I'll attempt to tell you later," Candi smirked. "After you."

Dropping Mile and Gio off at their ground level room, I asked that we eat in tonight and watch the movie, "Midnight In The Garden of Good and Evil." With no objections, I followed Candi up two flights of stairs to a Queen suite, complimented by a cast iron, slipper tub. I lucked out. Brownie points — that is if they are still allowed on this ride.

"Baby, do you remember … in Missoula, when I pulled you into a tub much like this one, clothes and all?"

I giggled. "I remember being elbow deep in you before you'd let me shed my clothes. What made you so amorous that night? Hold that thought. Oh, I remember — the book you were reading, 50 Ways to Get Laid."

Men are so clueless sometimes. "It was Fifty Shades of Grey, by E.L. James. You are acting so not Christian right now."

"Seriously, you're bringing up my personal beliefs? What have I done that was so bad?"

OMG! "D, Christian is the handsome millionaire male character in the book. It's on my iPad. You really need to read it. Maybe a little of Christian will rub off on you."

I took offense. "Did this Christian what's-his-name give away over a billion dollars trying to fix a situation commonly known in military circles as FUBAR?

"Did Christian unselfishly provide his sweetheart a meal ticket worth 10 mil, and in doing so make his life a living hell?"

I was rolling! "I bet Christian never got his girlfriend off on a motorcycle doing 50, maybe even 60 mph down the open roads with the wind in her hair — come to think of it, I did that twice."

He has a point. "OK, maybe Christian could learn a trick or two from you," she relented, remembering our first night on the bike cruising through the cornfields of Iowa.

"Damn straight." I huffed, "We've made love on just about everything that moves and floats — but to date, nothing that flies. I regret I've yet to introduce you to the mile-high club."

"Slut that you are, how many women have you screwed in the air? And another question that begs to be answered ... you do Victoria on the bike on the ride back?"

Dang, that was close! "Last question first...Hell No! As to the other one, I don't kiss and tell."

"Excuse me, Mr. Gigolo, you shared quite a few of your adventures when we first met. If you'd found the time to write, I wouldn't be surprised to find our exploits already in a bookstore somewhere. I can see it now, 'Candi... A Ride To Remember.'"

If she only knew...

Chapter 71

Taking in our well-appointed room, we were blessed with an inviting four-poster Queen bed, an oval mirrored antique dresser, two club chairs, and a mahogany, drop leaf legal secretary. None of which, other than the bed after being long on the bike, called my name. Laying down, it swallowed me, even before Candi crash-landed on my stomach, pushing me deeper into the plush goose down comforter.

"I'm hungry, D. What's for dinner?" After a long pause, she asked, "What's up with that? ... Where is the quick-witted man I remember?" Candi pouted. "There was a time when you'd tell me I could have you for dessert, first. And I did, too, multiple times."

"Girl," I caught myself and the word friend did not escape my lips. Victoria wouldn't understand. "You've said very little on the ride up today. Now you want to get frisky? I'm not being petty, but you've not hugged me, kissed me ... laughed with me all day." Damn ... I sound like a woman. "Now you belittle me and call me names. Tell me, Candice, are you angry, jealous, frustrated, PMS-ing… what? At least tell me something."

"Maybe all the above. D," she pleaded. "Can't you see it? The newness is gone along with the thrill of the chase. I chased you. You chased me. We lusted, we connected, we bonded… then poof, we disconnected. Now we're connecting again. I won't lie. It's harder than I thought it would be. It was much easier for me to dream of what we had, what we lost and what could have been when we were apart. You lived vividly in my memories of us."

"What you see is what you get, Candice Parker. I'm imperfect and flawed. I got it. You can look at my precious dysfunctional family and see that. We were individually looking for the same thing. We were just too self-absorbed to find it in each other. And we could have, mind you, if we'd talked more, hugged more, laughed more and loved more together, rather than apart."

I continued. "Life is not black and white. It's emotionally charged, gut wrenching shades of gray, hints of orange, smatterings of red and brilliant hues of blue. Collectively, these feelings cohesively tossed together becomes the formula that makes us into what we are today."

"D ... help me take us back to the way we were."

"You're not listening, Candi. ... It can't be absolutely the way it was. You're right... the newness is gone. And so is the chase now that we're together again. That's not always a bad thing. The emotional fluff is gone. If you're committed to make us work, our relationship can be deeper, healthier, stronger, but it begins at the foundation. The last time I looked that foundation, though chipped and dinged, is relatively strong. You're a spoiled brat, Candice Parker, who has always experienced life through rose-colored glasses. Me, I'm an imperfect man, subject to fail without notice, trying to redeem himself one day at a time."

"I don't want perfect, D. I want ... I want ... you... or someone like you, who makes me whole."

"There you go. If having me in your life makes you strive to be better, then we have in place the very cornerstone to build our future on." Bam, bam, bam ... I could tell by her knockers ... knocking ... Mile was at the door.

"D? Candice? Hungry?" bellowed Mile.

"We're not finished talking, Candi. I got it. Over the next couple of days, let's reacquaint and recapture us while having fun with the Italian stud and his filly. Speaking of ... please let Mile in."

Candi wasn't finished ... but she had to be for the moment. "Coming, Mile."

We ordered in, Maddiao's Pizza to be exact, complimented by two large Greek salads. And we dined fine, drinking Sam from a glass, no wine, watching director Clint Eastwood's classic, "Midnight in the Garden of Good and Evil" until eleven. "In the morning, say around eight, Candi time, I will take you to Clary's, the most delicious breakfast cafe, bar none, in Savannah. Established in the early 1900s, this restaurant has been a local favorite of mine for as long as I can remember. Oh, and it was featured in the movie we just watched."

"Sound good, not hungry..." beer burped Gio. "Cuz."

"You will be by tomorrow. Night."

"Good night, Mile. 'Night, Gio. Mile, if you're up early, beat on our door. We can all go for a walk, can't we, D?"

"Yes, Candi, we can," I replied, while my mind wandered, that is, if I can get enough rest sleeping beside this ice-cold popsicle in the making.

I dropped my clothes on the chair, slipped into bed in my shorts and turned on my side facing away. Beer and pizza is conducive to sleep. Serious late-night conversations, it is not.

How dare he? I pushed on his shoulder with both hands. "D, turn over! We're not finished talking."

"You talk, I'll listen," I assured her, two minutes before I woke myself snoring, on my side. ... Imagine that!

He's snoring already? ... I can't believe it! Snuggling up to him, I tossed my right leg over his, followed by my arm. This I remember most ... how safe I felt with him in my arms. My anger slowly subsided. Sleep quickly followed.

Chapter 72

I woke at five, even without Major's cold nose to prompt me. Candi, sound asleep on her side of the bed, coaxed me... no she downright begged me... whether she knew it or not to cuddle with her a few minutes longer. Sliding my hand under her tee, I stroked and massaged her breasts until I drifted back to sleep.

I was roused from a pleasant slumber with a hand on my breasts. Yes, this is more like it. D, spooning me, caressing me, holding me, not sexually, but lovingly. I closed my eyes and dreamed of him.

Knockers ... knocking ... jolted us awake at 6:30. "Mile's here," I announced. "You best let her in, Candi," I said, noticing my morning erection. "Trust me, I'm not decent."

"Not me, D. She's all yours."

"OK..." I stammered, "be right there, Mile." Opening the door, my little brain peaked out to confirm it was Mile, dressed in her skintight yoga pants and her short-short tee. "Come on in," I proudly announced, "Candi is still in bed."

Giving me the once over, then a second, Mile's eyes transfixed on well ... "D, you have problem?"

"Not at all," I grinned.

"I fix Gio's ... Candi fix you?"

"You'll have to ask her, Mile. I have no dogs in this fight."

Now wide-awake, Candi asked, "What are you two talking about? What problem am I supposed to fix?"

Walking backwards toward Candi, I stopped at the edge of the bed, before turning around, cheek slapping her with the rigid one-eyed monster, poking proudly out of my boxers. I pointed. She got it.

"Oh ... Oh!" *What was I supposed to say?*

Mile, seeing where this dog and pony show was headed, politely spoke up. "I be in lobby ... You come ... soon." Then she quietly closed the door.

Candi smiled. "You heard her, D. Come soon. Yesterday was all me ... this morning is all you." Laying her head over the edge of the bed, she welcomed me. One minute turned to two, then three, then four, then five. *My poor achy-breaky jaws throbbed.* She withdrew, rolled onto her stomach and asked, "What's up with you?"

I grinned sheepishly, "You Lovelace'd me. That was incredible. Why'd you stop?"

Exasperated, Candi clenched her teeth, "Why didn't you…"

"I didn't know you wanted me to. I'm sorry. I'll take care of it." Moving to the opposite side of the bed, I entered her from behind. Using my hands on her shoulders for leverage, I rose up and down, first slow, then fast, trying to find my rhythm. After a few minutes, Candi took complete charge, rising to her knees and rocking back and forth on the bed while flexing her extraordinary muscles until I came ... through. Resting against her, I breathed deeply ... then basked in my glow. This morning was all about me ... and I appreciated every glorious moment of it.

"Happy, D?"

"Happy," I whispered, "Mile will be happy, too. Problem solved."

"I got it. This was all about Mile and not the least bit about you?"

I nodded. "Let's just say you admirably accommodated the both of us," as a down pillow nailed me squarely in the face. "Thank you, Candice. Now, get dressed. Let's go take care of problem number two."

What about me? I tossed another pillow in his direction. "Excuse me, I'm your problem number two. Mile has been relegated to number three. You really need to take care of me! But, it can wait ... for now."

That was scary ... Candi sounded just like Victoria. What is it with this 'for now' stuff? Does it mean they're constantly unfulfilled or is there some business that needs replenished, repetitively? Admiring Candi gloriously traipsing bottomless to the bathroom, I deduced it could be a little of both.

Chapter 73

Joining marvelous Mile downstairs, the three of us took off down Habersham to West Bay Street, before dropping down to walk along River Street that meandered along the Savannah River. Restaurants, galleries and shops lined the entire length of the waterfront, many more than I remembered during my last trip here. A burgeoning robust economy was evident, driven by the charm of this historic city.

Circling back across West Bay St. we followed Abercorn St. to the Colonial Park Cemetery where we cut a diagonal through it before ending at the Cathedral of St. John The Baptist.

Caught up in the splendor of the church, Mile was speechless. "Beautiful … Like home."

"I'm glad you're pleased, Mile," I offered, "Would you like to go inside?"

"Much so … OK?"

"Candi, if you please, lead the way. Today, you're number one tour guide."

She smiled. "Nope, D. Remember, I'm number two, and don't you forget it."

Pointing the ladies towards the entrance, "I'll be right here." I sat down on the cold, hard concrete bench and waited. There was absolutely no purpose in me touring with them, listening to lively Italian banter that made zero sense to me. Ten minutes later they emerged and in another ten we were back in the Inn. Gio was dressed, but not ready. I made the call. We would leave from here.

"We shower, we pack, we go," I said. Candi took the hint and followed me to the room with a question.

"Mile would like to stay here another day, baby. Is that possible?"

"It is ... There's not too many things we can do with Gio, however. Too many stairs here in Savannah for all the places I'd like us to visit. I've reserved a three bedroom, oceanfront ground floor condo for us for the next couple of days. No stairs, just the beach, the sun, and since off-season... no people."

Sounds wonderful. "I'm for that, D. I'll politely tell her no.... hell no. I think she'll understand."

"Damn straight ... I would and I'm a slow learner." I showered, while Candi broke the news to Mile and was packed before she returned. "Waiting on you precious..."

"I'm taking a bath. Join me, D?" *I knew he wouldn't, but I had to ask.*

"Tonight, or tomorrow. You missed your window, Candi. We could bathe in the ocean."

"We could skinny dip. Do you remember our last night on Dale Hollow?"

"I do. The question is, do you? We had many firsts that evening. Any particular one that stands out? The sunset dinner cruise, skinny dipping in the dark, bluff jumping buck naked and almost landing in a bass boat filled with two horny fishermen or making love to me in the water under a moonlit sky?"

"All of them. The last one most of all. Now get out or get in the tub with me."

"I'm going. I'd best carry and pack Gio's and Mile's gear myself."

I had a delicious thought. "D," I purred, "before you leave, bring me my toy."

"Copy that," I grinned. "I love it when a woman takes matters into her own hands."

"Among other things, baby. Remember this morning?"

I walked down the stairs somberly thinking I should have stayed and drove the train. She had a problem, yet, she took care of it —I like that in her, along with the other things she referred to that continually draw me in. Sure, she's flawed, who isn't? Candi conveys an innocence that's refreshing and captivating. She's book smart in so many areas while her street smarts are still developing. She, like me, is a work in progress. We were two master-pieces in the making that were bound, more times than not, to compete, as well as, collide.

Stopping by the front desk on the way to Gio's room, I stood speechless before studious Anna, our morning innkeeper. She patiently offered a blank stare to match mine. "I'm sorry Anna, I forgot why I'm here."

"Oh, that happens to me all the time," offered Anna encouragingly. "What room are you in, maybe that will help?"

"I don't know that either. I can describe it for you. It has a four-poster bed and a cast iron slipper tub filled with water and a beautiful naked woman."

Anna blushed. "You're in room 301, under Parker."

"I hope so ... I think I came by to check out. We have two rooms."

"Are you OK, sir?"

"I am. Thanks. Too much on my mind."

"I bet it's that beautiful lady you left in the tub that has you discombobulated."

I nodded, walking away as I tried to remember the last time I'd heard that word.

"You're probably right. She does that to me all the time here lately."

Chapter 74

Gio was hobbling down the hallway away from me when I reached their room. Mile, by all indications, was still in process. "Gio, I'm right behind you. Let me get the door." I helped him negotiate the three outside steps and watched him mount his trike. It was hilarious. He had to approach the bike from the right, back into it, stand on the footboards and swing his right leg the opposite direction, before settling onto the seat.

Gio huffing, "Doc say cast off Friday. Happy ... Happy ... Change to strap on."

I choked — I could just see him in a strap on. Then I could call him Two Dong Long. "Yep, I got it," I smirked. "You can take it off to shower or do Mile without her riding sidesaddle."

"Si"

"It's a good time to talk since the girls aren't here. Ignore my texting. It's questions I need answers to. I'm sending them to you one at a time. So, ignore the text alerts you hear going off in your pants right now."

"First, as I told you, I'm coming to the party. Candi doesn't know it. Let's keep it that way. Second, I need you to go to the hotel on Friday and personally ask, bribe, forcefully persuade the General Manager to turn off the fire alarm system Saturday night at precisely 8 PM for twenty minutes. The hotel will not be in danger. Tell him it's to set up a prop that's part of our skit for the ball. I don't want the carbon monoxide alarms going off. I plan to make a grand entrance, one that will make you proud. Third, I need you to email me a copy of the video Candi made of Joseph. I mentioned it, but she didn't seem keen on sharing it. Fourth, how many people will be at your table? Joseph, Candi's mom? How many more? Will they have muscle? Will they be armed? Don't worry… you don't have to remember all this. That's what the texts are for. Answer them when you can. I know this is short notice, but I need all this by noon Saturday. Friday, late, would be even better."

"You ask lot … I get … I send. You tell me plan?" asked a considerably perplexed Giovanni.

"When it comes together, pal, you'll be the first to know, I promise."

Mile appeared on the stairs, toting one bag over each shoulder, followed by Candi with my day bag and her backpack.

Standing in the doorway, D, lost in conversation with Gio, seemed oblivious to us. Candi huffed, "Don't just stand there like a big stiff prick. Come carry Mile's bags!"

Giovanni shifted his gaze towards me. I glared at him in return. "Gio, I don't resemble that remark. I think Candi is talking specifically to you, stud muffin."

Standing up on the boards of the trike, "Cuz, leg no good … no help."

"Shut up, Giovanni, I'm not talking to you." Candi was trying her best to keep from laughing. "Let me rephrase that. I'm talking to the stiff little prick beside you. How's that?"

"Oh, why didn't you say that to begin with?" I laughed all the way to the steps. "Prickly this morning are we, Candice?" I asked, snatching all the bags in both hands. "BOA let you down?"

"Needs batteries… fresh batteries… but, mostly it needed you." she winked.

"Copy that. If you have the time… I have the chaps and the thong and the ride…"

There's that look. He's serious! "Not now!" Her skin tingled. "Maybe later, baby." She squirmed … *He saw it. Good!*

I stowed and strapped our gear, fantasizing about our last ride in chaps and thongs along the Beartooth Highway in Montana. Thrilling, as I remember it, would be an understatement.

"D, I think I know where your mind is," Candi blushed. "I can tell by the looks of your bulging jeans."

"You caught me," I confessed. "I do promise you, I am more than ready to recreate the ride with you, anytime…anyplace…anywhere."

"You're always ready to do it again, anytime, anyplace, anywhere. Slut that you are." she grinned. "Right now, I'm hungry … let's ride," she chimed, climbing onto the bike behind me.

"Your wish is my command, precious," cranking my engine with Mile and Gio following suit. "We ride."

I took us over the same route we had walked earlier this morning, across West Bay Street and along River Street, before catching Abercorn and riding it four blocks to Clary's Cafe. Experiencing only a ten-minute wait, we settled into a six top far away in the back. Hanging on the wall behind us were numerous autographed pictures from the stars, cast and crew of the movie; the most recognizable, Clint Eastwood standing with Patricia, the owner, and a native Tennessean.

"Does this seem oddly familiar?" Not waiting for an answer, "It should, you saw this setting last night multiple times. What you didn't see is their scrumptious food. My favorite is their Eggs Benedict Florentine. Gio you might like the Elvis … Peanut butter and banana, stuffed French toast." Mile chose that instead. Gio ordered Hoppel Poppel, made of scrambled eggs with chunks of Kosher Salami, potatoes, onion and green peppers. While Candi ordered Corned Beef Hash, eggs over easy, grits and whole wheat toast.

Thirty minutes later, we were stuffed and ready for a nap. I ordered a carafe of coffee and three mugs. "Driver's beware, we need a caffeine fix before we get on the road." Mile and Gio happily agreed. Candi wouldn't allow coffee to cross her lips if my life depended on it. Thankfully, she's not too particular about the other things that cross her lips ... number one of which was me. I gloated.

"D, Clary's deserves a five-star rating on Trip Advisor. Wouldn't you agree?" Candi asked, logging onto the website, checking all 5 stars, while raving favorably in the comment section.

"I'm glad you liked it. I can only hope you'll say the same about dinner tonight. We're going to the world-famous, Tybee Island Crab Shack."

With a generous tip on the table equal to our tab, we left Clary's much lazier than when we arrived. Riding through the streets of Savannah, I zig-zagged our way to U.S. Highway 80 east, before taking the Islands Expressway to Tybee. Disregarding the GPS for the moment, I led us to the end of the island, now a virtual ghost town since the tourists were gone and only the locals remained.

Quaint, costal small town, that's how I'd describe Tybee Island. Tapping me on the helmet, "Baby, I could live here. Couldn't you?"

My heart skipped a beat. "I could, actually. Or, some place much like it," I replied. "Be careful what you wish for baby girl. Remember, with me dreams have a strange way of coming true."

Paying attention to the GPS again, we rolled down Tenth, before hanging a right and driving straight to the ocean and our condo just beyond the black iron gates. Using the universal code provided when I booked them, the gates swung wide welcoming us to our home away from home. I could say that many times over. "Candi, do you realize over the last few days this will be only the second time I've stayed anywhere more than one night?"

Patting me on the shoulder, she whispered, "poor baby," into my ear. "For the next two days, I promise, you can relax, unwind, drink beer and screw."

"Screw? If we're gonna screw, we have to eat. You whose whole world revolves around food."

"By all means, D, that too."

Chapter 75

For the next two days, Candi was true to her word. The four of us relaxed on the beach, drank beer and — well, with Candi, the third one was a given… and fourth, we ate far too much seafood.

Watching pods of Dolphins, not 75 yards off the shore trail the shrimp boats through the bay was enjoyable, as well as relaxing. We parked Giovanni under a large beach umbrella in a reclining lounge chair and there he remained. Mile, in between waiting on him hand and foot, a beer readily in hand, worked to bronze her tan, before they returned to Italy next week.

By the morning of our third day, I felt used and abused … in a good way for a change … and rested. Soaking up the suns' rays of our last morning here, I followed up with Candi on our earlier conversation. "Baby, did you mean what you said when we arrived at Tybee that you could live in a small town like this, especially if it was on the coast? There are no large hospitals here. What would you do?"

"There are many things still on my bucket list, D. Nothing is set in stone. I could set up a free medical clinic. Thanks to you, it's not like I have to work. Besides, if I don't like it, I can always pick up and go somewhere else."

"What about your family?"

"They'll get by with or without me. As far as I'm concerned, the farther away the better."

"You say that now."

"I mean it, D. Why the third degree all of a sudden, especially about my family?"

"Choices, Candi. Sometimes we have to make hard choices… spur of the minute choices…and live with them. Could you follow your gut and just do it?"

"What exactly are you saying, baby?"

"I'm saying, sooner or later, there is going to come a time in your life when you have to move out of your family's shadow, live your life for you and let the chips fall where they may."

"I did that when I came looking for you."

"Not true. You always knew they were there to fall back on if you failed or ran into a problem that you couldn't overcome. Remember when you tossed your mom's name around, telling me she could control Standford? She didn't. More than likely, since I was involved with you, she didn't want to. Standford has been and is my problem. He has become the monster of my making. I will have to deal with him straight away at some point. Especially since all this running is making my head hurt every damn day."

"I was only trying to help."

"I know you were. I don't fault you for that. Last question and then we need to get on the road. If you had no Family ties that could deal with Standford and he remained a threat to me … to you … what would Candice Parker do?"

Don't let him see you hesitate, you know the answer, say it, "no question, I'd take him out anyway I could."

"That's what I wanted to hear."

"Now, please rouse Gio from his three-day nap and release Mile from her servitude. I'm sure he can't wait to get his cast off tomorrow."

Candi chuckled. "Two to one, I bet Mile wants it off a whole lot more than he does. After the last three days, she needs a break from him."

"Good point. We could leave him here," I said in jest. "Then again, because of his propensity to breed, Tybee Island would never be the same."

Our, three-hour ride back to Daytona Beach down I-95 passed quickly and was surprisingly uneventful. No one wanted to leave the ocean. I got it. Sadly, reality knocked more than once in Tybee. But I didn't want to answer. Today, once I dropped them off at the dealership, I had to.

With Gio and Mile turning in their bikes, Candi readily assisted me in loading mine, handing me the cinch straps, while I tied it down.

I've ignored this long enough. Here goes, "I can stay here with you, D. Gio and Mile can go back without me."

"No, you can't. Marcy is due in tonight. Remember? To have a friend, you have to be a friend."

I relented. "OK, you win. They all fly out Sunday after the All Children's Hospital Gala. I'll come back then. Where will you be?"

"Candi, remember, I'm a non-entity at the moment. Besides, you've single-handedly accomplished all you originally set out to do. You retrieved the ledgers and collected the reward. Realistically, there's nothing more I can do for you at the moment except involve you in my madness."

"That's not true. I wish ... I wish I could rewind the clock and never left Florida. Then again, I'd never have met you."

"What does your gut tell you to do?" She looked troubled and perplexed. I had put her on the spot. "You don't have to answer right now. There will come a time soon enough when I ask you the same question again. Think long and hard, then answer with the same conviction you conveyed this morning toward Standford. But, be prepared to live with it." I heard the clanking and clopping of Gio's crutches approaching. "Give me a hug, baby. We'll talk soon. By the way, where's your passport?"

"In my purse. I've yet to take it out from our ride. Why?"

"Just wondering. I ran across mine earlier and that made me think of yours."

"Are you going on a trip? Excuse me, are we going on a trip?"

"Baby, I've been on a trip all day, every day, since I first met you. Best you keep it close."

Moving to change her train of thought, I walked off the trailer and picked Mile up in my arms, kissing her squarely on the lips. "Thank you for not laying your bike down on this trip. It's bad enough taking care of Gio, let alone taking care of you, too." Ha, Mile kissed me back.

"D, happy. Good guide, good food, good fun," shared Gio, while giving me an Italian man hug.

I whispered, "Don't forget tomorrow. Whatever you have to do, make it happen."

"I will, D. You see."

Watching the three of them drive away pulled at my heartstrings. Over these last six weeks, the four of us bonded through the throes of adversity and formed ties we would carry to the grave. Gio cared deeply for Candi, that's why he joined us on our ride in Sioux City. My saving his leg and possibly his life didn't hurt, either. He has my back and I have his, of that I am sure.

Chapter 76

Finally, in the comfort of my truck en route to the Plaza Hotel, I envisioned Major calling my name, possibly using a litany of four letter words. Again, I had pawned him off to strangers. At least this time it was only for three days, not six weeks like before. I called the Plaza, confirmed my room for the night and asked them to notify the kennel that I was on my way to retrieve the dog.

Using Candi's iPad, the day before, I found waiting emails from Jim, Victoria and Greg. I didn't open them, but I would tonight. Over the last three days I welcomed a brief respite in the drama I've come to know as… my life.

To my delight, Major was bathed and brushed, and sporting a blue bandana round his neck when I arrived. The tech confirmed all his shots were current, his paperwork up to date. Major could travel anywhere with me in or out of the country, including Hawaii. "Thanks for taking care of it. With my travel plans continuously in flux, Major will be happy to know he can go anywhere the wind blows."

I checked into the hotel, took Major to the room, stopped by the bar and snagged two Sam's on the way to the business center. The first email I read was from Jim asking me where I was and to let me know all was quiet on his end. I skipped Victoria's and opened Greg's next. He wanted me to know that Missy was responding exceedingly better than expected in the trials. The whole town was grateful, so much so, they asked him about having a Candice Parker Day. And if so, would she come? Note to self ... I should ask her. Lastly, he wanted me to know he booked a trip to Hawaii and all the islands for the entire month of December, after hunting season. Of course, you did. I laughed.

Saving the best for last, I opened Vic's email.

> **Asshole! Why haven't you contacted me? It's been days! Where are you? How are you? When can I go home? I have a new phone, just for you. Here's the number… use it. Hugs.**

I put her number in the iPhone, hit send, then end to save it. Draining the last of Sam number two, I stopped by the bar, ordered an avocado burger platter, plus a side of green beans and had it sent to the room. Taking the bartenders last cold six-pack under my arm, I hurried back to the room where I had a long overdue date night planned with the D. O. G.

Twenty minutes later, I was nibbling at my burger, while he feasted on lamb and rice mixed with southern style green beans and a handful of crinkle fries. Moving to the balcony, watching waves crash on the beach at high tide, I downed another Sam in thirty-seconds flat — mostly for courage. Then I called Vic.

"Asshole."

"Guilty, as charged," I confessed. "Good evening to you, Victoria."

"It's good to hear your voice. It means you're alive. I was worried you might have been involved in that shootout in Illinois last week… the one involving the U.S. Marshals. You did hear about it, didn't you?"

I paused. "No, Victoria … I didn't read about it. Haven't paid much attention to the news since I left Sioux City."

He's lying…the S.O.B. is lying, I know it. "D, let me rephrase the question. Is it possible you didn't read about it because you were the one making the news in Illinois last week?"

Astute, isn't she? "You do an excellent cross, counselor. Let's just say I once again resemble that remark and leave it at that."

I knew it — ha! I won't press him. He'll tell me when he can. "D, when can I go home?"

"Sunday soon enough?"

"Yes, thank you." *I don't want to go there, but I will.* "Have you worked through your issues with Candi?"

"Not yet. We've made great strides. Much has changed since Calgary, Vic. I won't lie to you. I'm trying to work through them as best I can."

"How can I help?"

That's what I was waiting on — her offer to help. "I'm glad you asked. Get a pen and paper, please. Let me know when you're ready."

Vic rummaged around in her purse 'til I found a pen, "Go ahead."

"First, I want you to create a blind trust for the property in Tennessee, transferring it to my children equally. It can't be sold and is to be used to watch their kids and their kids grow up appreciating nature. Then, calculate how much money it will take to maintain it for the next fifty years. We'll set that money aside.

"If per chance, none of them want anything to do with it, then transfer the control of it to The Wounded Warrior's Project, where soldiers suffering from PTSD will have a place to heal. But, before that happens you'll need to make a run to Tennessee and retrieve two wooden crates and deliver one to Second Harvest Food Bank of East Tennessee, the other to The Wounded Warrior's Project in Nashville. You'll need the code to the safe. If you'll look inside the second to last page of your passport, you'll find it."

"Clever ... When did you put it there?"

"I don't remember, maybe while we were at Greg's. Which reminds me, according to Greg, Missy is responding better than expected to treatment. Looks like she's probably going to make it. Mistatim even wants to celebrate with a Candice Parker Day."

"You tell Candi that? Of course, you didn't. She doesn't even know you did it, does she?"

"It's not important, Vic. It's the thought that counts… that and the fact that Missy will get a second chance at life. Speaking of Missy, set up a college trust fund that will cover her expenses all the way through grad school. She impresses me as the type of child who will appreciate all those who have been there for her and will graciously pay it forward."

"I haven't heard those words in a while."

"You're right … I've been up to my eyeballs in alligators here lately. It's been hard enough trying to stay off radar without doing something magnanimous to bring attention to myself again."

"All this will take money, D. Do you want me to use what you've given me to get this rolling?"

"Heavens no. That's yours to use as you want. Which brings me to my next item of business. Find a no nonsense, no questions asked, commodities trader who deals in precious metals. He'll need to be bonded, say up to 20 million and should be able to convert into cash whatever is sent to him within 48 hours. Once you find him, I will ship you a crate which I suggest you divide and send him half to see how he performs."

"Crate…like the one in the safe at your house in Tennessee?"

"Yes. There were ten in total holding four, 27 pound bars. Which brings me to my last item of business. I want you to set up a non-profit 501C in Iowa, complete with a board of directors whose mission is to help people who have been defrauded by unscrupulous bankers and investors, or as I like to call them, crooks."

"D, who needs clients when I have you?"

"That's the plan. You'll do great…checks and balances, girlfriend. Checks and balances."

"Finally, I'm changing the subject on you. Put down your pen and close your eyes. I'm going to paint you a picture… a scenario if you will. Answer truthfully and honestly. There's no right or wrong answer here. Let's suppose you were given two choices on where you could spend your life. One is by far the most beautiful place in the world. Ideal year-round temps, blue waters, waterfalls, lush green forests in a small town with less than 1200 people, mostly mainlanders looking to retire in peace."

"Sounds wonderful, D. ... This is about Mayberry, isn't it?"

"It is, but now… it's so much more. The second place has mild summers, but harsh winters. Over fourteen feet of snow a year, blustery cold winds off the North Atlantic, an abundance of wildlife like moose and caribou and by far, 20,000 of the nicest, most unselfish, giving, genuine people you'll ever meet. Here's my question… which place would you choose?"

"Hands down, I'd choose the first one."

"Me, too, because it's almost perfect. Thank you, Vic. That's all I've got for now."

"Wait! Wait! When will I see you? I miss you, D. We had fun, didn't we?"

"No promises, Vic. Yes, we had fun, shared many laughs and shared even more tears. Kindred spirits that we are… we'll always have each other to fall back on."

Sounds like goodbye. I started tearing up. Damn, girl, get yourself together. "D, go find your Mayberry. Call me when you get there. I'll take care of every-thing on this end — checks and balances, I know. I know." I pressed end ... I didn't want him to hear me cry ... and cry I did, long into the night.

One answer down. One to go ... or was it two?

Chapter 77

Major and I slept in 'til six. After a quick walk with the dog, up and down the beach chasing crazy crabs, I fed him and left him piled up on the couch. Going downstairs for breakfast, I put a call in to Gen. Little while I waited for my food to arrive.

"Morning General, Jon David here. I told you I'd get back with you today.

"Good morning to you, Captain. What have you got for me?"

"As it stands right now, there will need to be an extraction of no more than two from the roof of the Marriott Waterside in Tampa at 1920 hours. Are you familiar with it? My sources tell me the building does have a helo pad, sir, I just don't know if it will be lit."

"No problem. I've stayed there. I'll make sure it's lit. My aide will notify them, anonymously of course, that a VIP is flying in tomorrow night before 1900. They'll leave the lights on. Don't like surprises. Do I need to bring security?"

"I don't think so sir. Better safe than sorry. I'll let you make that call."

"And where are we going from there, Captain?"

"Southwest Florida International."

"Copy that. Anything else I need to know, you call me, 1920 tomorrow. Marriott Waterside ... Confirmed."

I pushed my food back and forth across the plate until it was cold. I wasn't hungry. Too many details still to iron out left me hanging off the ledge. Seeking a small degree of solace, I called Candi ... It went straight to voice mail. I forgot Marcy flew in late last night. I sent her a text.

What I could control I did, stopping by the business center and confirming late night departures out of Florida International. I found the two I wanted, leaving non-stop at 22:05 and 22:45 p.m., respectively. They weren't full flights by any means. But, I was getting ahead of myself. This was a trip for two, better still for three, counting the dog.

By 0900, I had checked out of the Plaza and was on I-4 west driving to Ft. Myers, just a shade over four hours away. Passing through Orlando, trapped in the smothering highway congestion that the almighty tourism dollar brings, I had a major epiphany. Maui, my first choice, could eventually become just like this… God Bless Us, America. I pulled the trigger again. I should be going where I can blend in with others who unselfishly give more than they receive. I needed a second opinion

Major and I rolled into Ft. Myers sometime around two and drove straight to the long-distance shipper. Surprisingly, in less than an hour all the forms and paperwork were filled out to ship my truck, sans the trailer and the bike, west or north. What they needed the most, I couldn't provide… an exact physical address to ship to. That would have to come later.

I bought Major an oversized crate, complete with a memory foam fitted bed at PetSmart, along with two giant rawhide chews to keep him entertained during his confinement. Then I found a J.C. Penney and bought two pieces of luggage. Next, I checked into a ground floor room at the Holiday Inn on Airport Row. After unloading the dog, his crate, my clothes, my bags and the bike, I dropped my truck off at the shipping office. Nice enough folks, whose employees were kind enough to give me a ride back to the hotel to keep me from calling a cab.

While the dog and I waited for the surprise rain shower to quit, I texted Gio:

Hey Pal. Tell me what you know and what you don't.

After fifteen plus minutes, Gio replied with multiple texts in no particular order. I bet it took him that long to type. That's mean, even for a little prick to say.

Ciao D. What I know. We table of 4. Marcy come. Her Momma, Joseph, table 12. 4 heavy.

Heavy as in carrying concealed weapons, I surmised. Ha … I'm not as dumb as I look.

Mgr. do what I say. Big Tip. U Have Hr. No C movie … Candice say NO!

Which meant it was up to me to get her to say yes. Better still, if she could burn me two copies on DVDs to fit into jewel cases along with two very important CD's. I replied:

Thanks, Gio. I owe you. We'll talk tomorrow late. Meet me by pool at the Marriott, 6 PM sharp.

And then I rested my eyes watching Major break in his new bed. His sleeping, I soon discovered was contagious. I woke up at 04:30 and found three missed calls from Candi. For some dumb reason that now escapes me, I'd left the phone on vibrate.

Since I was still in my clothes, I took Major for his long overdue walk. I now remember why I never liked south Florida. It's as muggy at night as it is in daylight. We made two trips along Airport Row and back. My shirt, because of the heavy humidity, melted into my back. Yuck!

Since 05:30 breakfast was still an hour away, all I could scavenge was last nights' coffee. It would have do. Back in the room, I flipped on the news and zoned out, wondering what the day along with the night would bring.

When I put this plan together I was counting on shock and awe…the element of surprise, a room full of witnesses and a willing participant jumping at the chance to run away with me. What I didn't anticipate was the radical change in me that had occurred on my way here. I was now seeking service above solitude. Go figure. So much for writing a book.

Maui, Hawaii is by far the most beautiful place in the world by many standards, including mine. I spent seven glorious days in an Embassy Suites, watching hump back whales swim leisurely back and forth along the beach, not fifty yards from my room. Then there's the diamond in the rough. Hana, population 1200, is located four hours away from anywhere and offers a temperate climate, seclusion, privacy and unsurpassed beauty. I even believe Charles Lindberg retired and eventually, died there. Thankfully, I'm not ready to retire or die…not yet anyway.

Which brings me to my second and final option, Corner Brook, Newfoundland, population 20,000. Years ago, I persuaded three friends to go on a moose, caribou hunt on an island in the middle of Newfoundland, which, itself is an island in the North Atlantic. Long story short, our guns, our gear, our luggage never made it out of Boston. But we sure as hell did, never dreaming our luggage would never catch us, before we were dropped into a remote tent camp by helo.

Before us, an eight-day hunt. Behind us, our guns, our gear, our clothes sitting securely inside Boston Logan Airport, with no way to retrieve them. Within ten minutes of landing, Punch, our outfitter, passed around a yellow legal pad around asking us to write down our clothes sizes, shoe sizes, coat sizes as well as the caliper of gun we shot. Satisfied he had all the information he needed, he called in the supply chopper and disappeared. The next morning two choppers landed bringing us two of everything we listed, half of which was brand new. Seems the story of four stranded yanks went viral. Picked up by the radio stations, our dilemma passed through Corner Brook like wildfire and people from a fifty-mile radius delivered everything we needed for the week and more.

Newfie's, as they're commonly called in jest by other mainland Canadians, could very well use my gifts and talents, while offering me a like-minded community to establish new roots.

Paying it forward begins at home. Random, unselfish acts of kindness is a trait Newfoundlanders must be instilling in their children at birth. To me,

Corner Brook, and possibly all the rest of Newfoundland, is, to some degree, everything I've been searching for in my quest of Mayberry. Although, I dreamed of Maui, Corner Brook was calling my name, only louder.

Another lingering question… would Candi hear it, too?

Chapter 78

It was now half past six. Candice Parker, by my man-selfish calculations, had slept enough. I texted but got no reply. I rang three times, no answer. At least it rang. I huffed and puffed, then called again.

"D, do you know what time it is? Better still, you happen to know what time I went to sleep this morning? I tried calling you last night… five times. You didn't answer. I thought something bad had happened."

I brushed off my sympathy prose. "Candi, you care to know what time I got up?"

"Probably about the same time I went to bed. Marcy worried with me. Besides, we had a lot to catch up on."

"Time flies when you're having fun, huh baby?"

"I'm so tired right now. Can you please wait until I wake up before you start making jokes?"

"Grab a nap, then a shower. Call me later."

"I'll grab a shower…a cold one. I'll call you back, K?"

"Bye, baby."

I visited the breakfast room while I waited for Candi to call. This particular morning, nothing in their spread looked appealing. It wasn't the diverse food choices Holiday Inn provided, it was me. My appetite had waned since Candi left. I was apprehensive about tonight. Hard choices, harder decisions had to be made today, tonight. Otherwise, I would spend the rest of my life sleeping with one eye open.

My phone vibrated, then rang. "Morning, Candice, you awake now?"

"Not entirely ... But, it's all I can give you on three hours sleep."

"I'll take it. Remember, I told you there would come a time when you had to make some hard decisions? This is not the time. It will come soon enough. This morning, I'd like to ask you some hypothetical questions.

"Jon David, you woke me just to ask hypothetical questions?"

"The answers, excuse me, your answers are important to me."

Candi laid back on the bed and stared at the ceiling fan, "Go ahead, D. Fire away."

"I'm going to paint you a picture — a scenario if you will. Answer truthfully and honestly. There are no right or wrong answers here. Let's suppose you were given two choices where you could spend the next chapter of your life. One is by far the most beautiful place in the world. Ideal year- round temps, blue water, cascading waterfalls into shallow pools, lush green forests near a small town with less than 1200 people, mostly mainlanders looking to retire in paradise."

Aroused by the picture, D painted, Candi sat upright and propped herself against the headboard. "It sounds too good to be true."

"It's real, I promise you. The second place has mild summers and harsh winters; fourteen feet of snow a year, blustery cold winds off the North Atlantic, an abundance of wildlife, moose, caribou and bear; and by far, 20,000 of the nicest, most unselfish, giving, genuine people you'll ever meet. Neighbors who would give you the last of their food, even the coats off their back, if they knew you were in need. Here's my question, which destination could you choose to call home?"

Steeling herself, "before I met you, the scene you first described fit me to a tee, as in paradise. Once upon a time I dreamed of lounging in a hammock on a private beach, gazing out into coral, blue waters and spending my day sipping Mai Tais. The second place you mentioned sounds beautiful, yet brutal. But, it's the people you describe that live there that sets it apart from the first one. They sound so much like the qualities I've come to appreciate in you. Weighing them equally in both hands, I choose the later."

I exhaled. "You've grown up quite a bit since we met, Candice Parker. Who would have thought three months ago you'd choose substance over style? Go figure."

"What's this about, D? Are you going to tell me or not?'

"I am. Until then, I'm afraid I'm going to ask for patience and to trust me a little longer. That being said, I need you to burn two DVD's of the video you made with Joseph. Then I want you to give them to Giovanni."

"I can't, I won't. I'm sorry. I couldn't chance their getting out… ever."

"Candi, this is bigger than you, bigger than Joseph, certainly bigger than me. As long as I'm alive and you two aren't together, you know as well as I do, he won't stop looking for me."

"D, as far as he knows, you… are history."

"But, I'm not and therein lies the problem. One careless move, one casual photograph and the chase resumes. I watched three people die needlessly in a hail of bullets last week because of his jealously."

"You didn't tell me that. Was Donnie one of them?"

"Can't say… I'm sorry."

"I'll do it, D. But if this video gets out, Joseph's history."

"That's what I'm counting on. Not for him to die mind you, but for him to know that the risk he takes is far greater than the reward he receives."

"When will I hear from you again?"

"Soon, count on it. Kisses." I pressed end. I had my second opinion.

"Major, we're far from finished on this ride. Be patient with me a little while longer. I'm beginning to see a glimmer of light on the far side of the horizon."

Chapter 79

The rest of the morning was spent unloading my treasures from the saddlebags and the truck and packing it into my newly acquired luggage. I fed the dog, walked him and called a cab to take us, my bags, and his crate to the airport. Air Canada accommodated me in every way possible, assuring me they would take care of Major, until our flight left Ft. Myers. In dire need of solitude, I walked back to the Holiday Inn, feeling at times, lost, but never alone. There was an abundance of people who had my back. Tonight, I hoped I would not disappoint three of them, Gio, Mile… and Candi most of all.

I dressed in black leather and donned a red bandana in honor of Candi's infamous red thong. Confident I was ready to ride, I pumped my fist and shouted into the Heaven's… "Let the games begin!"

Traveling north into rush hour traffic, I planned to be at the Marriott before six to share the nuts and bolts of my convoluted plan with Giovanni. Thanks to clearing northbound congestion, I arrived shortly after six o'clock, along with hundreds of other attendees dressed in their finest revelry. With nothing to do but watch and wait, over the next fifty minutes, I made Sam Adams proud.

A few minutes shy of seven, I traded glass for plastic and found the pool. Giovanni, dressed in his finest biker rags, was waiting, holding two, jeweled cases in one hand, a red solo cup in the other. My hero.

"Welcome to the Gala, Gio. I'm glad you dressed down for it." Perusing his attire, Gio was wearing a ripped to the shoulder, black tee, emblazoned with the words, BITCH BEHIND on the front and STUD IN FRONT on back. His leather chaps covered most of the holes in his jeans, except where they didn't, in back, exposing his left butt cheek. I pinched it. He jumped, jostling his beer on the table.

"Ah… D. Too much sunshine?"

"The word's daylight, Gio. Maybe a little too revealing for the caliber of people gathered here tonight. In South Beach, you'd fit right in, San Francisco, too."

"South Beach… yes! San Fran…no!" replied Giovanni, passing me his beer, then taking it back and giving me the DVD's instead.

"Been drinking long?"

"Si," Gio giggled.

"How many?"

"Not enough"

"I heard that." Scoping out a far off, dry table, I pointed to it, "Follow me." Over the next two beers, I pitched my plan, revised it and with Gio's help, refined it, then dumbed it down… the simpler the better. Making my entrance after the awards portion of the event would put all eyes on me and the table I rode up on. All told, I had twenty minutes from start to finish to confront the mean queen and her dark knights, rescue the princess and ride off into the sunset.

I followed Gio into the banquet hall, located on the Mezzanine level and stood just inside the door, watching him weave his way through throngs of people in masquerades. Once he reached his table, he stopped, turned and walked to a large adjoining table, kissing a woman on the cheek, which I presumed was Candi's mom. Two chairs to her right, sat Joseph attempting to be, by all indications, John Travolta from the movie Saturday Night Fever.

Back to Giovanni's table, there were three women, two dressed in leather, the third adorned in a shimmery red dress that exuded elegance. She looked stunning, Candi. It was the first time I'd seen her looking so ... glamorous. Her hair was pulled back and wrapped tightly into a bun with what looked like a golden dagger holding it in place. Pretty woman/biker babe is that what Giovanni said?

For the first thirty minutes, I listened to Jeffery Whitehouse, the CEO/MC tonight, acknowledge all the locally famous people in attendance, as well as offer a brief history of All Children's Hospital, concluding with a litany of projects they hoped to launch from the proceeds of tonight's Gala. Glancing at the program, I noticed the next item listed was the Benefactor of the Year Award, recognizing the individual or individuals who best exemplified the heart and soul of All Children's through their charitable acts of giving and service to the community. Hopefully, my phone call to Mr. Whitehouse last week was successful in conveying such a person. I smiled.

"Ladies and Gentlemen," said Jeffery Whitehouse, "it is my pleasure to present the highest award offered by our foundation to one of our own. Stand with me and welcome our newest inductee into the All Children's Hall of Fame, Ms. Candice Parker."

I watched Candi lower her head into her hands, before catching her breath, while making a 360° sweep of the room to verify there was not another Candice Parker in the audience standing up to receive this prestigious award. The applause was deafening and continued to roar until she stood and walked to the podium, glimmering in her beautiful, red evening gown.

Mr. Whitehouse, reading her bio as she approached, got to the crux of the award as Candi reached the stage. "Dim the lights, please. Ladies and gentlemen, I direct your attention to the video screen on your right coming to you live from All Children's. Candice, someone very special wants to speak to you. Go ahead, Missy..."

I watched as Missy appeared, looking no longer frail, but vibrant and alive. "Ms. Candice, I'm Missy Bryan from Mistatim, Saskatchewan. We've never met in person, at least I don't think we have ... I mean, you could be an angel in disguise. Couldn't she mom?" asked Missy looking away, before turning back to the camera. "I want everybody out there to know I was dying a little every day. Then they said Candice gave so I could live. I'm alive today because of Candice Parker. And I'm going to Disney World!" Missy looked away. "It's true, Mom. D, promised. He said I get to meet Mickey, Minnie and Pluto. Vic said we're all going to Disney World. D said, I'm going to be a Princess."

My heart stopped beating. My eyes glistened. Victoria, girl, I wish you could see this. Then out of the mouth of a child, it came in waves — D said ... Vic said ... D said.

Turning back to the camera, Missy continued, "Ms. Candice, I love you. You come, too. Bye-bye," waved Missy as the screen faded black, before switching back live to the podium where Candi was standing, in tears. I watched Marcy vault from her seat and angle toward the stage with a package of tissues in hand. It wouldn't be enough. Throughout the banquet hall, tears of joy flowed for this blond haired, green-eyed little girl named Missy who captured their hearts this night like she stole mine a few short days ago.

Mr. Whitehouse grabbed a tissue from Marcy and patted his eyes before continuing. "People, this is what it's all about. Ms. Parker's generous million-dollar donation made this invaluable MDS trial possible for Missy and fulfilled Mr. D's promise to her and her family... she is going to Disney World. Thank you, Candice Parker. All Children's Hospital thanks you, everyone in this room thanks you."

I watched Candi accept the award with a gracious nod and hug before I disappeared from the festivities, ten minutes shy of show time. At precisely eight o'clock, I strapped on my helmet, brought my bike to life and rumbled through the startled guests in the lobby to the open elevator where Gio waited patiently. On the ride, up to the Mezzanine level, I handed him my last full bag of Standford's diamonds, mixed with hundreds of small clear glass marbles. That was my idea. Why couldn't we make this fun?

I rolled my bike off the elevator and waited for Gio to prop open the double doors. Taking a deep breath, I rumbled into the room as all eight hundred plus attendee's eyes, turned and focused solely on me. The silence was deafening.

Meandering my way through the maze of crowded, misaligned tables, I arrived at my destination at 19:10. Removing my helmet, I nodded to Joseph first. "Mrs. Parker, I presume. Candi has said so many things about you. I'm D… Jon David to you. Whatever you want to call me is fine. I'm not here to hurt or harm anyone, I'm here to make a deal. All I ask is two minutes of your time.

"OMG! OMG! Marcy, look … It's … It's—"

"I know who it is, Candice. I recognize the motorcycle. This is about to get interesting," Marcy said, watching Candi trip into a chair, before intercepting me at the large table.

I felt a hard pull on my left arm.

"D, you shouldn't be here, but you know that already. Don't you?"

I nodded. Laying two, jeweled disc cases on the table, I slid the one marked with a "X" to Joseph, the other marked with an "F" to Mrs. Parker. "Joseph, your ex-mother in law holds in her hand your second successful attempt at porn. Mrs. Parker, Joseph holds in his hand a copy of the infamous ledgers, along with the encryption codes that Candice worked so diligently to retrieve from me."

"I'm tired of running. I'm tired of trying to do the right thing. I'm really tired of watching people die, needlessly. So, here's the deal. I've retained two copies of each. Joseph, if something happens to me… yours goes straight to the head of the Family, as well as TMZ. No one in their right mind would own a lawyer with such a dubious past, especially one that is subject to blackmail and coercion. Mrs. Parker, yours on the other hand, will go directly to the DOJ and more importantly, the IRS. Family or not, lives will be destroyed… beginning with this nice little arrangement you have here in Tampa. Trust me, I have no desire to see that happen, either."

Reaching into my saddlebag, I lifted out a 27.5 lb. South African, solid gold bar and dropped it from two feet onto the table, rattling the silverware, knocking over the glasses and making a rather bold, pronounced statement. "This is for A.J. Standford. Tell him there are seven more just like it if he'll call off his witch hunt. If he says no," I laughed, "well then, there are three more just like it for the one who makes him go away…as in permanently." I glanced at my watch. "Speaking of going away, my two minutes of fame are up. Thank you for your time. I must bid you all, adieu."

Turning my gaze to the gorgeous woman in red standing on my left, "Candi, remember that decision I told you, you'd have to make at some point? I'm afraid that time is now." Firing off all cylinders, "I have to go, baby. You coming or staying? It's totally up to you."

D was right… the time had come. I could continue to live in the shadows of my family or make new dreams with him. "Mom, I'm sorry. I'll give the reward money back if I need to. It doesn't look like I'll need it anymore. I have to go with him. I love you."

My dreams were coming true in D. Joining me on the motorcycle, Candi lifted her dress, flashing a brief glimpse of my favorite red thong, as she settled in behind me. Tapping my shoulder, "Let's ride."

"Stop them," shouted her Mom, followed by Joseph's screams to take me out as the table erupted in my rear views. The stunned crowd before me graciously parted, allowing me to pass through the maze of tables, unencumbered. That is until Gio started screaming free diamond solitaires for everyone, tossing handful after handful of the shiny baubles into the air, mixed with the marbles to stop cold anyone giving chase. The chaos behind me was maddening. Passing through the doors to a waiting elevator, compliments of Mile, I mouthed, "I love ya, Mile. Tell Gio to take care of my bike." Pressing the 12th floor, I watched the doors slowly close behind us.

"So, where are we going, baby?" asked Candi.

"Up … We're going up, baby." At 19:18, the elevator doors opened. Taking Candi's hand in mine, I helped her off the bike and led her up the stairway to the roof and the waiting helo. Introducing her to my old friend, General Rich Little, we lifted off, flying south into the dark Florida sky.

Wait! ... Wait! "What about Major?"

"No worries, Candice Parker. I left the D.O.G. in charge. He's holding the plane…"

To be continued…

Read on for a sneak peek at book three: Ride to Retribution

RIDE TO
Retribution

Chapter 1

The thump…thump…thump of the helicopter's rotors overshadowed the engines deceleration, as General Richard Little powered back the throttle, beginning our decent into the Ft. Myers, Florida airspace around 21:30, before zeroing in on the helo pad, located a stone's throw left of Southwest Florida International Airport.

"General," I shouted, my voice vibrating in sync to the whump, whump, whump of the rotors, "thank you for making this extraction run as smooth as the skin in Candi's cleavage." Candi, rolling her eyes at me, clamped down on my knee with her left hand and squeezed deftly to stop my intimate sexual overtures from going into the eternal abyss. Candi, not to be outdone, removed her headset, leaned forward and kissed him sweetly on his right cheek.

"General Little," I cooed, "please ignore D's crude attempt of sexually charged humor at my expense. I'm grateful D has friends like you." I paused, gathered my thoughts collectively, then continued. "Can you imagine how fast my head was spinning, sitting on his motorcycle in an elevator climbing to the 14th floor? Thank you for rising to his call," I said, before kissing him again, this time on his left cheek. "We owe you," I whispered sweetly into his ear, while watching the goose bumps wash across his neck, followed by an abrupt, involuntary 'man' shiver.

"Don't mention it," countered Rich, with an 'Aw Shucks' good ole boy reply. "I'm glad to be of service. Call on me anytime, especially you, Miss Parker," stammered Rich, gazing longingly into Candi's ample cleavage, spilling ever so generously from her red evening gown. Deftly stroking his chin, he continued, "I don't know what you see in this man, but I certainly know what he sees in you!"

Look! Look! The awesome power of the Woo-Hoo strikes Generals, too! If I didn't know better, I'd think he's drooling over her. Abruptly changing his train of thought, I slapped Rich heartedly on the shoulder, dropping a small, velvet drawstring pouch into his lap, filled with a few shiny baubles, twenty-five to be exact. Roughly, 60 carets give or take, valued between 200K and 300K. These few conflict diamonds were a far cry from the 150-plus packages I mailed at the beginning of this ride, making whole, many of the poor souls Standford swindled in his massive Ponzi scheme. Still, it was enough to say thank you in a rather magnanimous way, if I do say so myself.

Stepping onto the tarmac with Candi in tow, I 'man hugged' Rich, after he'd unbuckled his harness and stepped from the chopper. Keeping my head low, cognizant of the blades whirling above my head, I shouted, "I owe you, sir, more than you know. Then again, we're brothers for life, aren't we?"

Rich nodded, "Don't mention it, Captain, I won't," he said with a wink. "Besides, it was fun," retorted the infamous Air Force, Black Ops Commander out of Hurlburt Field, before he climbed back into the helo, belted in, powered up and lifted off.

And then he was gone … lifting effortlessly into the starless, black shrouded night sky. *Chalk up another successful Black Ops Mission, even if this one happened to be off book.*

Urgently, encouraging this gorgeous lady to my right, "Hurry, Candi. We have forty-five minutes to make our flight," I bellowed, deeply breathing in the moisture laden, salty sea air, blowing inland from the Gulf of Mexico.

Clutching my luxurious red gown in both hands, I scurried along, while launching into a conversation between labored breaths, all the while trying to keep from falling flat on my face in these damn "man bait" heels. "D," I puffed, "all you said was Major was holding the plane. When are you going to tell me where we are going?"

Walking into the terminal directly to the Air Canada ticketing counter, I spun around facing her, gathering Candi's hands in mine and answered distinctly, "Canada."

Crossing my fingers, I was hoping Canada meant we were going to finish the ride. Who knows with D? I never quite know where his head is from one moment to the next. Then again, I know where I'd like it to be. Fond memories of our last, lust filled ride enveloped me, shivering me to the core.

"Candi, your passport?" I asked graciously, before passing it, along with mine, to an attractive, willowy blond Air Canada agent named Holly. "We have a 10:20 flight to Toronto, with a dog you're holding somewhere back there," I said, pointing through the double swinging doors behind her. "Can we make it?"

"Certainly, now that the flight has been delayed by thirty minutes. Your dog wouldn't happen to be Major, would he?" Holly asked, sporting an impish grin.

"He would," I nodded, "My guess is you've met him."

"Most definitely," Holly replied, looking a little to the right of flustered. "What a wonderful temperament he has. He's all male, that's for sure."

I turned to Candi and grinned sheepishly, "He does love women."

"And boobs," I breathed, just above a whisper, nonchalantly pushing my breasts together to show off a teasing glimpse of my cleavage, "just like his daddy."

"Copy that, Candi! Major's a boob man," I exclaimed, much louder than her whisper, bending down and kissing, ever so gently, her pronounced cleavage, magnificently on display.

Holly blushed because our sexual overtures had destroyed all that was left of her professional demeanor. "I have a note here that says since we don't have a full flight, Major is welcome to ride in the cabin with you. That is if you want him to."

"Gladly, he does love to ride shotgun, doesn't he, Candi? Not sure what we'll call this airplane arrangement, but it will definitely work."

"Please excuse me for a moment while I get him for you. Just so you know, I'm sending his crate on to your final destination," Holly stated poignantly, before swishing through the swinging doors, disappearing from sight.

Candi, girl, you're on. *Our final destination? Hmm... sounds kinda perma-nent. Not the best way to finish our ride.* "Baby, now that I've got your undivided attention," I cooed, playfully grabbing his crotch with no one outside our immediate circle the wiser. Well, maybe one the wiser, possibly even two, now that his little brain is awake and responding to my two-handed touch. "What is our final destination, Jon David?"

"It's a surprise, baby girl. After all we've been though, surely you still trust me?" I asked, then paused, while her left hand caught up with her right. Noticing how uncomfortable my jeans had become, I decided to give in to her seductive ways and share one specific location. "Later tonight, we'll be in Toronto."

I bit my tongue, purposely trying to keep from lashing out over his eva-sive answers. *Toronto is a great place to stopover, but not to stay long-term.* Reluc-tantly accepting this as all the answer I was going to get, I released my playful grip. "I'm with you and Major, my two favorite boys. Guess that's enough for now," I relented, before adding a pronounced caveat, "until it's not!"

Damn, did Candi just sound like Victoria? What's happening to me? Why is it when I'm with one of my two favorite women, memories of the other one clouds my terribly, twisted mind?

Hearing something explode in the distance, I turned to see Major vault-ing through the swinging door, leaping over the luggage check-in station and launching upward into Candi, planting his front paws on her boda-cious breasts. *That dog has ESP.* "Guessing he wants a hug, baby," I chuckled. "Oblige him."

Girl, you're blushing. "That's my Major, always wants to cop a feel every time he sees me," I shared exuberantly with Holly, as D looked wistfully away. *Is he jealous of the dog? Really?*

I had to laugh. "Like father, like son. Thankfully, I taught him to shy away from the Woo-Hoo, leaving it all for me!" As I was snapping Major on his leash, Holly, rendered speechless by my TMI comment, pointed us in the direction of the gate.

We were off! Next stop, Toronto; then onto Mayberry, AKA, Cornerbrook, Newfoundland.

At least that was my well thought out game plan...or so I thought...

Chapter 2

The Airbus A-320 was in the process of pre-boarding as we scurried to the gate. Sauntering down the gateway, Major vaulted toward the open door. Our seat assignments were in Business Class, row 3, seats A and C for Candi and me. While Major sprawled out across the aisle in seats D and F. Being the pampered labra-doodle he is, he acted like he owned the place. And, by the furious wagging of his tail, he was thoroughly happy to be here. Anywhere really, if Candi happened to be nearby.

Settled into our seats, after what seemed like an eternity of cloak and dagger mystery, I closed my eyes to rest. But only for a moment. Distracted by the distinct sound of clanking crutches approaching from the jet way, I was instantly on alert. It sounded like Candi's, cousin Giovanni's gait, compliments of a thigh to ankle cast, before he was refitted, not two weeks removed with a more versatile 'strap-on.'

It wasn't Giovanni, sadly enough. Instead I saw a 'high and tight' soldier and his family filling the aisle. From his appearance, he was most likely a Marine or a Navy Seal. Judging by his labored gait, I could only assume he'd been recently fitted with a state of the art prosthesis.

Whispering seductively to Candi, "Baby, since it doesn't seem to be a full flight, what say we move to the back of the plane? The Mile-High Club awaits us! It's gonna be easier to accomplish that feat from back there." I grinned, giving her my best impression of wanton puppy dog eyes blinking wildly, while pointing over my left shoulder.

You go girl! I rolled my eyes at him. *I'm not following him. Then again, we've made love on everything that moves, except a plane. There has to be a method to his madness.* Looking at the family of four ambling toward us, I realized in a flash that there was more to the request than D being D. "Gladly, baby," I replied. Securing Major's leash in my left hand, "Come Major, Daddy wants to get risky, frisky. Bet you're going to earn your keep by guard-dogging the door."

That's my girl! Rising quickly, by one sweep of my hand, I ushered the family of four into our recently vacated seats. "Guy's, it's your lucky day. We're moving to the back of the plane. Please take our seats," I directed, more so than politely asked. "It's because of the dog. We wouldn't want him to bother anyone in business class."

I retrieved my backpack from the overhead bin, receiving a respectful nod from the soldier/dad and a heartfelt hug from his wife. Feeling like we'd made a little difference for this family, albeit a slight one, I strolled toward Candi and the dog, thinking how proud I was of her for responding so quickly to my madness.

Two rows shy of the back, I found Major panting wildly and sprawled across three seats on my left, while Candi was seductively man spread across three seats on my right, her beautiful dress raised deliciously high enough on one thigh to reveal a glimpse of her exquisite, and up to now, elusive red thong.

Breaking out my best mischievous grin, "I know what you did, Jon David, and that's one of the many things I adore about you." Swirling my tongue across my Trixie-embossed lips, I added, "Does membership count in the Mile-High Club if we were to consummate the act… before we leave the ground?"

Feeling the prickly sensation of heat flush across my neck, "I'll get back to you on that, baby doll," were the only words I could muster, before Candi deftly pulled me on top of her and proceeded to take my breath away.

Chapter 3

Lust-filled and caught up in the moment, Candi and I were locked together in a tight embrace, touching, feeling, rapidly rediscovering sensations, at least one week removed, when a not so subtle, feminine voice broke through the passion, infused cabin air, enveloping us.

"Uh-hmm… Excuse me! I need you two love birds to put your seat belts on," directed Dawn, one of our Air Canada flight attendants, standing over us, one hand on the seat, the other patting the guard dog, who was lost in his own moment, panting from floppy ear to floppy ear. "You're my Business Class passengers. I saw you give up your seats to that soldier and his family, KUDOS. That earns high marks in my book." Almost apologetically, Dawn lowered her voice to a whisper. "Sadly, however, I must interrupt your love fest… until we get off the ground. She winked. "Work with me on this and I'll work with you. What you do after the plane takes-off is all you. Just keep it subtle, please."

Get your act together, girl. Rising up into a seated position in the window seat, while repositioning my breasts D had so expertly unleashed, I coyly replied, "Thank you, Dawn. It's like this, we're in lust. I promise we'll be good…at least until the lights are off." I winked back.

"Thank you, ma'am," chided Dawn, looking a little flushed herself. "I'm sure you'll be better than good, even great by the looks of things," she continued, staring purposely at my rather rigid predicament.

Now I was squirming. "Dawn, would you be so kind to round Candi and I up a blanket?" I pleaded, hoping to turn away her gaze and give me a moment to compose myself and shrink the one-eyed monster.

"Gladly," Dawn replied. "What say I bring you two, plus I'll toss in a couple of pillows?" She returned the wink to Candi, then disappeared aft.

I playfully nodded OK, before again turning my attention to the man beside me. "This paying it forward mentality is karma, D. I get it. You graciously give up our seats, Dawn sees it and returns the gift immediately … by not having us *thrown off the plane!*"

"I got it, Candi. But I didn't give up our seats just for a sexual rendezvous. I gave them up…"

"Out of respect for a Wounded Warrior and his family. Admirable, D, still you had an end game, didn't you? You always have an end game, like getting me away from prying eyes to get into my pants."

I nodded approvingly. She caught me. "Baby, this grey hair didn't happen overnight. My life lessons have been hard fought, teaching me a thing or two through the years. Specifically, learning how to make the best of any situation, like changing the best seats in the house for the second-best seats in the house, with benefits, mind you, complimented by your more than ample attributes," I concluded, softly caressing her breasts.

He knew how to make me laugh. "A poet with two brains," I replied, kissing D softly on the lips, responding to his touch by caressing his rigid little brain, screaming desperately to get out and play.

Out of nowhere, two blankets crashed into my lap, interrupting my lust laced, mildly wicked thought process, covering the man-sized tent of Candi's making. By all accounts, Dawn had struck again. Turning my gaze ninety degrees, "Major…what kind of watch dog are you?"

Defend the dog, Candi. "A great one, D. Major is the type of dog that mostly likes to watch," I interjected, blowing a kiss to Major, thoroughly caught up in our moment.

Settling into our seats, Candi and I reluctantly composed ourselves once again in time for take-off. I closed my eyes for the second time, trying to remember the last time I had been on a plane. Sadly, the memories that rushed in were not good ones, revealing the moment on the tarmac in Calgary *when Candi hung me out to dry….and kissed my ass good-bye. It still hurts. Her ruse to protect me and Victoria in Calgary worked. Sadly, however, its end game thrust us into the hands of others, before we found our way back. What a cluster, what a FUBAR!*

D, by the looks of things has gone off into La-La land. I poked him. "Baby, where's your head?" I asked, spreading one of the blankets across our laps and stuffing a pillow behind my head. Somewhat concealed, though the cabin lights were still on, I felt brazen enough to take his left hand and slip it between my receptive nether regions, while placing my right hand deliberately on him. *Surely, my moxie will rouse D from his current fog and back into reality with a nip /tuck of his fingers and a deliberate slip of my hand.*

I caught myself thinking out loud, a little too loud, considering our close proximity to each other. "I sure hope she's worth it," I exhaled, as Candi's right hand relocated mine, deftly placing it in a moist, all so familiar place. Her right hand, nesting restlessly on me, pounced. "Ouch! What was that for?" I screamed in sheer agony, as the whites of her eyes met mine, mere inches apart.

"Asshole! What do you mean 'hoping I'm worth it?' After all I've been through to get to you, plus all you've sacrificed to get to me, surely you know by now I'm worth it? Hell, D, even you're worth it!"

Asshole has a familiar ring, dick-wad, too, present company included. Victoria strikes again! "Excuse me for breathing. I was thinking about your last time on a plane and it wasn't pretty. Come to think of it, it down right sucked." I moved to smooth. Looking into Candi's beautiful brown eyes, "You're worth it, baby-doll. Every sacrifice I made, you made, to get us to this point is worth us being together again, right here, right now. It's totally up to us to not screw it up and make us work, yes?"

Nodding my head in approval, I thought, *there is no argument here.* "Yes, it is up to us to make us work and we will, D, as long as we're forthcoming in everything that concerns us; and I mean everything." *Girl, its gut check time. If you don't get your head on straight, you may wind up eating your words.*

Guess *that's my cue to jump in.* "Candi, we're going to Cornerbrook, Newfoundland, where the people are genuine and life is easy; albeit, the winters, notwithstanding."

"The hypothetical place you asked me about a couple of weeks ago? I got it… If it's everything you say it is, count me in." I sighed. *Then again, D dreams of apple pie in sky more times than not. His glass is always half full, mine, well, not so much.*

It was my turn to take a long, deep breath. "You hesitated, Candice. I saw your eyes slowly drift downward. Pray tell me why?"

I caught myself looking away through the plane's window into the night sky, before I answered him. "I was hoping when you said Canada, you were taking me back to Calgary to finish our ride. I can only imagine how beautiful the Icefields Parkway must be in the fall." I sighed again. "Excuse me, it's only a little girl's dream, D, when we had not a care in the world. Now however, a cold dose of reality has replaced that. Besides, you left your bike in the elevator at the hotel…Come to think of it, I left my leathers there, too." I sat up straight and proud, somewhat confident of what I was about to say, "Baby, if Newfoundland is where you've planned for us to go, then by all means, let's go."

Shaking my head dumbfounded, doing my level best to see the method in her madness, "I didn't know finishing our ride meant so much to you. I can always rent or buy another bike. As for your leathers…I have your old pair, along with everything you left in Calgary. It's packed securely in your luggage, Candice Parker." I grinned.

"You're awesome, baby! Then can we, can we, please finish the ride? We don't even have to do it on a bike." I blushed, clenching my lower lip between my teeth.…*Fondly remembering how thrilling it was to be riding with him. Plus, we'd done the deed on his bike, twice…so far.*

The amorous male in me interjected, "I liked doing it…you… you know what I mean…the ride on the bike, Candice Parker. My tongue thickened, then twisted. "You've flustered me again. You, of all people, go figure."

Thinking outside my girlish selfishness, "We can't take the bike, baby." Looking over at Major thoroughly engrossed in us, "Major can't go. Then again, we could rent a car for all of us, couldn't we?"

"Sounds like a plan, girlfriend. Let me work on it, at least until we land in Toronto. Besides, what else do I have to do for the next three hours?"

Coyly, the amorous woman in me answered him. "I'm sure something will pop up," my hand making its way a second time, mind you, under the blanket to caress his now disheveled little brain. *Little did he know these were the determined words of a woman not to be denied the opportunity to obtain her membership in the Mile-High Club.*

Chapter 4

ho would have thought the words I was about to utter would ever cross my lips in my lifetime? Especially with a beautiful woman in red, nestled beside me, her hand restlessly rummaging at the lifeless package, buried in the far recesses of my pants. "Please stop, Candi," I whispered. "I'm not in the mood. I have way too much to think about to make this new plan of yours come together." I pulled my Amex card from my wallet and swiped it beside the movie screen on the backrest, facing her. "Watch a movie, baby," I said, solemnly. "I've got work to do." With renewed vigor, I swiped my card again on my side to give me access to the plane's Wi-Fi connection.

I will not be denied, not tonight. "D, I refuse to remove my hand for the third time. Nope, it's not happening. You do what you need to do. I'll do what I need to do. Sure, I'll watch a movie. Just to be sure, know this now, I AM NOT DONE WITH YOU," I reiterated, clamping down on him with a woman's determination… an amorous one at that.

"Copy that," I replied, squirming uncomfortably, attempting to redistribute the tension streaming through my slightly tender testicles. Success! Kinda… "Hold that thought, Candi. In order to make your dream come true, I'll need my laptop."

"And?" I snickered.

"And, in order for me to grab it from my bag, you're going to have to release the pleasure pistol."

"That's a stretch, D. Tonight, it's acting more like a dilapidated derringer." Convinced I had made my point, I reluctantly released my grasp.

"Whew!" I sighed. "Thank you, Candice." Pointing at my lap, "my derringer thanks you." Standing up unencumbered, blowing her a kiss with my right hand. "We all thank you."

"You're welcome, D. Hey, Gone Girl is playing. I haven't seen it or read the book. Have heard however, its dark and twisted."

Hey, I resemble that remark. "Like me?"

"Naw…You're just twisted. Want to watch it with me, baby?"

"Sure, Candi, when I'm finished. You're a lot of work you know, but worth it." Tossing Candi, a set of headphones from my bag, I settled again into my seat, greatly relieved that her demonic hand had returned to her lap. With Candi engrossed in the movie, I began the arduous task of redirecting us west. *What's a few days, give or take, when we have nothing but time ahead of us? Then again, it's Candice Parker you're with, big boy. A niece of the Gambino crime family, an ex-wife to one very pissed off, jealous lawyer, also in the Family; and the blood cousin of 'Hung Like a Horse,' Giovanni, an Italian Stallion, Family member, who also happens to be my friend. What could go wrong?*

Changing thoughts mid-stream, I reflected how quickly technology has come to mainstream air. Accessing the internet on a plane was a welcome respite, when one has much to do and little time to do it. First things first, I changed our current tickets from Deer Lake, NF to Calgary, AB, leaving at 1005 tomorrow. Next, I booked a room for tonight at the Toronto Airport Marriott, generously welcoming pets for a mere $125.00 Canadian. Third, I notified my international shipper in Ft. Myers, FL to hold up on sending my truck, packed chock full of my stuff to Newfoundland. Fourth, since getting a bike this late in the season was not the best option, I booked, through Hertz, an SUV with a sunroof in Calgary, so that we could finish the ride in comfort. And finally, I checked my email. Waiting on me were three emails from Victoria, plus a plethora of others, relating to my recently departed life, BC (before Candi).

#1, from two days ago:

> D, I'm home safe. Getting back into the swing of things, beginning with all those items on your list. Hugs…Vic

#2, from yesterday:

> D, I heard from Frank. He's having a blast. Invited us to join him in Sweden. Says the women are beautiful there and it's amazing how appreciative that are of his (your) generosity. Oh, and I'm converting to a secure (NSA proof) server, compliments of you, my VIP client. I'll send you what I'm working on when it's up and running.

#3, from this morning:

> Congrats are in order, we are secure. Log into this new account (I've provided the link) and create a password. Once in, I'll have a message waiting on you… Say Hi to Candi for me. Tell her if she gets bored, I'm available at a moment's notice. LOL. Vic

I clicked on the link as instructed, whereby the site requested significant personal information for security questions, plus a ten-digit password I'd never used before. Once I set it up, I was in. Vic's message was waiting.

> #1, D, I can't put my finger on it, but thinking someone was/is monitoring my internet activity. Nothing really, just concerned with all Snowden's revelations lately. Anyone with Big Balls and lots of cash can track whomever they desire. Sound like anyone you know? FYI…I feel better now.
>
> On to business. I've applied for a 501C corporation, under the name of Mistatim Holdings, cute huh? Which reminds me, the renovation of the Mistatim Hotel is underway. Will has found a local contractor from Melfort, SK, who occasionally hunts with Greg. Small world, huh?
>
> And, I've located a trustworthy commodities broker in Chicago, through a law school classmate, now practicing in Denver. You can ship a crate to me anytime. Just give me a few day's heads up so I'll know to expect it.

I've attached a POA, which you'll need to print out, sign and notarize and snail mail the original to me. I need it to move all the utilities, taxes, and ownership of your lake property to the shell corporation, where I can manage from here.

That's all I've got for now. Write or call when you get this to confirm. I hope you're well and having fun. Me…I'm having almost having a blast, compliments of you.

Love Ya, Vic

She's on top of it, that's for sure. Who would have thought our first encounter on a catwalk where I mistook her for a Gucci priced call girl, in a casino in Sioux City, would have led to this? My confident, my friend (with benefits, I might add) and my attorney at law, Victoria R. Lawson, is now an invaluable asset in my rapidly evolving story…excuse me, my Ride.

I emailed Vic back, compliments of her new, secure server.

Hey girlfriend, Guess what? As of a few moments ago, Candi and I are finishing the Ride. Go figure? Trying to rekindle and recover what we seem to have lost once the insanity replaced the lust. Now don't go getting all excited on me. I'm doing my best to keep the little man from influencing the big one. There are some things I really need to work through. You were there, you know what I'm talking about. Remember the ferocious bear and the moonlit tree stand confessional?

Moving on, great news on the Mistatim Hotel, aka, Vic's 'Ho House.' Can't wait to see it when it's finished.

Please email Josie and ask her to hold a room for you tomorrow night, albeit us. I'd like to surprise her.

When you can, follow up with All Children's Hospital and Missy. If they give you a problem with all this HIPPA crap, tell them you've been retained by Candice Parker, her benefactor. Long and short, you and I promised the family a trip to Disney World. You'll have to go in my stead. Invite Greg and Debra, while you're at it. They'll come if it's not full-blown hunting season. Still might, since he thinks you're so smokin hot… remember?

Come to think of it, I still do. (:

Love ya more Girlfriend,
D

I hit send, then closed the Mac. Glancing over at Candi, I found her thoroughly engrossed in Gone Girl, watching by all accounts, a sexy, steamy scene in progress. Pulling an earbud from her ear, "Candi, I'm going to the Boy's Room. You need anything while I'm up?"

Of course, I need something while you're up! "My toy. You did bring my toy, didn't you?"

"It's your lucky day, baby. I have it in my bag, though the batteries may be a little on the weak side. I didn't have a chance to change them out since your last adventure, but you should be able to muddle through," I chuckled, 'til she punched me.

I punched him. "Go away!" *How dare him make fun of my pressing needs.* "But, leave my toy, please. I'm glad you never leave home without it."

"Me, too," I stammered. *Fondly, I recall, this little machine, affectionately known as the BOA (Baby Orgasmic Accelerator) is one well-traveled boy toy. And, thankfully, it is no respecter of persons, I might add. Let's see…I bought it for Candi on our six-week anniversary. Then I shared it with Vic…Oh…and somewhere in the mix, Gio shared it with Mile. Then Candi again…Then Vic multiple times…Then Candi again.* Holding it up to Candi, before dropping it into her lap, "This little boy has been in lots of tight spaces, I mean places, hasn't it, baby?"

Ignoring his snide comments, I promptly picked it up and twisted it to its highest setting, before answering him. "It has, D. And none more appreciative than this one," I cooed rather coyly, slipping it discreetly beneath the blanket and into a most welcome and receptive… me. Waving my free hand in the air, I motioned him away. "You can go away now, Jon David! I'm set."

Candi's verbal, along with her non-verbal communication allowed me to quickly exit stage right down the aisle, purposely shaking my head in the process. Greeting Dawn in the galley, making small talk, I almost forgot why I got up to begin with. Then it hit me, I had to go, bad. Slipping into the lavatory, no bigger than an oversized coffin, the plane began experiencing some minor turbulence, thoroughly preventing me from whizzing a singular straight line into a watermelon-sized hole. The Captain flashed the Fasten Seat Belt sign above my head. It didn't matter at this point. Stop, start, stop, start, just like the *Kegel exercises I'd come to adore, when practiced, not only by me, but others I had come to appreciate.*

Aw damn, girl! At least I was set, until three minutes into my self-administered appreciation, my toy launched into a slow-moving death spiral. Then this piece of crap had the audacity to up and die. I was so close. D, where's D? He can fix this. He has to fix this, now! Bolting from my seat, I went directly to the rear galley, properly introducing myself to Dawn, busily doing whatever stewards do, before I not so discreetly asked her which bathroom D was in.

"He's in the one marked occupied," chided Dawn, pointing at the sign on the door to the right. "You're welcome to use the other one ma'am. It's available as you can clearly see."

Dawn smirked at me! "I don't want to use that one, I want to use this one," I stammered. "It's a matter of… *Where was I going with this…* "life and death."

"You got it bad, girl, I'll give you that," Dawn confessed, sizing me up with her eyes, before continuing. "I'm going to the front galley, Candi … isn't it? I'll leave you to it. If you need anything, press the call attendant button and I'll come back… eventually."

Dawn smirked at me, again, walking away! I released my frustrations forth width. BAM-BAM-BAM! … I pounded the lavatory door with my fist, determined to get D's immediate, undivided attention.

Finally, the turbulence ceased. Beginning again for the umpteenth time, I aimed straight and true. Relief, I breathed aloud. It was smooth sailing from here on out, until over the engines humming, the BAM…BAM…BAM of someone's fists, vibrated the walls around me. "It's occupied," I shouted over my shoulder, with more than a hint of impatience. "Don't get your panties in a wad. I'll be out in a minute."

Trying to girl scream above a whisper is not possible in the rear of a moving plane I readily discovered. So, I knocked again, only harder, thanks to his panties in a wad comment. BAM-BAM-BAM! BAM-BAM-BAM! I power slammed the lavatory's door with both fists this time.

Finished, I had no more than put the little fella up when the incessant banging started again, startling me, mid zip. OMG!!! came to mind, and not in a nice way. My knee jerk reaction, propelled me forward, tossing the little fella out of my boxers and into the tracks of my copper, laced zipper, head first. Looking down in horror, I saw a nothing more than pink flesh, peeking through what looked like gigantic, devilish alligator teeth. It brought an abundance of tears to my eyes and an excruciating, gut wrenching pain to my little brain. With little to none big brain function, I pulled the slide and cracked open the door. "What?" I screamed, my free hand preciously covering my precarious predicament.

Candi, girl, you rock. That second time sure got his attention, because he's finally opening the door. "What do you mean, what, Jon David? Let me in this instant!"

I bit deeply into my lower lip, doing my best to keep the litany of bad words, begging to spew forth from my mouth, at bay. Lowering my head, speaking just above a whisper, "It's not a good time, Candice," I confessed rather meekly. "You really, really need to wait."

Not one to take no for an answer, I jerked the door open with both hands, then stepped into his current domain and slid the bolt shut behind me. Filling my lungs with jet fumes and disinfectant, I spun to face him. With mere inches separating us, I was swept up in his moment, suddenly aware of the tears cascading down his cheeks. Placing both hands on his bearded face, I swiped his tears away with my thumbs. "Oh baby, what's wrong? I'm here now.

It will be OK. What can I do to make it better? A little loving goes a long way," cliché after cliché rolled off my lips like water off a duck's back. Gazing into his tear stained, bedroom brown eyes, I lowered my hand to massage… his hand? *Why is he guarding his? …*

"It's really, really not a good time, Candi," I stammered, as she pushed me to arms- length, while she leaned back against the door, willfully brushing my guardian hand away.

"Oh… My… God!" I gasped, putting my right hand over my mouth, my eyes staring at something the size of a pink pencil eraser, protruding midway through his zipper. "Is that what I think it is? How did it happen?" *Never mind, I'm not going there. It's fairly evident how it happened. The question is how to fix it?* "What can I do, baby? I'm a nurse, remember?" My horniness swiftly abated, my countless years of medical training took over. *Though I can honestly say, I've never encountered a penis in a zipper, even when I managed the weekend late night ER shift. Stuck in a bottle maybe, possibly even a vacuum hose, but never a zipper. Although, I did see an assortment of objects up the butt-hole, but that's another story in itself, totally irrelevant to madness of his making I'm currently addressing here.*

Moving gingerly backward, I leaned far into the sink, inadvertently pressing the call assist button, while I retrieved a pen knife from my pocket. Thankfully, the powers that be in the TSA, relented when it comes to these tiny fingernail cleaners or I would be in a much darker place right now. Opening it, I pressed it into Candi's hand. "You're going to have to cut…"

The word cut flustered me. "I will not," I countered distinctly. "I am not cutting the tip off your penis. It will bleed like a mother and I'll have no access to it for a month." I grinned. "Selfish, aren't I? The last part I threw in to bring some levity to this situation." Patting his jeans softly, "I'm sorry, not feeling it, are you baby?"

I grimaced. "Nope, can't say that I am. I don't want that knife anywhere near the tip of my penis. What I do want is for you to kneel down and use the knife to separate the zipper just enough to release me from its death grip."

Following D's instructions, I had him sit on the sink, as I knelt between his legs and raised the knife to ever so gently extract him. Suddenly, without warning, the bathroom door popped open, jolting me from my perch. Dawn appeared, unwelcome if I say so myself, looking aghast at the spectacle unfolding before her.

"What do you think you're doing?" Dawn demanded, as the Captain of the plane appeared behind her, inquisitively peaking over her shoulder. "Someone pushed the call button. Is she attacking you, sir?"

I was puzzled by her comments, before I realized how totally absurd this must look. D, nodding yes, me, kneeling at his crotch with a small knife in my hand. I took control of the situation immediately, before it went south and the whole damn plane showed up to see what was happening in the rear lavatory. Wrestling into my big girl panties, "I'm an RN, did my initial training in an ER. Precious D here has zipped the tip of his penis, midway up his pants. I was about to extract it when you barged in. Dawn, if you have a first aid kit, please bring it, just in case he bleeds like a mother. And you Captain, if you're through laughing, I see you laughing, please, by all means, close the damn door!"

I must say, Candice Parker has a way with words. Dawn immediately disappeared, while the Captain, slowly, mercifully closed the door. "Go ahead, Candice, do what you do best, make my penis, once again, a happy man."

Skillfully, from a seated position on the loo, in very tight quarters, I began separating the zipper tooth by tooth, trying to maintain the integrity of D's precious package. Starting an inch below his now bluing flesh, I meticulously separated the teeth in the tracks, until I was two teeth away from success. Moving an inch above, I repeated the procedure. Now, all I had to do was maneuver the blade between his skin and the last two teeth of the zipper with enough pressure to release him. Using the dull side of the blade closest to his skin, I lubricated it with soap, then began the delicate procedure of extraction. Pushing downward, in less than five-seconds, the remaining teeth popped open, releasing D from the jaws of death that held him firmly in their grasp. "Success," I breathed, confident that he was going to be just fine.

"Relief, at last," I bellowed. "Thank you, baby doll, thank you. By the looks of things, my penis thanks you and adores you."

Reaching my hand into his jeans, I pulled D's pleasure pistol out to examine it more closely. Other than a purple and reddening spot, there were no ill effects from my extraction. As I bent over to kiss it, my way of saying, 'here baby, let me make it better,' the bathroom door swung open again. Filling the space was Dawn, standing at the ready, sporting a scowl, with a massive First Aid kit in hand. *Damn her, what is it with that smirk? She's jealous … has to be.*

"Guess you won't be needing this," plied Dawn. "From the looks of things, I'd say a little more privacy would be in order. By the way, welcome to the Mile- High Club," she chuckled, promptly easing the door closed.

"Was it as good for you as it was for me? Memories, that's what we're making, D, memories, enough to last us a lifetime. I must confess, it's the main reason I wanted into the bathroom with you, making Mile High memories in the Mile-High Club. But considering your predicament, I couldn't have timed it better."

Best to let sleeping dogs lie. I refuted not a word. Candi and I exited the bathroom to a rip-roaring applause, scattered across the minimally populated cabin. Seems word travels fast round here. Needless to say, Candi and I, according to the passengers, had re-upped our membership in the Mile Club tonight, for all the wrong reasons. Guess, in the end, it's really just the thought that counts.

From the Author

Thank you for taking the time to read Ride to Restoration, our second novel in the Ride Series.

Major and I welcome and encourage your comments, along with your fair and honest reviews on Amazon — as they will guide me in my continued quest to remake ... me.

My ultimate goal in this series is to entertain, as well as engage you, promoting selflessness, while generating more than enough sales to purchase at least a million meals through Second Harvest. We can do it, but not without you. Each month, one dollar from every e-book sale in this series is given to Second Harvest in your honor, our readers.

In the meantime, spread the word, pay it forward, volunteer where your heart is and encourage your family to be a part of it.

Many thanks — DJ Wilson
Email me: dj@dalehollowlakelover.com
Find me on Twitter: @dhlakelover

Visit my website:

www.dalehollowlakelover.com

About Second Harvest

Second Harvest Heartland works to reinvent hunger relief through leadership and innovation. As the Nation's largest hunger relief organization, our goal is not only to help our hungry neighbors today, but to provide the means for everyone to be fed tomorrow. We're known for distributing great amounts of food quickly and efficiently; in 2016 alone, we collected, warehoused and distributed more than 90 million pounds of food — but we're also constantly pioneering ways to reduce waste and better use the abundant resources available in this land of plenty.

Here's your opportunity to pay it forward. Make a contribution to Second Harvest where one dollar purchases three meals to those needing a little extra help.

www.FeedingAmerica.org